Barbara Howe lives on the third rock from the sun, while her imagination travels the universe and beyond.

Born in the US (North Carolina), she spent most of her adult life in New Jersey, working in the software industry, on projects ranging from low-level kernel ports to multi-million-dollar financial applications. She moved to New Zealand in 2009, gained dual citizenship, and now works as a software developer in the movie industry. She lives in Wellington, in a house overflowing with books and jigsaw puzzles, and wishes she had more time time to spend universe hopping.

T0288805

Reforging: Book 3

The Blacksmith

By Barbara Howe

The Blacksmith

ISBN-13: 978-1-925956-03-0

Printed in Garamond and Goudy Old Style typefaces.

IFWG Publishing International
Melbourne

www.ifwgpublishing.com

Journeyman

We buried my uncle the last week of August, the year after the Fire Warlock retired. When the news he was dead reached me, a day and a half down the coast, I left my gear in the smithy, promised the master to be back inside a week, and rode north through low clouds and drizzle, too wrapped up in memories and worries to think much about the road. The next morning, standing in the inn's stable door with a grey wall of fog outside, I couldn't avoid it.

"To get to Crossroads," the ostler said, "I'd go west, around the hills."

"That would take two days—"

"Three."

"I said I was in a hurry."

"You asked what I would do. I'm never in a hurry. But if you're that hot to get there…" He shrugged. "It's either the track over the hills—slow going and dangerous in the fog—or the road to Quayside."

Earth wizards kept up the Quayside Road, along the shore, as a favour to the Water Guild. Capped with paving stones all the way from London, it was a fast, easy ride. I could be in Crossroads with hours to spare.

Hard choice.

He said, "With the fog, you should be safe enough going through Quayside. We've had aristos complain that they've been to Quays and back, and never saw the damned thing."

My jaw dropped. "They can't have wanted to see it."

He laughed. "I said aristos. What'd you expect? They ain't got as much sense as a donkey. But even they don't go to Quays unless they've been summoned, or got kinsfolk on trial. I figure they want to brag that they've seen it and lived to tell."

"Fools." I led my horse out into the fog.

The ostler walked across the yard with me. "Don't you ever worry about robbers ganging up on you?"

I fingered the folded paper in my pocket, and grinned. "Not anymore, since an air witch gave me a charm for protection."

"Gave you? That lot never parts with anything for free. Sounds to me like you charmed her."

I pulled my collar up against the damp. "Wasn't trying to."

He snickered. "Aye, sure. What does the charm do?"

"Makes robbers see two of me."

The fog soon swallowed the noise he made laughing. Unwilling to risk a fall on stone, I led Charcoal on foot until the road curved to run along the shore, where I climbed on and rode out on the sand below the high tide line. Even with the light growing, everything past Charcoal's nose was lost in the murk. A steady breeze blew in off the North Sea, and we inched along the beach more by smell, sound, and feel than sight.

Finding our way kept me too busy to notice the wind picking up until it started punching holes in the fog. I rode into a gap, and the rising sun threw my shadow half a mile inland.

I hunkered down on Charcoal's neck and cursed. He was fresh and eager, even with a heavy load on his back, and surged into a canter. Any other day I would have enjoyed the steady duh-duh-duh, duh-duh-duh, but if I let him run he would wear himself out too soon, and we wouldn't reach Crossroads in time. And anything faster than a trot would draw too much attention. I reined him in sooner than he wanted, and he fought with me.

Ahead, fog still hung thick across the road and around the islands offshore. At a steady trot we might pass the causeway before the fog lifted. I looked away. I didn't want to see that castle hiding in the mist.

"If a wanted man tries to sneak past the Crystal Palace," Gran would say, "it will shine like a lighthouse, and pin him down with a beam as bright as the sun. Water wizards will rise out of the surf and catch him. He won't have a chance."

"Dad, is she telling the truth? A beam of light is fire magic, not water magic."

Dad didn't have much truck with some of Gran's stories, but this one made him look uneasy. "I don't know, Duncan. They say there's magic from all four guilds in the Water Office. It doesn't pay to count on the

Frost Maiden being limited to water magic."

I made the sign to ward off the evil eye, and pulled my hat brim down. I'd gotten rowdy sometimes with the other lads, and poached a few grouse, but I wouldn't have dared come this way with anything serious on my conscience. The Water Guild weren't likely to hunt me, as long as I didn't give the duke any lip.

Fat chance of that, with Uncle Will dead.

Across the water, a flash caught my eye. I looked up, and was blinded. I flung an arm over my eyes, and yelled. Charcoal reared. I landed, rolling, in the surf, and came up spitting sand. I lurched towards dry ground, but couldn't see where I was going. You can't hide from a wizard anyway. When they caught me...

I shaded my eyes and turned a full circle. No water wizards rose out of the waves. The only thing moving besides water and mist was Charcoal, galloping up the beach.

Damn his hide. He was running towards the causeway.

By squinting through my fingers, I made out half-a-dozen little suns on towers poking out of the fog. I heard Gran chanting, "Water Guild Hall, more glass than wall." Mirrors, that's all it was—goddamned, frostbitten mirrors.

I threw the old up-yours sign in the direction of the Crystal Palace, reached for my hat, and stopped cold halfway down. I couldn't see another soul, but that didn't mean they weren't watching. I'd probably just pissed off the whole Water Guild.

Dad used to say my big mouth would land me in a stinking mountain of trouble someday. I hadn't even opened my mouth this time.

I grabbed my hat before it floated away and walked with my heart thumping in my chest. Nobody except the Fire Warlock ever pissed off the Water Guild and got away with it. Even the king, who had bloody loud rows with the Fire Warlock, tiptoed around the Frost Maiden. That water witch had enough magic in her little finger to freeze everybody in Nettleton. She must like freezing people; she did it often enough.

I went from cold to hot to cold a dozen times. The Water Guild had no right to scare the devil out of law-abiding travellers, or to ruin my best clothes. Sand stuck to my proud new dark blue coat, and as it dried it turned splotchy with salt. Salt rimed my hat, too, and scrubbing at it with my sleeve didn't help.

The fog lifted before I caught up with Charcoal; the Crystal Palace glittered in the sun. I risked a glance, and straightened up, staring, until my eyes watered. Nobody ever told me it was pretty. But then, nobody in Abertee who did business in Quayside ever admitted seeing it. I'd heard folk living in Quayside got so used to it they didn't blink after a while. Seemed hard to believe.

If I had dared, I would've turned around and ridden south. The funeral could go on without me. Uncle Will was past caring. I didn't owe him anything.

Who was I kidding? I'd served my apprenticeship under him. I owed him just about everything. And turning around would look like I had something to hide. They would come after me, then, for sure, and show me how bad Water Guild curses really are. There was nothing for it but to brazen it out.

Boats were setting out from the wharves in Quays, out on the island, and traffic flowed in a steady stream from Quayside to Quays: merchants taking their goods to market and whimpering mundanes on their way to the courts, but no water wizards were in sight so early.

Once over the bridge into Quayside, a line of trees along the river blocked sight of the Crystal Palace. Silver jingled in my pocket and the smells of bread baking and bacon frying tickled my nose. I rode into an inn yard and got off Charcoal. The door opened, and a water wizard stepped out. I climbed back on. The water wizard gawked at me, then turned back to talk to the innkeeper. I rode through town and didn't stop until I was out of sight of the whole lot—Quays, Quayside, and the Crystal Palace. I stopped to eat my cold breakfast of oatcakes and mutton where the river curved for a good view of the grandest hall in Abertee, the White Duke's manor house. The first White Duke had started it and the family added to it over the centuries, until it was big enough to house a town. Built of the local granite, it would do a king proud.

The duke loved it, Uncle Will had said. His duchess hated it.

Off to the side, a mountain of yellowish marble the duchess had ordered hauled up the coast on barges sat, waiting. Had been waiting for three years, for her to make up her mind about the layout of her new wing. I hoped she'd lost interest. Maybe she'd come to her senses and realised the marble would look foul next to the granite.

As I rode closer, a work crew drove up with a wagon and unloaded more marble. Maybe she'd decided to pull down the old house and start fresh. I pulled my hat brim down and kicked Charcoal into a gallop.

I reined in at the new front gate. Master Hamish got the job after I'd left his smithy, and I'd not been this way since. I shook my head over the sloppy workmanship. He'd been pissed off, no doubt, and small blame to him—the duchess had been known to change her mind half-a-dozen times, and not pay for the extra work—but if they'd given me the job, I'd've done something to be proud of. Not that they would've considered giving that to a journeyman. Even for a master, jobs that special don't come often in Abertee.

Most local smiths called themselves lucky to get fancy work once or twice. If they knew I wanted more, I'd never hear the end of it. Getting above myself, they'd say. I heard enough of that already.

Across from the gate, workmen were laying granite blocks for a new jetty. She'd be paying Abertee's stonemasons for that. I went on my way, nursing a small sense of satisfaction.

Near midday I reached the fork to Drayman's Ford, and was a quarter mile down the wrong road before I remembered I was due in Crossroads and not home. I hadn't been home to Nettleton in months. Turning around was a wrench in the gut. Charcoal didn't like it either. I rubbed his head. "Sorry, old boy. We'll go home tomorrow, after the funeral."

From the fork, it would have been hours yet to Nettleton, but in the other direction, a few minutes to the bridge over the Tee, then an hour to Crossroads. I would get there on time.

Uncle Will's prodding, plus the lure of higher wages and more interesting work, had sent me away from Abertee, but I hadn't liked living among strangers for so long. I would go back to finish the job I'd started, but when that was done I would collect my tools, and turn back north. With Uncle Will no longer blocking it, the Blacksmith's Guild in Abertee would be sure to promote me to master.

On the far side of the river, cousins on their way to the funeral waved and yelled something I couldn't make out about the bridge. The day had turned sunny and warm. I would soon be among friends and family, I'd be home tomorrow, and the Frost Maiden hadn't turned me into an icicle. I started whistling a drinking song.

The village by the bridge was unchanged since I'd worked there, three years gone. I turned the corner to the bridge, and stopped.

There was no bridge. Water boiled around the support columns, but the roadway was gone. There weren't even heaps of stone messing up the river's flow. It was like the roadway had never been. I got off my horse and stared.

The smith's wife came out, wiping her hands on her apron. "Good to see you, Duncan. Wasn't expecting you to come this way. You'll have to go the long way around."

"What happened?" I said. "It was in bad shape, but…"

"The duchess sent out a crew to steal stone for her new jetty."

My mouth hung open. "You're joking." I screwed my eyes shut, then looked again. "You're not joking."

"She said she never comes this far out into this God-forsaken wilderness, so she didn't need the bridge, and she wouldn't pay for new stone to be quarried."

"That is just…" I couldn't find a word strong enough. Uncle Will had been after the duke for years to rebuild the bridge. The duke didn't keep up the roads and bridges like he should've, but he'd never broken one before. No wonder Uncle Will had had apoplexy.

I kicked at broken bits of stone scattered at the edge of the river. "How's your dad?" His house was within spitting distance of the bridge's other end.

"His pleurisy's getting worse, but he won't leave and move in with us. I had been crossing every day with soup, but now…" She shook her head. "We're collecting timber to build a makeshift bridge, but we can't start on it until they're finished with the old one and out of the way."

"If you don't finish before the harvest is over…"

"Aye, it'll be a hard winter. If folk can't pay their rent…"

After a while I climbed back on Charcoal and headed for the ford. The urge to whistle never came back.

Crossroads

We crossed the river, and Charcoal fought me when I turned his head west. Couldn't blame him—my hands on the reins told him Crossroads, but my knees said north, and Nettleton. I got down and walked him past the next bend. After I climbed back on, he plodded along with his head down, both of us wanting to turn around and run for home.

My grim mood lifted a little as we neared Crossroads. Even from a distance it was clear Uncle Will was getting the send-off he deserved. The crowd overflowed the church, the churchyard, and blocked the road. All our kin and every craftsman in the district must have come. I had been counting on sleeping in my cousin's house, but might have to settle for the barn.

Granny Mildred was waiting at the healers' guildhall. She walked out into the middle of the road, planted herself foursquare in front of Charcoal with her arms crossed, and glared. "Get down off your high horse, you young fool, and be polite. I'll not have any of your belligerence."

"Belligerence, my arse. I'm not the one in a lather." I slid down. "What should I be pissed off about?"

She jabbed me in the chest with a bony finger. "I'll not have you saying that if I hadn't been wasting time on the other side of the district, Will Archer wouldn't be lying dead in that church today."

"I wouldn't say that. Why would anybody?"

Her face, all wrinkles and sags, scrunched up tight. "Because maybe it would be so."

"Hogwash." I wrapped an arm around her and pulled her against me. "Tell me who's been saying rot like that and I'll have a word with them."

She bawled into my shirt. I gave her a shake. "Who?"

A soft voice behind me said, "The only one saying that is Mildred herself."

I glanced over my shoulder, and saw freckles splashed across a darling of a face. Where had she been hiding?

I gave Granny Mildred another shake. "Tell me what happened. The message I got just said he'd died of apoplexy and the funeral was today."

Freckles said, "We were away, treating children with chicken pox, when Master Will had his attack. He was dead before we got back."

The face under the freckles was even better on a second look. Not gorgeous, but the kind of face a man wouldn't get tired of looking at in a hurry. Cute little turned up nose…

I said, "Apoplexy wasn't a big surprise. She'd been telling him for years he was eating himself to death."

Granny Mildred mumbled, "Didn't do any good, did it? I told him so often he stopped listening. The lassies' mum told us about the broken bridge. We should have headed straight back here to tell Will, but we spent half the afternoon gossiping. If I'd been in town when he had his fit…"

Freckles said, "Mrs McAllister needed to talk, and you did her a kindness to listen."

I said, "Don't beat yourself up. You're a healer, not a fortune-teller. You couldn't have known—"

"I knew he'd be dreadful angry, and would march off to give the duke a piece of his mind. I should've kept an eye on him."

"Keep talking like that, and we'll think you're going soft."

She mumbled some rubbish about me being a good lad, and pushed away from me. Freckles handed her a handkerchief, and Granny honked into it.

Most folk get nervous when I loom over them. Freckles wasn't even looking at me. She was watching Granny Mildred. I watched Freckles. Her eyes were some funny colour I couldn't put a name to. Her mouth was begging for a kiss…

Granny Mildred poked me in the ribs. "Mind your manners, sonny. Be polite to my visitor."

I tipped my hat. "I'd be happy to stay and talk, but I've got to get to the church."

"Looking like that?" Granny Mildred said. "What've you been doing, you young scamp? Sleeping on the shore?"

"Fell off my horse."

She snorted. "You expect me to believe that?"

"Uh, nae."

Freckles gave me a sharp glance. Mildred brushed at my coat. The sand fell off; the dried salt disappeared.

"Thank you, ma'am." I held out my hat. "Can you clean this off, too?"

"Expect a lot, don't you?" She scrubbed the brim; my three-year-old hat looked as good as new when she handed it back. "Don't know why I waste my magic on the likes of you. Now get on with you." She gave me a swat on the arm. "And don't worry about being late. They heard you were coming; they're waiting for you."

Master Walter's lad came running to take Charcoal. The folk in the churchyard shuffled aside to let me through. If they'd known the light off the Crystal Palace had pinned me down, they would have run. I took a deep breath and let it out again before starting up the walk.

Cousin Ruth met me at the church door. "I knew you'd make it. You'd never let Dad down."

Her husband, two inches shorter than his wife and a stone lighter, gave me a broad grin and a firm handshake. "Except you are going to let Dad down. I'm glad I'm off the hook."

The pallbearers—three other blacksmiths and two farmers—could have passed for a squad of mountain trolls. We could handle Uncle Will.

Master Walter stuck out a hand. "I'm glad you're here, too. It'll be easier on the rest of us."

The pastor said, "Since the mourners won't all fit in the church, we're going to have the service out by the grave, instead of in here, so more people can hear."

I looked down at Uncle Will, and got choked up. When I could talk again, I said, "Any idea how much weight we're dealing with?" He'd been huge, even before he'd run to fat.

"Twenty-nine and a half stone," my brother, Doug, said.

"Frostbite," Cousin Jock said. "Sorry, Reverend. That's eight or nine stone apiece."

Doug gave him the gimlet eye. "Less than five. You can handle that much."

Master Hamish muttered, "I'm glad you're not doing my accounts, lad."

I said, "How did you get him here?"

"Wagon," Doug said. "Wheels on the bier."

"Wheels, eh?" Jock said. "We could wheel him right on out to the graveside."

Master Walter glared. "That's not the way it's done. Master Will was the most important man in Abertee—"

The pastor coughed. "After the White Duke, of course."

"Let's say he was the most respected man in Abertee."

"Can't argue with that."

"Fine. We're not going to let you, lad, or any other fool, trample on his dignity. Got that? Now, when I say 'heave', we're going to lift him up to shoulder height." Master Walter glanced at me. "My shoulder height."

We took our places. "Ready?" Master Walter said. "Heave."

Somehow, we got him out of the church and into the ground without any loss of dignity, his or ours. After the service, we had supper—a big spread—on the grounds. Nobody walked away hungry.

"The duke sent about half of it," Ruth said.

"Seems only fair," I said, "but still…"

She shrugged. "I don't blame him for what happened. Dad always called him a decent sort, but dim. It's that witch he married that's the trouble."

"I'm surprised she let him spend this much."

"She doesn't know. For his sake, I hope she doesn't find out."

Folk began saying goodbyes and drifting away before sunset, but even in the gloom a few groups still gabbed. I'd been with them, jawing with kin I hadn't seen in months or years, until it started to get dark. The inns and taverns were packed tonight. I'd had invitations to come along, but I wasn't ready to head indoors yet.

I sat on the cemetery wall watching the sky turn purple, then black. With Uncle Will gone, Abertee was in trouble. He'd been head of the Blacksmith's Guild in Abertee for thirty years, and there wasn't anyone who could take his place. A few wanted to, but they were just members of the local chapter. No other master smith had earned a certificate signed by a member of the Royal Association of Blacksmiths and Swordsmiths.

We could promote our own journeymen, and call them masters, but without a certified master we wouldn't have the royal guild's backing. The duke and duchess could demand our services and pay us whatever they wanted, and we would have to take it and say, Thank you, sir, Thank you, ma'am. A man could have more work than he could handle that way… and starve.

I'd spent the summer trying to get certified. Just as well I didn't have to explain to Uncle Will why I wasn't yet.

If I stayed out any longer, I'd trip over a gravestone in the dark and bash my head. I trudged towards the Shepherd's Arms, wondering why I was so tired. All I'd done for hours was talk. I'd be happy to sit in the corner and listen for a while.

The smell of Master Hamish's pipe met me before I saw him. He leaned against the tavern wall, in the shadows. "You look beat, lad," he said. "Come in with me, and I'll buy you a pint."

"Thanks, I appreciate that. I'm glad the day's over—I've had too many nasty shocks for my comfort."

I ducked under the lintel, got a good look inside, and would have backed out if Master Hamish hadn't slammed the door shut behind me.

Mildred Lays Down the Law

The tavern went quiet. Every head turned to stare at me. Master Hamish gave me a shove towards the big table in the middle, where Granny Mildred crooked a finger at me.

"Ah, hell, Granny, what'd I do now?"

"This time, sonny, it's what you're going to do. Sit down."

The crowd at the table—Granny Mildred, Doug, and half a dozen smiths I'd worked for since leaving Uncle Will's—jostled around the table with a racket of scraping chair legs, making room. Somebody at another table shoved a chair at me, and I squeezed in. Granny Mildred, the crown of her head no higher than the shoulders of the two men on either side, gave them each a shove. "You're crowding me, lads. Give me space." They crowded Cousin Jock out, but Mildred got elbow room.

Master Hamish handed me a pint, and sat down behind me. A gaggle of lasses waved at me from a table across the room. My sister Maggie's head stuck up higher than the rest. Her friend Fiona sat next to her. I craned my neck, but couldn't make out the others.

"We were discussing," Mildred said, "how we're going to fill the hole Will Archer left in Abertee—"

"And it's a big hole," Master Walter said, to groans all around.

I saw what was coming, and tried to back away from the table, but they hadn't left room to move.

"Right," Mildred said. "We need a spokesman. Someone who can stand up to the duke and tell him—"

"Fine," I said, though it wasn't. "If somebody has to tell the duke off, I'm the man for it."

"Whoa, lad—"

"He would, too," Master Walter said. "He's told off everybody else in Abertee."

Everybody, including me, laughed, except for Granny Mildred. She glared. "You think that would help? Forget it. We need somebody with authority. One of you master smiths is going to have to tell the duke he has to rebuild that bridge. He won't listen to a journeyman."

"Why's it have to be a master smith?" Master Hamish said. "Duncan's an Archer. That ought to do."

"Or Doug," the smith beside him said. "He thinks twice before he says something."

"And sometimes Douggie thinks three times," Mildred said, "and doesn't say anything at all."

Doug gave her a long look over his pint. Took a swallow and shrugged. I gave him not quite a wink. He gave me not quite a shake of the head in return.

"An Archer by himself won't do," Mildred said. "You've forgotten it's the smiths' guild charter that gives your guild head the right to tell the duke what he's doing wrong in Abertee, and he has to listen, even if he doesn't like it. Nobody else has that right. With Will gone, we need an Archer to get certified, so he can take over as head."

"Whoa," I said. "It doesn't have to be an Archer."

"It nearly always is. The head has to be somebody in good standing—"

Master Hamish guffawed, and pounded on the table. "Good standing, eh? You got that right. Nobody here with more standing, even sitting down, now that Will's gone." He kept cackling, until Jock cuffed him on the side of the head.

Mildred looked pained. "I meant, somebody whose family is respected, and has been for a long time. The Archers go all the way back even before the Fire Office, to when Charley the Great gave a third of North Frankland to the White Duke for his services to the crown."

Master Hamish said, "And the White Duke gave the Upper Tee Valley to that company of bowmen. Aye, we've all heard the story. The Archers could get away with needling the duke, because they were his strongest supporters."

"Being a duke's man meant something, then," I said. "Not now. Today we're the biggest thorn in his side."

"Aye," Master Walter said, "but he's used to it, and he'll take from the

Archers what he won't take from anybody else."

"There's Archer blood all over Abertee," I said. "We're cousins with every family that's been here more than a couple generations."

"But they don't all have the Archer name," Mildred said.

"Or the Archer size," Master Walter said. "That's why we need you, lad, to get certified by the royal guild, so you can deal with the duke the next time he lets us down. That's when, not if. Will had been saying for years you should get certified."

"Aye, but I don't—"

"He only ever said that to a handful of journeymen. Jed McAllister went on his own to Edinburgh to get certified, and the grandmaster smith there told him to go home and stop wasting his time. That he wasn't good enough and never would be good enough."

"And he was right," I said.

"Aye. You wouldn't have appreciated Jed acting high and mighty as guild head when he's not as good as you are. We're all agreed you're the best choice. You've already been journeying longer than most, and it's time you settled down. If your head gets any bigger—"

Granny Mildred said, "It's already two sizes too big."

"—Doug will knock it down to size, and you're the only journeyman we're sure can earn a certificate."

Granny said, "If you can keep your mouth shut."

The tavern wasn't as hot as a forge, but I wiped sweat from my face. "Maybe I could, if I got the chance to prove myself, but getting that chance isn't easy. When I left here in April, I went to Edinburgh. The grandmaster there said that after Jed, he'd take on a water wizard before anybody else from Abertee. I went to Newcastle next. That one said he had all the journeymen he could handle lined up for more than a year. He sent me to Leeds." If I clenched my fist any harder I'd break the mug. I let go and cracked my knuckles. Better not tell them that grandmaster had ordered me out after I called him a disgrace to his guild for trying to sell me a certificate. "Things didn't work out there, either. I was working my way back home when Uncle Will died."

There was a long silence. Granny chewed on her thumb. The master smiths studied the bottoms of their mugs. The tavern got noisier as folk at the other tables went back to talking to their neighbours. We ordered another round.

Master Hamish said, "You could go to Blacksburg. With two grand-masters there, you'd have a better chance."

"Forget it. This summer convinced me I never want to spend another day in a city, ever."

"Why the hell not? Lots to do there, I hear."

"You can't sleep in a city for the din. Cities stink. They're dirty, they're crowded, there's not enough grass and trees and birds—"

"Lots of pretty girls."

"We've got pretty girls here in Abertee. Fiona, for one." I grabbed my beer and shoved Master Hamish out of the way. "And she doesn't give me grief like some people I could name. I'm not going to Blacksburg, and that's final."

I wandered over and sat down between Maggie and Fiona. From the other side of Maggie, Freckles smiled at me. My head fizzed like I was on my fourth round instead of my second.

"What was that, Fiona? Noisy in here."

"I said, don't you want to be certified?"

I took a pull at my mug to buy a little time. Maggie said, louder than usual so everybody at the table could hear, "He does, if he has to be a master, but he'd rather keep on being a journeyman."

I choked on my beer. Several pairs of shocked eyes stared at us. Freckles cocked her head.

Maggie said, "When he's a master, he'll have to settle down and run his own smithy, and the only people he'll get to talk to will be the few dozen nearby doing business with him. Being a journeyman, he can go wherever he wants, whenever he wants. He's been sticking his nose into other people's business and flirting all over the north end of Frankland. Don't tell me he wants to give that up."

Fiona looked like I'd slapped her. Freckles reached across and patted her hand. "There's truth to that, but she's teasing you. Don't take it so seriously."

There was truth in it, more than Maggie knew. I wanted to be my own boss, and for the other smiths to stop acting like I was still a green apprentice, but maybe I'd never be ready to settle down.

I said to Maggie, "You're going to get me in trouble with their mums and dads."

Maggie leaned over and talked into my ear. "If they stopped pushing their daughters at you, would you mind? You keep complaining you haven't met a lass yet who didn't bore you silly sooner or later."

"Oh, aye, but still…"

Fiona said, "If you got certified, couldn't you go on to be a swordsmith?"

I overturned my mug. The beer dripped onto her skirts, and she flailed and yelled. The barmaid came running with a towel. Heads turned to see what I was bellowing about. The barmaid had mopped up and brought another beer before I stopped laughing. I said I was sorry, but it served Fiona right for asking such a fool question.

I said, "If it would help, sure, I'd jump at it, but I've got no chance of getting in the royal guild. None. I don't have enough magic to be a swordsmith, and even if I did, the only way to get in is to be the son or nephew of somebody already in it. Forget it."

She pouted. "Dad said you'd—"

"He ought to know better. Nobody from Abertee has ever been in the royal guild, so nobody from Abertee will ever be in the royal guild. That's how things work in Frankland."

"At least if you don't get certified it'll be because you don't want to. Hazel said—"

"Hazel?"

Freckles said, "That's me."

Aye, hazel. That was the colour. Not that I could tell now. In the dark corner her eyes were black, and as big as a calf's.

Fiona glared at her. "Hazel said the duke scares you. I don't believe it."

Time to leave and go to bed. I'd had enough nasty surprises for one day.

Freckles said, "I said it would be foolish for any commoner to not fear his overlord."

Maggie added, "And I said you were no fool."

I squeezed her shoulders. "Thanks, sis. So, Hazel, just visiting? How long?"

"Till the end of the week, then I'm off to another district. Granny Mildred's one of several healers wanting to retire, and I'm spending the summer considering where I'll go when I finish my training." Her voice was as soft as Maggie's. Funny that I could hear her fine, even though she was further away.

"Seems it a little early for that. Don't healers have a long apprenticeship, and you're, what, sixteen?"

She laughed at me. "Twenty-three. I only have one more year."

"Forget I said that. Tell me what we have to do to convince you to stay here."

She smiled. "Keep talking."

Later, on the walk to Ruth's, Maggie said, "You'd better watch what you say around that one. She knows when somebody's lying."

I said, "You sure? She caught you out about teasing Fiona, but that wasn't hard to guess."

"I'm sure. I saw her hat—it had a whole forest of those little trees on it."

"More than the three on Granny Mildred's?"

"Aye. Five."

Doug whistled. I sucked my teeth, and thought back. "I didn't tell any outright lies."

Maggie said, "You exaggerated how pretty Abertee is—"

"Did not."

"—and how friendly we all are—"

"Maybe a little."

She said, "Maybe a lot!"

"They weren't lies, exactly."

"Won't make any difference," Doug said. "A witch that powerful won't stay in a backwater like Abertee."

"Don't see why not," I said. "Anybody with sense can tell this is a great place. And she's got sense. Enough, anyway, to see that the duke, milksop though he is, is dangerous."

Maggie said, "Why doesn't Fiona see that?"

"Because folk here don't realise everything we've done for them. Uncle Will and Dad, and Granddad, and all the Archer's in the blacksmiths' guild, looked out for everybody, so folk here have had it easy."

"All the more reason for it to be some other family's job, for a change."

I said, "Speaking of that…"

Doug said, "Master Hamish and Master Walter are going together tomorrow to talk to the duke."

"Good. I'm off the hook."

"Until you get certified," Doug said.

"If."

"When."

I cuffed him, and he butted me back. Satisfied, we left Maggie at Ruth's door and staggered towards the hayloft. When we had settled down, with several of our cousins snoring at the other end, I told him about the Crystal Palace spooking me. The news woke him up. He shifted around on the hay.

"Ask Ruth for Uncle Will's maps. He doesn't need them anymore." Doug rolled off the hay and climbed down. He was standing in the barn door, looking east, when I went to sleep.

"When you get to Blacksburg—" Granny Mildred said.

"I'm not going to Blacksburg," I said. Charcoal nickered at me. I closed the stall door and rubbed his head.

"Or London, or wherever you have to go to get certified—"

"Forget it."

She peered at me through the slats. "Keep your eyes and ears open, your mouth shut, and your hands to yourself. Keep your nose out of other people's business, and don't draw attention."

I leaned over the door and reached for the bridle. "Tell me how to do that. I draw attention just standing up."

"Not much you can do about that, is there? I meant, don't draw any extra attention if you don't have to. Keep to yourself, keep out of trouble, and don't go doing people favours right and left. Don't be so damned-fool neighbourly to everybody."

"Why the hell not? I don't like it when folk aren't friendly to me."

"Because you're a soft touch, and they'll take advantage of you. People who are always friendly and helpful get noticed. Even short people. And if the commoners notice you, the Black Duke will, too, and he's nastier than our duke. If the commoners like you, he'll dislike you on principle. Don't let him know who you are. Get in, get that certificate, and get out. Got that?"

"Nae. You don't get it. I'm not going."

Doug led his mare out of her stall. "Morning, Granny. Can you give Master Hamish or Master Walter a message before they leave for the duke's?"

"Aye. You have some advice?"

"Aye. Don't waste their breath saying how much losing the bridge hurts us. Tell the duke how it hurts him. Master Hamish knows everybody that

19

goes past on their way to the Quayside market—he can count up how much the duke stands to lose when they can't pay their rents and taxes. And, if we can't get our goods to Quayside, the Water Guild will starve, and the Frost Maiden will come after him."

I said, "That ought to scare him shitless."

Granny cackled. "Thanks, sonny. I'll tell them. Now you—" She waggled a finger at me through the slats. "For God's sake, don't tangle with any witches or wizards, especially from the Water Guild."

I rolled my eyes. I planned on spending an extra day on my way south, to put the hills between them and me.

"Or the Air or Fire Guilds either," she said. "The Earth Guild's the only one you can trust to give a commoner a fair shake."

"Hey, now. I've got friends in the Fire Guild. They're all commoners themselves."

"They're the two-bit kind who make their living putting protection spells on houses, right?"

"Aye, but—"

"The higher ranking they are, the more they favour the aristos. Don't you forget it."

Doug called, "Duncan, you coming?"

"Aye. Be along in a minute." I pulled the girth tight and opened the stall door. "I'm not worried. I'm not going to meet high-ranking wizards and witches of any sort here in Abertee, which is where I'm staying. Sorry, Granny."

The group heading to Nettleton was already on the move. Doug and I trailed behind, leaving a big gap, and talked—one of those conversations I have with Doug where the gaps for thinking are longer than the talking.

"I don't need to get certified," I said. "I'd spend half my time, like Uncle Will did, listening to everybody's troubles and fighting with the duke for them. Every journeyman in North Frankland would be on my doorstep begging for work, and I'd spend my time teaching them and keeping them out of trouble, rather than making things myself. And it would mean six months to a year working for a grandmaster to earn that frostbitten certificate. No thanks, too much trouble."

Doug snorted. "Talking yourself out of it won't work. You'd have it already if everybody wasn't telling you to do it."

"Maybe. But now… Am I more likely to get in trouble with the Water

Guild if I get it or if I don't? If I get it, I'd have the guild at my back, but I'd draw more attention, too."

"Aye. If being pinned down by the light was an omen, it doesn't make much sense. There's nothing they could come after you for."

"Aye. They can't go over the duke's head except for treason—"

"Treason, my arse."

"Or murdering an aristo. Which must be somebody's idea of a bad joke. With the Fire Office shielding them, you can't kill the ones that deserve it. The Water Guild don't like commoners getting above themselves, but they've never gotten a toehold in Abertee to come after us for that. Uncle Will used to say the duke would never let them in—he's as scared of the Frost Maiden as we are."

"Tell me what you've heard about the duke's son."

I sucked my teeth. "He takes after his mum—mean, stupid, and as arrogant as the Frost Maiden. The duchess wouldn't let the duke have any say in raising him. He calls his mother's manor down south home, and doesn't give a mouse's fart about us. He'll let the Water Guild do whatever they like to us."

"Aye, and I've heard he sees red over the clause in the smith's charter giving you the right to tell him what he needs to hear. He's saying he'll revoke the charter when he's duke."

"He can't. The duke's dad tried, but he couldn't. Not without giving us a chance to bargain for what we want in a new one."

"The duke's dad wasn't an air wizard. His son is. Maybe he can."

"Meaning whoever's guild head when he gets to be duke is in for it."

"Meaning," he said, "what's good for Abertee and what's good for you may not be the same thing."

Abertee's problems faded as we rode through the gap at the bottom of the Upper Tee Valley. I grinned like a fool as we rounded the last bend, to where the valley walls opened up. Nettleton—home—was less than a mile away.

I knew every last soul in that valley, and every rock, tree, and rill in it, too. I didn't own any land here—Dad had left Doug the farm since I could make a good living as a smith, and that was fine with me, since I can't stand tending sheep—so it seemed silly to call it my valley, but it was.

Leaving again, after a few hours, made me ache. "Watch for me," I said. "I'll be back in a few weeks."

Maggie said, "We'll expect you when we see you. You're going to Blacksburg, aren't you?"

"Like hell I am. I hate cities. Crossroads is as big as I can stand, and being away from home at Midsummer stunk. Be iced if I'm going to miss Yule, too."

"But, Duncan—"

"Leave him alone, lass," Doug said. "He has to make up his own mind."

A long ride by myself helps with that. I rode into Crossroads determined to ask the local guild to promote me, and settle the question.

The smiths who hadn't already gone home were gathered around Granny Mildred's table, talking about the duke and the bridge. I counted enough noses for a regular guild meeting.

I nudged Granny. "Where's Hazel?"

"Off running some errands for me. Why?"

"Talk her into coming here to stay."

Granny gave me the gimlet eye. "Getting ideas, are you? Well, forget it. Hazel won't look twice at you. She'll never have you if you're not a master smith."

"What the blazes are you going on about? The guild will promote me, and I'll go back to Nettleton to take over for Old Malcolm when he retires, and—"

Master Hamish shook his head at me. "Sorry, lad, but we're not going to promote you."

"What the hell. I'm as good a blacksmith as anybody in Abertee."

"Better," Master Walter said. He wouldn't meet my eyes. None of them would.

"I talked to everyone here," Mildred said, "and most that already left, and got them to agree. They won't promote you, and let you off easy. If you want to be a master, go to Blacksburg and get certified. If you can't get that certificate, don't bother coming back."

Blacksburg

Blacksburg lived down to its name. With no wind blowing off the sea, smoke from thousands of cooking fires, lamps, and forges hung over the city like a shroud. The buildings were so dirty that one ten years old looked the same as one two hundred. Faces, trees, and even fresh-washed sheets hanging on the line looked drab and grey. The only bright colours were in the rich folk's clothes. The only white in the whole city was the duke's palace. Earth Guild magic, probably, paid for over and over again out of taxes. He should've paid the Air Guild to blow the smoke away, and make things better for everybody.

A deep breath of the smoke, mixed with the stink of night soil, horse manure, rotting vegetables, offal, sweat, and the heavy perfumes the women used to cover the other rot, made me double over, coughing and gagging. I got used to it after a while—mostly—but I woke every morning swearing that when I got back to Abertee I would pay Granny Mildred to purge the poisons from my system.

Blacksburg taught me one thing at least: not to laugh at people who couldn't follow directions. I could have found my way anywhere in Abertee, blindfolded. My first afternoon in Blacksburg, in trying to find a stable for Charcoal and a bed for myself, I couldn't have found my way out of a burlap sack. Everybody I asked directions of rattled off things like make a right where the cooper used to be and a left where the Horse and Hound burned down. If they said you can't miss it, I was sure to. The smith in the last town up the road had recommended a boarding house a few blocks downriver from the main city square; I must have passed within spitting distance of it half-a-dozen times before I found it.

The smith had warned me about the wee houses, and that most smiths

23

wouldn't have room for boarders, but I still grumbled under my breath as I forked over a week's rent. If the rates for journeymen in Blacksburg didn't cover room and board, I'd be in trouble. I unpacked my saddlebags in a room with none of the comforts of home, and lay awake working out how many weeks I could stay before I went broke if they paid me what I would've earned in Abertee.

I was the first boarder in the dining room, and had eaten half my breakfast before the next one showed. He returned my "Good morning" with a bleary stare and a mumble, and settled in the farthest corner. The others trickling in did the same. Only one bothered to talk to me, and that was to say, "New here, aren't you?" and to warn me that talking too much would make people nervous. Saying that much must have made him nervous, because he grabbed a boiled egg and a fistful of bread, and bolted. I finished without talking to anyone else, and went looking for the swordsmiths.

Later, I discovered that Grandmaster Clive's smithy was only half-a-mile from the boarding house. I must have walked four miles before finding it in a welter of narrow, twisting streets near the docks. I found it then only because, as I got close enough, I followed my ears rather than the directions.

Grandmaster Clive made a good impression even before I stuck my head in his door. The smithy yard was neat, well-tended. The sweet music of hammers said the smithy was full of men hard at work. I walked in and asked for the master. Without putting his hammer down, a journeyman jerked his head towards a dim corner. Sparks flew as metal scraped against a grindstone. I edged towards the corner, and waited for my eyes to adjust. The glint of light off steel hanging on the wall caught my eye, and I leaned closer for a good look.

A rack held a half-dozen swords: a lightweight one on top with a blade thin enough to bend if you touched it, several heavier ones in different sizes and degrees of finish, and on the bottom, one five-feet long that even I would have had to use two hands to swing. In the flickering red light from the forge, they seemed to eel across the wall like they were alive. My hands itched to take them down, to test out the balance, to see how much the blade of the lightest one would flex.

I bent down to study the inlay work on the biggest sword, and almost drooled. Guild symbols and writing—spells, no doubt—were etched into the blade as well. I couldn't read what it said, but it didn't matter—it was the prettiest blade I'd ever seen.

The grindstone came to a halt. The man sitting at it said, "I'm Master Clive. What can I do for you?"

I straightened up and introduced myself. "I've never seen swords like either the top one or the bottom one, or so many together in one place. The other grandmasters I've met either had only one in their smithy, or none at all."

"Who've you met?"

He nodded as I named them. "I'm one of the few that makes swords without a buyer already lined up. There's not much call for new ones, since they're for show these days, what with the Fire Warlock fighting all our wars, and the Frost Maiden scaring the nobles out of fighting each other."

"If they're for show, I guess that means they're not dangerous."

"Don't insult me."

"Sorry, sir. I didn't—"

"Of course they're dangerous." He wrapped a polishing cloth around the lightest sword's hilt. He pulled it off the rack and jabbed it at me. I backed away. "This one would poke through a chest even as thick as yours and out the other side, and if I got lucky and hit your heart, you'd be dead." He laid it back on the rack and hefted the two-handed monster. "This would cut through your thigh bone, no sweat." He grinned. "Not that I would. I don't want Her Iciness coming for me. Besides, it'd be a shame to dull the edge. But it'll chop through bone like my wife's kitchen knife through new cheese."

He slid the polishing cloth along the sword's blade, and let the sword settle into its felted slot in the rack. He wiped dust I couldn't see off the shiny blade and scrubbed at the hilt.

I said, "Why'd you make that one so heavy, if you weren't sure you'd find a buyer?"

"Because I can. I may never sell it."

"I would, too, I guess, if I could." Not that I'd ever get the chance, and there was no point in dreaming. The grandmaster pulled a sword from the middle of the rack, and carried it out into the yard. I followed. "What would it take to make that one shatter?"

He sat on a bench, waved me to a spot at the end, and began polishing the blade. "No idea. I beat the spell into it—I've beaten the spell into all my swords—but it's been centuries since we've heard of an aristos' sword shattering in his hands for lifting it against somebody he was sworn to protect. God knows there are enough stories going around about them treating everybody under them like dirt. I don't know if it means the aristos have stopped swearing to protect their vassals, or if we've forgotten something in the spell, or…" He shrugged. "Or maybe we swordsmiths aren't strong enough wizards anymore to make the magic work."

"Or maybe the aristos pay their lackeys to do the dirty work, instead of doing it themselves. If they're not actually using the sword…"

"That may be most of it, though there are some you'd think their swords would shatter just from being in the same room with them." He gripped the sword blade with the polishing cloth, and held it out to me, hilt first. "Here, give it a swing."

"I don't need a broken hand."

He snorted. "That story about them breaking commoners' hands is hogwash. It's the same earth guild spell you'd put on anything valuable. It breaks a thief's hand, but not the owner's, or anybody else he lets use it. Go on, take it."

I gripped it, and sure enough, it did me no damage. I swung the tip through a circle in the air. It felt alive in my hands, like part of my arm. I opened my fist, and the sword balanced flat on the edge of my hand. I gripped it again, and gave it a good swing.

Master Clive winced. "Guess you've never seen anybody swing one before. It's a sword, not a hammer." He took it back from me. "Not that I'm going to show you. I'm already in deep shit with the Black Duke, who thinks I'm too fond of my own work. The notion that any commoner has his hand on a sword keeps him awake nights." He shot me a keen look. "Enough of this. You didn't come to see me about swords."

"Nae, sir. I need to be a certified master. I'm hoping you'll take me on."

"You and every other journeyman in Blacksburg. I've got a full smithy."

"I can see that. If I stick around in Blacksburg, then when one of your journeymen moves on…"

"Then I'll have to take on one of the several dozen others already waiting. You could be waiting for a couple of years, or more."

"Fire and frostbite. I haven't got a couple of years."

"What's your hurry?"

I explained about Uncle Will, and Abertee needing a certified master.

He studied me from under bushy black eyebrows. "Sent you, eh?" He went back to polishing. After a bit, he said, "Ever been tested for magic talent?"

"Aye, when I was twelve, like everybody else. I've got a little, but nothing to brag about."

"Fire, or earth?"

"Both. I can light a fire, and dig a bit, and nothing else. I could've joined either guild, if I'd wanted."

"Can you hold a shield against the heat from the forge?"

"Nae."

"Shame. Would've been handy."

"Don't I know it."

"So why didn't you? Become a wizard, that is. Most boys think that's easier and more exciting than being a blacksmith."

"I don't mind hard work, and I was already as big as some men, and still growing. Uncle Will had agreed to take me on as apprentice, and I wanted to be a top-notch smith more than a one-flame wizard."

"If hard work doesn't scare you, there's another way to earn a certificate. Make a masterpiece, instead."

"What's that?"

"A piece of work just for show that's complicated enough, and has enough variety, to show you know what smithcraft is all about. Sign on with another master in town, work on it in your free time, and bring it to the guild meeting when it's done. The local guild, that is, not the royal association. If they decide it's good enough, they'll advise us to certify you. It would take months, but not as long as waiting for a chance to work for Randall or me."

I chewed on that. "I'd have to pay for it out of my own pocket, I suppose."

"Of course. You won't get it back either. Guild rules say you have to turn it over to them before they'll advise us to certify you."

"Frost it! That's a steep price for a bit of paper."

"Depends on how bad you want it. Other smiths have done it. Take a look at the masterpieces in the guildhall, and see what you think."

"I will, if Grandmaster Randall doesn't have room for me either."

"He won't. There's only one queue. There's a roster in the guild hall, which you should sign. Whenever a journeyman leaves either of us, we have to take whoever's next on the list. The local guild would have our heads if we didn't—they say that's the only way that's fair."

I groaned. "I'll head for the guildhall next, then, if you'll tell me how to get there."

"From here, easy. You can't miss it."

The clerk added my name without comment to a fat ledger.

"How long's the wait?" I said.

He scratched his nose and started counting backwards, working his way to a bookmarked page, where half the names had been struck through. "About two-and-a-half years, I'd say."

"How long would it take to make a masterpiece?"

"Not less than three months, if you're in a tearing hurry and work on it every day, including Sundays. Most take six months to a year."

My shoulder ached just thinking about doing nothing more than swinging a hammer, seven days a week, for months, but I was in a hurry. Even if I wasn't... "Why would anybody wait nearly three years if they could be done in less than one?"

"Most journeymen want the chance to learn from the grandmasters."

I'd trained under Will Archer, and he'd been the best. I'd be a better smith in three years, anyway, with or without their help. "I would, too, if I was starting out, but it's not enough of a payout for my time, when I'm good enough to be a master now."

The clerk gave me a long look over his spectacles. "Making a masterpiece is hard work, and it'll cost you—"

"But by being a master earlier, I'd make it up."

"Maybe. Assuming the Council likes what you've done. They might not, despite your high opinion of yourself. And when you turn it over to the guild to be judged, we strike your name from the roster. If they don't accept it, you'll have to sign the roster again, at the end—"

"Frostbite."

"Assuming they don't tell you not to bother, you'll never be good enough. They've done that, too. But if you want to try, take a look at the masterpieces here in the hall. Take your time."

I had already been eyeing the ironwork lining the walls. In the right place, a few would have been useful—a garden gate, or a candelabrum too big for anything other than a lord's manor house. A few others were nice to look at, like the statues the duke had in his garden just to make it pretty. But the others…

One freestanding monstrosity, taller than my head, was a mess of grape clusters, wisteria, thorny blackberries, and other fanciful vegetation that would never grow close together. It looked off-balance, too, but a light poke set it turning on its base. Not off-balance at all. Whoever made it, he was a damn good smith. Too bad it looked like a thicket in need of clearing out.

Most showed that the smith knew every trick any smith in Frankland had ever thought of, without being pretty or useful. In Abertee, we'd never had enough charcoal or coal, or pig iron cheap and ready to hand that we could waste on junk like this. Only the duke and a few other rich folk could afford ironwork just for show, and they made sure what they had was worth looking at. For the rest of us, anything tossed on the scrap heap got pulled back out and reused. And reused, until it rusted away or crumbled into pieces.

On the way out, I asked the clerk what they would do when they got a new masterpiece.

"Shove one of the older ones into the shed out back, along with the rest."

"There can't be more."

"Sure there are. These are the most recent, and a few older pieces the guild is most proud of. We've been collecting them for centuries. The basement's already crammed full, and we'll run out of room in the shed in another decade or two."

I left, shaking my head over the waste of good iron.

Grandmaster Randall's smithy door stopped me in my tracks. I gaped at the lintel. I didn't have to duck.

Inside, the grandmaster was obvious right away. Only a couple of inches shorter than me, his bald head gleamed in the red light. We measured each other for a moment. I liked what I saw—laugh lines at the corners of his eyes, a nose broken and healed without the Earth Guild's help, and a ready smile.

He turned that smile on me. "Welcome, stranger. It's rare I meet a man bigger than me."

"Aye, nobody's topped me since I was sixteen. Only my uncle and brother have come close."

His smile widened. "There're more like you? Good God. Where? You sound like you're from up north."

"Aye, sir. Abertee."

"Abertee, eh? You put me in mind of another man I met from Abertee, more years ago than I care to remember, when we were both journeymen in Sheffield—Will Damned-if-I-can-remember-his-last-name."

"That would've been my uncle, Will Archer."

When I left, a couple hours later, I had a good dinner under my belt, a sketched-out map in my pocket marked with the locations of other smithies that might take on a journeyman, and a pledge that he'd buy me a beer at The Hammer and Anvil some night after I'd had a chance to settle in. Maybe Blacksburg wasn't such a bad place, after all.

Master Hal

The next few days I roamed the city, keeping Charcoal reined in to a slow walk, chatting up anyone willing to talk—a rag picker here, a tinsmith there, pretty lasses everywhere. The friendliest of the lot, a green-grocer's daughter, lived on the same street as the boarding house.

But mostly I studied the ironwork. There was plenty—gates, fences, window grills, balcony railings, lanterns, hitching rings, doorknockers. You name it, it was there, and made to be pretty, not just because they needed it. Even the iron straps on the stable doors had three-lobed ends for show. Some looked hard, most didn't, but nearly all I could have done. Even the pieces I hadn't seen before were obvious, once I got a close look.

If not for the grill on its window, I wouldn't have given the shop a second glance. I had no more use for a store selling books than for one selling hair ribbons. Less—I'd bought hair ribbons for a winsome lass before. But after eyeing the grill, I started down the street, then backtracked and stared at the scroll behind the glass—a map of North Frankland, twice as big as the largest Uncle Will had.

I pressed my face against the grill, but reflections made it hard to see. On a closer look, inside, I drooled. This map was detailed enough to have Nettleton on it.

The shopkeeper told me what he wanted for it, and I walked away, grumbling. I never could see why something someone made while sitting at a desk all day should cost so much.

My foot was already in the stirrup before another idea sent me back in for a quire of foolscap. The charcoal I could get from a smithy. My head swam with ideas. The problem wouldn't be knowing what to put in a masterpiece—it would be deciding what to leave out, or I'd spend two years on it. I stuffed the paper in my saddlebags and went on surveying the ironware.

I had started at the edge of the city, and worked my way in. The biggest, fanciest pieces—the fence around the duke's palace, the Fire Guild gate, and the town hall's clock tower—were in the city square. I edged around the palace and eased out into the square, but jerked back out of sight. To get a good look at the duke's gate, I'd have to be in full view of the Water Guildhall. It sat catty-cornered to the palace, and on the same little rise, with a good view of the parade grounds in front.

Aristos went this way and that across the square, either thumbing their noses at the Water Guild, or they were so used to it that it stopped bothering them. Maybe it never bothered them. Her Iciness was on their side, after all.

After that I started looking for the smithies Master Randall had marked on the map. The first smithy's yard was weedy and untidy, the buildings needed repairs, and a couple of apprentices loafed around the side. I didn't stop. The second smithy looked more prosperous. I started talking terms with the master, but when I said I wanted to work on a masterpiece, he said, "Fine, but it'll be on your own time."

"That's what I'd expect."

"And you'll have to pay for every bit of charcoal and every scrap of iron you use."

"Fair enough."

"And don't think you can cheat me and get away with it. I keep track of everything coming in and everything going out, and I'll know if you cheat me."

Nobody in Abertee would say that to me and hope to get away with it. I clenched my jaw. "How many journeymen have cheated you?"

His mouth settled into a thin line. "None, because they know I'm watching. Anybody'll cheat you if they can get away with it."

"My Granddad used to say a man is quickest to accuse you of the sins he's guilty of himself. I mostly tell people off for being too big for their boots. See you." I walked out and didn't look back.

The third smithy was doing a brisk business in ordinary household hardware—pokers, hinges, latches, door pulls, and the like—but the master looked like he was chewing lemons. I was beginning to doubt Master Randall's judgement. When Master Hal said he could only promise work on a week-to-week basis, I said that suited me fine.

When I talked about making a masterpiece, and promised to pay him for everything I used, he shrugged. "You can if you want, but let me warn you—in the fifteen years I've run this smithy, I've had a dozen or so journeymen work on masterpieces. Most gave up after a while, 'cause it was too much trouble. Of the ones that finished, well…"

"The guild turned it down?"

"That, or the blacksmiths' guild approved it, and the swordsmiths still thumbed their noses at it. I've known some that got certified that way, but no one working for me ever did."

I needed work, so I shrugged it off. We came to terms without much trouble, he set me to making firedogs, and I dove in with a good will. It felt good to be back to work, even though drawing a deep breath made me cough. I stopped worrying and enjoyed myself for a while.

We closed early on Saturday, and he said, "You've gotten off to a real good start. Come on down to the pub with me."

"Sure. Where? The Hammer and Anvil?"

He made a face. "No, I don't go there often. I can't take the high and mighty attitudes of some of their regulars. It's the Three Horseshoes for me."

I followed him to the Three Horseshoes, where he introduced me to a tableful of farriers. They made room, but nobody offered to buy the newcomer a beer. Still, I wasn't having a bad time until the smith I'd called a cheat stomped in, and greeted Master Hal like his best buddy. He saw me, and went off in a corner by himself, where he gave me dark glares over his pint.

When the talk got around to women, as it usually does, that freckle-faced earth witch kept coming to mind, but she was far away, and I'd seen pretty faces in Blacksburg. It was still early…

The farriers got happy in their cups, and when one suggested heading to Mama Somebody's whorehouse, they said it was a great idea and staggered out into the street. They turned one way; I turned the other. Master Hal said, "Aren't you coming, Duncan?"

The farrier who'd raised the idea snickered. "Maybe he's not interested." Another said, "He's so big everywhere else, there wasn't anything left…" That set them all laughing.

I said, "I don't like paying for stale goods, when there's fresher to be had for free." They stopped laughing. I turned and walked away.

Plenty of people have accused me of acting high and mighty, and I don't deny it. Next time, I'd go to the Hammer and Anvil. Maybe I'd like that crowd better.

On Sunday, I rode Charcoal miles out into the countryside—far enough away to give my lungs and head a chance to clean out in the crisp, cool air. I stopped at a country inn for beer and beef pie. When the pie was gone, I fished the paper and charcoal out of my saddlebags, and started sketching ideas. After an afternoon's hard work, I tore them up and rode back to the city in a black mood.

Granny Mildred's advice, most of which I meant to ignore, rang in my ears. Stop being neighbourly, my arse. But keeping my mouth shut, I had to admit, was good advice. Too bad I hadn't taken it. You can't ask somebody if they took something you said as an insult if you think the odds are at least even they didn't, and you don't want them to start thinking maybe they should have.

Maybe someday I would learn to keep my mouth shut.

Come Monday morning, Master Hal acted as friendly as the week before. Maybe I shouldn't have worried. He asked me what I'd done on Sunday, and I told him about the torn up sketches.

He laughed. "Told you it was hard work. If you ask me, it's wasted time and money. Those certificates are to keep the competition down, so the smiths that have theirs can charge more than the rest of us. It's a scam. That's all it is."

That brought me up short. I'd heard muttering along those lines in Abertee, but not so strong, and it had always been from those who had no chance of earning one, so I'd not paid it much mind. I said, "Maybe you should have tried to get certified."

He scowled. "I did. I didn't do a masterpiece, but I worked for Brother Randall. He said I wasn't good enough. The hell I wasn't. I've got my own smithy now, apprentices and all. People buy what I make, so who's to say I'm not good enough?"

I didn't say it, not then. If he hadn't made a fuss, I wouldn't have given it any heed—plenty of good smiths in Abertee weren't certified—but I thought it more than once in the coming days. He was good at what he did, but what he did was limited. He didn't have the patience to make knives or dozens of yards of fencing, the eye to make something pretty, or the head to make a tool he'd never seen.

I didn't see all that right away. What bothered me at the time was his inclination to blame anyone but himself for his troubles.

"The Guild stinks," he said. "I pay a fortune every year in dues. If I didn't, I could have as nice a house as Master Paul."

"Master Paul pays the same dues," I said. "Maybe he manages his money better. And it's fair that everybody pays—the Guild takes care of us, we have to take care of the Guild."

"Takes care of us, my arse. Let me tell you what the Guild does for me: nothing."

"The Guild keeps the duke and the other aristos from taking everything you've made and paying you halfpence for it."

"They don't want the stuff I make, so what good does that do me? The Guild sets the prices too low for the things I do make. The apprenticeship fees aren't high enough, either."

"You earn the same off them as any other master."

"No, I don't. They're such a sorry lot they only give me half the work they're supposed to."

"Which is fair," I said, "since you're only teaching them half what they need to know."

It went downhill from there. A tailor came into the smithy one day, waving his hands and not using the right names for things. Master Hal was short with him, and would have sent him away empty-handed if I hadn't figured out he wanted an auger and a couple of clamps. Master Hal was happy to make a sale, but didn't like me showing him up. It didn't help that the tailor came back a couple of days later, asking for 'that chap who knows what's what.'

Master Hal didn't invite me to come along to the Three Horseshoes again. When we closed on Saturday, I went to the Hammer and Anvil. Master Clive was there, talking to a cutler. He waved me over, bought me a pint, and we talked knives for the better part of two hours.

When Master Randall showed up, he made good on his promise, and asked if I had started thinking about a masterpiece. I told him about tearing up the sketches, and he smiled.

"That's normal. Nobody gets it right on the first try. If you came up with a sketch and started on it that fast, I doubt it would be good enough."

"You've got a point. If you've got any advice, let me know."

"Tell me your opinion of the masterpieces in the Guild Hall."

"Not much. Most of them were showing off way too hard. But if that's what it takes…" I shrugged.

"What would impress you?"

"I'd've been more impressed if they were useful and pretty at the same time, without shouting about it."

"Then the only advice I'll give you," he said, "is forget about trying to impress anybody else. Impress yourself."

I rode out to the country inn again on Sunday, and made more sketches. When Master Hal asked again on Monday about my ideas, I showed him the best—a three-legged, six-armed lamp stand. Each branch and leg was different, to show off different techniques. It could be used— if somebody wanted to, and the Guild let them—but only an aristo, or someone else with more money than sense, would call it pretty. I couldn't figure out how to make it look good and still put in a sample of everything I knew.

But I'd bet franks to farthings Master Hal couldn't make it. Maybe it would do.

He didn't think so. He scowled at it, then started sketching in other branches. "You're not showing you can do splits. Put one in like this—"

"I can do splits. See here—"

"Not enough. They could overlook that."

"A little one with a spike through will be harder than the big one you just drew in. And if I have to do all that, it'll take me a year."

He threw up his hands. "I'm just saying, they want to see what you can do, so show them everything."

"And if I do, are you sure they won't turn it down?"

"How should I know? I told you, no journeyman of mine has ever gotten certified that way."

"If you don't know, then there's no point in taking your advice."

He gave me a dirty look. "Enough of this nonsense. Get back to work."

"Sorry. I didn't mean—"

"Sure you didn't." He walked away, muttering to himself.

His oldest apprentice said, so soft I had to bend down to hear him,

"The last journeyman who tried gave up after not getting a solid weld for more than two weeks. I dug clinkers out of the firepit every morning."

I sucked my teeth. "You're saying Master Hal poisoned his own forge."

The lad shrugged. "Don't know for sure. He said we'd been sold a load of bad coal, but it seemed funny that the problems only showed in the evening, when the journeyman was working by himself."

Master Hal kept giving me dirty looks, and grumbling about the guilds and their frostbitten certificates until everybody in the smithy was sick of hearing him. By Saturday I'd had enough.

"All week," I said, "you've been saying the certificates are too hard to get, and aren't worth getting anyway. Make up your mind which it is. If they're hard to get, that says to me they're worth something."

"Those what have them sure think so," he said. "Lording it over the rest of us. You act like one, and you haven't even got the frosted thing."

"Not yet, but I will."

"Sure of it, aren't you? I've had more of your attitude than I can take. Clear out your tools, and don't bother coming back on Monday."

"No problem. I wasn't interested in coming back, anyway."

The apprentice who had warned me about the clinkers said he was sorry I wouldn't be back. "You've taught me more in three weeks than he has in six months."

I said, "I'll have my own smithy before you set out as a journeyman. If you get as far north as Abertee, come see me. I'll take you on."

On Sunday, I reworked my sketches, without Master Hal's additions, and grumbled about time slipping away. October was on us already, and a certificate seemed as far out of reach as it had in August. I had no smithy to work in, and even if I'd had one, I couldn't start a masterpiece from scratch and finish it in time for Yule. That thought made me want to punch somebody, if I could figure out who.

On Monday, I went searching for a smithy that wasn't on Master Randall's list.

Paul Hammer

The yard was tidy, the buildings in good repair. A pair of apprentices sparred with quarterstaves, making beginner's mistakes. My hands itched to grab my staff and show them how it was done.

In the house, a lass was singing. Smells coming from the kitchen made my mouth water. I caught the master, Paul Hammer, finishing his dinner, and asked if he needed a journeyman. "Hammer's a good name for a smith, but I guess you're tired of hearing that."

He smiled. "Probably as tired as you are of fools asking how's the weather up there. The name fits because I come from a long line of smiths, going way back before anybody had to have last names. Why'd you come here?"

"Because the touchmark with the two crossed hammers kept showing up on gates and fences I liked the looks of. The clerk at the Guildhall said it was yours." And, when I had asked, the clerk said he had earned a certificate from Master Clive's father.

"Your timing couldn't be better," Master Paul said. "My best journeyman left at the end of last week, to go work for Master Clive. Let's see what you can do."

I followed him into the smithy. A journeyman and two apprentices banged away on a balcony railing, and another journeyman and apprentice, Master Paul said, were out for the afternoon installing fencing. He showed me his sketches for other jobs he had lined up—gates, fencing, railings. I liked the looks of it all.

He set me to work on a section of railing, and waved an apprentice over. "Sam, here, can be your striker."

About fifteen, and on his way to being tall and broad-shouldered, the lad was still at that stage where his arms and legs had outgrown the rest of him. Maggie might have called him cute, if he hadn't been sporting a fading purple and green ring around one eye.

It wasn't my business.

I heard myself say, "How'd you get that black eye?"

The lad's face closed up, and he mumbled something.

"Speak up, lad."

"None of your frostbitten business." That, anyway, wasn't mumbled.

I held up a hand. "Sorry. Being friendly, that's all. Forget I said anything." I made a few lame jokes, and he got less surly, but not talkative.

Master Paul's smithy lay across the square from the boarding house. I wandered through a maze of narrow streets and old houses, and had to make do on the scraps the other boarders had left from supper. The next morning I had just left the boarding house when the apprentice cut across the street ahead of me.

I caught up. "Hey, Sam, I guess you live nearby."

His face closed tight. "Yes sir, my mum runs one of the women-only boarding houses. Well, except for my dad and me. We live there, too." He scuffed along with his head down.

"You know your way around, then. The fastest way to the smithy must be across the square, but that's too open. I walked three times as far last night going around the duke's palace. If you're not cutting across, I'll follow you."

His head came up, the sullen look replaced by a grin. "Fine, since you're not calling me a coward for going around. The safest is past the Earth Guildhall at the other end. The trees and bushes block sight of the Water Guild."

"Lead on, then."

He loosened up as we skirted the square, talking about the rich merchants and aristos owning the fancy houses we passed on the way. Past the Earth Guildhall, the smaller houses weren't kept up as well. The fellow ahead of us would have looked out of place even if the sunlight glancing off his yellow silk suit hadn't made my eyes water.

I nudged Sam. "Who's the peacock?"

He shrugged. "I've wondered that, too. He's got five of those coats, in different colours. I told my mum about him, and she said Master Paul would have to work six months to earn enough for just one suit like that, and that was without paying room and board."

I whistled. "Have you seen him anywhere else?"

"Just between here and the wharves. He goes in and out of one of those houses like he lives there."

"Not likely, dressed like that. I'd guess he's got a wife in one of the fancier houses, and a girlfriend tucked away down here, out of sight. Although I'm surprised he doesn't slink in and out the back door."

"Why bother? His rich friends wouldn't see him leave."

"Not good for his girlfriend. Her neighbours would gossip."

"Why would an aristo care? Her problem, not his. They treat women—commoners, anyway—like dirt."

"Aye, they do." We followed him a quarter-mile, before turning towards the smithy.

We reached Master Paul's house and heard him through an open window, talking to his wife. Sam's face closed tight again.

I said, "Something wrong?"

"Glenn may be there already."

"Glenn?"

"The other journeyman."

A man wearing a scowl stepped out of the smithy as I reached it. A hefty fellow, his nose was level with my collarbone. His head snapped up, and he backed a step. The scowl deepened, his face got red, and he stepped forward, leading with his chin. "You must be the new journeyman."

"Aye. Duncan Archer." I held out my hand.

He crossed his arms. "Let's get one thing straight. I'm the ranking journeyman. You take orders from me when Master Paul's not around."

"You get something straight. I take orders from the master because he pays me. I take orders from aristos because I have to. I don't take orders from anybody else who hasn't earned my respect."

We glared at each other. He was a brawny fellow, with upper arms the size of hams—big even for a smith. I'd seen him at the Three Horseshoes, with the smith I'd called a cheat. If he stuck his chin out any further, it would run into my fist and break.

Master Paul called "Good morning." The journeyman backed down. "I see you've met Glenn," the master said.

The journeyman held out his hand. "Glenn Hoskins." We gripped, and he tried to break my fingers. Master Paul ducked on into the smithy with Sam on his heels. I let go. Glenn couldn't quite hide flexing his aching hand.

I ducked into the smithy, kept my mouth shut and my eyes open for the rest of the day, and watched Master Paul parcel out work one item at a time. Whenever somebody finished one job, he had to ask what to work on next. If Master Paul was talking to a customer, or had stepped out of the smithy, Glenn gave the orders instead.

He wasn't going to get a chance to give me orders. Master Paul was pleased enough with what I'd done, that when, at the end of the day, I rattled off a list of things I wanted to work on tomorrow, he said that was fine with him.

We walked out of the smithy with Glenn glaring after me, and Sam smirking. Once out of earshot, I said, "Glenn gave you that black eye, I'd guess."

Sam mumbled something I took as a yes.

"What did Master Paul say when you told him?... What was that? Speak up."

"I didn't, and he didn't ask. Master Paul doesn't know what's going on, because Glenn behaves himself as long as he's in earshot. I complained to Steve—the journeyman that just left—about Glenn, and he told me to stand up for myself, and not let anybody push me around."

I scratched my chin. "Holding your own against the other apprentices is one thing. But it's not fair when the fellow beating you up outranks you, or outweighs you by several stone."

"What do I do, then?"

"Good question. Master Paul should be keeping a better eye on his smithy. He ought to know he won't get good work out of you lads if you're spending your time looking over your shoulders, wondering when you're going to get hit next."

Sam's sullen look faded. Maybe all he needed was somebody to listen. Maybe he didn't notice I hadn't given him much of an answer.

A few days later the peacock stepped out of his gate as we walked by. I hailed him. "Good morning, sir. Are you heading down to the wharves?"

"Good morning to you, too, sir. I am indeed. And you?"

"We're headed towards Paul Hammer's smithy, about halfway down." I held out my hand. "Duncan Archer, journeyman blacksmith, and this is Sam Jackson, apprentice."

"Pleased to meet you, Mr Archer, Mr Jackson. Richard Collins, purveyor of luxury fabrics—silks, damasks, and the like."

"Aha. That explains the fancy silk suit."

"Certainly. I have an image to maintain. If I didn't look prosperous, I would scare away my clientele."

I looked over my shoulder at the shabby house. Clothes didn't mean much to me. I'd put my money in a comfortable home.

He smiled. "If I were in another line of business, I wouldn't dress as splendidly, I assure you. It's a good thing my clients don't see my house. I can't afford to keep up the image both in my shop and at home."

"I thought you'd be making a handsome profit dealing in luxury goods."

He made a face. "Who do you think my customers are?"

"Rich merchants and aristos, I'd guess."

"Exactly. If I could force the aristocrats to pay what they owe me, I would be quite well off."

"Huh. I guess you can't refuse to do business with them."

"Not if I want to continue to live in this city." He shrugged. "My paying customers are primarily merchants of other luxury goods, who also struggle to make ends meet. Someday soon we may all go bankrupt together."

I started on the base for my lamp stand, spending an hour or two in the smithy by myself, several nights a week. Glenn hung back one day until Master Paul left, to ask what I was doing.

"Working on a masterpiece, to get certified faster."

He frowned. "What makes you think you can get certified at all?"

I didn't bother answering.

"My name's near the top of the list," he said. "In another month or two I'll be working for one of the swordsmiths, and can stop kissing up to this idiot. I'll be certified before you are, even if you work your arse off on this piece of junk." He nodded at my sketches. "That what you're making?"

"Aye."

He picked them up and leaned close to the firepit. I blocked him. "You'll not go throwing them in the fire."

He scowled and flipped through the pages. "You sure got a high opinion of yourself. Someday, somebody's going to take you down a notch."

"Maybe. But it won't be you."

He flung burning papers in my face. I should've known he had a bit of fire magic; many smiths do. The bastard was gone before I had stamped out the flames, and finished the sketches' ruin myself, but his laugh echoed in my ears. I patched up my burns with an ache in my soul. Every smithy I'd worked in before Blacksburg had been a little piece of home. I'd never expected to feel homesick even in a smithy.

Belling the Cat

When I started, I did a poor job of planning the lamp stand, and would've had a devil of a time fitting some parts together, or adding some doodad without breaking something I'd already done. Now, after drawing the thing as a whole, I drew each leg and each arm by itself, thinking through every detail, and numbering every split, every upset, every bend, every weld, to remember what order to do them in.

After a week of that, I'd had as much as I could stand for a while, and went back to working on the base, although the drawings weren't finished. Glenn kept snickering at me, and telling Jack he'd be surprised if it was half done in two years.

The days were getting shorter, and the gloom hanging over the city seeped into me and sapped my spirits. I ought to have been spending every evening in the smithy working on that masterpiece, to get it done and go home, but I couldn't find the enthusiasm to keep at it. I couldn't even get up any enthusiasm to grab my quarterstaff and spar with the apprentices.

Early in November, when the greengrocer's daughter Annie suggested listening to a preacher who had been drawing big crowds, it seemed like a good excuse to spend time away from the smithy. I changed my mind after hearing him talk. Reverend Angus was a rabble-rouser—a fine talker who spouted a lot of nonsense while sounding like he was preaching the gospel truth. The worst of the nonsense was his opinion that the root of our problems wasn't the aristos, but the magic guilds and the four Offices. I agreed with him about the Water Guild, but his rants about the other magic guilds raised my hackles.

"Getting rid of the Frost Maiden sounds like a good idea," I said on the way back. "I guess you wouldn't like that, but—"

"Why wouldn't I?" Annie said. "She scares me, too. Being a woman doesn't mean much. She's not doing anything for her common sisters these days."

"How's that? She keeps the aristos from treating every pretty lass like a whore."

"Does she? Nobody's heard of one getting his privates frozen off in ages—"

"Aye, that's so, but—"

"And they get what they want. Maybe not by dragging a girl away by the hair, kicking and screaming, but they're doing something nasty. I bet they're using magic to make the girls think they agreed to it, so they won't complain to the Frost Maiden."

"But—"

"I know what I'm talking about. Until a couple of months ago, my cousin wouldn't have given the duke's nephew the time of day. Now she's hiding in his attic, crying her eyes out, but won't hear of complaining to the Water Guild."

That brought me up short. "Magic, you say."

"Sure seems like it."

"But that sounds like just another way for a man to force himself on a lass. The Frost Maiden shouldn't stand for it."

Annie shrugged. "I don't know why she does, but there are too many stories like that going around lately. You listen—you'll hear them."

I listened, and heard stories I wished I hadn't. My gorge rose, and my opinion of the Black Duke and his family sank. My homesickness got worse. Those kinds of things just didn't happen in Abertee.

Master Paul told the other journeymen and apprentices that if they finished a piece when he wasn't in the smithy, they were to ask me what to do next. Glenn looked ready to spit. Later in the day, Master Paul left the smithy to measure a customer's property, and Glenn knocked an apprentice into the wall. I caught it out of the corner of my eye, and swung on around.

"You'll not give me any more lip," Glenn snarled at Johnny.

"I didn't hear any lip," I said.

Glenn turned his glare on me. The apprentices froze, watching us. Jack, the other journeyman, kept banging away, pretending he didn't notice.

"I've been here for months," Glenn said. "You can't claim you know Johnny here better than I do."

Johnny was a snivelling arse-kisser without the guts to give anybody backtalk, but it's not fair to call people names when they can't stand up for themselves. "Maybe not, but I do know about lip. When I give somebody lip, the whole smithy, and the yard, too, knows it."

Glenn shoved his chin in my direction. "Don't you give me any lip, either."

"It's not lip when the other fellow isn't your better." I turned my back on him and kept working.

Turning my back may not have been the smartest thing I've ever done, but damned if I would let him spook me. Uncle Will would never have put up with a rotter like Glenn in his smithy. He called men like Glenn puny midgets, no matter what size they were. He'd never taken any lip from me, either, but then I'd never given him any. Never felt the need to. Everybody in his smithy had been proud to work for him.

God, I missed him.

The next morning I was thinking about Uncle Will again while shovelling coal. I didn't notice Master Paul wasn't in the smithy until Glenn got pissed at Sam. Glenn took a swing, the shovel flew of its own accord, and Glenn's fist slammed into the flat of the blade.

He was too shocked for a moment to even swear.

I plastered a smile on my face and lowered the shovel. "We'd all better watch those wild swings. Somebody could get hurt."

He let loose then, cursing me, my mum, my dad, and my cousins out to the fourth degree. He was still nursing his hand when he ran out of breath. I'd gone back to shovelling with a grin on my face.

I was asking for a fight, but didn't care. I didn't worry until he ducked out with an iron bar in his hand at quitting time. I told Sam to find a different way home, but wasn't surprised when he followed me. I would have done the same.

The next morning, Saturday, I got to the smithy with a split lip, half-a-dozen bruises, and a sore left shoulder. Sam sported a fresh black eye, a cut on his cheek, and a grin. He dropped Glenn's unbloodied iron bar on the heap, and set to pumping the bellows with more enthusiasm than I'd seen in him yet.

We'd been lucky. Damn lucky. Even expecting it, that iron bar had whistled past my ear closer than I'd been happy with.

Glenn never showed up that day. He looked quite a bit worse for wear on Monday. Whenever Master Paul wasn't looking, we eyed each other like a pair of circling dogs. I never turned my back on him that day, but it was too much of a strain, and I soon slipped back into old habits. The first notice I had of Master Paul stepping out was the crash behind me. I turned around to see Glenn sprawled across an overturned section of fencing. The apprentices wore grins, and Journeyman Jack sported a smirk. He reached down to haul Glenn to his feet. "Duncan must be bad luck for you, Glenn. You've gotten pretty clumsy since he's been here."

The gloom in the smithy let up after that. Nobody said anything, but we all took turns keeping an eye on Glenn, and with half-a-dozen burly lads who hated him finally working together, he didn't get a chance to cause trouble—not in the smithy, anyway. I worried he would be waiting for us on the way home again some night, and not by himself, either. We went a different way each night, including cutting across the square. Glenn wouldn't dare set foot near the Water Guildhall, so we often went straight past it. In the dark, it was just another building.

Daylight was another matter. I found the nerve to edge out into the square and inspect the clock tower, but we always went around the Earth Guildhall at the bottom of the square on our way to the smithy. If Richard Collins saw us he'd usually wait, and walk with us until we turned towards the smithy. It was Richard who prodded me to take the tour of the duke's palace offered to commoners on Sunday afternoons.

"Go," he said. "See what they're spending our tax money on."

With paintings, statues, wall hangings, and gold leaf everywhere, it was an eye-opener. The lady giving the tour prattled on and on about each painting's history. I stopped listening, and eyed the ironwork. She didn't mention that, but there was plenty, with Master Randall and Master Paul's touchmarks easy to spot. Somebody working for the duke knew and cared about good smithcraft.

The tour ended in a hall filled with statues—Greek marbles, the guide said. My eyes slid past the rest and locked onto the one at the far end—a gorgeous lass, turning her head to beckon to me. She might once have been alive, caught in mid-action and turned to stone by magic.

We walked the length of the hall and her eyes followed me. I couldn't tear mine away.

"And this," the guide said, waving at her, "is an ancient sorceress. She is said to bear a strong resemblance to our Frost Maiden."

I backed away with my heart hammering. The tour guide waved us out the door, and I tripped over the sill. Even outside, I felt her staring at me, through the wall. I muscled through the crowd to the street, and ran.

The weather turned cold early in December. Our breaths smoked in the morning, and we jogged along to keep warm, but with no wind it was tolerable. Richard Collins wore a wool cloak over his fancy suits; if we hadn't met him at his gate I wouldn't have recognised him.

"I guess you won't sell as much," I said, "but getting paid for everything you sell ought to help."

He said, "What?"

"That is, if your guild goes through with it."

"What are you talking about?"

"The Hammer and Anvil's bartender said the cloth merchants and tailors are going to stop extending credit to the aristos."

"We are?" He stopped dead. Sam and I jogged on a few steps, and had to backtrack to where he was standing, staring at us.

"The bartender seemed pretty sure about it. He said you'll vote at your guild meeting this week, and all the other merchants and craftsmen are betting you'll do it."

"This is the first I've heard of it." He tucked his chin down into his collar. "I'm always the last to hear anything about my own guild."

"It sounds like a good idea. Force them to pay for what they buy."

"Oh, it is. I've been saying for years we ought to."

"Why haven't you then, on your own?"

"Without the guild backing, I'd have been driven out of business. The only way for such an idea to work is for all the cloth merchants to agree, and for the guild to enforce it."

"I hope they do. Good luck."

"Thanks." He walked away with his head down.

If I had heard news that momentous about my own guild from an outsider, I would have been pissed off. He just looked sad.

The cloth merchants and tailors did vote to stop giving the aristos credit. Gossip said most aristos were furious, but the duke laughed, saying it wouldn't last. We—merchants and craftsmen in the other guilds—held our breaths, waiting to see what would happen.

Annie and I had gone back a few times to listen to Reverend Angus, the rabble-rousing preacher. The more I considered what he'd said, the more I thought we must both be wrong about the Water Guild, rather than agreeing with him about the other magic guilds. Maybe the Black Duke was paying him to make trouble for the magic guilds, to take the heat off the aristos.

I stopped going, but hearing other folk talk about how great he was rubbed me the wrong way. By the middle of December, I had gotten fed up. I went, without Annie, to hear him preach.

He said, "I propose a new set of laws that will apply when the onerous Water Office has been dismantled…"

We were packed into City Hall on a Wednesday night, not in church on Sunday. I shoved through the crowd. "Excuse me."

Heads turned. It wasn't the first time I'd been stared at for speaking out of turn, and it wouldn't be the last, but it was the largest crowd I'd ever had waiting for me to make a fool of myself. I said, "I'm all for getting rid of that frosted Water Office, but you remind me of the old fable about belling the cat. Tell us who's going to dismantle the Water Office, and how."

The preacher said, "Sit down, and be quiet. We don't need to address that problem tonight."

The crowd muttered. Nick Cooper, a journeyman cutler I'd drunk with at the Hammer and Anvil, elbowed through to the front. "It's a fair question. Answer it."

The preacher hemmed and hawed, dancing around the question.

I said, "You're talking about getting rid of all the Offices."

"Yes, they are all burdensome. Our country needs to be free of these ancient relics, and—"

"And you mean to drive out all the witches and wizards, and give everything over to the non-magic commoners."

"Yes, their privileges are injurious to a healthy society, where everyone is equal, and—"

"Do you have any sons?"

"What?" He stopped blathering and gave me a blank look. There were other puzzled faces in the room, too.

I said, "Do you have any children? Sons? Daughters?"

"I have two boys, the eldest not yet fifteen."

"If you drive out all the earth witches, tell me who's going to patch them up so they don't die of their burns."

"What rubbish are you—"

"If we don't have the Fire Warlock defending Frankland, they'll have to join the army. And since anybody who's anybody in the Empire is a witch or a wizard, they'll not drive out their magic folk. Our army will be sitting ducks for the Empire's fire wizards. In a few month's we'll be under the Empire's thumb, and they treat commoners with no magic even worse than here."

He drew himself up to his full height and puffed out his chest—it didn't help, next to me—and said, "Get out, and stay out."

"Fine, I don't like your ideas anyway." I jammed my hat on and left, with Nick on my heels. A rumble behind us surprised me, and we stopped on the other side of the street to watch, as half the crowd in the hall followed us out.

Master Randall said, "You're following in your uncle's footsteps, for sure." I answered his grin with one of my own. "How do you know? You haven't seen my work yet."

"I didn't mean that. I meant his habit of speaking his mind. You did Blacksburg a service by telling that preacher off. Word's gone around, too, that you called one smith a cheat and told another he didn't know what the hell he was doing."

"Frostbite." I set my mug down on the bar with a thud. "The preacher's fair game, but making enemies in the guild isn't a good move. I've got to stop saying the first thing that comes into my head."

"I don't know why you should care," the smith on the other side of me said. "They deserved it. It was all true."

"It's never a great idea to piss people off when you don't have to," Master Randall said. "A little tact can go a long way. But that's easier said than done. I'm twice your age and I'm still learning. You didn't say anything to those smiths I haven't said, and they weren't willing to hear it from me, either."

"Is that so." I gave him the gimlet eye. "Why the blazes did you send me to them, instead of to a respectable smith like Master Paul?"

"You told me you wanted to get certified. Those certificates aren't just about how good you are as a smith. They're also about upholding the guild's reputation. The guild protects us; we have to protect the guild. I won't certify a smith who will embarrass us by cheating or shirking his duties."

I leaned in closer, still glaring. "If you want men to behave themselves, don't set them a bad example."

"It's easy for a man to behave himself with me or Clive looking over his shoulder, but maybe that's not his true colours. If you could stomach Master Hal or his friends at the Three Horseshoes for long, you aren't the sort of man we want to certify."

The smith at my elbow clapped me on the shoulder. "But here you are at the Hammer and Anvil. Drink up, lad. You're doing fine."

For the first time in my life, I couldn't get excited about Yule. I'd made enough friends in the city I didn't have to spend it by myself, but even swapping stories over rum punch with half-a-dozen other journeymen at Master Clive's table wasn't as good as being at home. I crawled into bed that night, feeling sorry for myself, and missing Nettleton so bad it hurt.

The festive spirit finally came over me in early January, when Master Randall certified his top journeyman, and Glenn left to take his place. The other boarders gave me funny looks when the visions I had of Glenn kissing Randall's arse, and what he was likely to get for his trouble, made me laugh over my supper.

The next morning, Sam acted like a puppy chasing butterflies. I still had that frostbitten masterpiece to finish, so I was a bit steadier, but not much. Neither of us was prepared for the sick look on Master Paul's face when we stepped into the smithy.

"Duncan," he said. "I'm sorry. I should've…I don't know, done something…"

Jack and the apprentices ringed me with long faces like it was a funeral and I was the dead body.

"What the hell," I said. "Sorry for what?"

Master Paul nodded towards the corner where I had left the lamp stand. I flinched like Charcoal had aimed a kick at my head. Broken, twisted, hammered out of shape, the pieces were a blacksmith's nightmare. Putting them together would earn me nothing but hoots.

"I thought you were working late," Master Paul said. "My wife was nagging me to tell you to stop hammering so we could get to sleep when the noise stopped. I should've gone to see…"

Jack said, "At least he didn't break your tools, or steal them."

"That's because I paid the Earth Guild for protection spells. Didn't think I'd need them for this." I picked the pieces apart and flung them, one by one, on the scrap heap. "When I get my hands on Glenn, he'll—"

"Don't," Master Paul said. "You'll call down the magistrate on yourself, and you're too good to waste your time in the stocks. I'll report him to the guild. It's my smithy. He owes me, too."

"Yes, sir," I said, and set to dealing with the morning's work. An hour later, Master Paul sent me away before I broke everything I touched, so I saddled Charcoal and went for a hard gallop along the towpath upriver.

Returning at a walk, the cloud I'd been under while working on that silly lamp stand lifted. I reached the stable as giddy as Sam had been in the morning, and sang bawdy songs while currying Charcoal, until the head groom told me to shut the hell up.

Master Paul was right; I didn't need to lay hands on Glenn. The next time I saw him, I'd get my revenge by thanking him for doing me such a big favour.

Trouble Brewing

I whistled on my way to the smithy the next morning, breaking off now and then to yawn. I'd been up past midnight, making sketches by lamplight.

Sam watched me out of the corner of his eye the whole way, but I didn't offer to explain. We were the first ones in the smithy, so only Sam saw me toss the sketches for the lamp stand in the fire.

"Frost it, Duncan, you can't give up."

"Who said anything about giving up? Since I have to start over, I decided to make something better than that silly thing." I handed him the new sketches. "Take a look at this gate."

His eyes bugged out. "You can't do that."

"Sure I can. It's my masterpiece—I can do whatever I want."

"But I've never seen…I mean, you just don't…"

"Let me see those." Master Paul stepped through the door and reached for the sketches. His eyes widened. "This is different, that's for sure." He studied them for several minutes before handing them back. "I like the look of it better than that lamp stand, but it's just as well it'll be hanging on the wall in the guildhall rather than in somebody's garden."

"Why?"

"I try to balance a garden gate so well one of those fine ladies can swing it with her little finger."

"Aye. That's why I have the hindquarters coming out here, to balance the head."

"That'll make it balance in one direction, but with the head off-centre like that, sticking out to there, it's going to pull on the hinge a lot harder than the hindquarters."

"Frost it!" I snatched the sketches back and glared at them. "I didn't think about that."

"As heavy as that thing's going to be, it'll take a man with a good strong arm to shove it open. Sure you're ready to be certified?"

"Uh, maybe not."

He laughed. Sam said, "Duncan can make it balance."

Master Paul said, "I didn't mean what I just said. If you make that, whether it balances or not, you'll get certified. If it balances as well, I'll be impressed. Mighty impressed."

I spent a week making detailed sketches before starting on the ram's head, but I'd known while still on horseback what to do. The horns took shape almost by magic, and as soon as the first one was done, I hung it on the smithy wall where it caught my eye every time I pulled an iron from the fire.

That first week, I worked so many hours in the evening, that by Saturday night everything ached. I slept half the day away on Sunday, and Annie slammed the door in my face for not speaking to her all week.

Sam usually stayed late with me. So I wouldn't have to walk back to the boarding house by myself, he said. Maybe so he wouldn't have to walk home by himself. I didn't care. He made himself useful, pumping the bellows and juggling irons in the fire, and I told stories I'd heard from Uncle Will about famous smiths in Frankland's early days.

We were in the smithy one evening when Jack stuck his head in, a big grin on his face. "Master Randall kicked Glenn out of his smithy. Told him he never wanted to see his ugly face again, and to get his iced arse out of Blacksburg because he'd see to it the guild wouldn't ever promote him to master."

Sometimes, Blacksburg wasn't such a bad place, after all.

Towards the end of January, the Black Duke tripled the taxes on luxury goods. "To drive the cloth merchants out of business," Richard Collins said.

"It's affecting everybody," I said. "Master Paul's not going to hire another journeyman to replace the one that left. His commissions are drying up."

"That is unfortunate. I do hope the other guilds don't pressure us to give in. If we do it will make things worse for everyone in the long run."

"Aye. Have you ever thought about leaving Blacksburg and taking your business somewhere else? London, maybe, or Edinburgh?"

"Many times, but I've spent twenty years building my business here, and from the rumours I hear conditions aren't much better anywhere else. Some of my fellow merchants must think it worth a try, though. Several are talking about moving away."

"That ought to help you. Less competition."

He shook his head. "A smaller group is easier for the duke to pressure. If we are too few in numbers, the duke can revoke our charter, and rewrite it as he sees fit."

"Frostbite. And forget about complaining to the king that it's not fair."

One bone-chilling day in February, Master Paul said Master Randall asked him to come to the guildhall for a meeting, and to bring me along.

I asked, "What's the meeting about?"

"Taxes, I think. Some merchants are trying to get them lowered."

"Well, hell, I'm in favour of that. I'll come."

The cursing in Blacksburg about the Black Duke and his taxes had been worse than anything I'd ever heard in Abertee, even before he tripled the luxury tax. I was making good money, and being tight with it, but between the taxes, room and board, and two attempts at a masterpiece, I would leave Blacksburg with less money in my pocket than when I'd arrived.

How a man with a family to support could manage was beyond me. Many weren't managing. Beggars camped on every street corner, and journeymen were bailing. Rumours flew that this craftsman or that shopkeeper would leave as soon as they had a buyer for their shop.

The guild council and a few other smiths—a dozen total, all regulars at the Hammer and Anvil—came to the guildhall that night. I was the only journeyman. We were talking amongst ourselves, guessing what it was about, when Master Randall arrived without his usual smile, trailed by a couple of merchants.

"I'm glad all of you could come tonight," he said. "I asked you here because I know you are honest, hard-working men. You don't fly off the handle, but you don't fold when pushed, either. I want you to listen to what these men have to say."

One of the merchants said, "My colleague and I deal in luxury goods. I trade in gemstones; he imports spices. Luxury taxes and bad credit extended to the aristos have hit us hard."

A smith on the guild council said, "Hey, now, just because we don't handle those goods doesn't mean we aren't suffering. It's getting harder every week to pay my journeymen.

Master Randall said, "Hold on, he didn't say you weren't. But you're still making a living. They're not."

The gem merchant said, "We know you're hurting, too. Everybody in Blacksburg is. We're watching the cloth merchants feud with the duke, and it's making everybody nervous. We're talking to you because the duke has hired an air wizard, an aristo, to write a new charter that he wants to force on the cloth merchants." He paused, and we looked at each other.

"If he gets what he wants from them," Master Paul said, "who's next?"

"That's the question," Master Randall said. "Probably not the Blacksmiths' Guild, but it will be, sooner or later."

"That's why we've come to you," the spice merchant said, "hoping you'll back our idea. The only way we see to protect ourselves from the duke forcing charters we don't want on us, is for all the craft guilds and merchants associations to band together and present a united front to the duke."

"Safety in numbers."

"Exactly."

"Hold on," a council member said. "Our charter was written centuries ago, and some parts are way out of date. I don't want the duke forcing a new one on us, but I don't want the one we've got now enforced, either, because it would set rates that would beggar all of us."

"I wasn't finished," the spice merchant said. "I bet your charter has parts in it that the duke doesn't like either. He doesn't want to enforce it, any more than you do, does he?"

"Well, no, but—"

"My cousin in the Air Guild is willing to help. We're asking him to draft updated charters for all the craft guilds and merchant associations, without telling the duke what we're about. When they're ready, we'll present them to the duke all at once. If we all stick together, and agree ahead of time what parts matter most, he'll have no choice but to give us some of what we ask for."

"No choice, my ass. He'll call in the Fire Warlock, and he'll burn Blacksburg off the map for our insubordination."

"No, he won't, and this is the beauty of it. He will, if the rabble attack the palace with pitchforks and torches demanding relief from taxes. But if we ask the Air Guild for help updating the charters, there's nothing wrong with that. If we ask the duke politely to approve them, and he refuses, the Air Guild will tell the Fire Warlock we've been reasonable, and the duke hasn't. The Fire Warlock will light a fire under him, not us."

"Says who?"

"My cousin and his friends in the Air Guild. Those charters date from the days when 'fair as the king' still meant something. The kings insisted on them to make sure the duke treated us fairly, and the Fire Warlock respects that, or so they say."

"I believe it," Master Randall said. "When has the Fire Warlock ever sided with a duke? My friends in the Earth Guild say he'd love to set the Black Duke's tail on fire, and if we gave him an excuse, well…"

Nobody said anything for a bit. I eyed the other smiths. They eyed me, and each other. Master Paul cleared his throat a couple of times, but shook his head when faces turned towards him.

I said, "It might work. The magic folk say there's power in the guilds, and the bigger the guild, the easier it is to draw on that magic."

Heads nodded. "I've heard that often," Master Paul said. "And that if we take care of the guild, it'll take care of us."

I said, "Maybe somebody here could talk to the air wizard and see what he would do to fix our charter."

"And what they'd do to the other guilds' charters," the smith next to me said. "Without letting the duke know."

"How are you going to do that?"

"Magic," the spice merchant said. "My cousin says he can use magic to keep it a secret. If the duke finds out before we're ready, we'll be in trouble."

"No joke," someone else said. "But we need to do something, and I've not heard any better ideas. What about the Swordsmiths' Guild, Brother Randall? Are you in?"

"I wish, but our charter's from the king, not the duke. But we'll back whatever the Blacksmiths' Guild decides."

"We'd like you to pick one smith," the gem merchant said, "to talk to our air wizard, and come to meetings with the other guilds. It'll be safer if we can keep the meetings small."

"It would need to be a man," Master Randall said, looking up at the ceiling, "who's not afraid of speaking his mind."

"You know me," the smith next to me said. "You know I speak my mind. But I've got a houseful of mouths to feed. I can't risk it."

"I've got a family to support, too," Master Paul said, looking out the window. "We need a young man, who hasn't settled down yet."

Don't draw attention to yourself, Granny Mildred had said. Especially not from the Black Duke. Don't mess around with wizards or witches, she'd said. Especially not the Air Guild. They're trouble, she'd said.

"We need a man with good sense," another smith said, looking at me. There were all looking at me.

Good sense, my arse.

I said, "I guess you better give me a copy of that charter."

When we raised an elbow at the Hammer and Anvil after the meeting, I said to Master Randall, "Some things have been bothering me for a long time, and you might know."

He shrugged. "There's lots I don't know yet, but go ahead and ask."

"That old riddle: 'How is a king like a swordsmith? He has a hammer as well as a sword.' What the hell does that mean?"

He laughed. "Ice me if I know. Been puzzling over that for years. Grandmaster Henry—the head of the Swordsmiths' Guild—maybe he knows, but if he does, he hasn't told me."

"Shame. And why don't the aristos' swords break anymore? What would it take to make one shatter?"

His face darkened. "I don't know. Wish I did. My guess is it's our own fault. We've gotten weak and lazy. In the early days, there were powerful wizards in the guild. Thorvald the Mighty was a warlock, for God's sake. Now…"

"Now everybody with talent thinks they'll have an easier life in the magic guilds."

"Yeah, and they're probably right. And then, too, since no swords have broken in so long, too many of us think, why bother. If Grandmaster Henry ever found a sword without the spell on it, he'd rip the smith a new arsehole, but most just give lip service to it. I haven't made a sword in years—I'd have to go to Brother Clive and get him to remind me how the spell goes. Clive's one of the few that make them as a normal part of their business, and he's the only one I know that beats the spell in with every hammer strike, the way it's supposed to be done."

"His swords are good, then."

"The best. He's made several for the king. Damn, wouldn't the king be surprised if one of his shattered some day? I'd laugh myself silly."

"Master Clive would be pissed off over one of his beauties being ruined."

"Well, yeah, there is that. A crying shame, that would be, but it would be worth it."

"If it ever happened."

"And it probably never will."

The Luck of a Seventh Son

I flipped through the papers the wizard, a small man with thinning hair and a cleft chin, handed me, leaving sooty fingerprints. I handed it back. "Read it to me. I can't make heads or tails of your handwriting."

"Admit you can't read," the clerk said, "and be done with it."

"I can read, when the letters look like what I'm used to, and I know most of the words. But charters written by you air wizards have got to be full of long words I've never seen before." Even when I could read something, it always made more sense to me if somebody else read it aloud. But I wasn't going to tell him that.

He rolled his eyes, but read. When he finished, I said, "I can see why the duke doesn't want to enforce that any more than we do. That bit about us having the right to make charcoal in the duke's forests…"

"As big as the guild is now," he said, "you'd strip them bare in a couple of years."

Some words in the charter were old-fashioned, but it was plain language I understood. I said as much to the air wizard.

"That's the way it should be," he said. "A charter is strongest when everyone involved understands what's been agreed to. Your guild, like most craft guilds, has given up power by not requiring all new members recite it from memory on induction."

"Huh." I'd have to remember that. Uncle Will had drilled pieces of the Abertee Blacksmiths' charter into me, but maybe even he hadn't known the whole thing. "It's missing something."

"What's that?" he said, without looking up. He was scribbling notes in green ink along one side.

"The Abertee charter gives the guild head the right to tell the duke off whenever he does something that isn't good for Abertee."

"That's unusual." He chewed on his lip. "But an excellent idea. God knows somebody needs to get past the duke's flunkies and tell him some hard truths. I'll add that to the draft. The right to—"

"Right and responsibility, Uncle Will always said."

His pen stopped in mid-stroke. "Right and responsibility, both? That's odd. I wouldn't have expected your guild to accept responsibility for concerns outside your own craft."

I shrugged. "Well, we do. Everybody in Abertee looks to us to deal with the duke."

"I won't add that. Too big a burden. Not that this clause will be in the final version anyway."

"Why not?"

"Why not? The duke will never accept it, that's why not. But it'll be a useful bargaining point. We always throw in extras we're willing to drop, to protect the clauses that really matter."

I glared at him, but he had gone back to scribbling. "What's in it for you?"

"Eh?" He looked up again.

"I thought the Air Guild was full of aristos, except for the ones pretending they can predict the weather when they can't even stir up a stiff breeze."

He winced. "Sometimes, being an air wizard is embarrassing. I wish we could kick out those yahoos, but they're not as bad as the aristocrats. The Air Guild has a higher proportion of aristos than the other magic guilds, and I, for one, am damned tired of those rotters, like the one working for the duke, lording it over the rest of us, even in the guild, where we're supposed to be judged on our talent, not where we came from."

"Sounds like it's personal."

"I'd do this for my cousin anyway, but, yes, it is. That lordling has blown dust in my face too many times. If I can blow some in his for a change, it'll be worth it."

The days lengthened and my masterpiece began to take shape. The fight between the duke and the cloth merchants widened when the other merchant associations voted to join the cloth merchants in refusing to give the aristos credit. The duke vowed to see them all bankrupt.

The first warm Sunday afternoon, I ran into Richard Collins and his family in a park. We talked for a long time about the duke and the state of the city, and all the while we talked, he watched his children play with worry in his eyes. He still managed a cheery greeting in the mornings, but the lines in his face deepened.

Worried and angry faces were everywhere. The grumblings and mutterings grew louder and more constant, especially from Reverend Angus's admirers. Nick and I and a few others hounded him out of the bigger halls and churches, but he was still welcomed in some homes and taverns. I would have bet a week's wages the duke was paying him.

Don't draw the duke's attention, Granny Mildred had said. Too late now.

Leaving the preacher alone would have been smarter, but he scared me. If the fight with the duke went from words to fists and pikes, more folk could get hurt than the Earth Guild could handle. God help us if the fools listening to that preacher lost their senses and attacked the healers.

Glenn Hoskins scared me, too. He'd gone to work for one of Master Hal's friends from the Three Horseshoes after Master Randall threw him out. Gossip said he kept spouting off about the guild's unfairness, and the self-importance of the crowd at the Hammer and Anvil. We shouldn't stand for it, he'd say. We'll take control of the guild and show them a thing or two.

Other troublemakers were saying dark things to anyone who would listen. Some of them lived hand-to-mouth, and I couldn't blame them for being angry. With the Black Duke and his cronies living high on the hog off our taxes, breaking into his palace and eating his food must've seemed like a pretty good plan, even if it wasn't one I could agree with.

But some, like Glenn, were stirring up trouble out of pure meanness and spite, or so they could grab stuff that didn't belong to them rather than working hard to earn it for themselves.

If I'd had time to think about the damage they could do, I would've been sick with nerves, but I was so busy that, for a while, even homesickness had to wait its turn. Annie threw me over for a wheelwright who mooned around her every day. I wasn't surprised—I hadn't done more than wave at her for three weeks.

I don't know how much I helped in revising the charter for the Blacksmiths' Guild. I felt like an errand boy, shuffling between meetings with guild council and meetings with the air wizard and men from the other guilds. But I listened, and learned, and stored up ideas for the Abertee guild charter, if we ever got the chance to rewrite it.

The ram's hindquarters proved as hard as his head had been easy. I had gotten exactly what I wanted for the head, but when I made what I had sketched for the rear, even his dam would have called him ugly. Worse, as Master Paul had said, his rear didn't balance his head. When I built a rear that almost balanced, it stuck out farther than it should have. I lost track of how many attempts I tossed on the scrap heap. I lost track, too, of how many times I went to the guildhall to decipher the tricks in the off-balance thicket, but the fool clerk kept a tally, and snickered about it behind my back. In all, it took two months just to do the ram's hindquarters.

Sam helped. We both knew the masterpiece had to be all my work, but he couldn't sit still for two hours. He would pump the bellows, shovel coal, and juggle the irons in the fire. It wasn't long before he picked up a sledgehammer when he saw I could use a striker. I would work the apprentices for all I could get out of them when I was a master, so I couldn't see any harm in it.

We fell into the habit, at night, of the same teamwork that worked during the day, and I gave him more to do, or taught him things he'd not had a chance to try, working on railings day after day.

One night, I set him to work making a cluster of grapes. I watched, giving advice, while he worked. When he'd finally gotten a respectable grape, I turned back to my own work, and was struck dumb by the sight of Master Randall, leaning against the wall of the smithy like he'd been there a while.

He said, "I dropped by for a peek at that masterpiece Brother Paul keeps talking about."

"I'm not helping," Sam said. "Honest. Duncan was just showing me how to do what he was doing."

Master Randall smiled. "You think I can't tell an apprentice's work from a master's? I'm glad you're here, so I could see for myself Duncan meets one of the other requirements."

"Other requirements?"

"What do the certificates say?"

"I don't know. I've never read one."

Master Randall nodded at me. "You ought to know."

"The holder of this certificate," I said, "has demonstrated that he can, among other things…ah…oh, that he can pass on to junior smiths his knowledge of the craft."

"The craft guilds never have enough competent teachers. Keep up the good work," he said, and left.

Other smiths started dropping in. Some, like Master Hal, looked it over and stomped out. Others stayed to talk, and tell stories. Most stories they told on themselves, or other smiths, but other folk figured as well. One story I got a good laugh out of was about an aristo, trying to pass as a commoner by working as a groom, and making a hash of it.

Sam asked, "Why did he do that, when he didn't have to work for a living?"

"His father disowned him," the smith said. "Wouldn't pay his bills."

"I've heard of that," I said. "We can't stand them, and they can't even stand each other."

"That's so, but they usually find some other relative to leech off of."

Sam said, "They all ought to have to work for a living."

"It would be good for everybody if they did," I said, "but I doubt they could."

"Some do," the smith said. "You'd be surprised."

"I would be surprised. Name one."

"Well, a merchant here in Blacksburg is an aristo…"

"Go on. Which one? I've met most, and I don't believe you."

The smith scratched his head. "Damned if I can remember his name. I've never done business with him. Can't afford his goods. Cloth merchant. Clinton, or Collins. That's it, something Collins."

We got to Richard Collins' house early the next morning, and waited. When he stepped out, I said, "Is it true you're an aristo?"

He cringed. "Yes, it is true, much to my regret."

I gawked at him. "You're joking."

He grabbed my elbow and dragged me towards his house, insisting we come in. His wife poured tea and left us alone in the kitchen. He said, "You think a nobleman's life is one of wealth and privilege and easy living, don't you? It is, if you have the property to generate income and tenants to work for you. My family was the lowest rank of the nobility to start with, and nearly all there was went to my father's eldest brother.

"I'm the seventh son of a seventh son, and my share wasn't enough to live on. The furniture in the parlour—not this house itself or anything else—is the sum total of my inheritance."

I said, "But, but—"

"So, you see, I've had to work for a living, and being a…you-know-what has not helped. I've struggled to build working relationships with my suppliers and customers. I have had to be scrupulously honest and fair with every commoner I deal with because I can't afford the slightest whisper of doubt. If they find out before they know me well they think I'll cheat them or otherwise mistreat them simply because I can, and won't trust me. If they don't find out early, then they're angry and upset with me for having misled them, and I have the conversation I'm having right now with you, to persuade them to continue doing business with me."

I said, "I'm not angry, just confused. The seventh son of a seventh son is supposed to be lucky."

"I've had plenty of luck all right, nearly all bad. The only really good luck I've ever had was meeting my wife. She's a commoner, and her father let her marry me against his better judgment. He helped establish me as a merchant, and he did that out of concern for his daughter, not out of sympathy for me."

He tilted his head to one side. "Why aren't you angry?"

"Good question… We've haven't been doing business together, and even if we were, well, people don't often try to cheat me. I may not be the cleverest fellow you've ever dealt with, but my dad made sure I had enough horse sense to smell a swindle, and most people smart enough to pull a swindle are smart enough to back off when I give them the gimlet eye. If I have to I can pick a man up and shake him until his teeth rattle, and that's usually enough. The only man fool enough to think he could cheat me would be an aris… Sorry, I'm not half as smart as I thought I was."

He smiled. "At least you have the decency to apologise."

"But the taxes… Do you have to pay them? Don't you get any relief?"

"Possibly, no, probably, I could. I will not ask for it. Doing so would destroy in a day the trust I have worked half my life to build."

"Oh, aye. I see."

Sam asked, "Can't you give up being an, uh, you-know-what?"

"No. There is no provision, without the king's approval, for movement between the classes. My children are commoners since my wife is and I'm not titled, but I am...stuck. And I'm not alone. You may have met other impoverished nobles in Blacksburg, who hide their origins because they have to work for a living, and know they would lose customers and be shunned by their neighbours if found out."

I said, "That's not fair, either."

He shrugged. "As fair as the king. Saying it isn't fair is easy. Changing it is hard."

Sam said, "Why don't you take it to the king? He could help."

Richard and I both stared at Sam. He turned red. "I meant, couldn't he let you become a commoner?"

I said, "Sam, you've taken all those stories I've told too seriously. They're no more use than fairy tales. Fair as the king stopped being fair a long time ago. The one we've got now would bust a gut laughing at an aristo wanting to turn common."

Richard said, "If he listened at all. He listens to the dukes and barons, yes, but he's not interested in the likes of me. If even the Fire Warlock can't convince him of what's fair, what chance do I have?"

Touchmark

When Jack left in May, I was Master Paul's only journeyman. He turned away everyone who came looking for work. At least we were still in business. Every day some merchant was having a closing-down sale, or some craftsman packed up his tools.

"How much longer can this go on, without all the business in the city collapsing?" I said.

"Not long," Richard said, "and the duke will win. If two more cloth merchants go bankrupt, the association will lose its charter. I may be next. I've already had to let go nearly all my staff."

"They won't find anything else in Blacksburg now that pays a living wage. If your business survives, you can hire them back."

"If they don't move away, yes. Assuming, of course, I can make any profit under the terms of the new charter the duke wants to shove down our throats."

The air wizard was even gloomier. "The new charter is like putting a meat cleaver in the duke's right hand for him to use on his own left arm. He'll kill all business in this city, and tax every penny out of everybody who stays, to compensate for the taxes he'll lose from all the merchants and craftsmen he's driven away. There'll be riots, and everything worth anything will go up in smoke."

It wouldn't take much to get to that point. Talk on the street corners and in the taverns had a brittle, crackly edge to it like dry leaves. A spark would set the city ablaze, and I wanted out before it did.

Midsummer was coming, and when I realised I wouldn't finish my masterpiece in time for the guild meeting in early June, I got roaring drunk. As if that would help.

There's nothing like hammering on a ringing anvil to make a man ready to part with an outrageous sum for one of the Earth Guild's nasty hangover cures. I downed the potion, and my head and liver blew open. I slammed the bottle on the counter and bellowed at the wizard, "You poisoned me!"

"Did not," he said. "Scared the poisons out of your system. Worked, didn't it?"

After a minute or two, while the bits sorted themselves out and settled back into place, I had to admit it had, but I didn't want to ever do it again. Better, and cheaper, not to get that wasted in the first place.

There was no time for that, anyway. I put everything I had into finishing the masterpiece in time for the July meeting. The ram was done, but the pieces around him weren't. The stream of other smiths coming by for a look continued, but I didn't know how widespread the talk had gotten until one morning a pair of aristos charged into the smithy and fetched up in front of the gate.

Their clothes would have outshone Richard Collins. The one in the rear took care not to get close to anything that would leave smudges. "Filthy place," he sniffed.

The one in the lead didn't seem to care. He shook a finger at my masterpiece and started yelling. "What arrogant upstart commissioned this gate? I demand an answer."

"Nobody did," I said. "There's no buyer—"

"Damn straight there's no buyer, you impertinent wretch. If you expect me to buy something I didn't ask for, you have a lot of gall."

"Course not. It's not for sale."

Master Paul shoved in between us, explaining about the masterpiece, and that I would be handing it over to the Blacksmiths' Guild.

"Then why did he choose my family's mascot?" The cords in the man's neck relaxed, and he stopped shouting, but he didn't stop glaring at me.

"How would I know a ram is somebody's mascot? Who the hell are you anyway?"

The cords in his neck bulged and he went back to shouting. The other aristo smirked. "I told you, you're a baron, and nobody gives a shit about barons, even if you are rolling in money." That earned him a raised finger from his buddy, and he laughed.

I said, "I don't care if it is your family's mascot. There's no law stopping me from using it, too."

"No one else in Blacksburg would dare," he said. "How much do you want for it?"

"Eh? You just said—"

"Never mind. What do you want?"

"I told you, it's not for sale."

"Don't talk to me like that, simpleton. Of course it's for sale. How much are you asking?"

Typical aristo. Would be good for him to find out he couldn't have everything he wanted. I scratched my chin while I calculated. "Well, there's the cost of the iron and coal…" I'd kept a running total in my head of all Master Paul had docked my pay for, a total that made my head hurt any time I thought about it. "Plus my time…"

Master Paul and the apprentices stared at me like they couldn't believe I was even thinking about it. I winked at them and went on figuring. "Plus the spells I paid for after the first was ruined…" I came up with a number that would choke a horse, and tripled it. Considered that a bit more before speaking, and doubled it.

Master Paul's eyebrows rose, and he whistled silently. Everybody else gaped.

The baron closed his mouth and swallowed. "That's preposterous. Your guild puts limits on what you can charge for—"

"That's on pieces made to order," I said. "For a piece like this, I can charge whatever I want. You don't have to buy it."

"The hell I don't. I can't have it showing up in someone else's garden, as if I didn't know quality work when I see it, or was too cheap to pay for it. Everybody in this city—everybody who's anybody, that is, not a common idiot like you—would know. If you don't set a reasonable rate, I'll take it—"

"The hell you will. The spells against theft will break the hand of anybody touching it, if I don't let it go."

He snarled at me. "I'll pay you the going rate for a gate that size. I'll make you sell it."

"You can't. You're not my overlord. The guild charter says I don't have to sell to you."

"You made that up."

Master Paul said, "He knows what's in that charter, better than any other smith in town. If he says the charter says so, you can believe it."

The baron stomped out of the smithy. "We'll see about that."

He came back later, still snarling. "That gate belongs in my garden. If you don't sell it to me, I'll make sure no aristocrat in Blacksburg will do business with you when you have your own smithy. You won't sell another gate or any fancy work. Where will you be then?"

"Home in Abertee. I'm not staying a single day in Blacksburg once I'm certified, so I don't care what you do. It's not for sale."

Sam and I left the smithy most nights with muscles aching and Sam asleep on his feet. We dropped out of the sparring during breaks. I'd sit on the bench and shout advice as the apprentices went at it, but I was too bone-weary to grab my own quarterstaff and show them how it was done.

In his own way, the air wizard was working as hard. I never saw him between May Day and Midsummer without red-rimmed eyes, and ink stains on his hands and cuffs. Whenever his pen wasn't racing across the page, he was massaging his shoulder or flexing his wrist.

The secret meetings, working on the charters, put a strain on Master Randall, too. We stopped at the Hammer and Anvil late one night, after a long argument—one of many—with the other guilds about what was most important.

"I've been thinking about the royal charter a lot lately," he said. "What with all the other talk about charters. It's a shame it limits the number of swordsmiths. We could use some new blood in the guild. And spread out in more cities and towns, too. Frankland has grown, but we haven't."

"The king wouldn't think there's much call for swords these days," I said, "and doesn't understand what else you do."

"The king doesn't like us having the power we already do," he said, frowning down at the piece of bronze he was rolling between his fingers. "He knows what we do, and doesn't like it."

"What's that?" I said.

"This, my young friend, is the stamp I use to put the seal on those certificates all you youngsters are trying to earn." He flipped it up to show the swordsmiths' symbol carved into the splayed head. "They're numbered. See? Sixty of them, for the whole damned country."

"I've wondered what happens to one when the smith doesn't have a son or nephew to pass it on to."

"It goes to whoever he picks, as long as at least one other swordsmith will vouch for him. Mine's promised to a lad who worked for me about ten years ago. Well, he's not a lad anymore. A good man. But he'll be middle-aged before I hand it over. If the smith hasn't picked out another man to give it to, it goes to the next man on the guild's waiting list."

I lowered my mug. "I didn't know there was a waiting list."

"We don't talk about it much. It's a disgrace. Your uncle was on it for thirty years, and it never got to him."

He went back to frowning at his seal, and I stared down into my mug. I thought I'd known everything there was to know about Uncle Will, but I hadn't known that. Maybe he hadn't known.

The baron stomped into the smithy, looking like he had a bellyache, and slammed a bag—a heavy one, that clinked—down on my anvil. "This is half of what you asked, and it's robbery at that price. I will have that gate."

That was more money than I'd ever seen at one time. Ever had any hopes of seeing. The only noise in the smithy was the crackling of the fire. Master Paul stood with his hammer raised, his eyes wide. I could live in style on that for a long time. I could buy enough drink to make me forget I would miss another summer and autumn in Abertee. Maybe even another Yule.

I shoved the bag back into the baron's hands. "It's not for sale."

That moneybag haunted me. I should never have given him a price. If he wanted it bad enough to bring the full sum in cash, I wouldn't have any choice. I'd have to sell it to him, or he'd be within his rights to take it. My only hope was to turn it over to the guild as soon as possible.

In the meantime, he'd given me another worry. He'd made it worthwhile for someone—Glenn came to mind—to bribe an earth wizard to break the spells on the gate. If the baron laid his hands on it, I'd never see the gate or the money again. If I complained to the duke, the baron would claim he'd negotiated a better price with me. The duke would take his word against mine, and horsewhip me, to boot, for my gall.

I spent the rest of my money, plus a week's advance on my wages from Master Paul, on a Fire Guild spell.

July would be hot. Sleeping rough on the way home wouldn't hurt me.

I'd worry about feeding myself when the time came.

"Finished it, eh?" Master Clive's face split in a grin. "About time we heard some good news for a change. Let's see it."

We headed outside, everyone in his smithy following, to where Sam waited with the wagon. Clive and a journeyman helped wrestle the gate out of the wagon bed. The wide eyes and silent whistles when I unwrapped it made me grin. The apprentices and journeymen crowded around, stepping on toes and shoving each other, until Clive roared at them to back up and give him breathing room. "Take turns, you young fools. Duncan's not in a hurry. He'll let you have a good look."

An apprentice said, "I'd heard the ram was charging straight at you, but it's going off to the side. How come?"

I said, "You're looking at it straight on. Go unlatch it."

"It ain't latched."

Clive's eyes rolled. "Pretend it is. What would you do?"

The lad moved to the side and leaned forward. "Why, I'd—" His hand landed on the latch, inches from one horn. His chin was no further from the other horn—the one that had broken through the warped uprights. "Frostbite," he said, and backed up, to jeers from the other apprentices. "He is coming straight at me."

Clive's wife, at my elbow, said, "That would be unnerving if you weren't sure of your welcome."

"That was sort of the idea, ma'am."

Clive took his time inspecting it, running his fingers over everything, testing the sharpness of the thorns, the strength of the welds. Every time he yanked at something Sam winced. I didn't. I'd tested them myself. If they didn't give for me, they wouldn't give for Clive.

He found the touchmark, and squinted at it. Sam sucked in his breath. He hadn't wanted me to use it. Bad luck claiming to be a master before I was one, he'd said.

"Be proud of your work, lad," Uncle Will had said. "Never make something you're not willing to put your mark on."

"My cousin gave me the punch after my uncle died," I said.

"Thought it looked old. A new punch would leave sharper edges. Although it's still clear enough."

"Aye, sir. I don't know how old the punch is, but the Archer family sign is almost as old as Frankland."

"Why's the bow only half drawn?"

"Because we don't go looking for trouble."

"Then why nock the arrow at all?"

"Because trouble could come looking for us, and we always need to be ready."

He flashed me a look from under his bushy eyebrows, before going back to studying the gate. "What do you think?"

"About trouble?"

"About the gate."

"Oh. It's…" It was the best thing I'd ever done. It was better than anything in the guildhall, excepting the thicket. If getting certified was a race, I was cantering home while the lathered pack was still rounding the last turn. I was one of Frankland's best smiths, certificate or no certificate, and nobody could steal that certainty from me.

But say that in a yard full of journeymen and apprentices, when too many in Blacksburg already thought I was too big for my boots?

"It's good," I said.

Clive flashed another look at me. "Good, he says." He snorted. "All right. Back to work. I'm not paying you lot to stand around half the day and stare at another man's work." We wrapped it and loaded it into the wagon while the gawkers shuffled back into the smithy.

"It's more than good," Sam said. "It's the best. He won't have any trouble with the guild, will he?"

Clive leaned against the side of the wagon and stared past Sam towards the river. "If life were fair, the Blacksmith's Guild would've recommended that we certify him a couple of months ago. But life's not fair. We've seen plenty evidence of that lately." He pushed away from the wagon and trudged towards the smithy door. "Better keep that arrow nocked."

We parked the wagon behind the guildhall. Sam went in to fetch the clerk, and I let the tailgate down, then shifted the blankets to get a good grip.

"I'm turning my masterpiece over to the guild," I said. "Where do you want it?"

The clerk wiped sweat off his upper lip. "Carry it into the meeting room and leave it there."

"Do you want me to describe it to you for your ledger, or will you do that yourself?"

"Um, that's not necessary."

I turned my head to stare at him. "Eh?" He tugged at the neck of his shirt and didn't answer.

Sam said, "Uh-oh. Duncan."

I looked up. Glenn and Master Hal stood in the guildhall door, grinning.

Flashpoint

The smith I'd called a cheat and several of his friends from the Three Horseshoes leaned out the window of the guildhall.

"Sam," I said, under my breath, "climb back on. Get ready to drive, without making a fuss about it."

Master Hal staggered down the stairs. "Heard you finished it. We've been waiting for you—figured you'd need help carrying it in."

He lurched into me, and grabbed at the wagon. I got a good whiff. If he helped unload, the gate would land on somebody's foot—his own, odds were—and crush it. He poked at the gate with a finger. "Why didn't you paint it? Need to be careful with something like this, out in the weather. Be a shame if it rusted."

Sam started to say it would be hanging in the guildhall, but I rode over him. "Can't see why you would want me to sell it. You must've heard what that baron was willing to pay."

He snickered. "You don't know how much. We negotiated a better price. Three-quarters what you asked for, you arrogant bastard. It's mighty generous of you to make such a big donation to the guild." His cronies laughed, like he'd said something clever.

The clerk edged away. He wouldn't meet my eyes.

I said, "You're a bunch of cheats, the whole lot of you, but you won't cheat me out of that certificate. I'll take this away and bring it back for the meeting."

"No, you won't," Master Hal said, tugging on the gate. "It's the guild's now."

I had kept a firm grip on the gate ever since pulling the blanket off. It was still cold iron. I took a deep breath, and said, "Like hell it is. Take your dirty, thieving paws off my masterpiece."

He laughed. The iron flashed red hot under his hands. He screamed and fell backwards, knocking Glenn down.

I bellowed, but Sam was already swinging the whip. The wagon jolted over the cobbles. I ran after it. A glance over my shoulder showed Glenn and Master Hal sprawled on the stairs, blocking the way.

Sam kept up a brisk pace for a couple of blocks, but they were too drunk to give chase. We turned the corner, out of sight, and came to a stop as Master Randall jogged towards us.

He leaned against the wagon, wheezing and coughing. "Fifty-seven. Too old for this."

"You're too late." My voice wouldn't stay steady. I set my jaw and nudged Sam. "You tell him."

While Sam related what had happened, Master Randall hung onto the side of the wagon with clenched fists, staring off into nothing.

Sam said, "Why did they think they could get away with stealing it? The duke's hung thieves who'd only stolen a loaf of bread, and that gate's worth a lot more than that."

"They were playing me for a sucker. I haven't got anything worth enough—not even that gate—to see a man swing for. They knew I'd not complain to the duke."

"Maybe, maybe not." Master Randall came back from wherever he'd been wandering. "The story I heard was that they meant to wait until you'd handed it over to the clerk, and then spring their little surprise on you. You were lucky, son. If you'd let go, or carried it into the guild hall, you'd've been screwed. Sounds like they let the drink make idiots of them."

"But that's still stealing," Sam said.

"No, son," Master Randall said. "Once he'd handed it over, the guild could do whatever they wanted with it. I guess they figured they'd add enough to the guild's coffers, even after each taking a share for himself, that the guild would take their side instead of Duncan's. Especially since there'd be no getting the gate back once that baron had it in his garden."

I said, "If the guild council went along—"

"They wouldn't. The council takes the guild's reputation seriously, and they'll be furious. But the guild's fractured, and when the fight about this comes, and there will be one, I don't know which side will win. The guild could be in even worse shape than it is now. Just think, Master Hal could be on the guild council."

"Oh, God. If he is, they'll never accept my masterpiece. Then what the hell do I do? I need to be certified."

"That's not..." He stopped, stared, and bent over, laughing. He pounded the wagon sideboard with his fist, and howled.

I stared at Sam; Sam stared at me. I said, "Tell me what the hell is so goddamned funny about being cheated out of one of those frostbitten certificates?"

Master Randall straightened up and wiped his eyes on his sleeve. "Do you want to see our friends at the guildhall get what they deserve?"

"Does the Frost Maiden like ice?"

"I don't need the Blacksmiths' Guild to recommend you be certified. I can give anyone I want a certificate."

I blinked at him. "Eh?"

"The guild's recommendations filter out men who can't do the work, so we swordsmiths aren't run ragged by every journeyman coming through town trying to get certified. I don't know if this has ever come up before—the swordsmiths deciding to certify someone the blacksmiths haven't recommended—but we're free to use our own judgement. Clive and I have both seen the work you can do. Hell, Clive was about ready to certify you last autumn, just on the basis of the guild in Abertee having sent you."

"Then why the hell didn't he? Would've saved me a boatload of trouble."

"He wasn't sure, then, that you were telling the truth. And I figured there were a few things you still needed to learn. Weren't there?"

"Aye, I suppose so. About balance. And what being certified really means."

"And about when to speak up and when to keep your mouth shut?"

"Still working on that one."

"Ha! Me, too. But one of the times we have to speak up is when the guild is in trouble. I'm going to kick up a fuss at the guild meeting next week. I'll sign your certificate then, with or without their recommendation, and tell them why you earned one and they didn't. In fact, I've decided, don't turn over your masterpiece to them. Don't give them an opportunity to take the wind out of my sails."

I must've been grinning. "So I can do whatever I want with it?"

He grinned back. "Whatever will put their noses out of joint the most."

On the way back to the city from the baron's estate, Sam's eyes kept wandering down to the bag wedged between our feet. "Keep your eyes on the other travellers," I said. "Staring at it will just draw attention to it."

"Can't we go any faster?"

"Nae. We'd draw more attention."

"Don't you want to get to the Earth Guildhall as fast as we can?"

I patted my pocket. The Air Guild charm was still there. "I want to get to the Earth Guildhall as fast as we can with this bag just the way it is right now. It won't matter how fast we get there if we lose it on the way. That's why I'm driving and you're keeping watch."

He grumbled, but soon we would have been forced to slow down anyway. A work crew was building a barricade across the road. They waved us and the other incoming traffic through, but the duke's guards were crawling over the wagon at the head of the outbound queue, ignoring the curses the red-faced driver threw at them.

A cart further back pulled out of line. We had to wait while he turned around, Sam mumbling curses the whole time. We stopped alongside a wagon loaded with household goods, four children perched on top. A woman with another child on her lap sat next to the driver, giving him grief.

I said, "What's going on?"

The driver hawked and spat. "That son-of-a-whore duke. He's kicking beggars out, but from now on, anybody else leaving Blacksburg, except for aristos, has to pay an exit tax.

"Why the hell?"

He shrugged. "Too many craftsmen and merchants leaving. The aristos are having trouble getting what they need."

The woman said, "I told you we should have left last week."

I said, "How much is the exit tax?"

"A month's wages, or half the money you're carrying, whichever one's greater."

"Frostbite. Freeze his—"

"Watch your language, you lout," The woman had clapped her hands over the squirming child's ears. "There are children listening."

"Sorry, ma'am."

The cart finished its turn and we drove on, cursing under our breaths. Gran used to lecture me about fortune's wheel, warning me not to get too full of myself when I was riding high, because soon enough I could be at the bottom. The reverses were coming so fast it didn't feel like a wheel to me. More like a whip snaking through the air—a whip that hadn't finished cracking yet.

"**D**one," the earth witch said, waving her wand over the bag of gold. "Done, that is, as well as I can. No thief's going to creep into your room and take it from you, but the spell can't stop the duke from dipping his frostbitten fingers in and taking what he wants."

"Don't see why it can't. It's robbery, pure and simple."

"I know that, and you know that, but when he calls it taxes, the spell doesn't work."

I paid her and we left. "Good luck," she called after us, "on getting that out of Blacksburg."

We hid the bag in the safest place we could think of between the two of us—Sam's mum's root cellar—and I sent Sam back to Master Paul's with the wagon. I had another errand to run before going back to work.

My way passed the house where the head of the local Fire Guild branch lived. A couple weeks ago, Sam had suggested asking him for the Fire Warlock's help. Master Paul had said it wouldn't do any good—Blacksburg's fire wizard was an aristo, who always took the duke's side. Other people said the same, but so many stories had fire wizards locking horns with aristos it was hard to believe.

Maybe I spent too much time listening to the old stories, but I couldn't help it that they had better endings than the ones from recent times.

The map of North Frankland that had been in the bookstore window was gone. "Sold that months ago," the shopkeeper said, "but I have another copy. Let me find it for you."

He unrolled the map, and I traced the road from Blacksburg to Abertee, through Crossroads and on to Nettleton. It was June twenty-seventh. The next guild meeting was on July first. Just a few days more, and I would be on my way home. I paid him and left.

A lot can happen in a few days. Yesterday, that gate had left me poorer by a year's wages. I would've been glad to get the certificate and go home.

Even losing half the gold I had now, I would come out ahead. I had enough to buy the map without making more than a token fuss about the price. Giving some gold away to someone in need would've made me feel good, but having it yanked out of my hands by a rich aristo pissed me off.

Without selling the gate, I could've been stuck in Blacksburg for months, trying to save a month's wages. That thought sent shivers down my spine, and cooled my temper. Some other journeymen in town would never save enough. Especially since few masters were taking anyone new on.

With money in my pocket and a place to go, I was better off than most, and I had been pissed off. How angry would I have been if I couldn't get out?

The fire wizard's house was right in front of me. I climbed the steps and hammered with the knocker before I could change my mind.

"All supplicants have to walk the challenge path." The fire wizard waved a lacy cuff in my direction, without looking up from his book. "Talk to the guards at the gate."

"I'm not a supplicant. I don't want—"

"I'm not a supplicant, sir."

"Yes, sir. I'm not a supplicant. Sir."

"You said you wanted the Fire Warlock's help. Do you, or don't you?"

"I do, but—"

"Then you're a supplicant. Go away."

"Not for me. For all of Blacksburg."

He looked up then. It wasn't a friendly look. I wiped sweat from my forehead. The wizard's hat sported three flames. Granny Mildred had three trees on hers, and Granny Mildred could knock me flat on my back if she wanted to.

The wizard said, "And just what do you expect the Fire Warlock to do?"

"Talk some sense into the duke. Get him to drop that exit tax before somebody attacks him in the street."

The wizard set the book on his desk and folded his hands together over it. "His Grace the duke has matters in this city well in hand. You needn't worry about his safety; his guards would kill a madman before he could get close to the duke or his family."

"I'm not worried about them. I don't want some poor soul killed because he got so fed up he attacked the duke."

Sparks flew from the wizard's eyes. "Who sent you?"

"Nobody sent me. It was—"

"Nobody sent me, sir."

"Nobody sent me. Sir. It was my own idea to come." In fact, it had been Sam's idea, but it wasn't fair to point a finger at him.

"Which guild do you belong to? What's your rank? Does your guild council know you're here?"

"The Blacksmiths' Guild. Sir. They don't know. I'm still a journeyman, and—"

"A journeyman." He leaned back and sneered. "Did you really expect me to believe your guild would back you? Of course not. If it mattered, they'd send a member of the guild council. And do you think the Fire Warlock, with all his magic, knows so little about the state of affairs in Frankland that you, a mere journeyman craftsman from…from where? You don't sound like you're from Blacksburg."

"Abertee…sir."

"Abertee? Oh, God. Do you imagine the Fire Warlock can learn anything from a bumpkin?"

"Aye, if he's listening to you tell him the duke's got everything under control."

He shot out of his chair and screamed at me. "Get the hell out of my sight, you impertinent ass, before I flame you." I was halfway down the hall when he yelled, "Stop."

I edged towards the outer door. I didn't need to know how far he could throw flame.

The wizard stood in the door of his study, smoothing down his hair and tugging at his cuffs. He straightened his shoulders and gave me a smile that didn't touch his eyes. "There is something you can do if you do want to ensure Blacksburg remains a prosperous, orderly city."

"I'll do whatever I can, sir."

"Then the sooner we stamp out this dangerous nonsense from the craft guilds about rewriting their own charters, the better. What do you know about this ridiculous conspiracy?"

"C…c…conspiracy?"

"Gad. Why am I wasting my time? Of course they wouldn't have let a journeyman in on it. Get out of my sight, you hick."

I skidded around the corner of Master Randall's house, caught sight of a guard outside the smithy, and scrambled into the alley. A peek around the corner confirmed that the guard had had his back to me and hadn't noticed. I backtracked, and slammed into the wall at the touch of a hand on my arm.

"Gosh, Duncan," Sam said, "I sure am glad they haven't arrested you, too."

Riot

I saw a badger once, trapped in a cage. I'd felt sorry for the poor beast, but hadn't done anything about it. If I ever saw such a thing again, I'd be inclined to rip open the cage and let him loose.

Light coming in where the door didn't fit tight was the only proof I had that I'd not spent more than one night and part of a day in this hole. They had brought me breakfast, but I'd eaten that a long time ago, and was tired of listening to my rumbling stomach.

There wasn't room to stretch out on the floor, and the ceiling was too low for me to stand upright. I had to keep my elbows tucked in to not bang them on the walls. I'd already crawled on my hands and knees, feeling my way over everything, just to have something to do.

I should have insisted, yesterday, that Master Randall give me that frostbitten certificate right then. I could have left the gate with Master Paul, and been on my way home by now. Going home broke would have been better than this. Facing the duke's questions would be better than this. Facing an angry Fire Warlock would be better than this. Even facing the Frost Maiden… Nae. I went back to crawling around, running my hands over the walls.

When the door finally opened, I almost cried.

"Come out of that root cellar," Sam's mum said, "and have dinner. They're not looking for you."

"They posted a list on the church door," Sam said, "of the people they're looking for. Offering a reward. Your name's not on it. Master Paul says the duke doesn't know who he ought to arrest, and is just guessing."

"And he wouldn't guess an outsider, and a journeyman at that, would be involved with the charters," I said. I stepped out into the yard and reached for the clouds. Stretching had never felt so good. "But they went after the grandmasters because they've already spoken their minds to the duke more than once. Makes sense. Who else have they arrested?"

"Don't know for sure. All I know for certain is who's not been arrested. Both grandmasters are on that list."

"That's damn good news, but you said—"

"I was wrong. Master Randall's top journeyman said he slipped out the back when he saw the guards coming."

"What else have you heard?"

"All kinds of crap. I've been all over the city fishing for news, but one person will say one thing and the next will say the exact opposite. Except they all say the duke blew his chance. Everybody in Blacksburg has heard about the charters by now, and are helping hide the people he wants to arrest, even though he's offered a whopping big reward, especially for Master Randall. The duke doesn't have enough guards, either, to make arrests and collect the exit tax at the same time. I'd bet you could get out with all your money."

"Won't do me any good without that certificate."

We gobbled our dinners, then went to the Hammer and Anvil, on the off chance someone might have news. It was closed and locked. So was Master Clive's smithy. Most stores and workshops in between were silent and empty. Every soul in the city must have been out in the streets, making trouble for the guards, and pushing them back towards the palace.

We stopped at Master Paul's smithy to grab our quarterstaves, and while we were there, a noise, like a crowd cheering, rose from the direction of the wharves.

Mrs Hammer came out of the house, wringing her hands. "Have you seen Paul?"

I shook my head. "Sorry, ma'am."

"What are you going to do?"

"If I had any sense, I'd leave Blacksburg right now and not come back. Keep the children indoors, ma'am—don't let them get mixed up in this."

"I will. Be careful, yourself."

I hoisted my quarterstaff and headed for the noise, Sam following close on my heels. We reached the high street leading from the wharves in time to meet a group of men carrying guild banners marching towards the square. The crowd let them through, then fell in behind, carrying us along like a river. We added our cheers to the noise.

I shoved through the crowd and caught up to the group with the banners. The air wizard, his arms full of papers, led the way. Master Randall, carrying the Swordsmiths' banner, was right behind. I fell into step beside him.

"Sorry, son," he yelled. "Should've given you your certificate yesterday. I'll do it tomorrow, if I can."

I shouted, "We're taking the charters to the duke?"

"We are. You're not. Stay out of it. This isn't your fight."

I argued, but he wouldn't have it. "You're needed in Abertee."

We reached the square, and I dropped out of the stream of marchers to watch from the cover of the trees at the Earth Guildhall. The guards stopped the marchers at the palace gates, but the crowd was getting thicker, and pressing against the iron fence. People milled about, making as much noise as they could—yelling, screaming, pounding on the cobbles with quarterstaves or broomsticks, or banging on pots with knives. Glenn Hoskins ran past, shouldering a pickaxe.

The marchers with their banners were well-dressed merchants and respected craftsmen, but the folk at the edges, and the ones still pouring in, men and women both, looked like every cutthroat, pickpocket, thug, and other lowlife from miles around. Some had weapons or tools they could use as a weapon, but others carried rocks and cobbles. With a knife or a quarterstaff, you have a chance of dealing with the person behind it, but a rock can fly out of nowhere and kill with no warning. The sun was about gone, and it was cooling off, but I was sweating like I was at the forge. The Water Guildhall, almost due north, stared at me. I stood rooted to the spot, watching and worrying.

News rippled through the crowd that the duke had arrested the two merchants who had started the conspiracy, and turned them over to the Water Guild. In an instant, the crowd turned into a howling, bloodthirsty mob.

A section of iron fence rocked. Rocks flew, smashing windows. The guards waved their pikes, but there wasn't room at the front for the marchers to retreat. Other sections of fence rocked. The guards lowered their pikes and charged the fence. Master Randall was in the front row.

I grabbed Sam and ran. We swam upstream through the crowd, fighting towards the edge of the square. I watched over my shoulder as a section of fence went down. The guards, caught between hammer and anvil, had no chance. The mob ran them over and charged the doors. The vandals further out turned on the Water Guildhall and shops around the square. We dodged flying glass and ducked down the nearest side street, shoving through the mob. Some women in rags came out of a mansion with armloads of loot, laughing like they were proud of themselves. Where was that frostbitten Fire Warlock when you needed him?

We reached the cross-street Richard Collins lived on. Glenn Hoskins, coming the other way with a torch, was lighting rags and tossing them through broken doors.

I charged at Glenn, laying out looters in the way. Glenn took to his heels. Sam dashed into the Collins' house and flew back out pulling a burning rug. Richard, bloody, limping, and swinging a sword, followed.

For a moment he looked about to run Sam through, but then he pulled up short. His yell was drowned out by a huge, angry voice coming out of the walls, and the stones in the street. "THROW DOWN YOUR ARMS, OR DIE BY FIRE."

I dropped my quarterstaff. Sam dropped his a heartbeat later. Richard looked panicked; I knocked the sword from his hand with my fist. A looter grabbed it, brought it up to swing at me, and it went red-hot in his hands. He screamed and tried to drop it, but the metal stuck. Somehow, he tore away, and ran screaming down the street, but he'd left half his hand on the sword.

A river of fire roared down the street. I shoved Richard and Sam through the door, but the fire, hot as a forge, caught me. Flames poured over and around me and then they were gone, and hadn't hurt me, or set the house afire. I fell on my knees on the top step, and leaned against the doorpost, shaking.

Glenn, blazing like a torch, ran down the street towards the river. I clapped my hands over my ears, but couldn't block out his screams. The stink of burning flesh hit me like a punch in the gut. Glenn fell, rolled, and fetched up against a stone wall across the street, and lay there burning. Looters with burns on their arms or faces ran past him, howling.

I leaned over the side of the steps and puked. Sam flopped down beside me and added his. We lay side-by-side on the steps, heaving, until Glenn stopped twitching and the flames died down.

"Duncan," Sam said, "I hated him, but that's an awful way to die..."

"Don't feel guilty about it, Sam." Richard leaned out the door, looking green himself. "That was magic fire. You couldn't have saved him. You would have burned along with him."

By the Warlock's beard, I hoped that was the truth. I didn't need Glenn on my conscience. Maybe something could be said, after all, for the Frost Maiden's way of killing.

That thought came out of nowhere. I smacked my head with my hand, to beat some sense back into it. The riot hadn't killed us, and the Fire Warlock hadn't either, but she might yet…if the Black Duke didn't hang us first.

And if we did survive, what the hell would I do now, with Master Randall gone? I shouldn't have stopped to think. Thinking hurt.

I stood up, and pulled Sam to his feet. "Come on, we've got work to do."

Sam guarded the door while I carried Richard to his kitchen and shouted for his wife. "It's Duncan Archer, ma'am. I'm trying to help. We need to stitch your husband's leg. He's got a bad gash in it."

A head popped out of the pantry, and got a good look. She ran for the stairs and came back with needle and thread. Richard hunched over and hung onto the edge of the table while we worked on his leg. I cleaned the wound, then held it closed and talked while she sewed. "Somebody should tell those two bonny lasses their dad's going to be fine. The riot's over. The Fire Warlock's here in Blacksburg, and he won't let it happen again."

A pair of wide eyes peeked around the pantry door, followed soon by another pair. Mrs Collins said, "Come on out, girls, and say thank you."

They thanked me prettily, and watched while their mother finished stitching, then wrapped an Earth Guild bandage around his leg. "It should be like new by morning."

"Good thing you had those bandages," I said, "because the healers are going to be awfully busy the next couple of days. I don't know when you'd get anybody to come look at it."

He croaked out a thank you. He looked ready to pass out. I carried him into their sitting room and laid him on the couch so he wouldn't have to climb the stairs. The room was a mess, like the looters had smashed anything they couldn't carry. Sam and I shoved a couple of heavy wardrobes in front of the windows; if the looters came back, they'd not have an easy time getting in.

Before we barricaded the front door, I carried his sword in with the fireplace tongs and dropped it on the hearth. "You'd be better off with an axe or quarterstaff. That sword says 'aristo' as much as if you stood on the front steps and shouted it."

He said, "I know, but I have no other weapon. I've never learned to use a quarterstaff."

"Maybe you won't need to. The Fire Guild will keep a tight grip on everything going on in this city for a while."

"I certainly hope so. Are you still planning on returning to Abertee?"

"Nothing could make me stay here now."

He sighed. "I'd leave, too, if I had anywhere else to go."

He held out his hand. We shook.

He said, "Meeting you was the second most lucky thing that ever happened to me. Thank you, my friend."

It was full dark when Mrs Collins let us out the garden gate. She insisted on giving us a lantern. I didn't want to draw attention, but stumbling over bodies in the dark would've been worse. We took it.

We started down the lane but then our feet turned us around like they had minds of their own, and marched us towards the square. The Fire Warlock's voice was in my head, not all around, and it was ordering me— me, Duncan Archer—to come and account for myself.

The Fire Warlock

In front of me, Sam marched towards the square.

I said, "He ordered you to come, too?"

Sam nodded, and swallowed a couple of times. "Duncan, I'm scared."

"So am I. Only an imbecile's not afraid of the Fire Warlock."

The square stank of charred flesh. Bodies, dead or dying, lay scattered. Witches and wizards roamed about, snuffing fires and tending the wounded.

Our feet brought us inside the palace fence, to a bonfire of furniture and bedding. Nick Cooper marched in and joined us.

I said, "My God, man, how are you still standing?"

"What?" He looked down. "Oh. It's not my blood."

Other scared folk followed Nick. Some I knew, and respected. When there were eleven of us—eight men and three women—the Fire Warlock walked out of the bonfire.

Two of the women screamed. I dropped the lantern. My knees wanted to buckle, but I froze, as if I had any chance of escaping notice.

He stopped a couple of feet from me, and glared. At me. Eye to eye. His shoulders were almost as wide as mine, too. His big ring flashed red, and lit up the whole group. He raised his wand and tapped me on the chest. I reeled back, and stepped on Sam's feet. He yelped.

The Warlock growled, "It won't do any good, hiding behind the smith. I'm going to get a good look at each of you."

He walked down the line, tapping us on our chests. "Duncan Archer, Sam Jackson, Nick Cooper…"

When he got to the end, he turned around and glared. "Why, out of all the people in this city, can I only find eleven—eleven!—who went to somebody else's aid tonight?"

It wasn't easy to read faces in the flickering light, but everybody else looked confused and scared, too. Nobody spoke.

The Warlock held up his hand. "I don't expect an answer to that question. I called each of you here because the Fire Office took notice of your actions, and is demanding I commend you for your responsible behaviour and clear thinking. I suppose I'll have to, but I don't much want to thank a dozen twigs for staying out of a bonfire that didn't have to burn in the first place. Instead, I want an answer to a different question.

"If you are such fine, upstanding citizens with sensible heads on your shoulders," he roared, "then why didn't any of you frostbitten fools convince your guilds to ask for my help before this mess got completely out of hand?"

The others looked at me. I said, "Uh…"

He stalked back to face me, and folded his arms across his chest. The ring shining so close hurt my eyes. "Well?"

I wiped sweat off my face. "I'm just a journeyman, and an outsider, and—"

Spittle flew. "You think just because you're from somewhere else and planning on going back there that what happens here doesn't matter to you?"

"Nae, sir, I—"

He snarled, with his face a foot from mine, "That you have no responsibility to the friends you've made here—"

"Nae, sir, I—"

"And the people you've worked with, just because they're not your family. Just because—"

I leaned in until my nose was two inches from his, and yelled, "Nae, sir! You asked a question, sir. You want an answer? Shut up and listen. Sir!" He rocked back on his heels. I leaned forward, still nose to nose. "I tried to ask for your help, but I'll be iced if I know how. I went to the top fire wizard here, and he brushed me off, saying you wouldn't listen to a journeyman."

"Son of a bitch." The Warlock turned away and stared into the bonfire. The rest of the group had edged away from me—getting out of blast range, probably—except for one little woman who was poking me and whispering.

The oldest woman said, "I went to him, and he threw me out, too. Sir. Said not to bother my silly, little head about important matters a housewife couldn't understand."

I said, "If you're so concerned, you should've shown up sooner. Some of these bodies might still be alive."

The woman beside me grabbed my shirt and yanked. I looked down and she hissed, "Call him Your Wisdom."

"Don't bother." The Fire Warlock's voice barely carried over the crackle of the fire. "Calling me Your Wisdom tonight would be a joke. I've made so many mistakes lately you might as well start calling me You Dunce instead." The fight had gone out of him. His ring had dimmed, too.

He said, "You want to know why was I so late. I was down south, dealing with the riot that erupted after the Green Duke had a starving man's arm frozen off for stealing a loaf of bread."

I swallowed a couple of times, and cleared my throat. "Sorry, sir. I didn't know about the other riot. If I'd known…"

"You couldn't have known. Riots don't happen back-to-back. Riots don't happen at all in Frankland." He turned away from the fire and looked at us again. "Wouldn't have mattered, anyway. You had a right to expect I would come and stop it. The Frost Maiden and I had both warned the Black Duke not to arrest anyone over the charters, so I thought things here would keep for a day or two. My mistake. When I did get here, things were so far gone I had to burn people right and left until nobody was left standing. I hate it, but nobody asked for help in the way the Fire Office recognises, so it presumed the rioters were all no-good troublemakers."

He rubbed his eyes with the back of his hand. "I'd rather burn the nobles for their arrogance and greed, but the Fire Office won't let me. The Great Coven was full of nobles who didn't want it interfering with their control of their subjects. I can't step in on my own initiative until a revolt or riot is in full swing. Until then, about all I can do is talk. Been talking so much lately you'd think I was in the Air Guild."

I said, "You could take their swords away."

"I took the Black Duke's sword away, twice. But I have to hand it over to the king, and the king handed it right back to him. Fat lot of good that did. My hands are tied until the nobles lose control and people are getting hurt. Unless one of the chartered bodies has asked for my help." He rubbed his eyes again. "You should've listened when they said, 'Take care of the guild, and the guild will take care of you.'"

We all eyed each other. Nick said, "Sir. Your Wisdom. We've all heard that, but…"

"But you didn't know what it meant, eh? If you come to me on your own, complaining about your ruler, I can't do anything, but if a chartered guild asks for my help, that's good enough. I can revoke exorbitant taxes, pry people out of the Frost Maiden's clutches—whatever's necessary to calm things down. And if it does get violent, the Fire Office gives that guild the benefit of the doubt, and is less brutal to its members." He turned back to me. "There must've been other smiths who wanted my help. You could've asked them to back you."

"Rounding up the guild council for a vote would've—"

"Wasn't needed. If two smiths came together and said it was on behalf of the guild, that fool hothead would've had to send you on to talk to me. You know, respond first in an emergency, and ask for credentials later—and I won't ask. Doesn't have to be members of the guild council. Two journeymen would have done. But I guess you didn't know that."

His shoulders had slumped after I yelled at him. My own sagged now. "I didn't want to get anybody else in trouble. And that wizard…"

"Was a nobleman who didn't want to acknowledge the power you do have." He nodded at the woman who had said she'd gone to see the fire wizard. "You're not a member of a guild, but your husband is, and you have friends and neighbours who are. Spread the word, and you'll all know more about important matters than that ass. It's poetic justice the mob killed him. I'm glad I don't have to torch a member of my own guild for incompetence. I'm going to light a fire under all four magic guilds to do a better job of telling you commoners what the nobles don't want you to know."

He doffed his hat and bowed to us. "And now, I apologise to you for yelling at you, and I do commend you for your actions. Blacksburg would be in even worse shape without your help. Now go home."

My feet stuck to the cobbles. The others disappeared, mumbling thanks, leaving Nick and me standing.

Sam pulled on my arm. "Duncan, come on. What's the matter?"

The Warlock said, "Sorry, Sam, I have something else I need to say to your friend Duncan, and to Nick." He looked back and forth between us. "You two probably think the worst is over. It's not. In some ways the next few days and weeks are going to be even worse. The city will have to hunker down and lick its wounds, and it's going to be a long time—years, decades even—before it fully recovers.

"You two are newcomers. You've both gotten reputations for speaking your minds, and you've angered some people. Neither of you have been marked by the fire, even though many people saw you here tonight. You will both be in serious danger if you stay here, and I have enough else to do that I don't want to have to keep an eye on you.

"Go back to your rooms, pack, and leave. Tonight. Don't sleep again in this city, unless one of you keeps watch for the other. Understand?"

We looked at each other, and nodded. Nick said, "The exit tax?"

"Revoked." He cocked an eye at Sam. "You got any family outside of Blacksburg?"

Sam said, "An uncle, five miles upriver."

"Wouldn't hurt for you to leave, too. Go stay with him awhile."

I said, "The grandmasters. Are they... I guess Master Randall's dead."

The Warlock turned back to the fire and stared into it. "Yep, he's dead. Crying shame. He's over there." He pointed towards the downed fence. "The other one—Master Clive—is home, and likely to stay there." He turned and looked at me. "There's something else on your mind."

I gulped, and pushed my luck. "The merchants the duke handed over to the Frost Maiden. Can you do anything for them?"

"Ha. Them. Lucky bastards. If they'd been here they'd probably be dead, too."

"They will be, when the Frost Maiden's done—"

"No, they won't. Drafting a new charter's not a crime. She'll turn them over to me and I'll give them a slap on the wrist for keeping secrets. That's all. I'm glad I don't have to pick a fight with her over them—I don't feel like losing. Losing on too many fronts already. Now get going." He walked into the fire and disappeared.

We saw only Earth and Fire wizards out on the streets, but none of us felt like taking chances. We walked together to Sam's mum's boarding house—undamaged, thank God—and left him there, then Nick and I went to fetch our horses and the pack mule I'd bought a week earlier to carry my tools. The stable door was unlocked, with a couple of hands inside nursing burns. When they saw we weren't burned, I thought for a moment they would pick a fight, but we outweighed them, and they settled for cursing at us.

I was more than ready to take the Fire Warlock's advice and get out, but we had a few things to do first. We went back to the square, and began a job that will give me nightmares for the rest of my life. We pulled bodies from the heap by the broken fence and laid them out in a row. My clothes were as blood-soaked as Nick's before we uncovered Master Randall. If he hadn't been such a big man with a bald head, we wouldn't have been sure which one he was. The bodies had been gored, hacked, burnt, and trampled on. A team of oxen couldn't have done a better job of making a mess of them.

The stench of blood and death made both the horse and the mule skittish, and we had a fight getting Master Randall slung on the mule's back. We picked our way through the rubble and bodies, but hadn't gone more than fifty yards when Nick tripped and fell. I swung the lantern around, and set it on the cobbles because I couldn't hold it steady. What I had seen was, in a way, as bad as the heap we'd pulled Master Randall out of.

Nick had caught his foot under a pickaxe handle. The point was buried in a man's back. I squatted down beside the dead man, but couldn't bring myself to touch him.

Nick said, "You know him."

I nodded. Nick yanked the pickaxe out. After a little while I lifted the man's head out of the dirt and turned it to see the face. Nick brought the lantern close, but there hadn't been any doubt in my mind.

Neither of us said anything, just got on with loading him onto Charcoal. The horse was as ornery as the mule had been, but I wasn't in a mood to put up with it, and he gave in before I did. "Don't know why you're complaining," I told the fool horse. "He doesn't weigh as much as I do, and you're supposed to be a war horse."

Nick said, "How many children does he have?"

"Six, and another on the way."

Nick shouldered the pickaxe. "She can sell it. She's going to need every penny."

We left Master Randall with a blubbering journeyman, and walked into Master Paul's yard in the first grey light of early morning. Mrs Hammer came running.

"Paul? Oh." Her face fell. "Have you seen…"

"We brought him back, ma'am. I'm sorry, ma'am."

"Oh, dear God." She clapped a hand over her mouth and swayed. I steered her into her kitchen and made her sit down. She whispered, "Was he…was he burned?"

"No, ma'am. The riot killed him."

"Thank God for that." She covered her face with her apron and sobbed. I told her what the Fire Warlock had said and that I was leaving. I thought she hadn't heard, but after we had laid Master Paul on a bench in the smithy and were loading my tools onto the mule, she came out and thanked us for bringing him home. "I'm sorry you're going," she said, and kissed me on the cheek.

After that we went to collect Nick's tools. The sun wasn't fully up yet, but the master cutler was already in his workshop. He had a burn down one arm. After one look at us, he yelled, "Get out, and don't come back." He threw Nick's tools out after him, trying to hit him.

Nick said, "I have to admit, I'm glad you're with me."

I said, "Didn't anybody in this frostbitten city go to bed last night?"

Blacksburg, mid-morning on a workday, should have been a noisy place. Hooves striking cobblestones, wheels squeaking, hammers ringing on anvils, hawkers selling their wares—the din would sometimes make me stuff my fingers in my ears. Not so that morning. The quiet clink, clink of coins in my saddlebags was as hard to ignore as one of Granny Mildred's scoldings.

Three days ago, I'd been expecting to leave Blacksburg with less in my pocket than when I'd gotten here, and glad to get out.

Clink, clink.

I'd been lucky. Damn lucky.

Clink, clink.

After collecting Sam from his mum's, our path to Master Clive's smithy went past the Earth Guildhall. They, far more than the duke, would shoulder the burden of caring for the families that had been hurt. They would feed the widows and orphans. The duke wouldn't care if they starved.

Clink, clink.

A line of quiet people with makeshift bandages and blank faces stretched halfway across the square from the guildhall. One of the livelier sufferers was sweeping up glass from broken windows.

Clink, clink.

I yanked the bag of gold out of my saddlebags, fished out enough to get home to Nettleton on, and stomped into the guildhall. The healers were as battered and washed out as their patients. I couldn't tell one from the other except by who was doing the bandaging.

"Who's in charge here?" I said.

"Mother Astrid." A wizard waved without looking up from the lad he was tending. "Over there."

A witch straightened up, and wiped her hands on a bloodied apron. A witch with a splash of freckles across a darling of a face. I'd seen that face before.

"What is it?" she said.

Nae, not that face, but one thirty years younger. If she looked that good in her fifties…

"Speak up," she said. "I don't have time. If it isn't urgent, you'll have to wait in line—"

"Nae, ma'am." I shoved the bag into her hands. "This is for the Blacksmiths' Guild's widows and orphans. Make sure Paul Hammer's family gets a good share, and don't tell them where it came from. Wouldn't want them to know how soft I am."

I stomped out before the open-mouthed witch could ask questions, and gave the mule a hard slap on the rump. "Let's go, before I come to my senses and ask for it back."

Tools, pig iron, and charcoal lay scattered across the yard and trampled into the dirt. Looters had ripped the smithy door off its hinges and left it lying on the ground. One of the shutters was gone; the other swung open, creaking in the breeze. I poked my head through the window. The looters had stripped the smithy bare. Only the two-handed sword lay in the dirt. Some fool had kicked ashes over it.

"They came for the swords," Master Clive's wife said, from the kitchen door. She held a broom handle like a quarterstaff athwart the door. "They had a wizard with them."

"Master Clive couldn't stop them?" Sam said.

"He wasn't here, and I didn't try. I bolted the doors and thanked God they left the house alone."

"You were lucky," I said. "He couldn't have stopped them, either. Is he here now?"

"Why do you want to see him?"

"I meant to ask him for a favour." I kicked a few bits of charcoal into a pile. "Never mind, ma'am."

She gave me a long, narrow-eyed look as I walked into the smithy. I wiped the sword clean with my shirttail and hung it on the rack. When I came out, she said, "Come on in, Duncan. You other two, stay in the yard where I can see you."

She lowered the broom handle to let me in, and bolted the door behind me. Grandmaster Clive sat in the shadows at the far end of the kitchen. I tossed my hat on the table and started around the end to sit across from him, but his wife blocked my way. She pointed to the bench on the same side of the table as the master, and I sat down next to him. She poured me a cup of coffee without speaking, and backed into a corner where she could see out the window.

Glare from the window made it hard to see Master Clive. I raised my hat to block the sun, for a better look. His hands were clenched around a mug, and he stared straight ahead without looking at me. A muscle in the side of his face twitched.

I sipped the coffee, enjoying every hot mouthful. We sat for several minutes, and I wasn't sure he knew I was there, until he said, "Any news about Brother Randall?"

"He's dead. We carried him back to his smithy."

"I was afraid of that. I'll see to his funeral. He deserves a good sendoff."

We sat for a while longer. Finally, I said, "Damned shame about your smithy."

He didn't move, but the muscle twitched faster. After a while, I said, "They couldn't have got far with the anvils. There's lots of stuff scattered in the square and in the streets. If you ask a witch or wizard for help, you might get most of your tools back."

He snatched up his mug, and flung it against the side of the fireplace. "I don't care about the goddamned tools." He dropped his head into his hands. "All I ever wanted, since before I can remember, was to make swords. What the hell do I do now?"

His wife brushed past him and picked up the pieces of the mug. Tears ran down her cheeks, but she didn't make any noise.

I said, "You can rebuild the smithy. What's to stop you from making swords?"

He turned to stare at me, and showed what his wife hadn't wanted me to see. The other side of his face sported a burn, starting inside the hairline and running down his cheek to his mouth. The bottom dropped out of my stomach. His eyes slid away from mine.

He said, "You weren't burned."

"Nae, sir."

He turned away from me. Dark red rose from his throat until his whole face was the colour of a brick.

I said, "The royal guild wouldn't kick a man out if he says he's sorry, would they?"

"They've done it before." His mouth worked without saying anything, then he croaked, "And if they didn't kick out a smith who'd disgraced them, I don't know that I'd want to be a member."

Out in the yard, Charcoal kicked at the smithy wall. The other beasts stamped and rattled their tack. Nick cursed at Charcoal, telling him he was an impatient bastard. Sam asked Nick what was taking so long.

What was taking so long? I hadn't been home to Nettleton in close to a year. Going to London and making another masterpiece for another grandmaster would cost me another six months or more. The White Duchess would be making trouble, and I wasn't there to speak up for our rights.

But I couldn't kick a man when he was down. I just couldn't do it.

If I drank any more cold coffee, I'd puke. I pushed the mug away and stood. "When I get home to Abertee, and folk there ask me about my travels, I'll tell them I was lucky to have met Grandmaster Clive, one of the great swordsmiths. If you're ever in the neighbourhood, look me up."

I was pulling the door open when Clive's wife said, "Duncan, wait. What was the favour you wanted?"

Judging Men by Their Horses

Sam grinned like the certificate had his name on it instead of mine. "That's nice. That's real nice." He handed it to Nick who read it aloud, tracing the words with his finger.

"That's what a real master ought to be. Congratulations," he said. "I've got to admit, when we got here, I didn't think he'd be in a mood for doing favours for anybody."

I stowed the certificate in my saddlebags and climbed on Charcoal. Nick didn't need to know Grandmaster Clive acted like I was doing him the favour. "You can't leave without giving me a chance to redeem myself, even if just a little. Of course I'll sign it." His eyes met mine without sliding away. "God knows you've earned it, if anybody ever has."

We spent the night with Sam's kin, and the next morning the uncle and I went with Sam to the local smithy. The master was willing to take Sam on, on the basis of knowing the uncle and hearing my good word about how well Sam worked. Then Nick turned south, for London, and I took the old Roman road north.

For almost a year, homesickness had eaten at me. So why the devil, now that I was on my way home, could I not get my mind on Abertee and off of Blacksburg? When I closed my eyes, I saw blood and heard screams. I dreamed about the Fire Warlock yelling at me. The smell of a burnt pie in a roadhouse made me retch. The ring of hammer on anvil made me choke up.

If only I'd known a week ago what I knew now.

The skies were clear, but I plodded towards home in a fog, wondering what else the aristos—and maybe the magic folk, too—didn't want us to know. A day's travel short of Crossroads, I spent the night with a smith

I'd worked for a few years earlier. His news was the first since I'd left Blacksburg to make me sit up and take notice.

"A group of travellers staying at the inn were asking around if anybody was going to Crossroads. There's not enough of them to scare off the footpads, so I reckon they'd be glad to have you along. Although maybe they'd not need you now, since an earth witch on her own rode in not long before you got here. Said she's on her way to Crossroads."

"On her own, you say. Is she that powerful or that silly?"

"Doesn't matter. If I were a robber I'd not chance her making my privates shrivel up and fall off."

"Aye. What's she look like?"

He shrugged. "Didn't see her. My neighbour did. Said she had a whole forest on her hat."

I shoved my hat back on. "I'm going over to the inn. With a pack mule in tow, I'm not traveling fast, and I wouldn't mind some company tomorrow."

The taproom door was open, and raised voices spilled out.

"There's safety in numbers. We should wait for more travellers—"

"I'm not waiting. I need to get to Crossroads—"

"She said too many makes it harder—"

I ducked in. A group of men were waving their hands and shouting at each other. Standing in the middle, as calm as a pond on a windless day, was an earth witch with a little turned-up nose and freckles scattered all over her face.

Today was my lucky day.

I said, "I'm riding for Crossroads tomorrow. I reckon I'll make your party large enough to scare off just about anybody."

The man standing with his back to me turned, saying, "I'm worried—" He took a step back.

Without taking my eyes off Reverend Angus, I said, "I'd worry, too, if I were you."

Granny Hazel said, "I was explaining that the larger the group the harder it is for me to extend my magic to cover everyone." She smiled at me with devils in her eyes. "But if you're worried about robbers, Mr Archer, I'm sure I have enough magic to cover even you."

I stared down at her with a slack jaw. The innkeeper smirked and turned his back on us, making a show of polishing glasses. I said, "Thank you, ma'am. Very kind of you. I'll be happier with you along."

Her smile showed straight white teeth, not one missing. "That's settled, then. We'll leave in the morning, after an early breakfast. Good night, all." She walked out of the taproom, leaving the preacher glaring at me.

"Surely you, of all people," he said, "needn't be beholden to a witch for protection."

I shrugged. "I'm going to Crossroads tomorrow, with or without company, but what I said was God's truth. I'll be happier traveling with Granny Hazel. I'll even put up with you if that's what it takes."

The sun had already set, but the gloom I'd been under lifted. None of the lasses I'd mooned over, some prettier than Granny Hazel, had kept me interested for long, but an earth witch would have more to talk about than most women. Working as a healer, she'd earn her own money, too. She hadn't remembered me because she needed to snag a good provider. She'd have a man around if she wanted to, or not at all, and I'd heard stories about what an earth witch could do to a man she wanted to please. Walking back to the smith's, I felt like whistling for the first time in weeks.

The first horse out of the stable the next morning was a swaybacked nag. We'd be lucky if she could keep pace even with my plodding pack mule. The next one out made me smile—a sleek, high-stepping filly as pretty as any horse I'd ever seen. Charcoal and I both turned our heads to watch as the lad led her past.

"I don't know why you care, old boy," I said. "You couldn't do anything with her."

Charcoal snorted and rattled his bridle. I rubbed his head. "Can't help thinking about it though, can you. I guess it's in the blood."

While we watched the filly, Reverend Angus and his friends came out of the inn. One man I hadn't noticed last night fussed with the stirrups on the nag. The lad nudged him out of the way and got on with fixing the problem. The rider straightened up, and gave me a good view of his hat. I froze.

It wasn't too late to turn and run. Leave the mule. He'd never catch up on that nag—

A touch on my arm, and my blood stopped pounding.

"What's the matter, Duncan?" Hazel said.

I leaned on Charcoal's withers and took a deep breath. Let it out again, slowly. "You're using magic on me."

"You were panicking. What's wrong?"

"The water wizard. If I'd known…"

"Him? He's only a level two. What do you think he would do?"

"Drag me off to the Crystal Palace."

She gave me a startled glance. "Why would he? You haven't done anything, have you? That the Water Guild would care about, I mean."

"Not that I know of."

"I'd expect you would know."

"Then I must not have. Yet."

She stared at me with a pucker between her eyebrows. "You're planning to?"

"Nae, ma'am. But they act like I am."

The water wizard fumbled with his reins. She didn't even glance at him. "All I sense from him is embarrassment, and resentment that you're staring at him."

I turned away. "Maybe I've been seeing omens where I shouldn't. Sorry, ma'am. I wasn't making much sense, even to myself. Forget it."

"You won't panic again, will you?"

I took a deep breath and blew out through my lips. "I'd better not. That would draw more attention."

"Let's get on the road, then."

I gave her a leg-up onto the pretty filly. "I'm surprised the preacher's traveling with a water wizard."

"He wasn't. The wizard arrived late last night, and asked me at breakfast if he could travel with us."

"Oh. Thank you ever so much, ma'am."

She laughed. "Get on your horse. He won't bother you." She looked around the stable yard. "Everybody ready?"

"Yes, ma'am." "Certainly." "Right, ho." The water wizard looked a bit seasick, and muttered something, but nodded. The preacher, looking around, started and stared.

Hazel said something I didn't catch, but the mule pricked up his ears. Charcoal whinnied and stamped. Even the swaybacked nag raised her head.

The preacher cleared his throat and raised a hand, but Hazel's horse was already moving.

"Let's go," she said. All the animals moved. The preacher flailed, and grabbed for his saddle, but hung on.

I turned my grin towards the road and gave Charcoal his head. We caught up with the filly in a few paces, the mule almost crowding us.

"We'll have to walk most of the way," Hazel said. "That old mare can't manage the pace your horse wants to set."

"Charcoal will do whatever yours does." Charcoal was three hands taller than Hazel's filly. Talking to her was like talking to somebody down in a well, but if she minded me looming over her she didn't show it. I turned in the saddle and watched the parade behind us. The preacher and his friends left a generous gap between us and them—one of the few things I agreed with him on. He glared over his shoulder at the water wizard.

Maybe having a water wizard along wasn't so bad, after all.

Hazel's hat had four full-sized little trees, plus a sapling. I'd never seen that before. Most of my friends in the Earth Guild had two or three trees on their hats, and none could tell how a man felt from the other side of a stable yard, without even looking at him.

What else could she tell? It was a wonder she hadn't slapped me. "Are you an earth mother?"

Clouds came over the sun. I had to lean down to hear her. "No. I'm a level five witch. That would qualify me for the top rank in the other magic guilds, but not in the Earth Guild."

"Why not?"

"I don't meet all the criteria."

"All the what?"

"I'm one of the top healers in Frankland. I'm good at animal husbandry, too, and not bad at gardening, but I can't dig."

"So what? I can dig a bit. It's nothing special."

"Not to you, maybe, but I can't do it at all, no matter how hard I try. And believe me, I've tried."

"Sorry, ma'am. It doesn't seem important, next to being a powerful healer."

She sighed. "Thank you, but it means the guild won't call me an earth mother."

"That just shows the Earth Guild is as f—Sorry, ma'am—as messed up as any other guild."

She laughed. The sun came out from behind the cloud.

"You don't need to apologise to an earth witch for terms describing bodily functions. The Earth Guild invented most of them."

"Just because you've heard them doesn't mean I should use them." The stories said it was impossible to make an earth witch blush. I thought of a few things I'd be more uncomfortable saying than a healer would be hearing. Forget that.

"I'm surprised the Earth Guild would let an almost-earth-mother come to an out-of-the-way place like Abertee, instead of a city."

"I despise cities. I need hills and birdsong."

The more I learned about this lass, the better I liked her. "But I thought they'd want a powerful healer near lots of people."

"Isn't a powerful healer needed here sometimes?"

"Aye, but not as often."

"What do you do now when somebody needs something beyond what Mildred can do?"

"She calls on Mother Brenda from Edinburgh, and she pops in through one of the tunnels."

"And Mother Brenda will retire in a few years, too. After I'm established here, I'll pick up her work, until I cover her territory. Less powerful healers in Edinburgh and the other towns will handle the ordinary cases, and I'll handle the more serious ones. An earth witch can travel anywhere in Frankland in under an hour through the tunnels, so where we choose to live doesn't make a big difference."

"But why choose Abertee? I love it because it's my home, and I know every man, woman, child, rock, and tree for miles around. But I'd not expect you to think this was better than some other place with lots of rocks."

She shrugged. "My mother and I cast the runes, and they pointed here."

"Why? Don't they usually say something more than just, go there?"

"Yes, but…"

"What did they say? Sorry, it's none of my business."

"They weren't clear, that's all. My reading said Abertee needs me, but I don't know why me and not another healer. Mother's reading said I would be happy."

Because she'd have a big ox of a sweetheart? If not, I didn't want to know. "Why are you riding to Crossroads? Since you can go anywhere through the tunnels."

"The Guild Council encourages healers to do some traveling the long way. They say we need to understand what our patients have to deal with to be proper healers. Besides, one can't take a horse through the tunnels, and I like to ride."

"Do you? I'll show you the prettiest sights in Abertee, if you'd ride out with me on a Sunday."

The freckles disappeared under a wave of red. "I'd like that."

I was bewitched, and she wasn't even trying. Not even having Reverend Angus along spoiled my day. When we stopped for dinner, Hazel and I claimed a table outside the inn in the shade of a plane tree. The preacher and his friends marched into the dining room with their noses in the air. The water wizard seemed unsure of himself. Hazel ignored my muttering and waved him over.

Don't tangle with witches or wizards, Granny Mildred had said. Especially the Water Guild. But here was one sitting down across a table from me. I couldn't very well not talk to him.

I said, "I would've expected a water wizard to be chasing down highwaymen instead of acting like you're afraid of them."

He glared at me. "You obviously don't know the first thing about the Water Guild. I am afraid of them. Anybody but a colossal jackass like yourself would be."

My hand curled into a fist, but I'd been called worse names before. I would let it pass.

Hazel frowned at him. "Master Duncan was trying to make conversation. He's a respected man in Abertee. If you want to sit with us, be polite."

"Sorry," he muttered. "I just get tired of simpletons—"

"Ahem."

"Of mundanes hating the Water Guild because they think we spend all our time hunting them down."

"So, when one asks a question, instead of answering politely and trying to educate him, you attack?"

I said, "Everybody I know is afraid of the Water Guild because we think you hate us. You haven't done much to prove otherwise."

He turned red. "I didn't mean…"

She patted his hand. "Never mind. I'm sure you didn't mean any harm."

The serving lass clattered over, mugs in hand. "Here you go, then. It sure is good to see you, Duncan."

"That's Master Duncan, to you, Jill."

"Oh, is it now? About time, I should think." She bussed me on the cheek. "Even better, then, that you're back. The duke needs a rap on the knuckles."

I groaned. "I haven't even gotten home yet. What's the duchess done now?"

"Not her this time. Their son and his friends have been running wild. Somebody needs to tell them to grow up and stop insulting every pretty lass they lay their filthy eyes on."

I groaned again. "Frost it. Not that."

"Aye, that. Talk to Granny Mildred. She can give you an ear full."

"Thanks for the warning, Jill."

She left, and I turned back to the wizard. "You're right. I don't know much about the Water Guild. Why don't you tell me?"

He sighed. "I can keep people from drowning and fishermen's boats from taking on water, but that's about it. Without being next to an ocean or a lake, I don't have any magic I can use to protect myself from robbers, and even then, I couldn't do more than pull up a wave and hope it knocks them off their feet so I can run away."

"You can't kill a man by freezing him?"

"Of course not. Only the level fives—"

"The sorcerers and sorceresses," Hazel said.

"Only they can do that. It takes a lot of power, and they have to answer to the Water Office whenever they do, so nobody does it on a whim. I'm nowhere near that powerful. I'm just a two-bit wizard trying to scrape out a living by protecting fishermen."

I said, "You're going the wrong way to find any of them."

His lip curled. "I know that, you... Sorry. I'm going to my nephew's wedding, and when that's over I'll turn around and head home."

"Oh. What about the manhunts? If you don't have enough magic to protect yourself, you can't be much help with them."

"God give me patience. I never go anywhere near them. If the whole guild got involved we wouldn't have time for the things only we can do, like prevent floods and droughts and protect sailors and fishermen. The justice-related magics are a small part of what the Water Guild does. We were never supposed to patrol the highways, or do manhunts and the like in the first place.

"It doesn't take magic to enforce law and order—most of the time, at least. Magic's needed when you're hunting a wizard, or somebody so violent he'll kill the next person he meets for the fun of it. The nobles should handle most of it, and only come to the Water Guild for help in special cases, or as the court of last resort.

"We're doing more and more of what the nobles are supposed to do because they don't and somebody has to, but we hate it. Nearly everybody in the Guild is angry about it, but the Office doesn't have any teeth to force the nobles to accept their responsibilities."

I gaped at him. "You're telling me the Frost Maiden doesn't want to stick her claws—er, fingers—into Abertee?"

"That's exactly what I'm telling you. We're grateful the White Duke, unlike most of the others, has done a good job of taking care of problems himself and we haven't had to get involved."

Our food came, and I chewed without tasting it. Hazel and the wizard talked about other things while I tried to make sense of what he'd said. I wasn't sure how much of it to believe. Between him and the Fire Warlock, my whole world had gone topsy-turvy.

I started listening again when the wizard named the village he was heading for. "I thought you were going to Crossroads," I said.

He said, "I have to go past Crossroads to get there."

"Nae, we'll go within a few miles of it this afternoon."

"That would be great, but it can't be right."

"I'll show you." I went and got my map of northern Frankland, and spread it out on the table. Hazel's eyes widened. The wizard's eyes bugged out.

"I thought you were a blacksmith," he said. "Can you read? Who around here has books?"

"My brother has a few—the Good Book, Mr Marlowe's collected works, and some of the duke's castoffs. I listen while he reads them. I can read a bit, but it's hard work. The only things I've ever read through are guild charters, and those made my head hurt."

"Guild charters? Good God. And this map—"

"Books are hard, maps are easy. See, it's just pictures, like a sketch of a gate. Where the road's straight, like here, it's flat and easy going, but where it twists around, that's hilly. I've heard the names of most villages, so they're easy to figure out. Here's your nephew's, and we're here."

He squinted at the map. "That is what it says, but I don't know. These squiggles don't mean anything to me."

Hazel peered over his shoulder. "Master Duncan is right. It's not far from here."

"Well, if you say so."

I snorted and rolled the map.

He said, "But that map must have cost a lot. Whatever do you want it for?"

I froze, the map half in its case. Panic clawed at me. Tell a water wizard why I'd wanted it? Like hell.

Hazel's fingers brushed my arm. I shrugged. "My uncle and my dad had maps. They wanted to know where everything in Frankland was, and it rubbed off on me and my brother." I slid the map on in and latched the case. My hands weren't even shaking.

Hazel gave me a long look. I hoped she'd forgive me. It wasn't a lie.

We reached the track to the nephew's village by mid-afternoon, and rode with him the two miles off the Roman road to make sure he got there safely. The preacher got pissed off about going out of his way to help a wizard. Hazel didn't argue, but turned her horse off onto the track, leaving the preacher to follow or not. I was keen to get on to Crossroads, but willing to make the detour just to tweak the preacher's nose. And I didn't mind helping the wizard; he'd been friendlier, once he'd gotten past calling me names. When we left the village, he even thanked me for saving him half a day.

We got back on the Roman road with the preacher and his friends riding ahead of us. We were almost home, there were no water wizards behind me, and maybe, just maybe, I didn't need to be so scared of them.

The tune came out of my lips without me even thinking about it. The preacher turned on his horse to glare at me. I couldn't see why he minded me whistling a lively hymn tune. I switched to the bawdiest drinking song I could think of. He hunched over his horse's neck and kicked at it. The beast made a show of picking up the pace, without putting any distance between us.

Hazel laughed, and hummed along.

Every man, woman, and child in Crossroads must have shaken my hand, twice. They passed my certificate from hand to hand, read it aloud a dozen times, and handed it back to me only a little the worse for wear.

They should have been giving Hazel as much attention as they gave me—what's a blacksmith next to an almost earth mother?—but she wasn't interested. She smiled, shook her head when I tried to make a fuss over her, and faded into the crowd. I lost track of her.

I lost track of Reverend Angus, too. After the noise died down, I went looking for him.

Homecoming

Master Walter—Brother Walter to me now—and his lads helped search for the preacher. An apprentice spotted him in the Shepherd's Arms' dining room with his friends, finishing their suppers. I walked in and clapped him on the shoulder. "We have some unfinished business to talk about, don't we, Reverend Angus?"

The preacher stared straight ahead. "You and I have nothing to discuss, Mr Archer."

"That's Master Archer, to you. How long ago did you leave Blacksburg?"

"That is none of your business." He stood, turning away from me, and came nose to nose with Brother Walter.

Walter said, "Seems like a simple question. How long ago did you leave Blacksburg?"

The preacher glared, and turned. Walter's lads hemmed him in. He shrugged. "About a week ago."

I said, "You left Blacksburg before the riot, then."

"Riot? What riot?" The lads crowded closer. I waved them to silence.

I said, "Maybe you left before the exit tax, too."

The preacher shot me a smug look. "My friends in Blacksburg warned me about the exit tax. A pity yours were not so well-informed."

"Mine weren't working for the duke."

He turned red. "I was not—"

"Somebody was paying you. The duke, or another aristo, or maybe even the king. Somebody who didn't care that common folk got hurt."

The dining room had gotten quiet, except for me. I had gotten loud.

Walter said, "What are you talking about, Duncan?"

"This muttonhead preached in Blacksburg for months, saying Frankland will be better off if we drive out the witches and wizards. Some fools listened to him, and went for the magic folk in the riot. They threw rocks through the windows of both the Earth and Water Guildhalls, and beat the healers on duty. So, when commoners who'd gotten hurt came to the Earth Guild for help, they had to wait. Maybe some had to wait too long."

Nobody spoke. The other men at the preacher's table stared at him like they'd turned over a rock and found a snake.

"Most folk will do anything for a healer, so I figure the other guilds must've gotten it worse. Don't know for sure. I'm just glad you"—I poked the preacher in the chest and he backed a step—"are going on to Edinburgh."

"I am not. I have grown tired of cities. I intend to enjoy Abertee's fresh air for a time."

"Sorry, mate. You're not staying here."

"I have a right to express my opinions—"

"You've no right to stir up trouble."

"You have no authority to—"

"Oh, yes, I do." I waved my certificate under his nose. "The Blacksmiths' Guild sent me to Blacksburg to get certified so I could be the one who goes and talks to the duke whenever trouble's brewing." I poked him again, and he took another step back. "And you're trouble. Look around. These folk know me and trust me to look out for them. When I say I won't have you talking Abertee folk into rioting, who're they going to listen to, you or me?"

Somebody growled, "We don't want any witch haters here." The sweating preacher backed away. We'd backed him into a corner.

The innkeeper said, "He'll leave with the group going north tomorrow morning. My lads will see to it."

"Thanks, Charley."

"Anytime, Dunc—Sorry. Master Duncan."

I gave him a grin, and walked into the taproom. Brother Walter bellied up to the bar with me. "Tell us about this riot."

Granny Mildred gave me an earful next morning, and orders to talk to the duke about his son's friends, but I'd have gone home to Nettleton first, even if the duke hadn't been in Edinburgh, and not due back for a couple of days. For all I'd known since Uncle Will died that I'd have to

116

argue with the duke—and if I cared to admit it, I'd known far longer it would fall on me someday—I wasn't looking forward to it.

I was riding alongside the river, brooding on what I'd say to him, when Jake Higgins rounded the bend ahead, dressed like a duke's guardsman and carrying a battle-axe. Jake Higgins, that Doug and I had once dunked in a horse trough for bullying a lad half his size. The same Jake Higgins Uncle Will had thrown across the smithy yard for pawing Cousin Ruth. A low growl started deep in my throat.

He reined in, grinning, as I got close. "Well, if it isn't Duncan Archer, that fancies himself God's gift to women."

I kept my mouth shut. There wasn't anything I could say that would do any good. I'd be past in a wee bit and not have to listen.

He said, "All those girls eyeing you won't give you another glance after they see me in my uniform. But they can wait. Maggie will be all over me when I go to Nettleton. You'll have to smile and say, 'Welcome, Come on in', and let me make a woman out of her. Won't like that, will you?"

"I'm not worried. She could spend a week with you and still be a maid."

"You son-of-a—" We were side-by-side now. He raised the axe, but I had my hand on his arm, forcing it down, before he'd raised it chest high. With my other arm I grabbed his shirt front and hauled him half out of the saddle.

"You're not an officer, and you haven't got what it takes to be one. And you're stupid if you think you can attack an unarmed, law-abiding master craftsman and get away with it."

He was sputtering and turning red. I gave him a shake. "Stay away from my sister. She already made it clear she can't abide your homely mug."

He snarled, "You can't stop me."

"You don't have to answer to me. You do anything to her, and the Frost Maiden will freeze your stinking balls off. And I'll laugh when she does."

He was braver, or more foolhardy, than I'd given him credit for. He spat in my face. I hauled him off his horse and threw him in the mud. I gave the horse a smack for good measure and it ran for the stables.

I wiped my face. "It's just as well you're in the guards. When you cause trouble, I'll know where to find you."

The ache gnawing at me for more than a year began to seep out as I rode through the gap into the Upper Tee Valley. Abertee's problems, the Blacksburg riot—they all seemed small beer. I was whistling, riding through the narrow gap at the bottom.

Something called to me, saying I'd been away too long. I stopped to listen, but there wasn't any sound. Just a tugging deep in my chest, saying I'd had it wrong. The valley didn't belong to me. I belonged to the valley, it hadn't approved of me being gone so long, and I'd better not do it again.

Funny, that. Dad had said the valley had its own magic, but I'd never felt it before. I'd rather not feel it again. No reason why I should; even if I settled in Crossroads, I'd be close enough to come home often.

Smell of dinner cooking tickled my nose before I got within earshot. Doug waved from the upper pasture, and jogged down the hill. Maggie came running while I was only halfway up the lane. Jessie waved at me from the door.

The neighbours came in a steady stream. After a full day of hugging and kissing, hand pumping and back-slapping, little-tyke tossing, and oohing and aahing over my certificate, I was worn out. I slept better than I had in months.

The morning brought more visitors. I itched for a chance to talk to Doug alone, but had to wait until the dinner dishes had been cleared away. Maggie and Jessie were busy with housework and children, and weren't paying us any attention. I unrolled the map on the table.

Doug's eyes lit up. "Nice."

We traced the roads I had taken, and I recounted what I had learned from other travellers about the lay of the land south of Blacksburg. If I ever journeyed south, I knew enough now to bypass all the Water Guild haunts in North Frankland.

"It does mean going through a few cities, though."

"Rather not," Doug said.

"Can't be helped. The cities and towns are where the bridges are, or maybe the other way around."

I didn't have to tell Doug not to trust a ferryman. We'd heard the same stories. If the ferryman wasn't a water wizard, his brother probably was, and only a rank fool would ford or swim a river. Might as well shout, Here I am, arrest me.

"The good news is there are bridges all the way. We don't have to get our feet wet to reach the channel. The bad news is we have to use the Earth Guild tunnels to cross, and pray they won't turn us over to the Water Guild."

Doug scowled at the map. "I'd expect the Water Guild to keep an eye on everybody coming and going through those tunnels."

"We've heard stories of wanted men from North Frankland making it to New London. They got out somehow. The Earth Guild must have tunnels the Water Guild doesn't know about, but nobody would tell me where. Must've thought I looked too respectable. Like I'd tell on them."

"Keep looking. Do you have a map this good of South Frankland?"

"Nae. Just Uncle Will's." I rolled the map and slid it in its case. I hadn't asked the shopkeeper if he had one. For all I cared, the world stopped at North Frankland's shores. I wanted to know where everything was in North Frankland. Someday I'd see more of it, and come back to Nettleton when I'd had enough. Trying to find a way out was like a game—fun, as long as it wasn't real. God help me if it stopped being a game.

Doug eyed Maggie, busy at the spinning wheel. He jerked his head towards the door. I followed him uphill through a steady drizzle. We were a long way out of earshot before he said, "Tell me what you've heard about Fiona."

"Some rubbish I didn't believe about her making eyes at an aristo, and getting more than she'd bargained for. Granny Mildred wouldn't talk—not about Fiona, anyway. Gave me an earful about the aristo—Lord Edmund Somebody-or-other, some earl's son—insulting and mistreating pretty lasses, but she wouldn't tell me anything he actually said or did. Just ordered me to make the duke rein him in. I stopped at Fiona's yesterday morning, on the way home, but she wouldn't talk to me. Wouldn't even open the door. Yelled at me to go away and never come back. I'd've been pissed off if she hadn't been making eyes at me ever since she got old enough to know how. Got worried instead."

"Aye. Not talking to you—that's…bad."

"Something happened to her, all right, and worse than some whelp calling her names. I meant to ask Maggie about her, but with everybody coming out to welcome me home, I didn't get a chance."

"Don't bother. Maggie knows, but she's not telling."

"Won't talk, or can't? If the brat's using magic, maybe she can't tell."

Doug scratched his chin. "Wondered that. Not sure it matters. If Fiona complained to the Frost Maiden, her magic's strong enough to find out the truth."

"But she won't go, will she? There were women like that in Blacksburg, but I didn't think it would happen here. The Frost Maiden used to look after our sisters even when she'd frost us. Why doesn't she even care about them anymore?"

Doug didn't answer. He watched the house, water sliding off his hat brim. It was a warm day, but I hate the rain dripping onto my neck. I fiddled with my hat, and waited.

After a while, he said, "Maggie's talking about going to New London after she gets married."

I tugged my jacket tighter. The day had turned cold. "Let me guess. Since Fiona."

"Aye."

"How's her beau taking it?"

"He's not eager, but he'd do anything for her. If she says go, they'll go."

And rip part of my heart out when she leaves. I waited.

"Maybe we'll go, too, if she leaves," Doug said.

"You can't do that."

"I could. Better than waiting to be pushed out."

"You've never been away from here for long—you don't know what being homesick is like. I hated it. The valley tugged at me, all the time. The longer I was gone the harder it pulled. I could hardly stand it, and I was still in North Frankland. If I left Frankland, I think it would kill me."

Doug stared at me. "I've never heard you talk like that before."

"I'd never been so far away, and for so long, before."

"Earth magic?"

"Aye. And you're as much an earth wizard as I am. It might not let you go either."

We were both staring down the hill at the house when Jessie and Maggie ran out the door yelling. Jessie took off her apron and waved it in the air. Maggie gathered her skirts and ran uphill towards us.

Doug barrelled down the hill. I hurried after him. When they met, Maggie raced past Doug and shoved a little paper packet into my hands. It was lumpy, with something in it besides a letter. I turned it over in my hands. The only thing written on the outside was Master Duncan Archer, Nettleton, Abertee.

"Who brought this? I didn't see anybody come by the house."

"Nobody brought it," she gasped. "It came by magic."

"You're pulling my leg."

"I am not. There wasn't anything on the table after you rolled up your map, but it was there when Jessie sat down with her sewing."

Jessie, when we got to the house, said the same. "We've been here since dinner. Nobody else came in."

"Who'd waste magic like that on me?"

"How do we know?"

"Open it," Doug said, "and find out."

I shook it. The paper rattled. "Nae, I'll keep playing with it and wondering. Make the fun last longer."

Maggie stamped her foot. "Duncan!"

"Just teasing." I broke the seal, and tipped it up. A piece of bronze with a splayed head fell into my palm.

The Earl's Brat

"What is it?" Maggie asked.

It couldn't be what it looked like. Not a chance. I stared at it without moving.

"He's speechless," Jessie said.

"That's a first," Maggie said. She pulled the paper out of my hand. Unfolded it and waved it under my nose. "What's it say?"

I couldn't read the letter for the roaring in my head. The letters ran together, except for the end, where he'd written his name bigger than the rest. Clive.

I sat down and rolled the beautiful seal between my fingers.

Maggie snatched the letter out of my fingers and shoved it at Doug. "You read it. You read better than he does anyway."

Doug read,

> *Dear Duncan,*
> *I have heard from the Swordsmiths' Guild Council. As I expected, they are kicking me out, but I still have the right to pick my replacement, and I named you.*

I lost track of things for a bit after that. After a while, when Maggie and Jessie had stopped screaming, and my shoulder ached where Doug kept thumping it, he read the rest.

> *There are other men in the queue ahead of you, but it's my choice, and you're the one I think would be best for the guild. There won't be any argument about that, since Randall put your name on the waiting list. They will send you a letter with the guild rules, and will start to teach you about making swords at next spring's meeting.*
> *Congratulations, Clive.*

P.S. Don't worry about the magic. You've got enough to be a swordsmith. Trust me.

P.P.S. Don't give out any certificates until you've memorised the guild rules.

"A swordsmith in Abertee," Doug said. "Never thought I'd see that." Maggie kissed my forehead. "Dad would have been so proud of you. So would Uncle Will."

"A swordsmith, right here in Nettleton," Jessie breathed. "Everybody in Nettleton is going to be so excited. I can't wait to tell my auntie."

I looked up from the seal. "Uh, about that. Could you wait a day or two?"

Her face clouded over. "What's the matter, Duncan?"

I shook my head. "Nothing. It's just that… I hadn't gotten used to the notion I'm a master smith. I'd like some time to get used to the idea first, that's all."

"Oh, aye. I can understand that."

"When I'm ready, I'll let you spread the news."

"Deal," she said.

I set to work the next morning, fixing a broken stall door, but my mind was not on it. I'd work for a while, then take the seal out of my pocket and play with it a bit. I spent less time working than I did leaning against the rail, daydreaming about swords and gates the duke would be proud to show off. I'd have a smithy full of journeymen all answering to me. And a certain sweet earth witch's eyes would light up when she heard.

After a while I left the barn and climbed the hill to talk to Doug, alone. "It's a mixed blessing, you know," I said.

"Aye. I'd wondered if you'd see that. Should've trusted you would."

"Nobody comes to Nettleton on their way someplace else. There's not enough work in this valley to support a smithy full of journeymen and apprentices."

"Crossroads, then."

"Aye." I could put up with Crossroads. I'd never persuade Hazel to live anywhere else, anyway. With all the Earth Guild tunnels leading into town, that's where a healer belonged.

I must be far gone. I'd never before considered giving a lass any say in where I lived.

Doug said, "And then there's the duke."

"Aye. Maybe he'll see this as being good for Abertee…"

"He should."

"Instead of seeing me as a bigger pain in the arse."

"That, too."

"Aye, both at the same time."

"Keep in mind, if the Frost Maiden comes after you, even the Royal Association of Swordsmiths can't save you."

Doug's warning didn't spoil my good mood. I strolled downhill, waving at Jessie as she took the little ones to the village to see her mother, and headed for the barn, to set about fixing the stall door for real. I was whistling over my work when someone yelled, "Farmer!"

I dropped the hammer and chisel, and ran for the door, swearing. The clatter of horses on the track had been getting louder, but I'd been so lost in daydreams I'd not paid the noise any attention. I grabbed a hayfork on my way out.

Three riders trotted into the barnyard, between the barn and the house. Jake Higgins, on the second horse, grinned and waved.

Maggie should have been in the doorway, greeting the newcomers, but the house looked empty. "Wherever you are, Maggie," I breathed, "stay there."

The blue-blooded peacock in the lead walked his horse around the barn-yard, taking in everything with his nose pinched. Like there was something wrong with us. We weren't the ones wearing white for a ride on an upland track on a drizzly day. He saw me looking at the mud spattered on his fancy breeches, and his face twisted in a snarl.

"Farmer," he spat, "your landlord has better use for this property. You and your family have one week to vacate the premises. Anyone still here a week from today will be burned out."

"Landlord, my arse. We're freeholders, not tenants."

He scowled at me. "The White Duke says you must leave."

If he'd been a commoner I would have shoved his teeth down his throat. "The duke should've come to do his own dirty work."

"Your duke is busy, and I offered to do this errand for him." He walked his horse towards the house. Jake's horse was between us. I tried to edge around him, but he kept pace with me.

"Did you, now?" I said. "And who the devil are you?"

The aristo turned and glared at me. "You need not doubt I have the authority. I am Lord Edmund Bradford, second son of, and second in line to, Earl Eddensford."

My heart dropped into my boots. This was the aristo Granny Mildred had complained about, and he had the Fire Warlock's magical shields.

He said, "I hear you have a pretty sister. Where is she?"

Maggie, you should have already left for New London. I clenched the hayfork with both hands. "Not here. Gone fishing."

He got off his horse and walked towards the house. "You're lying."

I bellowed, "You gave us the message, now get out. You've no right to do anything else."

He stopped with his hand on the door. "I will do as I please. You have no power to stop me." He seemed to be waiting for something. I glared at him.

He said, "Don't you understand, simpleton?"

Shove his teeth down his throat and shake him until every bone in his body rattled. As if. I knew better than to hit a protected aristo. The shock the Fire Warlock would give my arm would make it useless for days, and then the Frost Maiden would cripple me—if I was lucky. I breathed hard and glared.

"Or don't you know how to speak to your betters? Say 'Yes, sir.'"

"I know how to speak to my betters. You're not one."

He turned purple. "You, there, horsewhip this insubordinate mongrel."

Jake Higgins raised his whip with a grin. "Aye, sir. A pleasure, sir."

I poked his horse with the hayfork.

By the time I had dodged flying hooves and weaved my way across the yard, the aristo had dragged Maggie outside by the arm. She cursed and landed a solid punch that made him yelp. I was proud of her, even if it would cost her plenty in the long run.

He swung her around and shoved her against the wall. I was almost to the house. The aristo drew his sword and brought the point to her throat. "Shut up, wench, and don't move."

I stopped dead, three steps away. Maggie squeezed against the wall. Her face, even her lips, went white.

The aristo looked her up and down, like he was studying a whore. "This

God-forsaken backwater might be worth my time, after all." He stepped closer to her, lowered his sword, and ran his left hand over her bodice.

I was on him, grabbing his arm, and yanking. He and his sword flew across the yard. "You'll not touch my sister like that again."

For a moment, everything went still. The aristo sprawled in the muck. Jake stopped wiping himself off and gaped. And I glimpsed a mountain of trouble even before the aristo scrambled for his sword.

He reached it before I got a boot on it, and came up swinging. I blocked with the hayfork handle, catching the sword and forcing it down. The tip sliced across my left arm. I dropped the hayfork, and clutched my arm with my other hand. Maggie screamed. Jake howled. The flunky still on his horse jeered.

The highborn brat swung at me again. I dropped and rolled. His swing carried him on around, and I came up on his right side. He shifted his weight for another swing, backhanded. I grabbed his sword arm with my left, pulled him down in front of me, and swung with my right. My fist caught the side of his head, hard enough to knock him into next week. He went down, and lay without moving.

He wouldn't move again, ever.

Flight

Maggie had picked up the hayfork and braced it against the stone steps. I lifted the aristo and slung him across his horse. Jake bolted for the gate. The other flunky was slow to realise what had happened, but he got a look at the brat's head and turned green. I gathered the horse's reins and threw them to him.

"Get out. Now." He didn't wait to be told twice.

Maggie yelled, "Duncan, don't move," and disappeared into the house. Doug and the hands ran down the path towards us.

I have a strong arm, even for a smith, and I had been hitting things all my life. That's what a blacksmith does, day in, day out: he hits things. When I hit something less solid than a lump of iron, it breaks, like the side of this aristo's head. I had felt it give as I hit him.

He was a dead man, and my right arm wasn't numb.

He was a dead man, and I'd be one soon, too, if I didn't run.

Maggie flew out with towels in one hand and needle and thread in the other, and we sat down on the bench under the eaves so she could stitch my arm. Blood poured from the gash, and it hurt like the dickens. A quarterstaff would have left a bruise, but the sword had sliced through muscle. Doug reached us and ran into the house without speaking. One of the hands went into the barn and the other ran down the hill to fetch Jessie. After Maggie finished stitching, she helped me change out of the bloody clothes, then I sat on the bench clutching my arm while they packed. I listened to Maggie telling Doug what the aristo had said, and tried not to think. Thinking made it worse.

Besides, we all knew what we had to do. This was the day we had planned for, and hoped would never come. I didn't need more time to get ready.

The hand led Doug's horse and Charcoal, both saddled, out of the barn. Doug came out with packed saddlebags and threw them on the horses. Maggie was crying so hard she couldn't see where she was going. She stumbled after him, arguing.

Doug grabbed her by the shoulders and shook her. "Shut up, Maggie. We can't all ride. We'll follow with the wagon, as soon as we can."

I said, "Get out before they come back. If they catch you, what I've done won't be worth anything. Follow the river to the coast then go south. When you get to the Crystal Palace throw yourself on the Frost Maiden's mercy."

She grabbed me, and buried her face in my shoulder. While she sobbed, Doug reached for the sword.

"Don't!" I said. "It'll break your hand."

Doug scowled at it. "It should've shattered."

"I doubt that brat ever swore to protect anybody."

"They oughtn't have let him have one then." He gave it a wide berth, leading the horse towards us.

I shoved Maggie at the horse. "Go. Run."

Doug gave her a leg up, and she kicked the horse into a trot. She rode away, still crying, without looking back. She was a sensible lass, and would settle down to do what she needed to do to protect herself. With a decent head start, her chances were good. They'd care more about catching me, anyway.

Doug said, "Maggie said he was second in line to an earl."

"Aye, that's what he said. The Fire Warlock should've protected him, no matter how hard I hit him. So why is he dead?"

Doug threw up his hands and shook his head. "I've given you all the money we've got, but it's not much."

I would have done the same for him. I gave him a one-armed hug. In return, he almost cracked my ribs. I climbed onto Charcoal, and he tossed me my coat.

"The swordsmith's seal and the letter are in the pocket," he said.

I looked at him, trying to think of something, anything, to say.

"Godspeed," he said.

I nodded, and turned Charcoal towards the uphill track, heading west.

The aristo's broken head swam before my eyes. I retched. May God forgive me for killing a man, because I wasn't sure I could forgive myself, even for one asking for it as much as that brat had. He'd been trying to kill me, but I'd just wanted to make him drop the sword. If I had known I could kill him, I wouldn't have hit him so hard.

Even as I thought that, I knew it was a lie. There's no time in the middle of a fight to think. I had done what I had to, to save my own life, and he shouldn't have died. The Fire Warlock's magic ought to have protected him, or maybe that was as much a fairy tale as the stories about swords shattering when they were raised against the aristo's subjects. Or that other fairy tale saying a commoner could go to the king or the Frost Maiden, and get a fair hearing.

If it was a lie, the duke should have known better than to send that bastard after my sister. Mostly he left us alone, so why had he tried to evict Doug now? The question troubled me, but gave me something to think about other than the dead aristo, or my throbbing arm. The red stain on the bandage grew, and every step jolted it.

We'd heard rumours of other aristos forcing tenants off their land so the aristos could run the better-paying sheep, but the White Duke hadn't tried that—yet. He was lazy and his greedy duchess didn't spend any more time in Abertee than she had to. The law said they couldn't force freeholders out, but Doug would have a hard time proving he owned the farm. Like everybody in Nettleton, we were proud freeholders, not grovelling tenants. We knew where our boundary markers were, and settled disputes amongst ourselves. We'd never had to prove it. If it came down to Doug's word, or even the whole village's, against the duke's, the duke would win.

The valley yanked at my soul. At the top of the ridge, I stopped and took a good long look to fix the sight in my mind. It seemed certain I would never be back.

And that earth witch… She had handed me a bag of hot muffins the morning I'd left Crossroads, and had promised to go riding with me on Sunday. Healers don't look kindly on barroom brawls or other commotions where folk get hurt. Even if the Water Guild wasn't hunting me, she'd not have anything to do with me, once she found out I was a killer.

I'm not ashamed to say I had to wipe my eyes and blow my nose, and it was a while before the hillside stopped blurring. I gave Charcoal his head and he plodded downhill. Two-thirds of the way down, angling south, we lost the track. A slip had wiped it out, leaving us no good way down.

The spring had been wetter than usual, and we'd had a good soaking rain two nights ago, so the fact that part of the hill had let go wasn't a surprise. There could be other sections where a footfall would trigger another slide, but we'd have to take our chances. I got off Charcoal and let him lead the way. He was more surefooted, and I hoped had a better nose for firm ground than I had, but I didn't want to be on him if the ground slid.

We picked our way downhill, and bit by bit got closer to the valley floor. I had begun to think that we would make it without mishap, when Charcoal's head snapped up. A heartbeat later I felt what he had felt, and cursed as the ground slid out from under our feet.

Hunted

Some would have called me lucky—I wasn't dead. I didn't feel lucky. I hurt worse than I'd ever hurt before. No hangover had come anywhere close. I would have lain still in the mud, hoping to die, if Charcoal hadn't been screaming. He lay half-buried under mud and rocks, thrashing around despite two broken legs.

That mercy killing was one of the hardest jobs I'd ever done. He'd been a good friend. He deserved better. Better than I could give him.

Getting my knife out and using it with my left hand wasn't easy either, but my right hand was on fire. Something broken there. More than one something.

When he was still, and I'd stopped heaving, I raised my head for a better look. We had been at the top of a small slip, and landed on the valley floor atop a pile of mud and rocks. If the rocks had landed on me, I'd have been no better off than Charcoal. Besides the hand, I had at least one broken rib, bruises and cuts everywhere, and my arm bled where several stitches had torn out.

I crawled to a boulder about chest high, and pulled myself upright. I couldn't have stood without its help, but the effort ripped out the last of the stitches. I was dizzy, and my left ankle complained when I put weight on it.

My knife, the clothes on me, and a few coins in my pocket were all I had left. My hat had flown clear, but after nearly blacking out when stooping to pick it up, I let it and the saddlebags lie. My coat, with the swordsmith's seal in its pocket, was lost, probably under Charcoal.

A swordsmith one day, and I was already a disgrace. Probably a new low for them. Master Clive, at least, hadn't lost the seal.

The half-mile to the woods was the longest journey I'd ever made. I'd lost my head start; the first search party climbed the ridge before I reached cover. On horseback against the sky, they were easy to see, but my clothes, caked with mud, blended in with the hillside. Even so, on foot and injured, I had no chance of escaping without help.

I sat down on a boulder and leaned my aching head against a tree trunk, hoping it would stop spinning long enough to let me think. I had planned on circling southwest, bypassing Crossroads. Now I had to go there, if I could. By the road, the town was a day's walk, even if I had been in good shape. Tunnel entrances were scattered around here and there all over the district, to let folk get to the Earth Guildhall when sick or injured, but most were in villages, and the nearest one I knew of was several miles away.

This morning, thinking about that bonny earth witch again had set me whistling. Now my throat closed up and my eyes stung.

I gritted my teeth and started walking.

Several riders went past on the track at the edge of the woods, but I stuck to a deer trail in the shadows and they didn't see me. When a bugle sounded from the ridge, I guessed they had found Charcoal.

By dusk I had walked less than two miles. I welcomed the dark to hide me from the search parties, but it also meant shuffling along, testing every step to avoid a fall. If I fell I might not get up again.

The drizzle changed to a cold, hard rain. In rough country a man can die of cold in the middle of summer if caught out overnight and unprepared. The headache and dizziness were getting worse, too.

I leaned against a tree and prayed aloud for help. A moment later a fox walked across the path. He trotted to the next bend and waited. I lurched after him. He didn't run. When I got close he trotted on ahead and stopped again at the next bend. He wasn't much more than a shadow among the brush. I wasn't sure I wasn't dreaming him.

The fox led the way for a hundred yards, heading uphill. We came to a rocky outcropping and he went halfway around, then dove towards the ground and disappeared.

I followed, and found a narrow gap between the rocks. I stuck my arm through and felt empty space. I edged in sideways, calling myself crazy for following the fox. Inside, it was pitch black and cramped, but no worse than Sam's mum's root cellar, and it was dry and warmer than outside. I sat down and leaned against the back of the cave, resting my broken hand on the cold rock floor.

Several minutes passed before I realised my back was against a wooden door. I raised my right hand, braced for pain to shoot through it, then thought about using my left hand. I knocked.

"Who's there?"

I gave the answers laid down in the old tales. "A wanted man."

"What do you seek?"

"Healing and shelter for the night. I mean you no harm, so help me, God."

The door jerked open and I fell in.

The Two Grannies

"For God's sake, you damned fool," Granny Mildred said, "we couldn't open the door until you asked for help. We thought you might die on us before you got around to it. What took you so long?"

I couldn't answer. The fall had knocked out of me everything I had left.

I lay half on, half off a blanket. Hazel grabbed the corners, tossed one end to Mildred, and pulled. If they hadn't been witches they would never have moved me, even the two of them together, but somehow they not only dragged me into a room with a fire, they lifted me onto a table and rolled me over onto my back.

Hazel slid warm hands under my shirt and stood without moving, head bowed and eyes closed. The saw blade in my side stopped its stabbing. If I'd been able to sit up, I would have kissed her.

Mildred was still swearing at me. "God Almighty, Duncan, could you weigh any more? If we use all our magic carting you around, you big lug, we won't have any left for healing."

"You're supposed to pretend you don't know me." I couldn't draw breath for more than a mumble.

She snorted. "When the whole district knows you're on the run? Not much point."

"But if anybody else comes…"

"Aye, that would mean trouble. You deal with him for a few minutes, lass. I'll set the spells on the tunnels so nobody'll come through tonight unless they won't last till morning." She poked me with her wand. "Be quiet and don't move."

As if she needed to tell me not to bother a healer at work, especially one working on me. Hazel moved her hands across my belly, and other pains went away. I closed my eyes and floated in the heavens. She pulled her hands out of my shirt, and put them on either side of my head. My head stopped hammering.

Something wet hit my chin. I opened my eyes, and watched another tear slide down Hazel's cheek and drip onto me. Of course laying hands on me would hurt a healer, as banged up as I was. I tried to push her away, and couldn't move, or talk.

She shivered, tears flowed, and that darling face screwed up tight. She let go and staggered to a stool with her head in her hands, sobbing. I watched, and cursed without sound.

Mildred came back. I glared at her.

She said, "Well, sonny, what did you expect? I told you not to talk or move. You got something to say? Say it."

"I meant it when I said I wouldn't harm you. You shouldn't have let her—"

"Don't be an ass. If we couldn't handle a little pain we wouldn't be healers."

Hazel straightened up and smiled. The smile didn't last long. "I've never dealt with anyone before who had so many injuries at once, that's all. Next time I'll be better prepared."

I said, "But you've got salves and potions and I don't know what—"

"Don't tell us how to do our job, sonny." Mildred picked up my hand, and it stopped hurting. I would have kissed her, too, wrinkles and all. "We use those where we can, but laying on hands is faster, and for some things it's the only way." She bent over, holding her own hand tight against her chest, and looking every one of her eighty-some-odd years.

"It isn't right. Men are supposed to protect women, not hurt them. Don't do that again."

They gave each other the look women have that says all men are idiots. Mildred said, "As if you could do anything about it in your condition. What happened? We saw that earl's whelp. That fight didn't do this to you."

"I had a fight with the hill. Rock slide."

"That's one fight you lost."

"Nae, you should see the hill. Those stones aren't getting up again." I couldn't smile; my face hurt.

Mildred snorted. "You must be feeling better. What did you do for him, lass?"

"Set three broken ribs, treated the bruised kidneys, liver, and spleen, stopped the bleeding from the sword wound, and cured the concussion."

Mildred whistled. "The Guild Council said you were good. Should've listened."

Hazel's smile lasted this time. "And since you're dealing with his hand, that's the worst of it. There are other bruises, and a slew of dirty cuts and scrapes, but those aren't urgent." She started pulling things out of a cupboard: sponges and towels, salves, wraps, potions, needle and thread.

Mildred said, "Get out of those filthy clothes so we can do the rest of it properly. Sit up and take them off, but don't use your right hand."

Hazel said, "He shouldn't use his left arm either."

Mildred sighed. "Well then, you lout, we'll get you undressed, this once, but don't think we'll make a habit of it. And it's all coming off. Don't try to be modest, we've seen it all before."

That was true, but I didn't have to like it. They set to work and I couldn't stop them, so I tried not to think about it and pretended my nether parts belonged to somebody else. By the time I was naked Mildred was doddering. She threw a blanket over me and sat down on a stool to boss. Like Hazel needed any bossing.

I said, "Tell me about Maggie."

"Sorry, lad, there's been no news about your sister." Mildred patted my arm. "Don't worry about her; she'll be fine."

"If she reaches the Water Guild before the earl's men catch her, you mean." I stared at the ceiling. She'd be fined for fighting back, but what he had done to her would offset most of it. So the old stories said. The newer ones worried me.

Mildred said, "Doug and Jessie were on their way before the duke's men got back, but moving slowly with the wagon. Everybody in Nettleton chipped in and bought the livestock, so they've got a little money."

God bless the neighbours. They couldn't have paid what the animals were worth, but it was better than leaving them to the guards' tender mercies. If the duke lifted the eviction order, Doug and Jessie would get the same animals back.

They weren't in immediate danger—I hoped. Right now, the Frost Maiden protected them, in one of the few times she was on our side. Taking revenge on people of any rank who weren't involved in a dispute, and who had witnesses to prove it, was sure to earn even an aristo a hex that would keep him cold a long, long time. Then, too, the duke had ordered them to leave the farm, and attacking someone obeying their lord's orders was another good way to earn a case of frostbite. Those laws were even older than the aristos' shields.

"Mildred, he said he was shielded. He shouldn't be dead."

Mildred and Hazel gave each other worried looks. Hazel said, "We've been wondering about that. Wasn't he second in line to an earl?"

"Aye. He made a point of saying he was second in line. But I hit him, and my arm didn't go numb. I didn't mean to kill him. He was swinging a sword at me and I wanted to make him drop it."

The worried looks on the two faces deepened. "Listen, lad," Mildred said, "don't beat yourself up over that nasty piece of work. What I want to know is why did they pick on your brother? It'd make more sense if you'd been back awhile, throwing your weight around, and they'd gone after you. And don't give me any backtalk. You know you act pretty highhanded sometimes."

"What do you mean, sometimes?"

"But if anybody here has a reputation for being decent, clean-living folk, and more willing to give somebody a hand than to pick a fight, it's you Archers."

"The duke knows that, but Uncle Will used to say the duchess thinks we're the loudest whingers in the district. Maybe she thinks she can get rid of Doug now that Uncle Will isn't around to stick up for him."

"Maybe. More folk have been asking him for advice, like they used to ask your dad, since his word is what convinced the duke to rebuild that bridge, but if she wants to drive him out, why didn't she do it last summer?"

"Because it takes a while to talk the duke into doing anything, and she'd forget about us while they're down south for the winter."

Mildred chewed on her thumb. "Maybe. If she's behind this, she's more a fool than I'd thought, and I didn't have a high opinion of her to start with. They've gone and stirred up more trouble themselves than any Archer has ever done."

"Aye. I doubt even I could piss off half the district in one go."

"Half? Everybody. And they're not just angry—they're all scared silly they're next."

"If they keep paying their rents and taxes, and keep their heads down, she ought to leave them alone. We're the pain in the arse she wanted rid of."

"For Pete's sake, sonny, are you that thick? Nobody else sees it that way. They know you lot have stuck up for the dukes, long after they stopped deserving it. If you're not safe, then nobody is, and they might as well raise hell now since it's just a matter of time till they're forced off their land, too."

I tried to sit up. Hazel kept me pinned down with one finger. I said, "Raising hell won't do any good. It won't hurt the duke. It just means other folk will be running for their lives, too." I rolled my head to get a good look at Mildred. "And I don't want to get you in trouble, either. I'll go as soon as you two are done working me over."

She snorted. "Don't be an ass, lad. You'll be in no shape to go anywhere for several days yet. We can hide you that long. And when you're ready to leave, we'll send you out an unmarked tunnel the duke doesn't know about, like the one you came in on."

"It's marked now. I left a trail of blood. As soon as they set the dogs on it they'll find it."

Hazel's head jerked up. "Rocks! What'll we do?"

Mildred said, "Move the last bit so the trail ends in the burn. I reckoned we would do that after he was asleep." She gave me a poke, none too gentle, with her wand. "And I'll thank you for not shooting your mouth off any more and scaring my assistant, or making me give away any more secrets. Come on lass. I'll show you some tricks they don't teach in the Warren." She threw another blanket at me. "Stay there, sonny."

As if I wanted to move. The next thing I knew, I was jolted awake, howling. Mildred was rubbing a lotion that stung like the dickens on a scrape across my shin. Hazel had a hand over her mouth, her eyes wide.

Mildred handed her the bottle and the cloth. "Told you that would wake him up."

Hazel mouthed, "Sorry," at me, but kept rubbing.

I held my breath until she stopped. "What the blazes was that for?"

"Cleaning dirt out of the scrapes," Mildred said.

"I thought I had a thick skin."

"You do. That's why we're using it full strength."

Hazel said, "Wouldn't want to miss anything." She started cleaning another scrape.

Through clenched teeth, I said, "Very thoughtful of you, ma'am."

She gave me a sweet smile and spread on a salve that killed the stinging. I worked at unknotting my jaw muscles.

Mildred said, "How did you find that door, anyway? I didn't know about that one."

"I asked for help, and a fox led me there."

"A fox, eh?" She screwed up her face. "Sounds like old Granddad Gavin's work, from four hundred years ago. Another period when the duke was acting too heavy-handed. Not a good time."

"At least when the king found out what the duke had done, he demoted that one. No chance of that now."

"Nae, 'fraid not. Where will you go when you leave here?"

I told her the route Doug and I had laid out. Hazel set down her jar of salve and listened. While I talked the two healers gave each other another long look.

Mildred said, "You didn't think that through today."

"Nae. Dad saw disaster coming years ago, when the duke first brought his duchess home. Doug and I have been thinking about it a long time."

"That's why you and Douggie have been so interested in those maps, isn't it?"

"Aye."

"Well...I take back what I said about you being thick. I was going to give you some advice, but it doesn't sound like you need it. My assistant doesn't need me to supervise her either. I'm going to bed." She gave me a squeeze on the shoulder. "I'll find out what I can about Maggie in the morning."

A tiny window, high in the wall of a tiny room, showed a red sky. I lay on a too-short, too-narrow bed, not knowing or caring why I was there, and listened to my belly growl like I hadn't eaten since...since yesterday's breakfast. Memories crowded in: Charcoal, Maggie with a sword at her throat, the lost seal, the brat's smashed head.

The sky faded to purple. I'd slept through an entire day, and those two grannies were in danger every minute I stayed in their house. I rolled to my feet, and grabbed at the wall to keep from falling down. My legs were as unsteady as a new lamb's. I sat down hard on the bed and put my head in my hands.

The door opened and Mildred came in with a lamp. I yanked the sheet over me before I remembered I was wearing a nightshirt, big even on me. Uncle Will's, Hazel had said. I didn't ask how Mildred had come by it.

"Maggie," I said.

"Safe and sound in Quays." She put the lamp on a shelf and sat on the bed beside me. Hazel followed her in with a tray, laden with enough food for two men. She sat on the only stool. If the room had been any smaller, she would have been in my lap. I wouldn't have minded.

"Is it safe?" I said.

"For now, yes," she said, "but you have to stay in this room. The mundane staff are in bed, and we've set alarms, but Mildred and I will have to run if anyone comes." She put a hand on my knee, and strength and life flowed into me, enough that I could face the world again.

Mildred said, "Douggie and the rest spent the night at a farm about halfway. They were in good shape when they left in the morning."

"Thank God," I said, and tucked in.

She waited until half the food was gone before telling the other news. "Word's gotten around, and feelings are running high. You're a lost cause, but Douggie... There's a crowd over at the tavern now talking about marching on the duke."

The roast beef I was wolfing down didn't look so tasty anymore. "To do what?"

Mildred chewed on her lip before answering. "To tell him that if he runs Douggie off his land, they'll burn his manor house to the ground."

"Frost it." I put the fork down. "That won't help Doug, and good people will get hurt."

"I know it." She patted my arm. "Eat, lad. Aren't you still hungry?"

Around another forkful, I mumbled, "If I could make trouble for her nastiness, the duchess, I would, but I don't want trouble for my friends and neighbours. Talk some sense into them."

"Me? Folk come to me about their aches and pains, and don't follow my advice about them. If they did, you'd eat more strawberries and peas and less shepherd's pie."

"I eat whatever the women serve me," I said, and finished the turnips.

Hazel smiled. My heart did a flip-flop.

Mildred eyed my clean plate. "And you're going to strip our larder bare, you big ox. If you ate like that all the time you'd get as big as your Uncle Will." She sighed. "It's a crying shame he's gone. He could've talked the duke into revoking that eviction notice. There's nobody else that can."

I stopped with an oatcake halfway to my mouth, considered it a moment, and set it down. "There is somebody else that can." I put a hand on her shoulder and gave her a little shake. "Somebody from Abertee—and by somebody I mean you—has to ask for the Fire Warlock's help."

Cinders and Ashes

Granny Mildred blinked at me. "Ask the Fire Warlock for help? Why?" "He can strong-arm the duke into doing the right thing by Doug and Jessie. It won't help me but it'll keep anybody else from getting hurt. Things will get worse—a lot worse—if they march on the duke. That's what I told Walter when we went to the tavern the other night. Didn't you hear the story I told him?"

"I heard it from his wife, and she didn't say anything about going to the Fire Warlock for help."

"What did you hear?"

"That you shouted down the Fire Warlock, and lived. I didn't believe it."

"Think I'm dead, do you?"

"Nae, sonny. You'd be cinders and ashes."

"Fine. But I did talk to him."

"I didn't believe that either. You'd better tell me the whole story. And tell it to me straight, you young scamp."

Telling the story took a long time. Even with her hand on my arm I had to stop twice—the first time, about Master Randall, and the second, about Glenn burning like a torch—and wait a while before I could go on. Knowing I'd lie awake all night reliving the riot didn't help.

When I got to the part about the river of fire, Mildred went white. "Well, laddie, you don't look like cinders. Go on."

By the time I'd recounted yelling at the Fire Warlock, and what he said after, Mildred had her head in her hands, moaning, "Cinders. Ashes." Hazel eyes were round and huge.

"I am not cinders and ashes, or a ghost either. This is what I was telling

Walter. The Fire Warlock is on our side. He promised to help if he can. If we don't ask for help the end will be bad, real bad. If folks are riled enough to attack the duke, somebody has to ask for the Warlock's help, before he turns Abertee into cinders and ashes." I glared at Mildred. "I can't, not anymore, and if Walter won't, well, then you're going to have to."

"Me? Are you out of your mind? I've got enough sense to be scared of the Fire Warlock, unlike some fools."

Hazel patted her hand, and the wild look went out of Mildred's eyes. "I'm sorry, Duncan, but neither Mildred nor I can ask for his help."

"Sure you can. You're guild members."

"Yes, but the magic guilds have special rights. We answer to the Officeholders, not the duke, so our asking the Fire Warlock for help would be outside interference, and isn't allowed. Otherwise, our Guild Council would have started advising us to ask for help centuries ago. Instead, a healer will get in trouble for telling a mundane what to do, since that's outside interference, too."

"Frostbite!" I beat on the bed frame with my fists while I chewed on that. "Fine. After I leave here tonight—"

"Forget it, sonny, you're not going anywhere yet. You're still shaky on your pins."

"Aye, but I can't stay. You'll get in trouble if they find me here, and I don't want—"

Hazel's touch on my arm was as soothing as a good night's sleep. "Helping the sick and injured, even convicted criminals, is the Earth Guild's right. As long as you're not fit to move, no one can come after you here, and no one will harass us for helping you, either. The Great Coven built a truce into both the Earth and Water Offices all those years ago, so the Water Guild won't try."

Mildred said, "Rocks, lass, talk about spilling secrets. Better watch your tongue."

Hazel shrugged. "There's no harm in telling that one. It isn't much of a secret."

I said, "But the duke or the earl—"

"Don't worry about them," Mildred said. "They'd get knocked back on their arses if they tried to come in the guildhall without our say-so. But once you're well enough to move, forget it. We can't protect you then. Nobody else in the Earth Guild can help either, unless you get hurt again."

"Fair enough." I put my head down in my hands. If Walter hadn't understood about going to the Fire Warlock for help, and Hazel and Mildred couldn't tell him or go themselves, keeping the peace in Abertee was back in my lap. Me, a wanted man.

I had to talk to Walter, but even without the danger of sneaking through town, I wouldn't make it out the door. If Mildred and Hazel thought I wasn't ready to go, they could knock me flat on my back and put me to sleep before I'd taken two steps. There was a way to talk to Walter, but I didn't like it. Even with the Earth Guild's rights, it would feel like shouting, Here I am, come arrest me. But if Abertee burned because I was a coward, I might as well turn myself in to the Water Guild.

I straightened up. "Mildred, go get Walter out of bed and bring him here so I can talk to him, and—"

Hazel's freckles stood out against white skin. Mildred screeched, "Have you lost your mind? Of all the damn-fool idiotic ideas you've ever had, you imbecile, that has to be the worst, even worse than any your dad and granddad had."

She had a knack for making me feel ten years old instead of nearly thirty. I talked through clenched teeth. "Somebody has to go to the Fire Warlock."

Mildred put her hand to her head and moaned. Hazel said, "We can't let anybody know you're here. They may guess you are, but we can't acknowledge it until after you're gone."

"But you said I was protected here."

"You are, while the truce holds, but your only chance of evading capture is slipping away through an unwatched tunnel. If we let any mundane know you're here, we break the truce, and the Water Guild will watch all the tunnels for you to leave."

"But she said—"

"I know what I said, sonny," Mildred snapped. "The duke's men don't know all the tunnels. If the Water Guild gets involved, they'll watch with magic, and they'll find them all, even the ones we've forgotten."

Ten years old, and an imbecile to boot, I felt like. "You're not making sense. The Water Guild is already involved."

"They're doing their damnedest not to be. When the duchess prods them, they're busy looking for you anywhere but where you're likely to be. But if we admit you're here, they won't have any choice. They'd have to come and set the triggers and wait for you to leave. Don't you understand? They don't want to catch you."

Hazel pushed my open jaw shut with a gentle finger. "Of course he doesn't understand, Mildred. How many times has our guild told us not to talk about this with a mundane? Duncan, most of the witches and wizards in the Water Guild are decent people who don't like what their Office orders them to do any more than we do. It wasn't supposed to be this way; something has gone badly wrong with the Water Office."

"It's broken, all right," Mildred said. "All four guilds play these silly little games dancing around each other, trying like hell to avoid calling down the Frost Maiden's full power. Nobody wants to see another good man frozen to death."

"Not even the Frost Maiden," Hazel said. "But we're not supposed to say so, because the Officeholders don't want ordinary people thinking they can flout the laws."

Mildred glared at me. "Did I call you a good man? I must be getting senile. Forget I said that." She stood up. "I'm going to bed, laddie. You make me tired."

I pulled her back down. "You're not going anywhere until we figure out how to make Walter go to the Fire Warlock."

"We'll do that tomorrow."

"There's no time. You said they were at the tavern tonight working themselves up."

"They won't march on the duke tonight. I know that lot. Jack Miller always works himself up into a fury until he pitches forward and falls asleep over his beer, and Billy Chandler can't walk in a straight line after he's had two, and he's so upset he's probably on his fifth by now. No, that lot's not going anywhere tonight."

"Do you know that because you're a witch, or are you just guessing because you know your neighbours?"

"I know my neighbours. That's not guessing."

"Mildred's right. There's time." Hazel eyes were closed and she was frowning. Mildred turned and stared at her. I stared, too, but I'd been doing that all along.

Hazel opened her eyes. "They're too drunk to go anywhere except home to bed, and most will have trouble getting that far."

My jaw hung open again. I closed it. "You can tell that from here?" She nodded.

Mildred said, "Huh! I was hoping you'd be as good as Mother Brenda in Edinburgh. Looks like you're better than."

Hazel's freckles disappeared under a wave of red. I said, "How do you know all that? Can you read minds?"

"Of course not. I read physical clues like their heart rates and the amount of alcohol they've drunk. Tonight, that's enough to tell me they aren't going far. I don't need to know what they're thinking." Her freckles were coming back. What would it take to make them disappear again? Not that I would be such a cad as to try.

"Good," I said. "I'm glad you don't know what I'm thinking."

Mildred whacked me on the arm. "She doesn't have to be an earth witch to know that, sonny. At least you stare at her mouth as much as you stare at her bosom."

I gave Mildred the gimlet eye. "There isn't anything about her that isn't worth staring at."

Hazel's freckles disappeared again. Mildred cackled. "You're going to have to work on that, lass. I'd almost think you were a fire witch, blushing like that." She yawned, and stood, one hand pressed to the small of her back. "Time we were all in bed."

I yawned. Yawned again. "I bet you tell your grandchildren to put on sweaters when you get cold."

"Great-grandchildren now. Of course I do. What kind of a granny do you take me for?"

Hazel moved the tray off the bed, but didn't follow Mildred out. "Lie down, and let me check that you're healing properly."

My eyes were already half-closed, and I'd been awake less than two hours. "If you're using magic to heal me, why am I so tired?"

Hazel said, "The magic encourages your body to heal, but you're doing most of it yourself. If we had to do it all, Mildred and I both would be abed for a week, after last night."

"Sorry, ma'am."

"Not your fault."

Everywhere she touched me I felt great. Mildred had never made me feel this good. She said, "I'm giving you more magic than you need to finish healing. This will help you stay healthy, and, if I do this a couple more times before you leave, will sustain you for about a month even if you don't get enough to eat."

"Thank you, ma'am. I appreciate it, every little bit."

"I've been racking my brains for other ways to help. When you were a child, did you ever play games pretending to be animals?"

"Oh, aye. Why?"

"What kind of animals?"

She looked dead serious, and worried. I scratched my chin. "Doug was a ram sometimes, or a stag. He tried being a fox a few times, but was too big to be good at it. I was usually a boar. Why?"

"Have you ever been tested for magical talent? You have affinities for both the Fire and Earth Guilds, don't you?"

"Sure. I could have been a halfpenny wizard in either. Most smiths have a little of one or the other."

"You've worked out a route to take, but have you given any thought to avoiding attention?"

"I have, and ice me if I can see how. I'm so big I always get noticed."

"You attract magical attention, too. Because you straddle the guilds, your magical signature, while weak, is unusual."

"My what?"

"The way you look to a witch or wizard searching for you by magic." She picked up the tray and gave me a long look. "Maybe there's a way to disguise it. We'll talk more about it in the morning."

The sun slanting in the window hit the other wall halfway up. Mid-morning. I rolled, and banged an elbow. Reaching out with just one arm, I could touch both walls. The grannies might not be in danger, but I had to leave—if I spent much time in this wee room, I'd go barking mad.

I swung my feet over and stopped, half off the bed. My coat, hat, and saddlebags lay in a muddy heap in the corner, next to the chamber pot. I blinked, and saw Charcoal. When Hazel came in, carrying a tray, I said, "How did you…," and choked up.

"The knacker found them. That's all you need to know. I'll clean them later."

"Thank you, ma'am," I said, around a bite of warm bread and jam. "For that, and for ordering me to sleep last night. I wouldn't have slept well without it, for all the troubles on my mind."

She sat on the stool, knee to knee with me, and pumped more magic into me while I ate, until I felt like I could run from there to Blacksburg.

"Mildred's gone looking for news," she said, "and to talk to Master Walter. You're healing quickly. You'll be well enough to leave tonight, after moonrise."

Kick me in the gut, why don't you? I set the bread down. Chewing somehow had become hard work.

She laid a hand on my arm. "Eat. You may not get another good meal for a long time after you leave here." I chewed. She looked down, playing with the hem of her apron. "I've been thinking about what you said, about pretending to be a boar. Maybe you can use the fourth magic to make you appear to be one. That will mask your signature, and as long as you stay deep in the woods everyone short of a hunting party will avoid you."

I stared at her, holding a jug of milk in mid-air. "I have no idea what you're talking about."

"I'm sorry, but we don't have time for me to explain the theory. Do you know anything about either shapeshifting or mindwarping?"

"Nae."

She said, "There are two ways to become an animal. The one that most people know about is shapeshifting, where your body transforms but you have a human mind."

An otter stood on the chair where she had been sitting, leaning with its front paws on my knees, and twitching its cute little nose at me. "Like so," said Hazel's voice.

I spilled milk across the bed.

"Sorry," we both said, and she was herself again, helping me mop up.

"Do that again. I promise not to run screaming out of the room."

"Not now. Shapeshifting takes a lot of power, and only a handful of level five witches and wizards can do it. I can't help you do that. What I can help you with is mindwarping, which is a lot easier. Your body stays the same, but your mind becomes like that of the animal. If done right, your altered image of yourself projects out to other creatures who see that image instead of the body you really have."

The lass holding the jug disappeared, and a giant otter, holding the jug, took her place. I turned into a blithering idiot and backed into the corner.

The otter disappeared, and Hazel came back. "I know I'm going much too fast, but this is the only thing I could think of, and we don't have much time."

"You're saying you can make me look like a boar. Ma'am, you're giving me the willies."

"I'm sorry. Are you willing to try?"

"If it will keep them from tracking me down, aye."

"Then let's see if you can do it with my help. If I guide you through it a few times, then after you leave you can do it on your own. I'm hoping, anyway."

She sat with her knees against mine, and her little hands in my big paws. I didn't mind that part, not a bit.

"Close your eyes and think about being a boar. What would you experience?"

"I'd have the smell of people in my nose, and nothing would look right." Out on the street, a wagon clattered past. "God, we're a noisy lot." I felt like I was standing on a cliff with her pushing. Nothing happened.

"You're thinking too hard. Stop thinking. Feel. How would you feel, right now, if you were a boar?"

"Trapped." Feeling that didn't take any effort. I was angry, too, and scared. She pushed me over the cliff and I fell down. Human stink slapped me in the face. I opened my eyes and huffed. The little otter with its paws on my hooves didn't bother me, but I had to get away from this human cage. I jerked up, pulling my hooves away, and was a man again. My head spun. I flailed and crashed onto the bed.

Hazel smiled. "Excellent. Let's do it again."

We held hands again, and closed our eyes, but I was unsettled, and couldn't calm down. Her smell was in my nose, and she smelled better than honey cakes, or Jessie's roses. I peeked. Her face was inches from mine, her eyes closed, her mouth open a little. I closed my eyes, but she was still there. I was on a different cliff this time, one I'd seen other men walk off of, but never gotten near myself.

I leaned forward. She tasted better than honey cakes, too. For a moment I was lost, but then she pulled away.

I stepped off that cliff on my own. "They'll need good healers in New London, too. I can send for you when I get there." She stood, but I had her hands and wouldn't let go. "They don't have aristos. I've heard it's a fine place to raise a family."

Her freckles stood out, sharp. "No, no, I can't." She jerked her hands away, and stumbled out, slamming the door behind her.

Grounded

"What did you say to my assistant that upset her so much?"

"None of your business." I dug my face deeper into the pillow. I'd been a fool for thinking a wanted man could talk an earth mother into following him. Especially when the runes said she would be happy here. After I left, she wouldn't even miss me. "Leave me alone."

"It is too my business." Granny Mildred gave me a hard whack on the shoulder. "I'll not have the best healer Abertee's ever seen driven away by some dunderhead. Talk to me, or don't you want to know what Walter said?"

I rolled over and sat up. She prodded me with a bony finger. "Hazel."

"She's not leaving Abertee—not on my account, anyway. I said New London needed good healers, too, and she ran away, without so much as a by your leave."

"Oh, laddie." Mildred patted my shoulder. "No wonder. She can't leave Frankland."

"Why not?"

"She's an earth mother, you ninny," Mildred said. "Despite the silly guild rules that won't let us call her one. That's why not."

"You mean the Earth Office won't let her go because she's an important healer."

"Nae. It's not the Office; it's the land. We're all tied to the land we're born on, to some extent. An earth mother will die if she stays away from home too long."

"But she didn't grow up in Abertee."

Mildred shrugged. "An earth mother's territory is big. She said she could live anywhere in North Frankland that's not flat."

I stared at the wee patch of blue sky showing through the window. Dying of homesickness I could understand. "Will the Upper Tee Valley kill me when I leave?"

"What's this about the valley?" Mildred chewed on her thumb as I explained. "Sounds like the same thing, in a smaller dose. Nae, lad, you won't die of homesickness. The valley's not big enough on its own, and you're not enough of a wizard for it to feed on. It'll make you unhappy, but it won't kill you."

I mumbled, "Thanks for nothing."

"Going to New London will be best. The valley can't maintain its grip that far away. It'll be harder if you stay in Europa." She sighed. "Enough of that. You wanted news, didn't you, lad? It's bad, all the way around."

"Go on. I want to hear it."

"Men have been coming into Crossroads this morning from all over the district. They're planning on marching off in a couple of hours to see the duke. I talked until I was blue in the face, but the ones that'll listen aren't running things. Walter, at least, has some sense. He asked for my advice. Said he'd been thinking about your story, and you were right more often than not—"

"Decent of him."

"Aye. As far as he's concerned, you're still guild head, and you'll be an honorary member for life, even after they replace you."

"He said that?"

"Aye. And he's willing to go to the Fire Warlock—"

"That's good news. You said—"

"I said he was willing, even if he is scared silly, but nobody's willing to go with him."

"Not even one of his lads?"

Hazel knocked on the door and came in, carrying my clothes, clean and mended, and sporting red-rimmed eyes. "When you wake next, get dressed. You'll have to leave tonight."

I nodded, and made room for her on the bed.

Mildred said, "Walter's lads think you've got a hole in your head and brass-plated steel balls for talking back to the Warlock."

Hazel ducked her head but didn't quite hide a snicker. "Why are they afraid? They'd be doing what the Fire Warlock wants."

Mildred shrugged. "Nobody in Crossroads seems to be thinking straight today."

"Duncan," Hazel said, "the person backing him doesn't have to go along, does he? Didn't the Fire Warlock imply that if you had said someone was backing you, the fire wizard would have had to send the message to the Warlock?"

I scratched my chin. "Aye, he did say that. So if a single journeyman agrees with him, that ought to be good enough. Tell him to get moving."

"Whoa," Mildred said. "That was one problem. Second problem: where's he supposed to go? The nearest Fire Guildhall is in Edinburgh. He can't get there in time."

"You said it; nobody is thinking straight today. Hazel said an earth witch can go anywhere in Frankland in less than an hour. Let him use the tunnels."

Mildred glared at me, breathing hard. "God give me strength. You reckon I didn't think of that? We can't. Only members of the Earth Guild belong in the tunnels. Nobody else can go through unless they're sick or injured, and looking for a healer."

"That's not so," Hazel said. Mildred's head snapped around to stare at her. Hazel went on, "A member of the Earth Guild can escort a mundane anywhere in the tunnels. It happens all the time. You've taken people to Edinburgh to see Mother Brenda, and then back home, once they were well. And the Guild Council lets the Fire Guild use them, too. I've met fire witches and wizards in the tunnels by themselves, more than once."

"Really?" Mildred gawped at her. "I never…"

Hazel patted her hand. "I've travelled more than you have, even if you're past eighty and I'm only twenty-four. Duncan's right. In an emergency, which this is, Master Walter would be allowed through the tunnels on Fire Guild business."

Mildred said, "He'd get lost in the tunnels and never come out—"

I said, "On his own, sure, so you'll have to go with him—"

"Whoa, laddie." Mildred had gone wild-eyed again. "I'm scared of the Fire Warlock, too."

"I'll take him," Hazel said. "I'm not afraid of Warlock Arturos—"

"Who?" I said.

"The Fire Warlock. The Fire Office was built to protect Frankland's women and children. It won't hurt me for helping. Besides, I know the way to Blazes, and I have friends in the Fire Guild. I can get to the Fire

Warlock more easily than most people can."

"Get going, then."

She nodded, and left.

"Pity." Mildred patted my shoulder. "That lass has nerve. She would have made a fine Archer."

Night had fallen when I woke, but a lamp burned on the shelf. I bounced out of bed, dressed in clothes mended so well I couldn't tell where they'd been ripped, and peeked out the door.

"It's safe," Mildred called. "Come on down to the kitchen."

My head said time to go. My body said the sooner, the better. My heart said stay put, fool. I crept down the hall like a prisoner on his way to the Crystal Palace. Hazel and Mildred sat side by side on the settle, with Hazel cooking by flicking her wand at a frying pan on the fire. Mildred had her feet up, and they both looked worn out.

Mildred said, "Douggie and Jessie reached Quayside safely, and the Water Guild gave them a place to stay until things get sorted out. The Water Guild's not happy about the duke evicting law-abiding freeholders, either."

"Good. The Fire Warlock?"

Hazel said, "He sent another warlock who met the marchers before they reached the duke's manor house, and scared them into dispersing. A dozen men got singed. We treated them and sent them home. And that's all that got hurt."

"Thank God," I said. "It could have been a lot worse."

"Yes, and Warlock Quicksilver talked the duke out of evicting Doug and Jessie. When word spreads, Abertee should calm down."

"It will," Mildred said, "if the duchess doesn't bully the duke into changing his mind."

I added, "Uncle Will always said he didn't have a backbone."

"He doesn't. The question is, who is he more afraid of: the Fire Warlock, or his duchess?"

Hazel handed me a plate of bacon and eggs. "I found out why Lord Edmund died. He wasn't shielded."

"But he said…"

"He was wrong. His brother married in secret, and the wife had a baby

158

a couple of months ago, so he wasn't second in line anymore. The brother hadn't told the rest of the family yet."

Mildred said, "So it's normal human folly, not the Fire Office breaking down? That's a relief."

"Yes. Apparently even his own brother couldn't stand Lord Edmund."

Mildred snorted. I flexed my hand. No wonder my arm hadn't gone numb. Maybe I'd gotten luckier than I'd thought. If he had been protected, I couldn't have stopped him from running me through and doing whatever he wanted with Maggie. That didn't bear thinking about.

"And I asked Warlock Quicksilver," Hazel said, "if the Fire Guild could help you, Duncan. He said anything they did would make matters worse. Once the Water Guild heard, they'd stop playing games, and mount a real search, just to spite the Fire Guild."

"Figures," I said. "I didn't believe it when they said, two years ago, that the bad blood between those two guilds was over."

Mildred went to bed, saying goodbye with a pat on my shoulder. "Good luck, laddie. I'm going to miss you, you big lunk." She shuffled down the hall, wiping her eyes and muttering something that sounded like "going soft."

"Moonrise is in two hours," Hazel said. We sat down for another lesson on becoming a boar. We did it again and again, until all it took was a gentle nudge. Then she said, "Do it without my help."

I couldn't. Half an hour later, my head was pounding. She looked like hers hurt, too. "We're out of time," she said.

"Aye, ma'am." She held a hand to the side of my head, and it stopped hurting. She handed me my belongings, repacked into a bag I could carry on my back. My coat was a dull brown instead of blue, but otherwise it looked as proud as the day I paid for it, instead of the year-old relic, dragged through mud and salt-water, that it was. I felt in the pocket. The seal, and Clive's letter, were both still there.

"I didn't mean to pry," Hazel said, "but they fell out while I was cleaning the coat. Duncan, I am so sorry. I wish I'd known, when we went to see the Fire Warlock."

"It wouldn't have made any difference. Swordsmiths are still commoners."

"But I should let him know. When word spreads that a swordsmith is a fugitive, that will raise tensions."

"Maybe not. I mean, word may not spread. The Royal Guild will probably kick me out as soon as they hear."

"Why?" Her voice wasn't soft, for once. She was almost as loud as Granny Mildred. "For defending yourself and your sister? That's ridiculous. That's—"

"That's Frankland," I said.

"Sometimes," she said, "I want to go to New London." She turned her back to me and fussed over the supper dishes. She sniffed a couple of times, and wiped her face with the tea towel.

"Stop that," I said, "or I'll not be able to leave."

She ran away, down the hall. I put on my coat and hat, and shouldered the bag. She came back a few minutes later, and led me down a tunnel without looking at me.

"Mildred said this is the best one. It ends beside a forest brook in the district's southwest corner. Not far downstream it crosses a deer track. If you follow that south, you'll come out of the forest a little west of the way you had planned. I'll come with you as far as the deer track."

We walked downstream, going quietly until I misjudged a step and landed on a branch that cracked like a shout in the still night. Hazel hissed. Uphill someone yelled, "What was that?"

I crashed through the brush along the stream, grunting and squealing. Putting distance between me and those nasty humans was better than hiding. I ran for several hundred yards before daring to stop and lift my snout. I was downwind, but couldn't smell human stink.

The otter stuck her head out of the water. "Oh, Duncan, I knew you could do it. You became a boar by yourself this time. All I did was surprise you."

Snout? Squealing? Barking mad. I would've been proud of myself if I hadn't felt so silly. "You mean there was nobody there."

"Not within half a mile. Come on, we're almost to the deer track." She swam away.

She was perched on a rock beside the stream when I reached the deer track. "Use the boar illusion when it will help, but not often. If you overdo it, you'll stop thinking clearly. Spend more than half your time as an animal, and you risk never returning to human."

I sat on my haunches so that my face was about level with the otter's. "I'll remember that. Thank you, Mother Hazel, for everything you've done for me." The trees were blurring; I screwed my eyes tight shut.

A lass's lips touched mine. "Godspeed," she said. There was a splash, and she was gone.

I waited until I could see again, then climbed the bank, heading south.

An Offer Rejected

Apprentices filed out of the smithy and sprawled in the shade of an oak tree. A journeyman followed them out and sat on a bench, picking up in the middle of a story. The master closed up, and disappeared into his house. I watched, and waited, from the cover of brambles at the edge of the woods.

A farrier's apprentice came by with a handful of old horseshoes, and they began a game. I didn't mind. The shadows were getting longer, and I'd be safer after dark.

I had found the brambles in the grey light before dawn, and lain there in the morning, but the lad's uncle had come with him on his way to the farrier, and given me no chance. I had slunk deeper into the woods and gone hunting, but had one skinny rabbit to show for a day's labours. My stomach hadn't been full since leaving the Earth Guildhall, two weeks ago. The penalties for poaching didn't scare me. If I got caught, the Frost Maiden had first dibs. I'd be an icicle before the local lord got his chance to whip me.

The game of horseshoes went on forever. I waited.

It was dusk when the lad finally jogged down the lane. I hissed at him, "Sam."

He stopped and looked around. I rose to a crouch. "Over here. It's Duncan. Duncan Archer."

"Duncan?" He came closer, peering into the undergrowth. "Sorry. Master Duncan—"

"Shh. Keep your voice down, and don't call me by name."

"What're you doing here? What's wrong? You look like a…"

"Like a tramp." I grabbed his shirt and steered him deeper into the forest. "Don't be polite. I smell like one, too. Cause I am one." I scratched at my chin. "God knows I hate having a beard in the hottest part of the summer, but it can't be helped."

"But what—"

"I had a fight with an aristo."

"Oh, shit." His shoulders sagged. "Not you…"

"Aye, lad. Me. And I need your help."

"Well, sure, I'll… Wait." His eyes bugged out, staring white in the gloom. "Did you kill an earl's son?"

"How the hell did you know about that?"

"It was you? God almighty, Duncan, you must be the strongest man that ever lived, to break through the Fire Warlock's magic."

"That wasn't what happened. How did you—"

"I'd heard the stories, but I—"

"What stories?"

"From travellers stopping at the inn. About a blacksmith up north somewhere killing an earl's son. It's all anybody's been talking about for days."

I dropped onto a tree root. Breathe in. Stop. Breathe out. Stop. Breathe in…

"I never thought about you," Sam said. "You'd rather chew an aristo out than hit him. And you aren't usually that, er…"

"Stupid," I said.

"Er, yeah. Nobody seemed to know who did it, or where. Just that it must be so, because the aristos are acting like the trumpet's blowing for the Last Judgement. Barricading themselves in their castles. Screaming at the sight of a woodman with an axe. Throwing out any tenant with a temper…"

"Frost it," I said.

"And the commoners are talking about forming armies and marching on the aristos, if the Fire Warlock's shields aren't so good, after all."

I put my head down in my hands and groaned. "Sam, he wasn't shielded. He thought he was, but he wasn't. His big brother got married without telling the family, and his wife had a baby. A son. That's all."

"Be damned," Sam said. "That's it?"

"That's it, lad."

He sat down beside me on the tree root, and I told him what had happened.

He was quiet for a bit, and then said, "I guess I oughtn't say this, but I'm glad he's dead. He deserved it. And it's about time a commoner won a fight, for a change."

"Sorry, lad, but that fight had two losers. More than that, if the stories you're hearing about troublemakers being evicted are true."

"I guess you're right." He stood up and brushed himself off. "Let's get out of here before it gets too dark to see."

"If your aunt has any bread left over…"

"I'll see what I can find." I followed him to his uncle's barn, and settled down to wait in an empty stall. A pony in the next stall blew softly in its sleep. Further away a horse nuzzled its feed bucket. The loudest noises were coming from field mice digging in the straw.

In my head I heard burning, children screaming, women crying. How could it be so quiet here in the barn, when the whole country seemed about to burst into flames? A lifetime ago the Fire Warlock had commended me after the riot. If he saw me again, he'd throw lightning bolts at me, for making things worse. Guess I'd better not go near the Fire Guild, either.

At least I hadn't pissed off the Earth or Air Guilds. Yet.

The stars were out when Sam came back to the barn with a dark lantern, and his arms full. "There's bread," he said, dropping one sack. "And meat, cheese, apples…"

"There's enough here for six men," I mumbled, around a mouthful of bread and cold pork. "Take some of it back, or you'll get a caning when your aunt and uncle notice."

"Will not. My aunt picked it all out."

"She did what? For God's sake, you didn't tell her—"

"I said a friend of mine was on the run. Didn't say who."

"Both of you can get in the stew for helping a wanted man."

"She's done it before."

After a bit I remembered to chew. "She's done it before."

"You're not the first wanted man to come this way."

"But, still…"

"What would you do if a wanted man came by your place?"

I thought about it, and admitted, "I'd let him sleep in the barn, and send him on his way with a full stomach and more food in his bag."

"Thought so."

I stopped arguing and ate. When my stomach was full, I leaned back with a sigh. "Tell your aunt she's the best cook in fifty miles, and as big-hearted as an earth mother. But there's something else I need your help with. In fact, this is why I came looking for you." I pulled Master Clive's seal out of my pocket. "Do you know what this is?"

He nudged the lantern open a little further and peered at it. "No."

"It's a swordsmith's seal."

"A what? Oh!" His eyes went wide. "You are the best, Master Duncan. I knew it. How did you get it? Master Randall didn't have a son. Was it his?"

I shrugged. If that's what he wanted to think, I'd let him.

"Oh, but..." His face fell. "It's not doing you any good, is it? Her Iciness is still after you."

"'fraid so. The Royal Guild can't help, and they might not, anyway. They're probably pissed off at me for disgracing them."

He closed the lantern until just a sliver of light was showing, and sat with his arms around his knees. "What do you want me to do?"

"I don't have any right to take the seal out of Frankland, either. Hide it for a month or so, until I'm long gone, then take it to Master Clive. He'll know what to do with it."

"Can't. Master Clive left Blacksburg. That's what I heard, anyway."

I rolled the seal in my palm. "Not surprised. Where did he go?" Sam shrugged. "Did he take that monster sword with him?" Another shrug.

I said, "If he's not there...take it to the Air Guild and ask them to send it to the swordsmiths."

He wouldn't take the seal. "I'm coming with you."

"The hell you are. That would be a damned fool thing to do."

He beat on his knee with a fist. "Why should I stay in Frankland, when not even a swordsmith can get a fair deal? There aren't any aristos in New London. Life's got to be better there."

"It may be, but we've got to get there first. If you come with me, you'll get in trouble."

"If they catch us."

We argued, circling the same ground dozens of times, until his head was lolling and his eyes wouldn't stay open. He kicked off his boots and lay down in the straw. "Talk about it in the morning," he mumbled. I blew out the lantern, and stared into the darkness while I waited for his breathing to get slow and regular.

I needed sleep, too, but Sam's family was in danger with me here. I found his boots by feel and dropped the seal in one, then picked up my pack and the sacks of food and eased out of the stall. At the door I stopped and listened. Nothing moved. Even the mice must have gone to sleep.

The fuss over the earl's brat would die down, too, sooner or later. They always did. There were enough stories about manhunts fizzling out that Mildred and Hazel must be right. If the Water Guild didn't think a man likely to kill again, they didn't work hard at finding him. The longer I stayed free—and the further south I got, where no one knew me—the odds of staying free got better. As long as I didn't do something stupid, like falling in a river, or stepping on a water wizard's toes. Or taking on someone else to be responsible for, and losing any hope of using the boar magic to escape capture. Having somebody to talk to would make the journey easier, and I liked Sam's company, but it was too dangerous, and I already had too much on my conscience.

Maybe someday, if I was lucky, I'd see Sam again. Even after leaving Frankland, I'd have to work a year, maybe two, to earn enough to pay for passage to the New World. He could finish his apprenticeship, sail out of Liverpool, and be in New London before me.

Maggie and her beau might be on their way already. That brat pawing her was probably all the push she needed.

And I wouldn't get there if I didn't keep moving. I pulled the door closed and walked away before I could change my mind.

My eyes are better than most at seeing on a moonless night. Starlight and glimmers off the river were enough to let me follow the towpath into Blacksburg. I held my breath slinking across the bridge, but no water wizard rose up to block my way. Once across, I turned south, away from the river, and dove into the welter of narrow streets.

Blacksburg at night is darker than the inside of a mole's belly. The houses all jammed together block out the moon, when there is one, and starlight isn't strong enough to cut through the murk. The night watchmen carried lanterns, but I couldn't very well ask them for help. Here and there lamplight or candlelight through a window would show where some unfortunate soul couldn't sleep, and I'd thank them under my breath for lighting my way while I dodged from shadow to shadow.

Where I couldn't see, I moved by feel and memory, and barked my shins and banged my head and cracked my elbows and stubbed my fingers and bloodied my nose and cursed under my breath. I made enough noise I was sure the watchmen would raise an alarm, but the only people that seemed to notice were a pair of footpads who ran from me like the devil was chasing them and a drunken whore who called me darling and started singing loud enough for half the city to hear. The watchmen did come for her, but I was two streets away by then.

By first light I was on the southern outskirts, and deep into farmland by late morning. I walked across fields and stiles until I was dead on my feet and my eyes were full of sand. I stumbled into a sheltered hollow under a stand of trees, and settled down to eat my lonely dinner and sleep until dusk. I spread out my coat on the ground and tipped up the bag of bread. Master Clive's seal fell out, and rolled across my coat.

Stone Soup

I reached into the bag and crammed a roll in my mouth without taking my eyes off the seal. The leaves overhead moved in the breeze, and the light caught it, making it shine against the rough brown.

Only magic could have made it jump from Sam's boot into my pack. Of course something that valuable would have a don't-lose-me spell on it. The day was already hot, but I shivered, wondering what other spells it had.

The Swordsmiths' Guild had had some powerful wizards in its early days. What would they have thought about the trouble I'd caused? They'd be disgusted, I should think.

After a while, I put the seal in my pocket, and lay down to dream about the Fire Warlock chasing me with lightning bolts.

South of Blacksburg I didn't know the lay of the land, and had to stick close to the road. After several days I figured I was far enough south nobody would recognise me, or know I was on the run if they did. Acting fearful, like I had something to hide, would draw the wrong kind of attention, so I stopped slinking along behind hedgerows and dodging from tree to tree, and walked the road like I owned it. And whistled, like I was on holiday, but every step further south was harder to take than the one before. Sleeping outdoors in my clothes didn't help my looks, but except for my size, I blended in with the growing flocks of beggars, tramps, and evicted tenants carrying all they owned on their backs.

Every day the roads got more crowded with hungry families streaming towards the cities and towns. At first, every new story pissed me off, but after a while I went numb. The newcomers pouring into the towns made it easier to slip through without notice. I was grateful to them, and hoped they never realised I was the one who had scared the dickens out of their landlords.

We were all hungry for news, as well as food. A week or so after seeing Sam, word spread that the dead aristo hadn't been shielded. Talk about marching on their overlords died out, and commoners began treating the flap over the dead earl's brat like a great joke. The aristos knew we were laughing about how gullible they were, and hated it. They started forcing out freeholders as well as tenants, and arresting mums and dads in front of their children for no good reason. Gossip also said they were calling in the Frost Maiden, and laughing when she was nastier to the commoners than she'd ever been before.

And then there was the story about the king going berserk and screaming at the Fire Warlock for not helping the Frost Maiden catch Lord Edmund's murderer. I flinched when I heard that; I didn't want the Fire Warlock any more pissed off at me than he already must be. No one else acted like it was bad news. Most seemed to relish the idea of a commoner tweaking the king's nose. At first only a few brave men, or fools, said that outright; most snickered in their beer. They got louder, though, after the rumour started that the Frost Maiden had looked the king in the eye and called him a halfwit for insisting she catch the man.

Why any fool would believe such rubbish was beyond me. The claptrap that started in early August that the magic guilds planned to take apart and remake the Water Office was worse. Whenever that came up I'd shake my head, thank them for their time, and walk on down the road.

The magic Hazel had pumped into me ran out the second week in August, and my luck along with it. In normal times, a man could work his way down the length of North Frankland chopping wood, mending fences, reaping—whatever needed doing—in exchange for a meal. There was always someone eager to hear the latest news, and most people knew not to ask questions a traveller might not want to answer.

But these weren't normal times. With so many being forced out, many farms weren't being worked, and where they were, farmers were running out of patience with strangers asking for handouts. I spent more and more time hunting for food. I pulled in my belt, and had to learn to call a day a good one when I got five miles further south, or my stomach didn't gnaw at me.

The townsfolk were getting fed up, too, and put guards at the gates to keep out the riffraff. I would have been happier going around, but the bridges were in the towns, and I didn't have any choice. When the guards hassled me, I pulled out my master's certificate and waved it under their noses. "I'm a master blacksmith," I'd say, "on my way to London after a tramping holiday." Raising my voice and demanding to see the nearest alderman usually bought me passage through, but at the cost of attention I didn't want.

One night I stumbled across several families camped in an apple orchard, and added to their soup pot the grouse I'd brought down with my slingshot and the sack of peas I'd helped myself to from an abandoned garden.

"I'd've felt guilty about helping myself," I told the woman doing the cooking, "if there hadn't been pods rotting on the plants."

"Nobody to pick them, I suppose," she said. "Forced out of their homes, just like us."

"It's a crying sin, the waste is. There'll be a lot of hungry people this winter."

"It's not all going to waste. We hauled a load of cabbages to town this morning. Sold them all. Yesterday I picked beans and Jack dug onions. Sold them, too."

Her husband grinned over his bowl. "And the best part of it is, the lord doesn't know we're here. We're not paying any rent. Taxes, either."

"Good luck with that," I said. "He'll notice, sooner or later."

"Not until the middle of September, at the earliest. I promised Hannah we'd be gone by then."

"Why not til then?"

"You hadn't heard? The king ordered all the aristos to Paris for a meeting at the end of the month."

"Did he now?" I scratched at my beard and tried to remember when I'd last seen an aristo on the road, or wrecking a farmer's wheat field galloping after a fox. "That would explain why I hadn't seen any lately. But the lord must've left somebody in charge."

"The steward here is a lazy bastard who won't put one foot in front of another when his lord's not watching. We're safe enough."

"What's the meeting in Paris about?"

"What I heard," Hannah said, "is that the Fire Warlock wants to knock some sense into the aristos. They're going to hang a magic mirror and show the aristos what really happened when that swordsmith up north killed that earl's whelp."

I choked on my soup. Several minutes of coughing later, I managed a strangled, "Swordsmith?"

"That's what they're saying in town."

"It makes sense," Jack said. "Nobody short of a wizard or a swordsmith would've dared talk back to an aristo in the first place."

When we had emptied the soup pot, I moved away from the fire and sat with my back to an apple tree. Don't draw attention to yourself, Granny Mildred had said. What could I do now? After that meeting, every aristo in the whole frostbitten country would know what I looked like. If I stuck to the roads, my days as a warm body were numbered. I would have to slink through the woods, and use the boar magic, even more than I'd used it on the way to Blacksburg.

Hazel had warned me not to overdo it, but odds were I wouldn't have much choice. I was wondering how it would feel to get stuck thinking like a boar, when another tramp wandered into camp, and killed my hopes of leaving Frankland alive.

"The king is offering a reward," the man said, "for capturing the murdering swordsmith—"

"Murdering?" Hannah's voice rose. "And him a swordsmith? King Stephen's got a lot of nerve calling a respectable man like that a murderer."

"Hey, don't yell at me. I'm just repeating what the town crier said."

"You didn't have to repeat it word-for-word. That aristo sounded like the one doing the murdering, and I'm glad he got his just rewards."

"Look, woman, I'm just saying—"

"Well, watch how you say it. What else?"

"The murd—sorry, the town crier said the man they're after is a swordsmith from Abertee named Duncan Archer, and he'd be easy to spot. Brown hair, brown eyes, square jaw, good teeth, and the girls say he's good looking. Arms like tree trunks, a chest like a barrel, and so tall he has to duck going through the church door. Can't be many like that."

Hannah edged between me and newcomer, her skirts blocking the firelight. "Never seen him. Even if I had, I'd not—"

"They're offering two hundred and fifty gold franks for him, dead or alive."

Two hundred and fifty franks? More than what anybody at the campfire could expect to see in their entire lives. Nice to know I was worth that much. Would've rather found out some other way.

Everybody around the fire went quiet. Thinking about what they could do with that money, no doubt. Then Jack said, quiet and slow, "There'll be murdering done, and not by that swordsmith either, if anybody collects on that reward."

The newcomer shrugged. "Maybe. The townsfolk didn't like the news. They threw things at the town crier and shouted him down."

Hannah said, "Huh. And there I thought they didn't have any sense, living in a town like that."

I stayed with my back against the tree, moving only to finger the seal in my pocket, until well after they had banked the fire, and everybody had settled down and started snoring. Then, moving as quiet as I could, I walked towards the road. I stepped out from under the trees and stopped. A flash of light, like moonlight off a knife, had caught my eye. The flash came again. The shadow behind it separated from the deeper shadows and eased into the open.

"Can't sleep?" I said, no more than a whisper.

"Not tonight." Jack's reply was no louder. "Not for worrying about my neighbours' health. A man might think he could wander into town by himself in the middle of the night. He could get hurt that way."

"Never a good idea to travel at night," I said. "Lots of trouble out there."

"Speaking of trouble." The knife disappeared into the man's boot. "I've heard that out west, in Cornwall, there are tunnels under the channel the Water Guild will never find. Idle talk, maybe. Never been there, myself."

"I'll keep that in mind," I said, and stepped onto the road.

He said, "If you ever see that swordsmith, thank him for me, will you?"

"For what? Scaring your landlord into throwing you out?"

I thought he grinned. "I've been wanting out from under his thumb for years, but I couldn't get Hannah to move. Now, I don't think she'd go back even if we could. But what I meant was, for showing us how little it takes to scare them. We won't all be so cowed anymore."

He slipped into the shadows. I turned south, and walked until dawn.

Some demon pounded my head with a sledgehammer on every jolt of the wagon. I couldn't see, but heard other horses, other wagons. We were getting close to the town. I would be mighty glad when we left this rutted cart track. With one final jolt, hard enough to make a sack of turnips fall over and bounce on my head, we were off the track and onto cobblestones. With a clacketa-clacketa-clacketa, the sledgehammer turned into a hundred finishing hammers going at me all over.

My boots had gotten me into this fix. My left big toe had poked out a hole before Blacksburg, and other stitching had been coming loose, so it wasn't a surprise when I caught the left sole under a root and ripped it apart. I'd tied it up as well as I could, but didn't have the tools to fix it proper. I limped along through forest for a few days, but after a sharp rock sliced through both the leather thong and the side of my foot, I went looking for help.

The old charcoal burner I met in the woods acted like I was doing him the favour by asking him for help. Don't go to the nearest cobbler, he'd said. That greedy bastard would sell out his own mother. But the old man's nephew's sister-in-law's cousin was a cobbler. His son-in-law had had an arm frozen off for poaching. He'd help.

So here I was, lying in a wagon, sacks of turnips and beets and onions and garlic hemming me in and a wool blanket covering me on the hottest day of the hottest August in memory. I'd been riding for a day and a half, handed off from charcoal burner to nephew to sister-in-law's son like a load of firewood. I hadn't given out my name or where I was going, but they all seemed to know.

As grateful as I was for their help, having to trust strangers stretched my temper to the limits. If the ride on this ball-busting wagon didn't end soon, I'd go berserk.

The clacketa-clacketa gave way to clickety-clickety. A gap in the floor-boards showed the smoother stone of a bridge. I held my breath until we were back on the cobbles.

The driver said, like he was talking to himself, "Almost there. That was the last bridge."

We might get there before I drowned in my own sweat. More than once over the past two days I'd thought freezing to death didn't sound so bad. I'd considered turning myself in to the Water Guild and being done with it all. Collecting the reward myself and having them send it to Doug and Maggie would mean it went to somebody who deserved it. Even while thinking that, I kept riding in the wagon until my teeth rattled, because I didn't want to disappoint that charcoal burner and his relations.

The wagon stopped. The driver climbed down. With my eye against the gap, I watched his feet disappear into an open door. I fought down the urge to stand up and heave sacks of turnips after him. In a few minutes, he came out, climbed back on, and drove the wagon into an alley. We stopped in the shade. The smell of leather made its way past the sweat and garlic that had been in my nose for hours.

The blanket was yanked off me. I sat up, and blinked at a face that reminded me of Uncle Will. "Whew," he said, "you look like a drowned rat. Smell pretty ripe, too. Mary!" He bellowed over his shoulder. "Bring us a pitcher of ale. We've got a man dying of thirst here." He turned back to me. "Let's see those boots."

In a short while I was sitting on a bench in the cobbler's garden with a cold pork pie in one hand and my second pint in the other. A high wall and trees blocked out nosy neighbours. The wagon was gone—the driver had waved goodbye and set out for home, looking pleased with himself. Mary, the cobbler's daughter, eyed me from the door and giggled.

The cobbler's apprentice shambled over, measured my feet, and walked away grumbling about the cost of leather. I would have paid the cobbler for fixing my old boots, but not only wouldn't he hear of it, he insisted I spend the night with them, so he could make me a new pair. "You won't get as far as South Frankland with these. I'll sew them back together, but next time the leather will give out."

He hadn't told me anything I didn't already know. I finished the pie and pulled the map out of my pack. Too far east, I needed to plan a new track. Honeybees buzzed around the garden. Butterflies danced across the flowers. Squiggles danced across the map.

I gave up and put it away. Feeling more at ease than at any time since leaving Mildred and Hazel, I pulled my hat brim down and lay down on the bench.

"Wake up." Mary shook my shoulder, hard. "Please, Master Duncan, wake up."

"Huh? What—"

She shoved my old boots into my hands. "You've got to go. There's a wizard looking for you."

Persuasion

I jammed my feet into the re-stitched boots and snatched at the laces. The sun had fallen halfway down the sky. I'd been asleep for hours.

The cobbler's wife dropped a basket of wet laundry onto the grass. "Too late, he's here." She pushed at me with both hands. "Lie down, and don't move."

I lay down on the bench and brought my feet up. The two women snatched a sheet from the basket and flung it onto a line overhead. A breeze caught it, and slapped me across the eyes with the wet corner. The women pulled darned socks out of the basket and hung each one like it was a treasure. The wind played with the sheet. Slap, slap, slap. My eyes stung. I didn't move.

The cobbler's heavy stomp said he was pissed off even before he growled, "See for yourself. I'm not harbouring any murderers."

The lighter voice fit the lighter tread. "I didn't say you were. All I said was, someone had seen the swordsmith here, and—"

"That someone should be ashamed of himself. If that smith was here, I'd not turn him over to Her Iciness. She could freeze me, and—"

"I don't want the Water Guild to get him, either. Get that through your thick skull. The Fire Guild is trying to save him from her clutches. We won't turn him over to the king, either."

In the silence that followed, Mary whispered to her mother, "He's just a boy. What's the Fire Guild doing, sending a boy out after a man his size?"

Her mother whispered, "He can't be on guild business. He must be trying to collect the reward himself."

The cobbler said, "Nice try, but I don't believe it. You wizards are all in it together."

The boy's voice rose. "The hell you know. When has the Fire Guild ever been that tight with the Water Guild?"

"I thought the point of that big bash a couple years ago was to tell us you weren't fighting anymore."

"Oh, for… We're wasting time. If you do know where that swordsmith is, warn him there's a water wizard on the way. He'll be here in less than ten minutes."

The light footsteps retreated. A door slammed. I rolled upright and yanked at my laces. Before you could say, Freeze my arse, I was out through the garden gate and following Mary through the alleys at a run. She was out of breath and looked like she had a stitch in her side when we reached the edge of town. I snatched a kiss by way of thanks and left her grinning as I ran for the woods.

I slowed down when the path led uphill through a field of boulders. Slipping into the boar magic made scrambling over them on all fours easier. I was almost to the top when a voice above me said, "About time you got here. Took you long enough."

A skinny, bareheaded lad of about fifteen sat on the highest rock, a wand in one hand and a peach in the other. I growled at him.

"Hey, cut that out," he said. "I'm trying to help." He waved the wand, and I was jolted out of being a boar.

"Frost you. Who are you, and what do you want?"

He took a bite of the peach and wiped juice off his chin with his sleeve. "I need to talk to you."

"Not with a water wizard on my tail." I climbed past him.

"He's not that close. You can give me a few minutes."

"How do you know?"

"Because I'm a warlock, you ass. You wouldn't be here if I hadn't warned you he was coming."

I turned around and took a good look at the lad. If he was a warlock, I was the tooth fairy. "You knew I was in the cobbler's garden?"

"Of course I did. Don't hide behind a sheet again; it doesn't work. I nudged you out of there so we could talk without having to explain it all to them, too."

"Is there a water wizard?"

"Well, yeah. He picked up your trail a few minutes ago, and—"

"Frostbite." I scrambled over the top of the hill and started down the other side.

He yelled after me, "Hey, stop. Come back here, drown you."

I barrelled down the hill, jumped the stream at the bottom, and started up the next. I came to a clearing about halfway up. He was waiting for me, and not out of breath either.

"Stop," he said, "or I'll burn you."

"Better than being iced."

I'm not a master smith for nothing. I warded off the fire shooting out of his wand and kept going. He bounded after me, shouting, "Frostbite, Master Duncan. I'm trying to help. What am I supposed to tell the Fire Warlock—that you're too thick to know what's good for you?"

I took another good, hard look at him. "The Fire Warlock sent you?"

"Yes. He'd come himself, but he's busy."

"All right then. I'm listening."

"Stop. I can't keep up with you."

I stopped. "Fine. One minute. Talk."

He talked so fast he would have beat a squirrel chittering. "In a few days the magic guilds are going to fix the Water Office. We're going to take it apart and re-forge it, and when we're done we'll need test cases to prove it's been fixed, and the Fire Warlock said yours was the best, so we've been looking for you for weeks, and I only found you because after the king posted the reward Granny Hazel told us where you were going and that she'd taught you mindwarping. So now you know, I'll take you to the Fortress and you won't have to worry about the Water Guild until it's time for your trial and I'd've taken you there already, but Quicksilver said it was better if you volunteered. See?"

He reached for me. I swatted his hand away. "Keep your paws off me."

"I can't take you to the Fortress without a hand on you."

"You're not taking me anywhere."

"You'll be safe there."

"Not if you're turning me over to the Frost Maiden."

"I didn't say—"

"You said Hazel told you how to find me."

"Yeah, after the king offered the reward. She figured—"

I didn't stay to listen. "She can go to hell."

"Hey! Didn't you hear—"

"And you can go kiss the Fire Warlock." I didn't look back. Thirty miles later and close to dawn, I went to earth in the lee of a hill. There'd been no sign of wizards for hours, but I kept running, weaving in and out of field and forest, and switching back and forth between boar and human, until I wasn't sure which I was. Maybe I could have stopped earlier, but running was easier than thinking about what the fire lad had said—that the Fire Warlock wanted to hand me over to the Frost Maiden and Hazel had turned on me for the reward. The rest of the rubbish he'd spouted hadn't made any sense, but I'd understood that much. If I'd lost Master Randall and Uncle Will and Charcoal all on the same day, it wouldn't have hurt as much.

The early sun stabbed me in the eyes, and I came wide awake, snarling at the entire human race. Within seconds I was scrambling through the underbrush, intent on getting away from people. Thinking like a man again didn't come for more than a hundred yards. I sat down on a tree root, blowing hard.

I had never before gone to sleep thinking like a boar. That was far too close for comfort to that place I shouldn't go, where I couldn't get back to human. I shivered. If I couldn't think straight, I'd be a sitting duck.

Maybe the gossip was true, and the Water Guild wasn't working hard at following me. The fire lad might be working harder, but he was inexperienced. There was a chance I'd shaken them.

Even if I had lost them for a while, they now knew what district I was in and could make a good guess where I meant to go. They knew about the boar magic now, too. This might be my last day as a warm body.

Not that I cared, when even Hazel had turned on me.

After climbing a hill to get my bearings, I angled southwest, and stumbled across a shady path threading between fields and the edge of the woods. I followed it, keeping my eyes moving, my ears open. The only noises besides my own footsteps were the rustle of leaves, birdsong, and the sound of a stream off in the distance. A few famers were picking peas and melons before the sun got too hot. Rounding a bend in the path, I caught up with a townie, ambling along with his head down and his hands together behind his back, like he was thinking hard, feet moving out of habit.

He glanced over his shoulder, smiled, and nodded. He should've been nervous—I made people nervous before looking like a tramp—but if he was he didn't show it. A wizard? Frostbite. Too late now not to speak. Short, skinny, and early thirties, he wasn't carrying a wand, and was dressed like an ordinary craftsman. Ten years ago I'd have called him a lightweight and not paid him any more attention, but I'd learned better since then.

He picked up his pace, and something about the way he walked, light and surefooted, reminded me of a cat. He said, "Are you in such a hurry, friend? If you slow a bit I will walk with you."

Not doing a good job of looking like I was out on a carefree holiday, was I? If I acted like a boar and he was a wizard, I was dead. I slowed. "Where're you headed?"

"Nowhere in particular. I do my best thinking while walking, and today I have to talk to an important man—a highly respected and influential man—asking him to undertake a difficult task. I have been pondering how to approach it."

At least he wasn't looking for me. Thinking about somebody else's problems would be better than thinking about Hazel or the Frost Maiden. I kept my eyes moving across the fields while listening with half a mind.

He said, "My protégé already broached the subject with him, and made a hash of it. He dismissed the boy out of hand. I had intended to speak to him at the first opportunity, but now my task is doubly hard."

"The lad could tell the fellow he's sorry."

He shrugged. "Yes, but at the moment it seems unlikely the man would listen. He is a forceful individual of heroic stature, not overly tolerant of foolishness or incompetence, but he has proven himself generous and willing to put himself at risk in the defence of others less capable."

"That sounds like a man I could look up to, like a hero out of an old story." Uncle Will had had quite a store of tales. Get him started, and he'd tell one after another, long after we should have been in bed. We'd be bleary-eyed the next day, and he'd chew us out for not letting him get enough sleep. The memory made me smile.

I said, "I used to love hearing those stories. Maybe you noticed a lot of the heroes were blacksmiths. I was real proud to be apprenticed to a smith." I rubbed my eyes. Shouldn't have said that. "I was a young fool. Thought by being a smith I'd get a chance to be a hero. Life doesn't work like that. Not anymore."

"Suppose this man had an opportunity to save others' lives by risking his own, but would not take it. Would you still consider him a hero?"

"Nae."

"Even if he did not believe he could?"

The sound of running water was getting louder. I searched the woods for signs of water wizards. "Somebody ought to rap him up the side of the head. Knock some sense into him."

"But those he trusts do not believe either. Only a few, myself among them, believe he has the power to save those lives. He does not know me, nor has any reason to trust me, and the story I must tell him is so far out of his experience he would be justified in laughing in my face."

I scratched at my beard. "Hard problem you've got there. Can't expect a man to be a hero if he doesn't see any point to it. What are you trying to get him to do?"

"Avert a civil war."

I whipped my head around and stared down at him. "Eh?"

"Surely you have felt the tensions rising, the rage against injustice, the desperation of families forced to leave their homes."

"Aye. Kind of hard to miss. Like Blacksburg before the riot." Frostbite. Shouldn't have said that either.

"Indeed. When it breaks, it will be worse than a riot. If the Frost Maiden executes that fugitive swordsmith, Frankland will erupt into full and open class warfare."

Great. Something else to add to my guilty conscience. "You can't know that. That's never happened in Frankland."

"That it has never occurred before does not prove it cannot occur. Let me introduce myself." He held out his hand. "Master Jean Rehsavvy, historian. You need not give me a name in return. Better to keep silent than to lie."

I eyed his outstretched hand. After a moment I shook it. "Pleased to meet you, Master Jean."

"I have studied the conditions leading to war in many times, many places. Frankland is long overdue for corrective measures. The four Offices are too rigid to allow the gradual, non-violent corrections that should have taken place centuries ago, but if changes are not made, Frankland is doomed. We cannot continue on the path we are on, and hope to avoid violence."

I put one foot in front of another, not watching for wizards. Not watching where I was going, either. Nothing ever changes in Frankland. How many times had I heard that? "A lot of people could get hurt."

"Many will be hurt."

"If the Frost Maiden ices the swordsmith, you said. You'd better pray, then, that she doesn't find him for a long, long time."

He shook his head. "The Water Guild will find him soon, but his life is not in immediate danger."

"The hell you say. With the king offering that reward, he's got no chance."

There was no snicker, no chuckle, but something about his eyes made me think he was laughing. "He should have been captured weeks ago. That reward was a stroke of genius. The most extensive manhunt in Frankland's history has been sabotaged by the king himself."

"Eh?"

"The response to the offer of a reward has overwhelmed the Water Guild. Reports of sightings have flooded in from across Frankland— hundreds each from Paris, London, Blacksburg, Edinburgh, and every other city. Thousands from South Frankland. Dozens even from Abertee, where he could not possibly be. The Water Guild has redeployed its witches and wizards to areas with the most sightings, leaving one wizard to cover central Northern Frankland. The one region where he most certainly is has produced only four sightings."

I smacked into a tree. "You're joking."

"I am not. The people have spoken, and they do not want him found."

The path went round a bend, and dipped down to a stream too wide to jump. Crossing meant trusting slick steppingstones. I backed into a pea field.

Master Jean's laughter faded. "Sadly, the one remaining water wizard is a zealot. The swordsmith's capture is imminent."

I fought the boar down, and turned on him, snarling. "How the devil do you know that?"

He held up a hand, palm out. "Peace, friend. I am not a water wizard."

"You know too much. You've got to be a wizard. What kind? Fire? Earth?"

"Fire. I—"

Flames belched beside us. I yelled, and whipped around.

Master Jean grabbed my arm. "Do not move."

The fire lad stepped out of the flames, wild-eyed. "The Water Guild spotted him. She's coming."

My feet wouldn't budge. Master Jean pushed me like I had no more heft than a scarecrow. I sprawled in the peas. My hat went flying. The fire lad fell across me.

"Keep him warm," Master Jean said.

A man and the most gorgeous woman I'd ever seen rose out of the stream. I'd seen her before—she had called to me across a crowded room in the Black Duke's palace. Blue light, so bright it hurt my eyes, flashed from her ring, but I kept staring at her, unwilling and unable to tear my eyes away.

The Frost Maiden lifted her wand. Ice poured from it, straight at me.

Fire and Ice

Water, not ice, splashed my face. The bravest man I've ever met stepped between me and the Frost Maiden.

She said, "Stand aside, Jean, you are harbouring a fugitive." Her voice chilled me more than the water had.

He spread his hands, palms out. "I beg your pardon, Your Wisdom, but he is under the Fire Guild's protection."

The hot blue August sky turned black and the wind howled. Ice, snow, sleet, and freezing rain flew at us. She threw hailstones as big as chicken's eggs, and icicles a foot long and as sharp as a dagger. They met a shield of fire centred on the wizard's outstretched hands. The ice and snow melted, running down onto the peas, or went sizzling and steaming into the air, or flew out to either side or over our heads.

The attack went on and on, and snow and ice settled around us in snowdrifts taller than Master Jean. His face was down, and his hair and shoulders were white from snow, but it wasn't building up. Cold water ran off him and pooled on the ground, trapped between mounds of snow.

The fire lad wedged his legs under me and tilted my head out of the rising water. We both lay in it. Where he touched me I was still warm, but elsewhere was like being stabbed with cold knives. The lad was shaking, and his lips were turning blue.

Freezing to death in August, or drowning—I didn't approve of either choice.

My hands and feet had gone numb, and the water lapped my chin when, over the noise of the wind, a voice bellowed, "Hey, Jean, what are the magic words?" I'd heard that voice before, and would never forget, as long as I lived.

Master Jean yelled, "I pledge by the Token of Office…to deliver this fugitive…to the Water Guild for justice…or see him dead or in exile within one month."

The howling and the freezing barrage stopped. Master Jean grabbed my shoulder. Heat and life flowed into me, like Hazel had her hands on me. I got my arms under me, and pushed my shoulders out of the water. The fire lad rolled, slipped, and went down backwards over his head. Arms and legs flew. I grabbed an arm and stood, hauling him with me. Master Jean smacked him on the back and water shot out of his nose and mouth.

The lad swore like he'd learned it from the guards. He wasn't drowning then, anyway. I let go, and felt in my pocket. The seal was still there.

Mountains of ice and snow boxed us in, except for a narrow gap in front. Master Jean shouldered through, the ice melting and steaming away like he was red hot. The fire lad followed him. I had to squeeze through sideways. Somebody offered me a hand, and I came out face to face, once again, with the Fire Warlock.

He clapped me on the shoulder. "You all right? Good grief, you're a mess."

I croaked at him. The next thing I knew I was dry again.

"Good. We wanted you alive and kicking. Do you understand what I just did?"

"Nae, sir."

"I guaranteed your good behaviour until you are either dead, or out of the country, or handed over to the Water Guild. Now, I do not want to see you dead. Understand?"

"Aye, sir! Thank you, sir!"

"Good." He pushed me towards a grassy spot beside the path, where the fire lad lay face down, shaking. Master Jean was on his knees with a hand on the lad's head, talking to him.

The Fire Warlock pushed down on my shoulder. "Sit down here and don't move while I—"

I roared, "Like hell I will. Sir. He told me not to move and I nearly drowned. You give me an order and I'll do it, but don't make me not move again, or…"

"Or what?" He leaned in, glaring. I held my ground.

"Peace, friend." Master Jean was on his feet with his hand on the Fire Warlock's arm. "I offer my apologies for leaving you in rising water, but between holding off the Water Office and summoning the Fire Warlock, I had little attention to spare."

"Sorry, sir," I mumbled. "I know you saved my life. I don't mean to be an ingrate."

The Fire Warlock said, "You'd never live down letting him drown."

Master Jean said, "I am aware of that."

"I can see the history books now. Warlock Quicksilver's primary claim to fame: drowning a fugitive."

Master Jean's stony glare would have made me duck, for all I was twice his size. The Fire Warlock grinned.

Master Jean said, "I cannot blame Master Duncan for anger at being prevented from protecting himself. If our roles were reversed, I would be livid."

"Well, then," I said, "why…"

"Because I did not have time to warn you of the consequences of running or fighting back. Either would have drawn a swift lightning bolt from the Fire Warlock."

"He put you under the Fire Office's shield," the Fire Warlock said. "If you reject that, it'll make me kill you. I wouldn't like it, but I'd do it. That's why you're going to sit down here and not move until we straighten things out."

"Nothing doing," I said. "I promise I won't run."

The two wizards looked at each other. After a moment the Fire Warlock shrugged. "You'd better not panic, either." His grip on my shoulder cut into me like a vice. "You're no good for me, dead. Understand?"

"Aye, sir!"

He let go and walked away. I took two steps after him before I stopped cold. The Frost Maiden stood like a statue, knee deep in the stream, staring towards the north. Her arms hung loose at her sides. The water wizard who had come with her stood on the far side of the stream, tugging at his robe, his head swivelling back and forth between her and the Fire Warlock. He edged away as the Fire Warlock got closer.

The Fire Warlock looked down at the stream and made a face, then walked into it and put an arm around the Frost Maiden's shoulders. "It's all right, Lorraine. No riots today. Thaw out, already."

My jaw went slack. So did the water wizard's. At least somebody else here didn't understand was what going on, either.

I dropped onto the grass beside the fire lad. We watched as the two fire wizards talked to the Frost Maiden. I clamped my arms around my knees and wondered how many days it would be before either of us stopped shaking.

"Who is he?" I said.

"He, who?"

"The wizard who called himself Master Jean."

"Oh, him. He's the retired Fire Warlock."

I glared at the lad. "Stop spouting rubbish at me, and tell me something I can believe, for a change."

The lad swelled up, and looked ready to throw fire at me, but Master Jean gave him a hard stare over his shoulder. The lad settled for glowering and muttering curses.

The Frost Maiden stepped out of the stream and curtsied to Master Jean. "Thank you, Your Wisdom, for your forbearance. I trust you have not taken offence."

He bowed to her. "Certainly not, Your Wisdom. You are not to blame for the Water Office's deficiencies. This incident has reinforced my belief that the Office's presumption of a fugitive's guilt is a tragic flaw."

"I agree with you, Jean, and we shall fix it, but it may take generations before any but the most stalwart or naive commoners do not believe their only hope is to flee the Water Guild."

The Fire Warlock said, "I want another change, too."

"What change?"

"Toast those iced—er, sorry—damned pass phrases. Let me say 'Stop!' and make the promises later."

"Certainly. That will be better for both of us, I assure you."

She climbed the bank towards us. I put my hands down, ready to scuttle backwards like a crab. The lad grabbed my sleeve.

"Don't panic." His voice was a high as a girl's.

The Frost Maiden stopped. "Master Duncan, are you injured?"

I shook my head. Couldn't get my mouth to work.

"Good," she said. "I am sorry I frightened you. I do not enjoy frightening people. Warlock Snorri, I trust you are well."

I looked around for another wizard, but she was talking to the fire lad. He swallowed, twice. "Yes, ma'am. I slipped in the ice water, that's all. It was my own fault."

The Frost Maiden turned towards the water wizard. "Cornelius, what were you thinking?"

Her voice raised goose bumps on my arms, on a scorcher in August, and he was on her side. The water wizard sputtered, without giving a clear answer.

She said, "Did you not see the beacon Warlock Snorri set on Master Duncan's head last evening?"

"Yes, ma'am. That's how I found him again."

"Why did you demand my attention when Warlock Quicksilver already had him in hand?"

The fire lad said, "Probably thought he could claim part of the reward."

The water wizard turned red. The Frost Maiden's own cheeks grew red spots. She shrieked at him. "Fool! Wretch! How dare you sully the Water Guild's reputation. Have you no concern for our safety?" She splashed across the stream, grabbed him by the ear and twisted. "I promise you will not see a halfpenny of that reward." She dragged the howling wizard into the middle of the stream, and they were gone.

Don't draw attention to yourself, Granny Mildred had said, a long time ago. Don't mess around with wizards or witches, she'd said. Too late now.

My stomach growled. My last meal had been hours and miles away.

The Fire Warlock held out a hand. "We'll all feel better with a good breakfast under our belts. What do you say to that?"

I kept my eyes on the middle of the stream and my arms clamped around my knees. "Why the blazes did you bother to rescue me from her today, if you're going to turn me over to her later? You could've let her get what she wants now."

Master Jean said, "She does not want to execute you." He sank down onto the grass in front of me. The Fire Warlock flopped down beside him.

I said, "You can't expect me to believe that. She sure tried hard."

"Not so. If she had wanted to kill you, you would be dead. Her Office wanted you dead; she did not."

I glared at him.

"The Water Guild has two ways to kill," he said. "The more ostentatious method is the one she used today, throwing ice and snow until the victim is buried under the weight and freezing from the effort of melting it. But even under a mound of snow dozens of feet thick, freezing to death is not guaranteed. The air in the snow locks in heat, and a warm body can survive some time under it. Many animals survive the winter asleep under a blanket of snow.

"The Water Guild's other method of killing, the one used for executions after a trial, is to suck out the heat. That method is quiet, subtle, and merciless. If I pump heat back in as quickly as the Water Office draws it out, I will kill the victim with burns. I could, perhaps, outlast it, but that would take hours, perhaps days, and the victim would be long dead. If she had wanted to kill you, she would have done so, and I could not have stopped her. Instead, she chose the method I can protect against, and she knew it."

"You're going to say you weren't fighting back, either."

"Certainly. I was not. Everything I did was strictly defensive, to protect you, my protégé, and myself. I made no offensive moves towards Sorceress Lorraine. None. I have no interest in acquiring the distinction of being the first retired Fire Warlock executed by his successor for treason."

The Fire Warlock lay down on his back in the peas with his hands over his face. "Bloody hell."

Master Jean put a hand on the Fire Warlock's arm. "We survived, my friend. As I believed we would."

"I'm sure glad you think fast on your feet. And remembered the magic words. We could have been here for hours if it had been up to me."

Master Jean smiled. "You have no idea how many times in the past century I practiced those pass phrases. It gave me great pleasure to steal someone away from the Water Office's grip, on the few occasions I could use them." His smile went away. "I never imagined I would feel sympathy for Sorceress Lorraine on such an occasion."

My stomach growled. The Fire Warlock said, "You ready for breakfast yet?"

I took a hard look at the glittering mountain of ice and snow melting in the hot sun. My hat was under there, somewhere, and flat as a dog's tongue, probably—a lost cause. I went back to staring at the stream. "Tell me why she was so pissed off at that water wizard."

Master Jean said, "A dozen members of the Water Guild have died or been gravely injured this summer, either by mobs, as in the Blacksburg riot, or by individuals driven to seek revenge. The Water Office shields her from such violence, but she fears for her people, and for Frankland. She believes, as do I, certain events could trigger nationwide retaliation that would cast the destruction in Blacksburg into the shadows. A water wizard collecting that reward would be such an event."

Finally, he'd said something I understood. I'd seen the wreckage of Blacksburg's Water Guildhall.

"You've got to wonder," the fire lad said, "if that wizard has water for brains. Their guild council should've told them it wouldn't let them collect on that reward. We did. The Earth Guild Council did, too."

"Certainly the Water Guild Council issued that edict," Master Jean said. "They are the most in danger. But men hear what they want to hear, and greed makes fools of many. Perhaps he hoped to buy protective spells from the Earth or Fire Guilds. Perhaps he cannot believe the entire Water Guild is in danger. That has never happened, therefore it cannot happen. This is, after all, Frankland. Nothing ever changes in Frankland."

That had always been true before, but I'd seen enough changes this summer to make me dizzy. It seemed they weren't over, not by a long shot. I said, "Who is the reward going to?"

"A soon-to-be-former cobbler's apprentice, may the wretch have no joy of it."

The lad's eyes bugged out. "Did you just curse him?"

"Certainly not. He has done that to himself. The lore is full of such greedy fools."

My stomach growled. I looked at the Fire Warlock. "You said breakfast."

He nodded. "You two, take him to the Fortress. I'll be along in a few."

The fire lad said, "Why? What are you going to do?"

He grinned and pointed. "I'm going to stroll over to that wagon and tell the farmers hiding behind it to spread the news that the swordsmith is alive and kicking after the retired Fire Warlock snatched him from under the Frost Maiden's very nose. That's one story I'm going to enjoy hearing repeated."

With a wash, a shave, and a good breakfast under my belt, I ran out of excuses for not listening to the fire wizards. They'd even found clean clothes big enough for me—the Fire Warlock's cast-offs, only a wee bit snug across the shoulders.

The Fire Warlock told me to sit, but he went to stand at a window in

191

the room he called his study. The red light flickering in his ring didn't look angry like it did the night of the riot, but watching it made my eyes itch. I perched on the edge of a chair, and watched the other wizard. "What am I supposed to call you?"

He raised an eyebrow. "Master Jean is one of my titles."

"I wondered if I was supposed to call you Your Wisdom."

"You may call me that if you prefer."

"I don't. You may be more than a century old, but you don't look older than me, and it doesn't seem right."

"Then call me either Warlock Quicksilver or Master Jean. They are the oldest of my titles, but ones I am still proud of."

"Good. I've never liked having to say 'sir' and 'ma'am' and 'my lord' and so on to people who think they're my betters but don't act like it."

He didn't flame me. "Nor do I. The measure of a man is what he has done with what he has been given, not where an accident of birth places him."

The Fire Warlock turned away from the window and dropped into a chair. "Sorry. More problems. A duke throwing a tantrum. He can wait."

Master Jean said, "Tell us what you understood of Warlock Snorri's confounding explanation."

Hazel had turned on me. None of the rest of it had made any sense. I crossed my arms over my chest and stared out the window at empty air. "You're going to turn me over to the Frost Maiden, and she won't pass up a second chance to ice me."

"Whoa," the Fire Warlock said. "Right there. We're not going to turn you over to the Water Guild. Not unless you volunteer."

"Are you a frostbitten moron? No way in hell would I do that."

He laughed. "How is a swordsmith like a king? He's the only other fool in Frankland that calls me names to my face and thinks he can get away with it. But look, Duncan, this is the part you didn't get. Come the first of September, we're taking the Water Office apart. Stripping it all the way down and re-forging it. Fixing it."

I stared at him, then at Master Jean, who nodded.

"Fixing it, you say. You can't fix it. Those Offices were supposed to stand for all time. If you can rebuild it, you should've done it years ago, before things got out of hand."

"We could not take it apart," Master Jean said, "until the Locksmith appeared. For a thousand years, no other witch or wizard in Frankland has had the ability to unlock the Water Office. We do not know with certainty that even she can, only that Frankland is in mortal danger if she cannot."

"And what do you mean by fixing it?"

"Two things. Making it more flexible, so that it responds to the living citizenry, and the judgements it issues change as times change. And reducing the influence of the nobility, that commoners may once again believe its judgements to be fair."

I snorted, and scowled at the window.

The Fire Warlock said, "The king has demanded a trial, once it's been put back together, to show to everybody's satisfaction it's been fixed."

"You mean all the aristos'," I said. "If they're happy, the rest of us won't be."

"Well, yeah, that's what the king means. But we want a trial commoners can see is fair, and where the nobles can't argue with the judgement, even if they don't much like it."

"Good luck with that."

"That's why we need you."

I said nothing.

Master Jean said, "The contrast between you and the late Lord Edmund Bradford could not be greater. His life was the most repellent I have ever had the misfortune of examining."

"The aristos won't see it that way."

"We think they will," The Fire Warlock said. "I commended you for helping a noble in the riot, remember. Most of them couldn't stand that brat Edmund either. You've done more for them than he ever did, and we can show it."

"And if I don't knuckle under and volunteer?"

"I'll take you to the border, give you the fare to New London, and send you on your way. Feelings are running too high in Frankland for me to make you do it. Of course, if you don't, Frankland will be screwed, but you won't care. You won't be here."

I gave him a look that would've made most men back up and spout sorrys. He didn't blink. I went back to staring out the window.

"It is unfortunate," Master Jean said, "that we cannot show the nobility the value of your position. Since Edmund Bradford's death, Abertee has been aboil with anger and resentment, but it had been the most peaceful district in Frankland, largely due to your guild's relationship with the White Duke. The clause in the Blacksmith's Guild charter giving you the responsibility of talking to the duke was a stroke of genius."

"Genius, my arse," I said. "Maybe for the rest of the commoners in Abertee, but it makes us Archers look like troublemakers. Wish I knew which wiseass thought that up."

"It was the first White Duke."

"Eh?"

"The duke did not trust the lackeys and advisors who depended on him for their livelihoods to tell him the unvarnished truth about conditions in his domains. He insisted on that clause in the charter to force the plainspoken blacksmiths he did trust to report issues to him before they grew too big to handle easily. That clause was not for your benefit; it was for the duke's."

I gaped at him.

The Fire Warlock said, "We can't use that. None of the nobles understand. Not even the current White Duke."

Master Jean said, "You may find he has begun to appreciate it, even if he cannot articulate the reason."

The Fire Warlock shrugged. "It won't help."

"Not with the nobles, true. But it will bear weight with the Water Office, and it is the Water Office we must convince first."

"Forget it, then." I stood up. "The Water Office has never given the likes of me an even chance. You might as well throw me out of the country now."

The Fire Warlock said, "No dice. If I throw you out, the Office won't let me bring you back in when you change your mind, and I'm betting you will. I'll ask you again on the first of September, after the Locksmith has unlocked the Water Office. In the meantime, don't set foot outside the Fortress. It you do, the Frost Maiden will ice you before you even know she's there."

The housekeeper, a Mrs Cole, offered me a room near the top of the Fortress, but I said I'd rather be in something simpler and smaller, so she led me down the stairs to the guards' barracks, as far away from the Fire Warlock's study as I could get.

The sweet music of hammers on metal filled the air in the space behind the walls. After the housekeeper left, I followed my ear to the smithy. I ducked in, and it went quiet inside. Everybody turned and stared at me.

"Get back to work, you morons," the master smith bellowed. He nodded at me. "You the swordsmith?"

"Doesn't seem right to call me that. I'd only had the seal one day before I had to run. Never even saw the guild rules."

"Guild rules. Eh." He spat into the forge. "Ever make a helmet?"

"Nae."

"Grab a hammer. We'll show you."

When I followed the smiths into the hall for dinner, it went quiet, too. I sat down at an empty table, but they filled in around me, talking about getting ready for the meeting in Paris. They eyed me, but didn't ask questions. I wouldn't have known what to say about why I was there, if they had.

Being back in a smithy was a relief, and I put in a good day's work. Thinking about helmets was better than thinking about standing trial, or thinking about Hazel. I had lost muscle tone in nearly two months on the run, and went to sleep that night on a real bed, almost big enough, with a sore back and an arm like jelly. Not even the heat and thunder, or fretting about the fix I was in, kept me awake.

The next morning, I had just gotten into a good rhythm when one of the Fire Warlock's servants stepped in. "Master Duncan?"

"That's me."

"The Flame Mage wants to see you."

The Flame Mage

"Do come in." The wizard dropped his pen and held out a hand. "I'm Master Sven. Oh, wait." He grabbed a rag and wiped his hands, leaving blue streaks. "Sorry. Ink gets everywhere."

"Aye," I said. "Like soot. Mine aren't clean, either."

He shrugged, and we shook. He moved a stack of books from a chair onto the windowsill. "Have a seat."

"Those spindly legs couldn't hold you up, much less me."

"The Fire Warlock usually throws himself into it. If it held up for him…"

The chair didn't break when I eased onto it. It didn't even creak. Magic. Had to be.

He said, "I didn't expect you so soon, or I would've cleared a spot."

"The fellow that delivered the message said the Flame Mage wanted to see me, so I figured I'd better get my arse on up here."

His cheeks got red. "He said that?"

"Nae. He was too polite to say arse."

"I meant, calling me the Flame Mage. That was very…I mean, I'm honoured. I'm the junior Flame Mage, after the Fire Warlock Emeritus."

"The who?"

"Warlock Quicksilver. The retired Fire Warlock."

"You just called him three different things, besides Flame Mage."

"That's true. And all I'm known for is having my nose in a book. Maybe that's why…" He shrugged. "Anyway, I didn't mean it to be a summons you had to respond to immediately. The Fire Warlock thought you would have more questions, and asked me to answer them, if I could, since he and Quicksilver are both busy."

"Oh. Well, I do have a few."

"Fire away."

"Start with reminding me what a mage is."

"Ah. A wizard has magic talent, but may not give a hoot about theory—how the magic works. A scholar of magical theory cares about how it works, but may not have any talent himself. A mage is both a ranking wizard and an authority on the theory."

"So you're a warlock, too."

"No, I'm a level four, just short of being a warlock, thank God. I can't walk through the fire."

"Thank God, you say. I thought all you fire wizards want to be the Fire Warlock."

"Not me. I'm glad I've escaped that horror. Oh, I admit it would be more convenient to jump through the fire than to take the stairs or wander around lost in the Earth Guild tunnels whenever I need to travel. And there are times when I find it galling that a woman and a boy half my age can do things I can't. But I want a normal family life. Play with my grandchildren. Put my feet up in my old age and die in my sleep. Not spend my life as a celibate warrior fighting with the king and spending every hour wondering who's trying to kill me now. Or which will get me first, the Empire, or the Fire Office."

"Huh. Guess I'd never thought about it."

"You thought it would be great to have everyone cower whenever you get angry and jump to do whatever you want."

"Folk already cower when I get angry. Can't say I like that much."

He grinned. "You won't get that response often in the Fortress or Blazes. Fire wizards tend to only fear more powerful fire wizards."

"I can believe that. Even if you're not a warlock, I gather you're in on this madness about rebuilding the Water Office."

"Yes. I've been studying the spells these past two years, getting ready."

"Then tell me this. If you're going to take it apart, why the hell put the frostbitten thing back together? Stop while you're ahead, and give the commoners a break."

"Would it be good for the commoners? If the Water Guild didn't administer justice, who would?"

"I thought…"

"No, you didn't think. Somebody, somewhere, has to make sure murderers and rapists and arsonists and all the other misanthropic cretins don't run amok and destroy all that's good in Frankland. The other Offices, for one, and the king, for another, would insist on somebody picking up the slack. And who would that be?"

"Uh…"

"It would be the nobles—that's who. The king would be ecstatic over taking it away from the magic guilds, and he wouldn't let the commoners have a hand in it. Would Frankland be better off with justice in the hands of the nobles, and only the nobles?"

I stared out the window, clenching and unclenching my jaw. "There's got to be some other way."

"Not that I can see, and I've been studying this problem for two years, Warlock Quicksilver and the Frost Maiden for decades. Given the constraints imposed by the other Offices, those are our two choices: the Water Guild or the nobles. I trust the Water Guild more than I trust the nobles."

I gave him a hard look. "My ears are playing tricks on me. I just heard a fire wizard say he trusts the Water Guild."

"Hard to believe, I know. I compared them to the nobles, so that wasn't saying much. And no, I'm not happy with all that authority in the hands of a gaggle of prissy, frigid water witches. But…look, the Water Guild is three-quarters commoners. Their Guild Council is all commoners. They have friends and relatives who aren't in the guild, and they're not a bit happy about the broken Water Office, either. They're the ones pushing the hardest to fix it, and they're defying direct orders from the king to leave it alone."

"I'd like to believe you, but…"

"I've had a hard time coming to terms with it myself. Nothing ever changes in Frankland, you know. But things are changing, whether we see them or not. Whether we like them or not. What we're trying to do is make the changes go in the direction we want."

We, he said. Wizards and witches, he meant. I hadn't heard them offering to share power with commoners, and I'd not believe them if they did.

"Did the Frost Maiden really call the king a halfwit?"

The mage grinned. "I wasn't there, but that's what the Fire Warlock said. The only surprise is that she said it to his face."

"I've got another question for you." I dug in my pocket. "About the swordsmith's seal. I tried to send it home to the guild, but it came back to me. I was wondering…"

"For God's sake, don't send it away again. It might not return to you a second time."

"The swordsmiths can't be happy with me hanging onto it, pretending I'm one of them."

He snorted. "They're not upset with you. They're angry at the king. That royal charter gives them—you—special privileges he's trampled on. Grandmaster Henry, the head of your guild, said they'll back you whichever choice you make."

"Decent of him."

"So hold on to that seal. Strong magic backs the Swordsmiths' Guild, and it could tip the balance in your favour if you do agree to be the test case."

I turned the seal over and over, rolling it between my fingers. "Strong magic, you say. What other magic is on this seal?"

He held out his hand. "Let me see." He closed his fingers over it and leaned back, staring at the ceiling. "The usual Earth Guild spells to foil theft. It won't wear out. Or leave an impression for anyone but its owner." He handed it back. "That's all I can detect."

"So where's the strong magic? Grandmaster Clive said I have enough magic to make a sword, but I don't have much."

He rolled his eyes. "A swordsmith, of all people, ought to know better. It doesn't take magic to make a sword."

"Eh?"

"The royal guild is about control of the swords, not making them."

"You're joking."

"I am not. Any good smith could make a sword. You don't because you've been told so often that you can't. The nobles told everyone that centuries ago because they don't want Frankland flooded with swords."

I closed my mouth, and swallowed. "But the spells…"

"Well, yes. The swordsmiths do beat spells into the swords. But they don't have to. How is a sword different from a big knife or an axe? They're all pieces of steel with sharp edges. Any of them could kill without magic."

"Aye, that's so." An army of commoners with unmagicked swords… That would be—

"But don't get any ideas about arming commoners. Think what the Fire Office would do to them."

"Aye. Kill all us troublemakers, not just leave nasty burns that scar over."

"Right."

"Shame."

"And now I've let the cat out of the bag. The Swordsmith's Guild will have to keep you."

I shrugged. "It won't matter. I'll be out of Frankland before long. But I am curious. What happened to the spell that makes the aristos' swords break? You know, when they're used against the folk the aristos have sworn to protect. Why haven't any swords shattered lately?"

"Now that's a good question." His fingers drummed on his desk. "A very good question."

"What's a good question?" The fire lad shouldered open the half-closed door and dropped a load of papers on the desk. The mage winced.

I said, "Why don't the nobles' swords shatter any more? I've not heard of one shattering in centuries, and God knows, they ought to."

"If we had time," the lad said, "we could find out, but we don't. We have to get ready for tomorrow."

The mage sighed. "I know that."

I went to the door. "Time for me to leave."

"Afraid so. Tomorrow will be a busy day. I'll be happy to talk to you again, afterwards. In the meantime, I can arrange for Granny Hazel to come here."

"Don't."

His eyebrows rose. "She's been quite worried. I'm sure she—"

"Nae. I don't want to see her."

The mage and the fire lad exchanged looks. The mage shrugged.

The fire lad dropped a stack of books from the windowsill onto the chair, and scrambled into the window. "Do me a favour. When you get back to Abertee—"

"If."

"When."

I leaned against the doorjamb. "You're pretty cocky. What makes you think I'll ever get back there?"

"I'm a wizard. Some wizards are seers, and—"

The mage snorted. The lad grinned. "All right. I'm not one. But the Fire Warlock is, and he says you'll—"

"He hopes Master Duncan will," the mage said. "He doesn't know. His visions stopped when he became Fire Warlock."

The lad's eyes went round. The mage went on. "No reliable seer has had foreknowledge of the events of the last two months. We're groping in the dark."

The lad was turning green. I took pity on him. "Supposing I get to go home. If you fix the Water Office, and I do what the Fire Warlock wants, and it all works out all right—and those ifs are as big as Storm King. Supposing all that, what do you want?"

"Shut that snake, Reverend Angus, up before I go and torch him."

"The hell you say. I told him to get out of Abertee."

"You botched it. You should have sent someone you trusted with him to Edinburgh. He left Crossroads with a group headed there, but two hours north he left them and doubled back. Been preaching against witches and wizards ever since. Hey, don't hit me."

I pushed a fist against the wall. "Sorry, lad. I'm not pissed off at you. That good-for-nothing is nothing but trouble. What has he got against you magic folk anyway?"

"Envy," Master Sven said. "He's a disappointed air wizard. You've heard him talk. Nothing he says makes sense afterwards, but he's persuasive while he's talking. For a few minutes, he almost had me convinced we'd be better off without the Water Guild. That's air magic, and strong, too."

"If he's an air wizard, why isn't he in their guild?"

"They wouldn't take him. He can't stir up a breeze, and that's their minimum requirement. As far as they're concerned, he's nothing. Fools. Not that the Fire Guild is any better. We won't accept anyone who can't light a candle."

"So now he hates all wizards because they wouldn't admit he's one."

"Yes. Does that surprise you?"

"Nae. I've seen it before. So he's still in Abertee. Are folk listening to him?"

"Not many in Abertee," the fire lad said. "Not after you told them about Blacksburg. He's been staying at an inn on the Roman road, preaching to people passing through. The Fire Warlock's had me keeping an eye on him, and after listening to him a couple of times, I was ready to shove him in the volcano."

"The Fire Warlock ought to do something about him."

"He'd love to," the mage said, "but he and the king are already nose-to-nose on too many other issues, and the king's protecting the son-of-a-bitch. Claims he has a right to express alternative views. Ass!"

"Stirring up trouble like he does… Encouraging folk to riot ought to be a crime."

"It is. Sedition. Incitement. Sorceress Lorraine—the Frost Maiden, that is—would love to sink her claws in him. But until the Water Office is fixed, it won't do any good."

"And if you think I can do something about him, you're nuts."

The fire lad said. "Maybe you can keep people from going to hear him."

The mage flipped through the stack of papers. "Unlikely, and we're wasting time. As you reminded me, we have work to do for tomorrow. Master Duncan, wait!"

"Aye?"

"I will put a spell on the kitchen fire tomorrow morning so everyone here can see the proceedings at the meeting in Paris. You should watch."

"Thanks, but nae. I know what happened. I've no stomach for seeing it again."

"Yes, I understand that, but there are surprises in store for the nobles. For the commoners, too."

I shrugged. "Fine, but not interested. It won't affect me."

"I beg to disagree. It will affect you."

The fire lad added, "You'll be sorry if you don't watch."

Maggie and the Frost Maiden

The forge was cold, the alleyway empty. The guards—every single one stationed in the Fortress, as far as I could tell, except for a lone man at the main gate—had gone to Paris. I set to work at the grindstone, putting an edge on a battle-axe, but kept sneaking glances over my shoulder at the empty smithy, and before long set the axe down and rode the stairs to the kitchen. Might as well see what the surprises were. I didn't have a good excuse not to.

Officers' wives, the Fire Warlock's lackeys, and several dozen others crowded around the fire. I looked over their heads, and through the fire saw a ballroom packed with aristos.

Mrs Cole counted stragglers. "Good, that's everybody. It's time, and Master Thomas has something to say before they start."

The man beside her waved a folded paper. "Master Sven asked me to read this to you. I don't know what it says either; he bespelled it so no one could read it too early."

He unfolded it and read, "No man in Frankland, royal, noble, wizard, or commoner, can force himself on an unwilling woman and hope to evade justice. We learned this at our mothers' knee, and we learned a lie. Nobles can, and do, rape without penalty."

I swung around from the fire and gave him a hard look. He stopped reading and stared at the paper.

"That's nonsense," someone said. "Isn't it?"

"Maybe not," I said. "It would explain a few things. Keep reading."

Master Thomas cleared his throat, and read about the magic the aristos were using that let them get away scot free with doing what any man who'd ever loved his mum or his sister ought to be ashamed of thinking about. He read on, giving dates for Lord Edmund's crimes.

It hadn't taken much brain power to figure out he'd helped himself to Fiona, and what he'd had in mind for Maggie. I'd wanted to believe it wasn't so. Hearing it from a mage put paid to that forlorn hope. When I hit the brat, I swear I didn't intend murder. If that blow hadn't killed him, I'd go after him now, with intent.

I left the kitchen and went back to the barracks, where I took an axe to a pile of firewood and made matchsticks. I was still swinging when Master Thomas and Mrs Cole came down.

"You haven't heard, have you?" she said.

"Heard what?"

"Your sister's on trial for slander."

Maggie was part of the counter-magic, they'd said. She'd wanted every Frank to know that earl's whelp deserved what he got, they'd said. She'd made her accusation, that Lord Edmund had raped five women, in front of the king to make sure the aristos' dirty laundry got a good airing, they'd said.

What they didn't say was how Maggie came to be in the counter-magic, rubbing shoulders with warlocks and mages, but I could guess. Maggie was friendly with Hazel, and Hazel was friends with the Locksmith. When they needed a dupe to stand trial for them, they had picked an Archer. Naturally, given what fine, upstanding suckers we are.

I stayed by the fire all that long, hot day, shelling walnuts from a sack an officer's wife handed me. Needed for pastries, she'd said. Keep my hands too busy to break the crockery, she'd meant. No doubt Mrs Cole could snap her fingers, the shell would crack open, and the nutmeats would throw themselves wherever she wanted them.

Men and women drifted through the kitchen, stopped for a few minutes to listen to the lawyers wrangling, and drifted out again. Late in the afternoon they trickled back in and gathered around the fire. Mrs Cole inspected my work and offered me a venison pie. My belly rumbled, but I turned it down. I had no stomach for it.

The royals paraded back into the ballroom, and the trial began. I kept on shelling walnuts. I couldn't bear watching the filth on display. Listening made me glad I'd turned down the pie. Several watchers ran, heaving, from the kitchen.

When the Frost Maiden summoned Maggie, I moved closer to the fire and watched my baby sister kneel at that unfeeling witch's feet.

"The Water Office finds you guilty of slander," the Frost Maiden said. A roaring drowned out anything else she said before everything went black.

I lay flat on the floor beside the kitchen fire. "What the—"

"Quiet!" Mrs Cole snapped. She pinned me to the hearth with her wand, without looking down. I couldn't roll over or sit up, or make the slender rod budge. I turned my head to the fire and stared. A riot was in full roar in the ballroom, under the Fire Warlock's nose. Boots and cabbages flew. The mob howled. The Fire Warlock bellowed. Flames shot across the room. An aristo burned like Glenn Hoskins.

Mrs Cole waved a hand at the fire. The noise died. "That's enough. Out of my kitchen, all of you. Find something useful to do. They'll be bringing wounded guards home soon."

When the kitchen was quiet, with only Mrs Cole and Master Thomas leaning over me, she said, "You can talk now. I'll let you up if you promise not to go berserk again."

"My sister's in that mob."

"No, she's not. She's here in the Fortress. Warlock Quicksilver is grabbing everybody who can't protect themselves and bringing them here."

Master Thomas said, "Did you hear the sentence?"

"Nae. Just that she's guilty. Guilty, my arse! She told the truth."

"Yes, and after today it will be impossible for anyone, even the king, to argue the Water Office isn't broken and needs to be fixed."

"Is that why she was there? As whipping boy? So the magic folk in this re-forging nonsense could get the king's approval?"

He shook his head. "I don't know."

"Maybe they think they're clever, but it isn't fair to my sister."

"No, of course not. It doesn't seem like something Warlock Quicksilver would do. He's subtle, and devious sometimes, but fair."

I lay with my arm over my eyes and took long, slow breaths. "Tell me the sentence."

"She has to pay a whopping fine, and serve the earl for the rest of her life."

After a long silence, Mrs Cole lifted her wand from my chest. "When you're ready to see her, she's in the ballroom."

The ballroom was ablaze with lights. I tiptoed from one shadow to another on the walkway outside, looking for Maggie. I held my breath passing the knot of people around the king, but they watched the riot in the magic mirror on the far wall, and no one turned to look out the window.

Maggie sat on the floor, crying, beside a glass door. Hazel was on her knees beside her, stroking her hair.

I put my hands flat on the wall between the door and the last window, and leaned against it, breathing hard. If I dared show my face to the king, I'd walk in and tell Hazel off. It was bad enough she'd turned on me. She had no right to ruin Maggie's life, too.

Maggie scrambled to her feet. I peeked around the doorframe; an old woman and the new earl—Lord Edmund's brother—were coming.

Be damned if another highborn lout would get his paws on my sister. My carcass was due to be iced anyway. I grabbed the door and drew in a good breath, getting ready to roar.

Green light flashed, and I couldn't move or make a sound. I was off-balance, and should have fallen over, but stayed upright, unmoving, with my fist gouging splinters from the doorframe. All I could do was swear in my head like Old Nick, while the bastard ordered my sweet baby sister to...

While he ordered her to go home, do whatever she wanted, and not bother him again.

How was I supposed to know a louse like Edmund could have a brother that acted like a...well, like a nobleman?

Green light winked from the old woman's hand. The Earth Mother, that's who it was. Her magic held me still. The yank I'd given the door would tear if off its hinges if I didn't stop it when the magic let me go. The green flash came again. I leaned in, and caught the door full in the face.

I rested my head against the door and felt for my nose. The Earth Mother tut-tutted, and waggled her fingers. My nose snapped back into place, and the blood pouring out disappeared.

"Thank you, ma'am," I mumbled.

Great. The king wanted me dead, and I'd made a fool of myself in front of three of Their Wisdoms. If the head air wizard showed up, no doubt I could make it a full slate.

Nobody besides the Earth Mother seemed to have noticed. She walked away with the earl and his mouth-watering wife. Hazel whispered to Maggie, who spun around and threw herself at me. She laughed and cried on my shoulder. I held her, kissed her hair, and watched Hazel walk away without turning to look at me.

When Maggie's sobs dwindled to little hiccups, I said, "What are you doing, mixed up in this mess?"

"I hated what that miserable aristo did to Fiona. What he almost did to me. Hated people laughing when I said you were trying to protect me. I hated all the lies. I—we—thought getting rid of the lies would make things better."

"Doesn't look like it did."

"No, it didn't." She mumbled into my shoulder. "I don't know why not."

"Guess I can't give you grief—much, anyway—for trying to help. I'll save it for Hazel."

Maggie straightened up. "Are you out of you mind? Why?"

"For talking you into it. Those witches shouldn't have dragged a no-magic lass like you into their mess."

"They didn't drag me. You think I can't poke my nose into trouble on my own? I'm an Archer, for God's sake. You, of all people… Hazel tried to talk me out of it. Said our family had already lost too much. But I insisted—I wanted to help."

I patted her hair. "Sorry, sorry. I'm proud of you for telling the truth. You did fine. It's just that…I don't know what to think. I've been wondering for days now why Hazel turned on me, and then you get mixed up in this. You know—you piss off a witch, and things go to hell…"

Maggie pulled away. The light from the ballroom lit up one angry eye. "Turned on you? What gave you that idea?"

"She told the Fire Guild how to find me."

"Aye, but—"

"And the runes said she'd be happy there, so it must not have bothered her much."

"Happy, my arse. When Granny Mildred found out, she sent her packing. Between that and fretting over you, she's making herself sick, crying."

"Serves her right for ratting on me."

Maggie slapped me. "Duncan, you are an idiot sometimes. Here you are in the Fortress, where the Frost Maiden can't get you, and the Fire Warlock willing to take you to the border and save you God-knows how many months and pairs of boots, and you're pissed off at Hazel for helping you get here? When the fuss started, with the king ordering everybody in the Water Guild out on the hunt for you, and offering a reward big enough to buy half of Crossroads, we were sure you were icicles. When Hazel told us she'd taught you mindwarping, and asked for Doug's advice, he said she should tell the Fire Guild."

My own family had turned on me? Nae, I couldn't believe that. "Doug what?"

"He said you'd be safer with the Fire Guild than on your own. I had a hard time at first believing he said that, but he was right. I don't know what he would have said if he'd known what she didn't tell us."

"What didn't she tell you?"

"I heard it today from a water witch. Teaching you mindwarping magic counts as aiding and abetting a fugitive. Hazel has to stand trial, too."

I reeled backwards. "Nobody told me... She didn't say..."

"Of course she didn't, you halfwit. If you'd known, would you have let her teach you?"

"Hell, no." I ran along the line of windows. Only a few people were left. I charged in and grabbed the fire lad by the collar. "Granny Hazel—where is she? She was here."

"She left for the tunnels a while ago."

"Which way?"

He jerked a thumb. "By the Fire Warlock's study."

The magic stairs had seemed slow, but they sped up as I ran, taking them three at a time. Near the top I was almost flying. I yelled, "Hazel, wait. Granny Hazel."

The landing at the top was empty, and cold. A knock on the Fire Warlock's door brought no answer. The breeze made no noise. The only light came from stars and a quarter moon. There was no sign an earth witch had been through only a little earlier. It would have been easier to believe no one had set foot there in a hundred years.

Stepping onto the stairs to go back down felt like falling off the edge of the world.

Maggie and Mrs Cole were waiting at the ballroom. Mrs Cole promised to have Warlock Snorri take Maggie home in the morning, and they left together, to find Maggie a room for the night. My footsteps echoed in the empty ballroom, but the magic mirror was just a mirror. When I walked out onto the terrace, the lamps blew out behind me. Other lights glowed, here and there in the Fortress, and down in Blazes, but they were far away. Even sleeping rough in a forest or hedgerow, with the Water Guild after me, I'd not felt so alone. There were always small bodies—foxes, field mice, rabbits—making soft sounds in the night. Here there was nothing, not even a breeze.

I sighed, and turned away from the ballroom. A woman, silver in the moonlight, waited by the stairs. I froze.

"Grandmaster Duncan Archer," the Frost Maiden said, "I beg the favour of a word with you."

September First

That fool Fire Warlock said I was safe in the Fortress. I backed into the wall.

"Do not fear," the Frost Maiden said. "Even if I wished you harm, which I do not, I hold no authority here. The Fortress shields you, as it has shielded other men, far more wicked than you."

The Frost Maiden I'd heard stories about would have iced me, Fortress or no. I edged towards a door. "I wouldn't know about that, ma'am. Your Wisdom. What do you want? Er, sorry, ma'am. Didn't mean to be rude."

A flick of her hand sent blue light dancing along the walls. "The current and former Fire Warlocks have both asked you to be the test case when we demonstrate for the king the soundness of the re-forged Water Office. On the Water Guild's behalf, I add my voice to theirs, and ask you, nay, beg you, to reconsider your refusal. You are Frankland's best hope for a verdict that will satisfy all classes."

Her face was in the shadows. Maybe she meant it. Maybe she wanted another crack at icing me. I felt behind me for a latch. "Why me?"

"We have identified few other test cases fit for the purpose and, in comparison to the lives of the other accused men and women, yours is head and shoulders above the rest."

A Frost Maiden with a bent for bad jokes. Who would've believed it?

"Further," she said, "powerful magic is gathering around you."

"Burn it." My hand found the latch and eased the door open. "I'm not a wizard."

"You are a wizard, but not a powerful one on your own."

"On my own... Look, ma'am, you know what happens when somebody tries to use magic more powerful than they can handle. They're cinders. Or ice."

"Not always. The king has no talent, but the magic of his position is at his command. The magic of the common mundanes was also at his command once, but as he abandoned them, their magic has abandoned him. That magic is not visible, but it is real, and strong, and has been seeking an outlet. This summer, the commoners adopted you as their new champion, and the magic is striving to use you to accomplished its ends."

"Frostbite! Oh, damn. Sorry, ma'am. Er, Your Wisdom."

"Should I take offence at your language? If so, three quarters of Frankland would be shivering by the fire on this, the hottest night of a torrid summer. I have lived for more than a century with the names of my guild's tools the most provocative terms in common use, more offensive even than references to sexual acts or eternal damnation. If I dared let such language wound, I should never have shouldered the burden of this frostbitten Office."

I gaped, then closed my mouth and swallowed, twice. "Sorry, Your Wisdom, but I don't know what you were talking about just now. Commoners haven't got magic. That's why we're commoners."

"Nonsense. All living creatures have spirit, and will. That is the essence of life, and of magic. An individual mundane has little, but large numbers acting together have much."

"Aye, sure. If you say so. And how do you use it?"

She spread her hands wide. "I do not know. That magic falls in the Earth Guild's domain, and they do not share their secrets with the Water Guild."

"And they'd share them with me instead? Nae." I started to shake. The door rattled. I let go. "What you're saying, ma'am, is if the Water Office doesn't kill me, this other magic that's building up will, because I won't know how to use it. I'll be in the way when it starts pushing."

"That is…possible. More probable is that the magic will shield you, and somehow you will bring it to bear on the Water Office."

"But you don't know how."

"No, I do not."

"It's not your life at stake here when things go bad, and you've already had your claws in me and mine—first Maggie and now Granny Hazel. Sorry, ma'am, but you better find some other dupe. You've convinced me the smartest thing for me to do is to hold the Fire Warlock to his promise to take me out of Frankland and make tracks for New London."

Maybe I imagined her shoulders sagged. Very softly, she said, "If you will not, who will?" Water spread out at her feet.

"Wait! Ma'am…"

"Yes?"

"Granny Hazel. Does she…are you…"

"That wretched earth witch. The Water Guild owes her a debt for saving your life, but the Water Office will not let the Earth Guild suppose it will ignore others overstepping the bounds of the truce. She must pay a penalty for teaching you mindwarping. I hope you can understand that."

"No, ma'am, I can't. You want me to help you. If I do, will you let her go?"

She lifted her hands, fingers splayed out wide, rigid. I held my breath.

Her hands sank back to her sides. "The Water Office does not bargain. You cannot pay for her transgressions."

"But she was just trying to help. She's a healer. Frankland needs her. Icing her would—"

"Icing her? Don't be ridiculous. We certainly will not deprive Frankland of a fine healer. Aiding a fugitive is not a capital crime."

I grabbed the doorframe and held on, before my knees buckled. "Thank you, ma'am. Did she really save my life?"

"No, fool, she has to stand trial because we enjoy making people miserable." She drew in a sharp breath, held it for a few seconds, then let it out. "I beg your pardon. That was uncalled for."

"It's all right, ma'am. You're sounding more like, uh…"

"As you expected? Thank you so much."

I winced. "Sorry, ma'am. It's hard to know when you're joking, when everything you say comes out sounding as cool as spring water."

"The Fire Warlock has expressed the same complaint." She sighed. "If Granny Hazel had not been instrumental in enabling you to evade our net, we would not need to charge her with aiding a fugitive, would we?"

"Nae, ma'am, I guess not."

"And later, her advice to the Fire Guild let Warlocks Snorri and Quicksilver snatch you away from that fool, Cornelius, whose zeal would have brought disaster down on us. One can never say with absolute certainty what might have been, but in this case it is more than fair to say, yes, she saved your life, more than once."

"Thank you, ma'am. I'm real glad to know that. But the penalties…"

"Her trial will not be held until after the Water Office is rebuilt, and I will not conduct her trial myself. That is all I can do for her. Goodnight, Master Duncan."

Water lapped my shoes, and she was gone.

On the last day of August, the open air seared like a blast from the forge. I walked the western wall in the shadow of Storm King's shoulder, and beat on the stone blocks with my fists. The Fortress ignored my puny strikes, and bruising my hands didn't help shift the weight from my shoulders, or shake the homesickness. I was stuck on the southern flank of this bloody great mountain; I couldn't even look in the direction of Nettleton, frost it!

A whistling guard below butchered one of my favourite tunes. If there'd been loose stones, I might have dropped one on his head. I couldn't remember the last time I'd felt like whistling.

I should have agreed to do what that water witch wanted. Being stubborn wasn't doing me any good. If the Fire Warlock threw me out of Frankland, I'd never go home again, ever. If I were their test case, at least they would bury me in Nettleton.

Wasn't much of a hero, was I, now that I had the chance? I didn't like being pushed around, that was all, and first the Fire Guild, and now the Frost Maiden, too, were pushing pretty hard. The Fire Warlock I didn't mind too much. Risking his life for Frankland gave him the right to ask others to. But the Frost Maiden…

To be fair, she wasn't supposed to risk her life, and God knows, I'd be ashamed if a woman got hurt while I stood by and did nothing. But when the riots came, she'd be safe in her Crystal Palace, far away from the mobs. The rest of the Water Guild would be in danger, if they couldn't get there in time, but frost me if I would risk my life for the likes of that ass Cornelius, who had done his best to see me iced.

Even after sunset, hot air filled the space between the mountain and the curtain wall with the weight of wool blankets. I cursed the weather, the Fire Warlock, the king, the forge, and the guard at supper who'd commented on Maggie's good looks. Lying down turned my bed into a sweaty bog. I picked up my pillow and mattress and rode the stairs. Two flights short of the Fire Warlock's study, the air turned cool. I bedded down on the landing and dreamed of water witches, cold beauties luring me to my doom.

Daybreak's hammer-strike jolted me awake, and I rolled to my feet, swearing. The guards' quarters behind the wall were still in deep shadow, and would be for another hour, but I had no hope of getting back to sleep. Today was September first, the day the Fire Warlock was going to demand an answer. As if I had a real choice. The answer I'd have to give made my head ache and my heart pound. And folk called me brave. Fools.

At breakfast, the cook handed out scorched toast and sludge for coffee, and barked at everyone who complained. Guards who had ribbed each other at supper traded glares. A pair of sergeants came to blows when one made too much noise agreeing with the other.

Sweat fouled our grip and by mid-morning made the smithy stink like Blacksburg. The master growled at his striker and the striker snarled back. The lad working the bellows mumbled curses until a smith cuffed him for talking too much.

A lightning flash caught me in mid-swing. Blinded, I froze. Other deafened, blinded men hunting for the way out smacked into me. When I could see again, I pulled everybody's irons out of the fire before following them out.

Babbling craftsmen and guards filled the lane between curtain wall and mountain. An officer elbowed through and climbed onto a barrel, waved his arms, and yelled for quiet. "Clear the lane. Get back to work."

"Meaning he doesn't know what happened either," the smith next to me grumbled. We drifted towards the smithy, not eager to go back into the airless oven.

"It was the coven unlocking the Water Office," another man said.

"No," a third said, "it was lightning. The Fire Office wouldn't let them."

A farrier said, "It's a sign we'll be punished for our arrogance."

I left them arguing and ducked in, but I'd not had my mind on my craft, and this hadn't helped. An hour later, when the Fire Warlock's voice in my head ordered me to the ballroom, I was ready to get it over with. I pulled my work out of the fire and put my tools away. The other smiths were doing the same, or raking out the firepit. We walked out into the lane, and joined the queue for the stairs.

In the ballroom, the guards lined up along the back wall. I took a spot in a corner, under a balcony, and looked over my shoulder at the gilt-edged mirror. Better not get too close, or Mrs Cole would chew me out for fouling the mirror with soot.

The townsfolk swarmed in on our heels. Even hurrying, almost an hour passed from the summons until everyone was packed in.

A tower of fire rose and died. The Fire Warlock stood on the stage, holding up a hand for quiet. His ring gave off waves of light, red as blood.

Blood? That was silly. Cinders don't bleed. A corpse the Frost Maiden had iced didn't bleed either.

The Fire Warlock crossed his arms, with the ring tucked in. "Sorry to," he croaked. He cleared his throat and started again. "Sorry to drag you away from your work, but you need to know what happened. You felt that magical lightning bolt a while ago. We didn't warn you it was coming, because we didn't know what would happen. That was the lock on the Water Office being released."

He waited with his arms crossed, unsmiling, for the noise to die. "When you leave here, make a holiday of it. It's something to celebrate. The biggest change Frankland's seen in a thousand years." He walked across the stage, tugging at his beard. "I hope someday I'll be able to join you in celebrating, but it won't be today.

"The first Locksmith cast a black magic spell on the Office to attack the Officeholder responsible for releasing it. We knew there was danger involved, but we didn't know exactly what it was, and Sorceress Lorraine insisted we keep it quiet to prevent rumours and panics. We had some wild rumours anyway. What actually happened wasn't as bad as it could have been, but it was bad enough."

He wiped his eyes. "Sorceress Lorraine looked like she'd run into a lunatic with a meat cleaver. She has dozens of gashes on her right side— her torso and leg, but the worst…"

He stood still for a few seconds with his eyes closed. "The worst was her right arm. It was hacked to bits. It isn't there anymore."

With my eyes closed, I saw a woman awash in blood. I backed into the mirror and put my hands over my ears, but couldn't block out his voice.

His voice shook. "The Locksmith was burned, all over, the worst I've ever seen. All that's left of her right arm is charred bone. The power needed to release the lock was tremendous—much more than she had ever handled before—but no one else could.

"Those two witches came close to dying, but they're going to live. Warlock Quicksilver... My friend Jean..." The ballroom might have been empty, it was so quiet. "Quicksilver let down his own shields to take the brunt of the blast for his wife. We don't know yet if he's going to live or die."

The Fire Warlock pulled out a handkerchief and blew his nose. Turned his eyes towards the ceiling. "Sorceress Lorraine and the two warlocks were the only people injured. For which we should be grateful, I suppose. The Earth Guild has its best healers at work on them. It will be a while before we know what they can do."

He walked to the back of the stage, then returned to the edge, facing us. "There's something else you need to know. The Locksmith read the spell two years ago and warned us about the dangers. Both witches have known for two years that releasing the lock might kill them, but the country is in so much trouble they said we had to go ahead and do it. Don't let anybody tell you someone made them do it. It was their decision. They told the rest of the coven they believed they had to. This is why the Locksmith and Warlock Quicksilver have been calling down the lightning every night since they got back from their honeymoon. They've been building up the amount of power she could handle to give her a chance of surviving. He expected to die today, and would have considered it a fair price, as long as she lived.

"These three are the biggest heroes Frankland has had in centuries. Anybody who says anything disrespectful about any of them, Sorceress Lorraine included, will have to answer to me. Understand?"

Heads nodded. Voices whispered, "Yes, sir."

He roared, "Do you understand?"

We roared, "Yes, sir."

"Good. Any questions?"

A wizard near the front raised a shaking hand. "What about rebuilding the Water Office? Can they do that without the Frost...Sorceress Lorraine, that is?"

"It'll be better if she can help, but she has a trained apprentice, and the Water Guild Council knows what's needed. She made sure beforehand they could handle it without her, since she thought she might not survive.

"Everybody involved is in too much shock—and the Earth Guild is too busy—to start on it today. They'll tear it down as soon as Mother

Celeste decides she can spare a mage from tending the wounded."

A guard a few paces from me was next. "Is there anything we can do for Miss Lucinda, uh, I mean, Mrs, uh, the Locksmith?"

The Fire Warlock said, "She'll blister your ears, George, if you ever stop calling her Miss Lucinda. But no, there's nothing you can do. You'd just get in the healers' way."

"But you said her arm was ruined. If the Earth Guild could put it on her, I'd let her have mine."

I gaped at the guard. The townsfolk turned to stare.

Another guard yelled, "That's a damn-fool idea. How'd she look with your big, hairy arm on her little shoulder?"

Other guards shouted the second one down. "She can have mine. I'm smaller—it'd fit better." "The Frost Maiden could have my arm."

"Quiet!" the Warlock roared. "George, that's very generous of you, but it wouldn't work. The fit matters—matters a lot, I'd guess. I hadn't been planning on saying anything yet, but the Earth Guild is trying to regrow her own arm."

The muttering grew to a roar. A captain shouted over the din. "Your Wisdom, we've all sworn to serve the country, at the cost of our own lives if necessary. I think I speak for all my men, that giving up a hand or an arm seems like a small sacrifice..."

Pompous ass. The guard, now, I respected him. It couldn't be easy to make an offer like that. If I lost my arm, I wouldn't be a smith any longer, and I wouldn't know how to be anything else. Might as well be dead.

The Fire Warlock disappeared. I rested my head against the mirror and stared at the painted salamanders dancing across the underside of the balcony. They turned disgusted eyes on me, calling me coward.

Silver perfection, she'd been, in the moonlight. Whoever had set that wicked spell must be burning in Hell. It's a mortal sin to ruin something so beautiful.

A door slamming echoed in the empty ballroom. I hadn't noticed them leaving. I caught up to the stragglers, waiting their turn on the stairs, but my feet carried me past and put me on the stairs going up. I came out of my daze only when I reached the door to the Fire Warlock's study. I tilted my head back and gawked at the lintel far out of reach. I should have noticed when I'd been there before, but I'd had too many other shocks then. The only reason to make a door that tall would be to scare the dickens out of everybody coming to see the Fire Warlock. I set my jaw. I didn't have to prove it worked.

The doors swung open. The Fire Warlock said, "Come on in, Master Duncan."

I marched to his desk and looked down at him. His eyes were bloodshot, his face haggard. He had his chin on his left hand, staring down at the other, stretched out on his desktop. His ring's deep red pulsing made my eyes water.

The Warlock slapped his left hand over the ring. "What do you want?"

"You don't need to ask. You knew I was here."

"I'm not a mind reader. Nobody steps on that last flight without the Fortress letting me know they're coming. That's all. What can I do for you?"

"Oh. Well. You said you were going to ask me again after she'd unlocked the Water Office. When you said come to the ballroom, at first I thought that's what you wanted."

"Yeah, I did say that." The Warlock frowned at his hands. "I hadn't thought about you at all today, until just now. You should be grateful. So, what's it going to be?"

"If you'll do something for me, you can take my case to the Frost Maiden, Your Wisdom."

His expression lightened. "I knew you'd come around. Didn't have much choice after today's news, did you? Couldn't let yourself be bested by a guard, or worse, a couple of women."

"That'll make it easier to live with, sure, but I guess I made up my mind a couple of days ago. I just kept hoping to find a way out of it."

The Warlock leaned back and studied me. "Why did you decide to do it? And I shouldn't get excited until I've heard what you want in exchange. I'm not making any promises."

I stared at the wall behind the Warlock's head. "Somebody's got to do it, sooner or later. If you think I have the best chance, I'd be a coward to run away and stick it to somebody else…"

"And?"

Sweat trickled down my nose. Never, ever, lie to a warlock. "It's the only way I can see of ever getting to go home again."

"You're right about that." The Warlock let out a long sigh. "Going home. I could use something so simple and straightforward to keep me going." He unclasped his hands and flattened both on the desk. "I've always expected to die from a lightning strike, like seventy-one Fire Warlocks before me. Maybe I've got mush for brains, but it doesn't seem as awful as those knives. I hope I have as much guts as Sorceress Lorraine, when it's time to unlock the Fire Office."

I yelped, "Not the Fire Office, too."

"Not now. Calm down. Think I'm a fool? Don't answer that."

I dropped into a chair, breathing hard. "You bastard. Don't scare me like that."

He smiled. "God, I hope you survive. You're about the only one outside of the Fire Guild Council that doesn't tiptoe around me."

"The king calls you names, too."

"How is a king like a swordsmith? He calls the Fire Warlock names? Well, no. The king means them."

"The Fire Office…"

"Has problems, too, and needs to be fixed. But that won't be for years yet. Assuming that Lucinda—the Locksmith—recovers, and is willing to go through this again."

I laughed. I felt guilty, later, but right then the relief was too strong. "Go through that again? You're nuts. A woman's not…"

The Warlock snorted and rolled his eyes.

"…not that stupid."

"You have a point. Now, you said you wanted me to do something for you."

I laid my hands flat on the desk and leaned in until my nose was only a foot from the Warlock's. "Find out what son-of-a-whore was responsible for setting that bastard on my sister and make him pay for it."

A flame burned in the Warlock's eyes. "I can't promise the Water Office will be fixed. That's what bringing this test case is all about."

"Aye. But promise you'll make an example of him in front of the king and aristo, too."

"You betcha." Fire crackled in his voice, though he wasn't loud. "That's one promise I'm happy to make."

Fortune's Whip
Cracks Again

A walkway, wide enough for three to walk abreast, ran along a line of bedrooms. Several guards stood at an open window like mourners at a funeral. The guard who had offered his arm was there. I got off the stairs and walked across to join them.

The Earth Mother and half-a-dozen healers sat in chairs around a bed, with their hands on the two bodies lying on it, both wrapped in white cloths. Earth Guild burn cloths, they had to be, not burial shrouds. Healers don't waste magic on dead bodies.

The healers were hard at work—eyes closed, nobody moving a muscle, except for one old wizard with an eye twitching. Hazel made no move to wipe away the tears streaming down her cheeks. An old witch with the same splash of freckles sat at the foot of the bed. My eyes moved on, then went back. I'd seen her before, in Blacksburg. She'd aged a quarter-century.

Another group of healers came along the walkway. We moved aside to let them into the bedroom. One newcomer joined the circle, and with a deep sigh, the old fellow with the twitch let go and stood up, carefully, like he was a hundred years old and all his joints hurt. He stood by the bed for a bit, running his hand over his right arm, then came out onto the walkway, leaving the door open. We surrounded him, whispering questions. I listened, and watched Hazel.

The second newcomer joined the circle, and after a moment, Hazel let go. She lurched to her feet, nearly knocking over her chair, threw one wild look towards me, and ran into the cold fireplace and disappeared.

Nobody was watching me. I followed her. With a push, the back wall of the fireplace swung open like a door to a cool cave, empty except for

Hazel. She hunched over on a chair and sobbed.

I'd heard the warnings; everybody has. Never touch an earth witch when she's carrying someone else's pain. But I'd been bounced around in a landslide, and walked away from it. I could take a lot. I touched her shoulders, and jerked my hand away, strangling a scream. A landslide was one thing. Grabbing an iron straight out of the forge was something else.

Hazel's head jerked up. "Duncan! What are you doing?"

The skin on my hand was red. It should have been an ugly mess of charred meat. I gritted my teeth, held my breath, and picked her up. Hell's bells. I whimpered like a kicked puppy but didn't let go, or pass out.

She beat on my chest, and tried to push away. "Duncan, are you mad?"

I saw stars, but the pain was already easing. I breathed again, in long ragged breaths, and sat down, holding her with my right arm and wiping sweat off my face with my left. I flexed my right hand. The blisters were already shrinking.

She stopped trying to push away. "Duncan, you shouldn't have done that."

"Just trying to make you feel better."

She blew her nose. Her tears had slowed. "You did, but you weren't prepared. The pain could have killed you. Made your heart stop."

"Aye, but it didn't. I figure I owed you."

"Owed me? For what?"

"For thinking you'd… Well, never mind."

"For giving you away?" Her tears flowed again. "But I did. I was so frightened for you. When the king offered that reward, I was beside myself. I didn't know what to do."

"I know. Maggie told me."

Her handkerchief was a sodden mess. I handed her my dry, sooty one. "Sorry it isn't any cleaner."

She smiled and blew her nose. Hiccupped a couple of times. My heart flipped over.

She said, "Warlock Snorri said you were angry, and I couldn't blame you."

"Shh. Don't kick yourself. You did the right thing. If you hadn't gone to the Fire Warlock, the Water Guild would have gotten me first, and I'd be dead."

"They might have, but—"

"Would have. The Frost Maiden said so."

Her eyes got huge. "You talked to Sorceress Lorraine?"

"Aye. She said the Water Guild owed you for saving my life."

Hazel breathed, "She said that?" Her eyes were big enough for a man to get lost in. Her mouth was open a little, begging for a kiss. I obliged.

She wrapped an arm around my neck and melted against me. For the length of a half-dozen hammer swings, I forgot the Frost Maiden, the Fire Warlock, even how far away Nettleton was. Then her grip went slack and she slid away. When her head came to rest on my shoulder, she was asleep.

I looked down at the sleeping lass. My lass. My witch. For an earth witch she was a featherweight. The Fire Warlock had said to make a holiday out of it. I had time to wait until she woke up.

Rustling skirts made me look up. Mother Astrid was walking towards me, rubbing her right hand, and scowling. I looked down at Hazel's freckles, up at Mother Astrid's, and tightened my grip. Whatever was coming, I'd be in deeper trouble if I dropped the lass in my arms.

Mother Astrid let out a long sigh. "I'm not angry at you, Master Duncan. I saw what you did. It was gallant of you. Not wise, but gallant."

"Thank you, ma'am. I never claimed to be wise."

"I appreciate what you did for my daughter, even if it wasn't wise." She frowned down at Hazel for a moment. "Sleep is what she needs most right now. I need sleep, too, but I would appreciate a few words with you, and there is nowhere better than this private chamber. Wait here."

Like I was going anywhere. I looked around at this cave as big as a ballroom and wondered where we really were. Not next to a bedroom, I was certain of that, but somewhere in the Fortress. Wrought iron chairs and scorch marks on the floor and walls stamped the room as Fire Guild property. It was too dim to see the ceiling, but there had to be scorch marks there, too.

I shifted my weight in the chair. Competent workmanship, but not comfortable. I could do better. Would do better. I kissed Hazel's hair, and dreamed.

Mother Astrid came back with a load of bedding. She spread a pallet on the floor, and after I laid Hazel on it, led me a distance away to another pair of chairs.

She stared at me as if she could read my soul. "You've agreed to be the test case."

"Aye, ma'am. I may be Frankland's biggest chump, but I said I would. How'd you know?"

"Powerful magic is gathering around you—"

"Frostbite! Sorry, ma'am. That's what the Frost Maiden said, too, and the idea of that pushing me around scares…" I stopped. Something had changed. The weight still pressed on my shoulders, but not as heavy, and I wasn't afraid, any longer, of being afraid. I'd be terrified on the day, but that didn't make me a coward.

She laid a hand on my arm. "You have done what the magic required, by agreeing to be the test case. It wants to break the royal's grip on justice in Frankland, and no one else has what it needs. If you had refused…" She shrugged. "It might have weighed you down so you couldn't leave Frankland. But you wouldn't have refused. It knew that when it picked you."

"Tell me about this weight, ma'am. The Frost Maiden said it was Earth Magic."

"It is. Haven't you heard, 'How is the king like a swordsmith?'"

"Aye. 'He has a hammer as well as a sword.' That's never made any sense to me, ma'am."

"The hammer is the weight of public opinion—the source of the king's authority, and the power he controls. If used wisely, it is a force as powerful as any of the four Offices, but it has abandoned him, as he has abandoned us."

"I've felt for months like there's a weight on my shoulders I can't shake off. Ever since my Uncle Will died. He used to say he felt like he was carrying all the souls in Abertee."

"He was. The Blacksmith's Guild in Abertee has assumed that responsibility. When you shouldered responsibility in Blacksburg as well, the king's abandoned magic found you. Being in favour with three of the Offices has also channelled the magic towards you."

"Three? The Fire Warlock did commend me, for whatever that's worth, but that's just one."

"The Earth and Air Offices took note of you in Blacksburg; the Air Office for your work on the charters, and the Earth Office for your gift to the widows and orphans. Your generosity has done a world of good."

"Well, ma'am, I'm glad about that."

"And now that you have agreed, of your own free will, to be the test case, the Water Office should also hold you in high regard. Garnering the favour of all four Offices is not a trivial accomplishment. Don't be afraid of the magic around you; if you hadn't been able to carry it, it wouldn't have come to you. It will protect you as well as use you."

"But I don't like being pushed around. What else will it push me into doing?"

"I don't know."

I studied her. She had looked real good the first time I saw her. "Ma'am, you look awful."

She gave me a weak smile. "How very flattering of you."

"You're still cute as a kitten. You look like you need to sleep for a day and a half, is all I meant. And you were scowling when you came in. If you weren't pissed off at me, then what?"

She sighed. "Scowling was better than crying. That wicked Locksmith— the first one, that is—had no right to inflict such pain."

"I'm glad you're regrowing the Locksmith's arm. Are you regrowing the Frost Maiden's, too?"

"No. She won't need it to rebuild the Water Office, and she is so old the strain would kill her. Humans aren't made to regenerate, like starfish, once adult. Even with Frankland's best healers at her side, it nearly killed Lucinda—the Locksmith—and she is—was—a young woman in robust health. Every healer's first concern is to do no harm, and each of us purposefully inflicted harm—great harm—on that poor girl. It was dreadful."

Earth mothers aren't supposed to cry, but her eyes were brimming. "But, ma'am, you were just trying to help her."

The tears flowed. "No, we weren't. It would have been kinder to amputate the charred stump and let her live with one arm. She's a warlock; she would have made do without it. The pain we inflicted on her was intolerable, literally intolerable. She tried to escape, and we wouldn't let her die."

She sobbed into her handkerchief. I put an arm around her shoulders, and she didn't shake me off. Like I had any power to comfort an earth mother. "I'm sorry, ma'am. I shouldn't have said anything. Go lie down next to Hazel and rest."

"Oh, my poor, darling Hazel. She's too young for this. She had never worked with a sufferer who wanted to die, and the Locksmith is a close friend. I hope she finds the grace to forgive Hazel. I hope Hazel forgives herself."

"But, ma'am, if regrowing an arm hurts so much, why do it?"

"Because she's the first talent in a thousand years who can unlock the Offices. Frankland needs her more than it needs anyone else right now, Fire Warlock and Earth Mother included. She can't survive unlocking another Office, and she won't dare try, until she can control the lightning, and to do that, she has to be hale and whole. Even then, it will be dangerous and difficult. Without an arm, she would waste so much power compensating for it, even if she tried not to, that calling down the lightning would kill her."

"Are you sure it will be all right again?"

She shrugged and blew her nose. "The best healers in the country reached her within seconds. Most of what's needed has already been done, but we won't know for several days if her arm will regrow straight and true. Only one healer at a time needs to stay with her from now on, thank goodness. This has put a serious strain on the Earth Guild, but Mother Celeste ordered us to do everything possible for the three injured, even if it meant other people died for lack of attention."

"You'll take turns sitting with her? Hazel will be around for a few days, then."

She lowered her handkerchief and frowned. "You know she has to stand trial for aiding and abetting a fugitive?"

I pulled my arm away. "Aye, ma'am, and I'm awfully sorry. I didn't mean to get her into trouble."

"Do you know the standard penalties in such cases?"

"Nae, ma'am."

"After their training, most healers return to the communities they came from. Usually, the healer aides someone she is close to: brother, father, beau. The punishment the Water Guild has deemed fitting is banishment. She is sent to another district, and may never again contact the man she helped, or his family."

The roaring in my head drowned out the rest. "I'm sorry, ma'am. What did you say?"

"Please, don't come to see her again. It would be cruel to raise false hopes."

I walked over to the sleeping witch and stared down with a lump in my throat. My lass? That had lasted a long time. Cruel? Damn straight.

"Aye, ma'am," I mumbled, and stumbled down to the barracks without any idea how I got there.

Walking into Winter

Every waking hour I spent at the forge, for want of anything else to do, and thinking about smithcraft helped block thoughts about the trial, or Hazel, or what Frankland would be like with nobles handing out sentences. But not even the smithy kept me from being homesick for Nettleton; that tug was always there.

The fire lad dropped by the smithy every evening to report on the progress rebuilding the Water Office. "Master Sven and I have had some free time," he said one day, "and we found the answer to your question."

"You did, eh? Which question?"

"Why haven't any swords shattered lately?"

"Because the guild doesn't have enough wizards?"

"No. Making a sword shatter takes a lot of power, and the smiths who set up the guild knew they couldn't count on all swordsmiths being strong enough wizards for it. They made the magic work so even a true mundane can pound that spell into a sword."

"That so? Where does the power come from, then?"

"From the king's hammer. It's tied in with the Great Oath. The swords stopped shattering when the kings stopped taking the oath, because the oath gives them the hammer."

"You're making it sound like that hammer's a real thing."

He shrugged. "'How is a king like a swordsmith? He has a hammer as well as a sword.' That sounds to me like something real. It may not be a hammer you can see and feel, but that doesn't mean it's not real."

"If it's real, tell me where is it, and how he uses it."

He threw up his hands. "Beats me. We didn't find out much else. Earth Guild secrets, as far as we can tell."

I hefted the hammer in my hand. "This one's real, and I might as well get back to swinging it. Because from what you said, we're never going to see a sword shatter. Not while Stephen's king, anyway."

"Come in and sit down," the Locksmith said. "Don't stand in the doorway gawking."

"Sorry, ma'am. Didn't mean to stare." With piebald pink and white skin, she was not a pretty sight. She had gone from being a sweet armful to thinner than was healthy, and her right arm, wrapped in bandages, was inches shorter than the left.

Master Jean was worse. He hadn't had any padding to start with, and she at least had a scarf hiding her naked skull. His new skin stretched tight over bones, all the knobs and sharp edges showing. I tore my eyes away and watched the fire lad juggle live coals.

"Please, Master Duncan, take a seat," Master Jean said. "I asked you here to explain what to expect at the coming trial."

"Aye, I'd like to know a few things, starting with: how soon?"

"Perhaps another week, and less than a fortnight. The rebuilding is almost done, but Sorceress Lorraine is not yet ready for the rigours of a trial. She tires easily."

I could believe that. The Locksmith and Master Jean looked like sitting up was wearing them out.

"Ideally," he said, "she should be given months to recuperate, but we cannot hold the king off that long."

"I'm sorry for her, but I'd rather get it over with, too. And I'd like my brother and sister there."

"Of course. You need not fear for lack of support. We will send for anyone you request, and you will be represented by Frankland's foremost authorities on both law and magic: the Company of Mages, backed by the four magic guild councils."

"Uh-oh," the fire lad said. "Flint's going?"

"No." Master Jean smiled. "I told him his presence was required. Warlock Sunbeam also declined, albeit politely."

"They didn't want to see Injustice Hall?"

Master Jean gave him a sharp look. "Be careful how you refer to the courtroom. Much depends on the outcome of this trial, and needlessly antagonising the Water Guild will do our cause no good. No one alive today is responsible for the miscarriages of justice that have taken place there."

"Yes, sir. I won't call it that…there."

"Change how you refer to it here, and in your own mind, and you will be less likely to slip, there."

The fire lad made a face. "Yes, sir."

I said, "Why are you talking about Injust—the Crystal Palace? The Fire Warlock said Paris."

Master Jean shook his head. "The king wants a demonstration of the outcome of the trial and the justice of the sentence. He does not insist on the trial taking place before his eyes. We will hold the demonstration in Paris the day after the actual trial, to give ourselves time to implement an alternative strategy if the trial shows the Water Office is still broken."

"What alternative strategy? Taking it apart and not putting it back together?"

"If necessary, we will rebuild it without the sentencing functions, but we must consider that the last resort. Moreover, I must warn you, even if the reforged Water Office behaves as we expect, and does not order your execution, the king may still override the Water Office's verdict and order your death. He has that authority."

I rolled my eyes. "What makes you think he won't?"

"Custom, laziness, and the judgements favouring the nobility have kept King Stephen from ever exercising that authority before now. If custom and laziness continue to hold sway, he may not remember that he can override a sentence, or if he does, the exemplary quality of your life should persuade him not to."

"Fat chance. You know as well as I do the king hates commoners, and will stick it to us any way he can."

Master Jean frowned. "I know no such thing. Beware calling the king your enemy, lest you draw the Fire Office's attention."

"Fine. But he thinks we're his."

"He does not."

"Eh? But—"

"In naming someone your enemy, you acknowledge your foe has the power to hurt you. The king does not rate you so highly. He does not consider commoners at all, neither as individuals with the same needs and desires he has, nor as groups with power that can be channelled towards constructive purposes. He notices commoners when they become mobs, and blames the magic guilds for not keeping the rabble under control."

"That doesn't make sense. He's paying that rabble-rousing Reverend Angus to stir people up."

"True, but he expects their ire to be directed towards those he does consider his enemies: the magic guilds. The damage the mobs did to the nobles shocked and frightened him. He cannot understand his own role in the disaster."

"But—"

He held up a hand, palm out. "I say 'cannot' advisedly. King Stephen is an unintelligent, unimaginative man in a role demanding both. He is foolish, not evil, and the counsellors he trusts are equally foolish. Supporting Reverend Angus was not his idea, and he does not understand what the man does. He continues to pay him because he knows we despise him."

"And if you hate him, he must be doing something useful." I shook my head. "It doesn't seem right. Kings and Fire Warlocks were always at each other's throats, but the kings used to be happy with the other magic guilds. What happened?"

"In Frankland's early days, when the king enjoyed the people's love and respect, the king was more powerful than the Fire Warlock, whose role was limited to defence. The kings' power waned as they forgot it sprang from the consent of those governed. King Stephen's father became so bitter over what he saw as the rise of the upstart talented that he forced his son to swear imprudent oaths, including one to never take the Great Oath, simply because we wanted him to." Master Jean raised his hands, and let them fall. "When, as Fire Warlock, I learned of this, I despaired. How can Frankland ever be restored to balance, when the king's oaths trap him as surely as the Fire Office traps the Fire Warlock?"

On the morning of the trial, I prowled the Fortress walls long before dawn, and was the first one in the mess hall when it opened. When I asked for eggs, the cook shook a knife at me. "Three eggs! Four sausages! What's the matter with you, boy?"

"I guess I'm a bit off my feed this morning."

"You've eaten four eggs every morning since you got here. I'm fixing you four eggs and six sausages, and you're going to eat 'em. We can't have you fainting from hunger in front of Her Iciness. How'd that make us look? She'd think we didn't know how to feed a man."

Maybe he was right. I did feel better after eating my regular breakfast, but I shovelled it down and left the mess hall as fast as I could. Most guards coming in wished me luck or told me to give 'er hell, with a handshake or a slap on the back or a punch on the arm. Much as I appreciated the support, it didn't help steady my nerves.

Neither did Mrs Cole dragging me to the ballroom and handing me a top-drawer new suit. I said, "I won't know how to behave wearing such finery."

She tut-tutted. "You'll soon forget what you're wearing, you'll see, and you'll behave like the respectable craftsman you are. I'm not worried about that."

"But that's just it. I'm a craftsman, not a gentleman. You're dressing me up like a gentleman. Those water witches will expect me to talk and act like a gentleman, and I can't. They'll laugh at me and call me uppity. Not that I'd care, usually, but I don't want to make things worse."

She thumped me on the chest. "If you know what's good for you, you'll sit quiet and let their Wisdoms do the talking. If you aren't dressed up, you'll look so out of place you'll draw more attention, and they'd sneer at you for not talking the occasion seriously. Trust me on this. Besides, you never get a second chance to make a first impression. So make it a good one."

"Yes, ma'am," I said, and took the clothes. When I'd gotten dressed, I said, "What kind of magic is in these clothes? I look like an earl."

She smiled. "Don't kid yourself. You look better than most earls. You look like a prince, or at least a duke. If there's any magic involved, it's the normal magic of good health, good muscles, and a good chin."

I tugged at my cuffs and watched myself in the mirror. "I'll be the best-looking cold corpse Abertee has ever seen."

She sucked in her breath and scurried away, sniffling.

By the time we walked through the fire to the Crystal Palace gates, I was ready to bolt. Being close enough to Nettleton to walk home by nightfall hurt like a broken rib stabbing my chest. Sunlight bouncing off the windows stabbed my eyes. A year ago, when the light had pinned me down on the shore, I had watched for water wizards rising out of the surf, though they had nothing on me then. Now the charge was murder, and I was standing at the gate, handing myself in. Fool.

The Fire Warlock gave my shoulder a hard shake. "Never thought I'd see a fellow as big as you look like a scared rabbit. The magic's stronger if you walk in on your own than if I drag you in, but if I have to, I will."

"You said it was my choice."

"Too late—we're on their home turf. If you turn around now, you won't live long enough to wish you hadn't."

Master Jean put a hand on my arm. "Take heart, my friend. No one here, either within or without, wishes you dead."

"Aye, sir. I'll walk in on my own."

The Locksmith took my other arm. "I don't like walking in there, either. We'll go together."

I lurched up the ramp, a warlock on either side. Once inside, out of the glare, walking forward got easier, but stepping into the shadows chilled me like walking into winter.

Injustice Hall

Master Jean was talking to a dozen other wizards at the waiting room's far end. He had put some weight on; he was skinny, but not a bag of bones. It didn't hurt to look at him anymore. The other wizards were experts on law and magic, to provide support and counsel, he'd said. The advice they'd given so far was to tell the truth, all of it, when the Frost Maiden asked questions. Like I didn't have enough sense to know that.

Maggie had a vice grip on my arm and wouldn't let go. I didn't mind that. It was when she asked what the wizards said about my chances that I shook her off.

"How's Hazel?" I said. "Is Granny Mildred still pissed off at her?"

The look passing between Doug and Maggie said they didn't like my question, either.

"Come on," I said. "You know that isn't right. I told Warlock Snorri to tell Mildred to come see me, but she wouldn't. Maybe she knew I was going to chew her out. But if she won't talk to me, you're going to have to do something about it."

"Do what?" Maggie said. "I don't want to fight with Granny Mildred, even when she's wrong. I don't want half of Abertee mad at me, too."

"Somebody's got to tell her she's wrong about Hazel. Guess that means you, Doug."

Doug had a hangdog look about him. "It's not right to disrespect our elders. You know that."

"It's not right to disrespect an almost-earth-mother, either, and that's what Mildred's doing. I'm not saying you have to tell Granny Mildred off in the Shepard's Arms with all of Crossroads listening. Just tell her in private that Hazel saved my life turning me over to the Fire Guild, and she ought to thank her for it."

"I tried that," Maggie said, "and it didn't do any good."

"Why not?"

"She said you being on trial showed you jumped from the frying pan into the fire. That when she heard the Fire Guild was looking for a test case, she held her breath, because you're the big-hearted, damn-fool, would-be hero they were looking for. She really laced into me, saying after my brush with the Water Office, I should be the last person sticking up for Hazel. So I went crying to Cousin Ruth, and she sent me packing. Miserable day."

"Well, hell." I gave her a hug and a kiss on the cheek. "Thanks, Maggie. At least you tried." I glared at Doug.

He shrugged. "Wouldn't do any good now."

"Why not?"

"Her trial's this afternoon," Maggie said. "We're not likely to ever see her again."

The water wizard, Master Charles, led the way to Justice Hall. Master Charles didn't look dangerous, but neither did Master Jean. I'd better not slip and call the place Injustice Hall. Guaranteed to make a water wizard go berserk, I'd heard.

We stopped just inside the door, and gawked. On our right, rows of benches climbed higher than a two-story house, forming half of a bowl. Sunlight slanting in through windows set high up sparkled on white marble and dark blue tiles.

On our left… I twisted my neck and moved further out to get a good look at the wall. King Charlie the Great and the first Frost Maiden, three times larger than life, stood on rocks in front of pounding surf, holding a magic mirror between them. The king raised a sword in his right hand. The sun picked out gold in his crown and her ring. In her left hand, she held an hourglass.

I wrenched my eyes away and bumped into Master Jean. "Sorry, sir. I figured you would have sat down already. You must be used to it."

Without taking his eyes away from the wall, Master Jean said, "I have seen paintings of this magnificent mosaic, but I have never been in the Hall of I… Hall of Justice before, either." He strolled closer to stare up at the king. Master Charles glared at the back of his head.

Turning away from the picture of the hourglass brought me face-to-face with silver scales and a real hourglass on a stand. I cursed under my breath, and couldn't move. Despite the chill, I was sweating.

Master Charles grabbed my sleeve and tugged me past. "Royalty and nobles, when they are here, sit in the middle, there, with the talented on either side. Commoners sit in the higher rows, except for immediate family." His voice echoed in the nearly empty hall. The empty benches dwarfed the magic folk in the bottom two rows.

I wiped sweat from my face. "Where is everybody?"

"Specifically uninvited. Only the witches and wizards involved in the rebuilding are here. This is a trial trial, you might say."

Mother Astrid, looking thirty again, nodded to me from a flock of healers. The Flame Mage and the fire lad gave me thumbs-up. The Earth Mother, Fire Warlock, and Locksmith had chairs below them, on the floor of the bowl. The Locksmith was grey. They shouldn't have let her out of bed.

At least the Water Guild was treating her like royalty, giving her a padded armchair and footstool. The two Officeholders only rated straight chairs. Everybody wore woolly hats and winter coats.

I went where Sorcerer Charles pointed: the prisoner's bench. Doug and Maggie filed into place behind me. Their bench had a cushion. Mine didn't. Not that I cared to complain.

Master Jean and the Air Enchanter slid into place on either side. I said, "They should have given you an armchair, too."

Master Jean shrugged, "They offered. I declined. We shall not be here long."

The Enchanter said, "I wouldn't have minded a cushion."

A gong cut off Master Jean's beg-pardon. We stood. Double doors on one side of the hall opened. The blue-robed Water Guild Council filed in and lined up before an unpadded bench under the mirror.

The Frost Maiden floated through the double doors. I stared. The ancient Greek goddess in the Black Duke's palace had stepped off her pedestal and taken Sorceress Lorraine's place. No, it was the same witch I'd seen before; gorgeous, but as cold as ice, as pale and hard as marble, and as perfect as that statue.

Nae, a broken statue, with one arm gone. I shuddered.

She stopped at the short bench, directly in front, between the scales and the hourglass. We got to sit. Master Jean gave a soft sigh. He should've taken the armchair.

The Frost Maiden said, "Let me remind you that in the administration of Justice the Water Office operates in two phases: first the determination of guilt and innocence, secondly the issuance of penalties. The first phase has not been problematic, and nothing there has changed. The second phase, which has been issuing penalties increasingly at odds with the first phase's verdicts, has been the source of our troubles. We will now perform the first phase: determination of guilt and innocence. Let us review Lord Edmund's death."

The mirror came to life, showing the three horsemen entering the barnyard. I ducked my head. Awake or asleep, I had seen Lord Edmund die a thousand times since then. Maggie leaned forward and rested her head on my shoulder. I reached back and squeezed her hand.

She whispered, "Excuse me, Your Wisdom."

Master Jean leaned back. "Yes?"

"The problem is the Water Office's right hand doesn't know what the left one is doing? The left hand dishes out penalties the right hand said weren't deserved?"

"That sums it up rather well."

I muttered, "But her right hand's the one that's gone, and the left hand is the one with the teeth in it."

"What a repulsive metaphor."

"Sorry, sir." But her right hand was gone, and I couldn't tell if she even missed it.

Did a goddess ever feel anything? Anger? Love? Pity for the poor louts she'd destroyed? She'd risked her life, but maybe she was so cold she didn't know how to be afraid. She'd talked a fine story that night in the Fortress, but I hadn't heard it in her voice or seen it in her face. I wished I could see something there besides ice.

I ducked my head lower and kept my eyes on the floor. The marble was easier to take than her, or the mirror, or that frostbitten hourglass.

When the mirror went blank, the mages got into an argument about manslaughter I didn't try to follow. She asked a few questions I answered with "Aye, Your Wisdom" and "Nae, Your Wisdom."

Then she said, "We charge thee, Water Office, according to Frankland's laws and customs, to show those assembled here a just verdict."

I looked up. The scales held two dolls: a big one looking like me, smaller one looking like Lord Edmund. I held my breath.

She said, "In the confrontation at the Archer farm, which man's actions, if either, indicated he intended murder?"

The pan holding Lord Edmund dropped. The air whooshed out of me. A few healers cheered.

The Frost Maiden shook her head. "This is as we expected. No one, other than perhaps the king, believed the murder charge justified. There are, however, lesser charges we must consider." She asked a few more questions, the scales bobbed up and down, and then she said, "The Water Office has determined Master Duncan was justified in acting to protect both his sister and himself. Nevertheless, he did cause Lord Edmund's death, and even the accidental death of a noble is a serious matter. We must now perform the penalty phase."

The Water Guild Council gathered around her. When they all had a hand on her shoulders, she said, "Ready? Begin." The stone in her ring, now on her left hand, throbbed with blue light, no faster at first than the hoofbeats of an old nag at pasture. The witches and wizards looked like ghouls in the flickering light. No one spoke, no one moved. For a long time, nothing else happened, except the throbbing quickened to a trot, then a gallop. Then the beats ran together, and the stone in the ring flashed bright blue, brighter than the sunlight coming in the windows.

With a roar like surf beating on rocks, the sea in the mosaic came alive. Cold water poured out, spread across the floor, and rose to hip-high in seconds. I scrambled to my feet and reached for Maggie. A chest-high wave hit me, and I went under.

The Frost Maiden's voice cut through the roar of rising water and froze me in place. "Be still. You will not drown, nor be swept away. Let the flood pass over you."

My bones ached with cold. Then the water drained away, more quickly than it had risen. My teeth chattered. The Fire Warlock sat down, hunched over, and shook so hard his chair rattled. The fire wizards crowded together. Mother Astrid's freckles stood out against white cheeks. The Air Enchanter floated down from the ceiling. Even up there, somehow, he'd gotten soaked.

Master Jean and the Locksmith were the only ones outside the Water Guild who hadn't panicked. She hadn't even moved. She looked pissed off, not scared. Weren't members of the Fire Guild all supposed to be terrified of drowning?

Master Jean hissed under his breath, "For God's sake, Lorraine, there are warlocks here."

The Air Enchanter mumbled, "The rest of us didn't like it either, you know. What was that?"

Master Jean's eyebrows rose. "A flood?"

The Enchanter glared at him. "I meant—"

"I beg your pardon. I do not know. They do not seem to know what to make of it, either," he said, nodding at the coven around the Frost Maiden. They waved their hands and argued with each other, but I couldn't make out the words. The Frost Maiden sat with her eyes closed, looking even more like a statue, while they chattered around her.

"It was a magic flood, anyway," I said. "There's no mud." There were no drowned mice, either, or scattered leaves, or any of the other usual mess a flood leaves. The walls and floor gleamed like they'd just been scoured.

"A good omen, perhaps," Master Jean said.

Somebody or something was working magic on us. The water trickled out of my hair and clothes, faster than it should have. My shoes were still awash, but my shoulders were already dry. Master Jean tapped me on the arm, and made me warm for the first time since walking into the Crystal Palace. Soon, even my shoes were dry, and the last of the water disappeared. The water coven stopped arguing, and went back to the bench under the mirror.

The Frost Maiden said, "We have witnessed an event the Great Coven expected would happen frequently, but that has never happened since the Water Office was created. We have been privileged today to see the Water Office correcting itself, washing away the detritus of centuries of bad precedents and unjust decisions. This is as we had hoped. It remains to be seen, however, if the new judgements are more just than the old. The death of a noble is still a serious matter. Penalties must be paid." She laid her hand on the hourglass.

My heart stopped. One hour to say goodbye. To make my peace—

"But today," she said, "we have no need of the hourglass."

Maggie squealed. I can't recall quite what happened after that. Sparks filled the air. Grinning wizards pumped my hand. Mother Astrid kissed me—I'm sure about that. Healers I'd never met hugged me.

Maggie tugged my sleeve. The pinched look on her face brought me back to earth. I couldn't hear what she said for the noise, but I followed her eyes. She was watching Master Jean. He wasn't celebrating with the other fire wizards. He seemed carved from the same marble as the Frost Maiden. He watched her. She watched me. Our eyes met. Ever so slightly, she shook her head.

My skin crawled. I slid down onto the bench beside Master Jean. The gong sounded, and sounded again before the healers stopped chattering and returned to their seats.

The Frost Maiden said, "I understand your desire to celebrate. We are no longer bound by the barbarism of an eye for an eye and a tooth for a tooth, where the eye and the tooth matter only if they belong to a nobleman. Nevertheless, the Water Office is still constrained, more tightly than we had understood, by the privileges of rank afforded the nobility by the other Offices, in particular the Fire Office."

Master Jean made a noise like she'd hit him. She said, "Yes, Jean?"

He gripped the edge of the bench with white knuckles. "I beg your pardon, Your Wisdom. Please, continue."

"The death of a dishonourable noble still matters more to the Offices than the death of an honourable commoner, and the penalties for killing a noble are not light."

The hall went dead quiet. I shivered.

"Master Duncan, I will not call you, today, to step forth and hear your fate. The judgements will not take effect until I do so at the meeting tomorrow in Paris, but I will tell you today what is in store for you.

"There are three aspects to all Water Guild judgments: deterrence, recompense, and retribution. That is, preventing the crime from happening again, making things right, as far as is possible, for the wronged parties, and, if need be, further punishments as befits the gravity of the situation.

"First is the matter of deterrence. The Water Office will not take away from you the ability to kill another person. It cannot do so without also depriving you of your livelihood, and your right to defend yourself. However, I warn you, if ever you strike the first blow, you shall suffer the same injury you deal to your opponent. If you kill again, you shall die at your own hand."

I flexed my hand. Men had lost arms for lesser crimes, and starting a fight was nearly always a bad idea. I wouldn't mind getting a shove away. "That's fair, Your Wisdom."

"Second, there is the matter of recompense. A man's death may leave a family struggling to survive, and the Water Guild will not establish a new precedence that does not include this."

Drown me. I should have expected blood money, but the Water Office didn't demand money from a cold corpse. Maybe I hadn't really believed they could fix the Water Office.

"To ensure the debt is paid promptly, you may not return to the Upper Tee Valley until the full amount is paid."

She'd sucker punched me. Of all the bad things the Water Office could do, I'd never considered this. Could I pay it off before I died of homesickness? Oh, God, what was an earl's son worth?

Doug hissed, "We'll help you pay it."

I wanted to tell Doug my nephews shouldn't go without, but the words stuck in my throat.

"Mr Archer," the Frost Maiden said, "your generous offer to help your brother is predicated on the assumption you have a choice. You do not. The king will require the debt be paid, if not by Master Duncan, then by the entire Archer family. Everything you, your brother, your sister, your spouses, and your children own or earn will be forfeit until the debt is paid, nor may you leave Frankland to escape the debt."

Maggie choked. Doug's hobnails scraped on stone. I couldn't bring himself to look at them.

"The king determines a nobleman's worth," the Frost Maiden said. "Lord Edmund was an earl's son. For his death, you must pay Earl Eddensford one thousand gold franks."

One thousand. This must be her idea of a joke. I stared, waiting for a real number, and jumped when the Fire Warlock bellowed.

"One thousand. Goddamn bloody Hell. They can't pay that. Nobody short of another earl can pay that."

"Of course they cannot," she said. "The Water Office does not approve—"

"I thought you were going to fix the damned thing." The Warlock was on his feet, and putting out heat like a forge. He shook off the Earth Mother's hand. The healers on the bench behind slid away. The Frost

Maiden shielded her face with her hand and leaned back.

"Come clean," he roared, "and call this the Hall of Injustice yourselves."

It got colder. Mist rolled out of the fake sea and billowed around the Water Guild Council. They crowded around their mistress. Her voice knifed through fog. "Silence, fool. You—"

"Beorn, sit down and be quiet." Master Jean's order cracked across hers. The Fire Warlock dropped into his chair. A leg snapped. He listed, teetered, and came to rest, glaring, on the other three.

"You forget yourself, my friend," Master Jean said. "You are not master here. I beg your pardon, Your Wisdom, for my interruption."

Jagged flashes from the stone in the Frost Maiden's ring turned the angry water witches and wizards into fogbound ghosts. With a snap of her wrist, she sent them back to their seats. With her hand still raised, she scowled at the Fire Warlock. They were both breathing hard.

The fog turned to frost. I strained not to shiver, not to let my teeth chatter. The healers huddled close to the still-burning Warlock.

The hall got colder. I turned my collar up and tucked my hands in my armpits. The Water Office hadn't iced me, but the Fire Warlock was trying to. That was a fine state of affairs.

The Frost Maiden closed her eyes. Gradually, she stopped breathing so hard. The lines in her face faded, returning to smooth marble.

Be careful what you wish for, Dad had said, for you will surely get it. I should have known better than to wish to see some feeling in her face. Master Jean had been right, back in that ruined pea field. If she had meant to kill me, I'd be dead.

"Lorraine, dear," the Earth Mother said. "Er, Your Wisdom. My nose hairs are crackling. Must it be so cold in here?"

"I will chill the hall no further," the Frost Maiden said, "but I cannot return the warmth. Perhaps the Fire Guild will oblige."

The hall warmed. The Frost Maiden opened her eyes. "You did not need to apologise, Jean. I thank you for your intervention. A test of strength today between fire and ice would be disastrous. Would you please explain? He will listen to you."

"Certainly, Your Wisdom," he said, without looking away from her. "The Water Office has attempted to correct a perceived injustice, and would have done so, but the magnitude of the payment demanded is not under its control. The payment required has been established by the authority of the line of kings with the Fire Office's support, and is the amount due on the accidental death of an earl's son at the hands of another noble. The Water Office is not to blame. Is that correct, Your Wisdom?"

"Quite so, Jean. The Water Office does not approve of the sum required. The original purpose of blood money was to ensure a family would not starve after their breadwinner's death. It did not measure the worth of a human life, although the nobles have come to view it that way. Nor was it intended to beggar others as they struggled to pay off a debt to a wealthy family not needing their support.

"Lord Edmund Bradford left no wife, and, as far as we know, no children to support. His brother, Earl Eddensford, does not need a smith's assistance to survive, and taking away Master Duncan's ability to support a family of his own ill-serves the country. The Water Office does require a penalty commensurate with the offender's ability to pay, to remind everyone involved of the seriousness of taking another person's life, and to prevent the needs of dependents from ever being forgotten, but strictly speaking, no payment to the earl is necessary. If the Water Office were capable of emotion, I would say it is furious. It does not want to re-establish the precedence of requiring onerous payments where they are not needed."

The Fire Warlock said, "That settles it then. We're fucked."

The Frost Maiden speared him with a cold blue eye. "Your language is appalling, but the sentiment is accurate."

He ducked his head and stared at the floor. "Sorry. And I shouldn't've yelled at you."

"Apology accepted. Your reaction was understandable. You are a commoner as well as a wizard, and understand how the commoners will see it." She turned and raked the line of water witches and wizards on the bench behind her with her eyes. "Those of you who took offence at the Fire Warlock's derogatory term for this place must forgive him; he spoke the truth. This has become Injustice Hall."

She rose from her bench and sailed out the door. She disappeared while we were still scrambling to our feet.

Maggie said, "Is it over?" I flinched at the tears in her voice.

The Air Enchanter said, "Yes, Miss Archer. You and your brother should go home and rest, if you can. Tomorrow will be a gruelling day."

The members of the Water Guild slid out of Doug's way as he marched out, Maggie on his heels. Neither one looked back.

The Road to
the Palace

The iron railing glowed red, turned yellow, then eye-blistering white. The Fire Warlock tore chunks out with his hands and with a wordless roar, hurled one after the other at the mountainside.

The younger mage, the fire lad, and I stood shoulder to shoulder, flat against the wall, glad he was throwing them at Storm King—like it would even notice—rather than at us. The fire lad chewed his nails. The Locksmith watched, frowning, from the centre of the balcony. Her husband paced tight circles with their winter coats over his arm.

When the Fire Warlock finally stopped, leaving only a few glowing support columns, bending under their own weight, the Locksmith said, "Feeling better now?"

"No. I feel like a two-year-old, and that pisses me off, too."

"At least you've calmed down enough to talk."

"Maybe."

"You must," Master Jean said. "We have much to do, and little room to manoeuvre. Master Sven, you and Warlock Snorri worked wonders in August disseminating the truth about the injustice of rape trials. Can you perform another miracle and reach the members of all four magic guilds before the demonstration tomorrow?"

The two wizards frowned at each other. "Most," Master Sven said. "We can't find them all in one day."

"Do what you can. Concentrate on the Water Guild."

"What's the message?"

"All talented not needed for riot control must seek a safe place: the Fortress, the Warren, or the Crystal Palace. Not the Hall of the Winds. If they cannot reach one of those three, go to earth. Leave Paris. The Water Guild

Council will supply those safe havens with magic mirrors for watching the proceedings. No commoner in any magic guild is to attend tomorrow's audience with the king without their guild head's approval. On the Fire Warlock's orders… That is, of course, if you concur, Your Wisdom."

The Fire Warlock saluted, with a weak grin. "Not used to being second in command, are you? As he says."

"We're on it." The mage and the fire lad dove for the stairs.

"Mother Celeste will talk to the queen," Master Jean said. "Lucinda and I will pay a familial visit to the Eddensfords. As soon as you are able, offer the Water Guild a thorough apology. We must be in accord at this afternoon's trial, and tomorrow."

I pushed away from the wall. "Aren't you going to take the Water Office apart again?"

Master Jean frowned. "Why?"

"You promised you'd do that if it wasn't fixed the first time."

"It has been fixed. You are still with us."

I leaned over him with fists on my hips and elbows out wide. "Like hell it's been fixed. It still looks broken to me." I tried to stare him down, and failed.

"It won't look fixed to other commoners, either," the Locksmith said, "but it is. The king and the Fire Office are conspiring to make it appear still broken. That's why the Fire Warlock is so angry."

"Reforging the Water Office without the justice magic will not help," Master Jean said. "We cannot let the king take the judiciary out of the Water Guild's hands and turn it over to the nobles. Aside from problems of flagrant bias in sentencing, the nobility do not have the Water Guild's magic for ferreting out the truth of guilt or innocence, or their scruples to do so."

I leaned my head against the wall and closed my eyes. "When you asked me to be the test case, I thought it was about me living or dying. Being a debt slave for the rest of my life isn't much better than dying, and if I'd thought it could ruin Doug and Maggie's lives, too, I wouldn't have agreed to it, ever. I won't say I'd be better off if she—it, I mean, the Water Office—wanted me dead, but at least it would have been quick."

The Fire Warlock said, "God knows I'm sorry, Duncan. You would have been better off. It wouldn't have gotten the chance to kill you."

"Eh?"

"If it had ordered you dead, it would have given you an hour's grace. I would have taken you to the border with Espana and thrown you out. You would've been on your way to New London by now."

"You son of a bitch."

He grabbed my fist a foot from his face. "Whoa. Remember what she—"

"You could have told me so. She scared the devil out of me. You—"

"Peace, friend." The Fire Warlock hadn't forced my arm down; Master Jean did. "We did not dare tell you. The magic in your favour was stronger if you believed your life at risk. The Water Office would have been wroth had it suspected you disdained its authority."

"But it wouldn't have touched Doug and Maggie."

"No, it would not have."

"Tell me how you're going to clean up this mess."

"We will attempt to persuade or coerce the king to be merciful." I snorted. He said, "If that fails, our only hope is to limit the damages."

"Aye, and hell will freeze over." I charged down the stairs towards the barracks. After shedding my new suit, I pounded the smithy's pile of scrap metal into ragged heaps of slag. The guards stayed out of my way, and even before the orders came down from their captains, picked up the pace prepping armour and weapons for the coming riots.

"You're alive," Doug said. "That's something."

We were a grim group, waiting for the Frost Maiden in the Earth Guild's Paris hall. Maggie had been crying. Doug's eyes were bloodshot, his mouth a tight line. I couldn't bring myself to tell them what the Fire Warlock had said. "I can't blame you for being pissed off. God, I'm sorry."

Doug nodded and walked away.

I said, "What about Hazel? Have you heard?"

"I'm sorry." Maggie leaned against me and talked into my shoulder. "I was so miserable I didn't think about asking Warlock Snorri when he brought us here. Wouldn't the Fire Warlock know?"

He would, but I didn't want to ask. He looked ready to burst into flame if anybody poked him. Master Jean, arguing with the Earth Mother, looked like he was nursing a pounding head.

"No, Jean," she said, "I will not hide in the Warren. We have to present a united front, and my bones say you're going to need me."

"I respect your desire to help, Your Wisdom, but perhaps you under-estimate the danger." He looked up and met my eyes. "Excuse us, please." He took the Earth Mother by the arm and marched her out of the room.

The Frost Maiden sailed in, trailed by a trio of water wizards, and stopped in front of me. I took a step backwards.

"When I entered Jus—Injustice Hall yesterday," she said, with a flick of the eyes to the Fire Warlock, "I sensed someone close to an untimely death. I thought then that was you, Master Duncan, and I worried we had missed something crucial in reforging the Water Office. I sense violent death today, even more strongly." She paused and focused on the Fire Warlock. "But I do not know who here today is most at risk. I will do what I can to deflect danger, and I applaud you all for your courage in being here."

Master Jean and the Earth Mother came back. His face was hard as granite.

The Frost Maiden brushed past him. "They will be waiting. Shall we go?" The water wizards followed her out the door.

"On that note of optimism and good cheer?" The Air Enchanter said. "I'd rather not. But no one has suggested I stay away."

The Earth Mother looked up at him with her hands on her hips. "I'm not in hiding; you shouldn't be either. Besides, I still think we can persuade King Stephen to be reasonable."

"If you think so, madam, you are deluded."

"I am not. I believe in marvels and wonders. Don't you?" She took his arm and dragged him towards the door. We followed them out to the coaches waiting to take us to the palace. I was in no hurry to climb in. The Frost Maiden and her sorcerers were climbing into the first, drawn by a matched team of four white horses. As pretty a display of horseflesh as I'd seen anywhere.

The other three Officeholders and Master Jean queued at the next coach, drawn by a team of matching black horses. I smiled. I liked black ones better. Before he'd bleached from years in the sun, Charcoal had looked as good.

I ducked my head and climbed into the third coach without glancing at the chestnuts pulling it. One thousand franks for that wretched weasel. I'd never own another horse. Never ride out on a fine day. Never enjoy a gallop over the green turf. A fire burned deep in my chest.

Maggie and Doug climbed in behind me. When we were rolling, I repeated what Master Jean had said about persuading the king or limiting the damage.

Maggie said, "Could they do it? Make the king tell us to pay only what Lord Edmund was worth?"

Doug snorted. "They'd be paying us."

"Something, anyway, we have a hope of paying off?"

"Master Sven said the king has turned noble families into beggars before." I shrugged. "If he did it to them…"

"Can't the Fire Warlock make him?" Maggie said. "With all that magic behind him… And the old Fire Warlock can do anything he wants, they say."

The crowds lining the streets were as silent as a funeral—mine, and I wasn't even dead yet. The silence weighed me down. In a riot, the mob would attack the palace. We'd be trapped. "No dice. He kept the Frost Maiden at bay without breaking a sweat when they caught me, and didn't show any sign of nerves two weeks ago when he was expecting to burn to death. Today he's as taut as a pulled bowstring."

Master Jean lined us up outside the palace ballroom and gave us our final marching orders. We waited for several minutes as the last of the lower ranking nobles found their seats. I passed the time slamming my fist into the stone doorpost and twitching my shoulders, trying to shake off the weight on them. The weight of public opinion, Mother Astrid had said. Like that made any sense.

"Whatever happens today," Master Jean said from behind me, "you must not lose your temper. Remember that."

I whipped around, but he wasn't talking to me.

The Fire Warlock glowered. "Yeah, right. Like I've got any chance, after yesterday."

"You must not. The stakes are higher today."

The doors to the ballroom opened. The two wizards shook hands, and the Fire Warlock mumbled, so soft I wasn't sure I'd heard him right, "Goodbye, old friend."

Master Jean slipped into place in the queue, and we began our march up the aisle. I ducked through the door, and the aristos nearest the aisle shrank away. I clenched my jaw and kept my eyes on Sorcerer Charles's head.

On both sides of the stage, rows of seats faced inward towards the thrones in the middle. Master Jean and the water wizards marched into the last row on the right—four straight chairs with cushions. We filed into the middle row—a hard wooden bench. Maggie rolled her eyes. Doug shrugged. The four Officeholders filed into the first row—four plush armchairs.

The dukes followed us in, and lined up on the left side of the stage. In the front row, the White Duke was sweating. He stared down at the floor, the throne, up at the magic mirror, the balconies, anywhere other than at me, or at his wife and son in the first row at the foot of the stage. His son smirked. I gave him the gimlet eye. The ass's smirk widened.

The Earl of Eddensford, in the second row on the stage, met my stare, and nodded.

The king and queen appeared, along with the prince, a lad about twelve years old. They strolled up the aisle together, taking their own sweet time.

The water wizard behind Maggie grumbled about not being able to see. She turned and whispered to him behind her hand, "Sorry. Our dad was an elephant."

He melted. "I guess you can't help it."

The royals took their places, the prince on a smaller throne behind his mother's, and the sergeant-at-arms said we could sit.

The king said, "We have called the nobles and the powers of this land together today to hear the holders of the Fire and Water Offices account for themselves. You, Frost Maiden, claim to have taken apart and rebuilt the Office of the Northern Waters. You, Fire Warlock, have been haranguing our kinsmen about their supposed disrespect for the law at the same time you have been harbouring a killer. You will explain yourselves, and demonstrate that you haven't broken the Water Office. You will bring this murderer to justice, here in full view of all, rather than hidden away in that cold hall where none but members of the Water Guild dare go.

"To that end, we have asked His Wisdom, Enchanter Paul, holder of the Air Office, to review the events around Lord Edmund's death and his murderer's trial." He broke off and glowered at me. "Why isn't the prisoner in chains?"

The King's Hammer

M aster Jean hissed in my ear, "Do not respond."
I growled but clamped my mouth shut and glared at the king. No matter what the Frost Maiden said, if they tried to put chains on me, I'd kill someone.

The Frost Maiden said, "What prisoner?"

The king gaped at her for a moment, then pointed. "Him. The man that killed Lord Edmund. That blacksmith."

The Fire Warlock said, "The swordsmith is here on his own accord. I gave him the choice of exile or submitting to the Water Office for justice. He chose justice."

Thank you, Your Wisdom, for telling everybody in Frankland what an imbecile I am. All those aristos staring like I was a two-headed calf made me sweat, even while my hands and feet were freezing.

"Besides," he said, "the Fire Office commended Grandmaster Duncan for coming to a nobleman's aid during the Blacksburg riot. The other Offices have commended him for other selfless acts. They demand he be treated with respect."

Several dukes gawked with eyes popping out of their heads.

"Nor is his the only trial we will review today," the Frost Maiden said. "The actions of three men, two living, one dead, have drawn the attention of the Water Office. The other living man is also here on his own accord."

Good. Nail the bastard that sent the earl's brat to us. I'd been so wrapped up in my own troubles I'd forgotten the Fire Warlock's promise. He hadn't bothered to tell me who he'd found.

The king blinked at the Frost Maiden. The queen nudged him and whispered. He said, "Oh, yes, of course. As we were saying, Enchanter

Paul will conduct today's meeting. In our dealings with him on treaties and trading contracts, Enchanter Paul has been a model of dignity and decorum, and has shown he understands the privileges of rank and the positions of the nobles. We trust him to be impartial. At least, we trust him more than we do the other Officeholders, who act like enemies of the nobility."

Doug snorted. Guess they hadn't bothered to tell the king a few things either. The Enchanter walked to the edge of the stage and began talking about principles of justice. A few feet away, aristos wore the same sorts of angry looks commoners in Blacksburg had worn in the days right before the riot.

I perched on the edge of the bench, searching for a bolt hole for when things got ugly. I would grab Maggie and run. The magic folk could take care of themselves.

"...shall examine the lives of two men: Lord Edmund Bradford and Grandmaster Duncan Archer."

The magic mirror clouded over, then cleared to show Dad giving orders to a work crew putting a new roof on the Nettleton church. He'd kept my sixteen-year-old arse busy hauling new slates up the ladder. The men on the roof laughed at the steady stream of bad jokes that came with each new load. Down below on the stage, I squirmed.

The second scene showed me wading into the middle of a bar fight. I'd yanked two sots apart, and held up in the air the one who'd started it, a little fellow taking wild swings at everybody in sight. "If you hit me," I'd said, "and I find out about it, you're in big trouble."

Folk in the balconies laughed. Fire and frostbite, that was an idiotic thing to say. I must've been half drunk. I leaned forward and hissed, "Thank you, Your Wisdom, for making me look like a fool. What the hell does this have to do with Lord Edmund?"

The Fire Warlock growled, "We're showing you're good-natured and a good neighbour. Shut up before you prove it's not so."

Twisting my neck to watch the mirror hurt. I watched the aristos instead. Some yawned and fidgeted, and small blame to them. When the happenings in the mirror didn't make me squirm, they were boring: the everyday things any decent man does to take care of his neighbours and get along with those he works with.

The bored aristos came to attention. I looked up. Lord Edmund thumbed his nose at his tutors and bullied the servants.

That went on for a while: a few glimpses of me, then one of Edmund being a rotter. The only scene where he was polite, to an old man, gave way to one where he sneered about sucking up to the old fart.

The king's hand rested on the pommel of his sword. His head jerked like he was dozing off. I fumed. I shouldn't have felt guilty that the country was on the edge of riot and war. Edmund had more to answer for than I had. Even dead, the brat was nothing but trouble.

The mirror showed a bloodied girl in ripped clothes, crying. Edmund smirked while he buttoned his breeches. A wave of anger from the balconies hit us like a blast from a furnace. The Earth Mother cringed. I beat on my thigh with a fist. One thousand franks. The price on my head had been a quarter that, and I'd done more for Frankland than this brat had. A lot more. Any fool could see that. The old earl should've paid the Water Guild to take him off his family's hands.

They got to my stay in Blacksburg, and showed me telling off the cheat. Working on the charters. Hounding Reverend Angus out of the big halls. Forging my masterpiece. Edmund raped more women and made his brother's life hell.

The king's fingers beat a tattoo on his sword hilt. Master Jean's mouth was a thin, lipless line. His eyes flickered across the nobles, the balconies, the dukes, the king, back to the nobles.

The weight bearing down on me grew, became more solid. When the Frost Maiden announced the penalty, there would be riots. I didn't believe Master Jean could persuade the king. Master Jean wasn't acting like he believed either.

In the mirror, I'd sold my masterpiece, and walked away with a bag of gold. Doug went rigid. Maggie goggled. "You didn't tell us about that. What happened to it?"

I put my head down in my hands. I should have kept the money, dammit. It wasn't one thousand, not anywhere close. Doug would still have lost the farm, but it might have saved my nephews from debt slavery.

"And now," the Enchanter said, "we come to the events at the end of June—the Blacksburg riot."

The aristos who had been yawning perked up and paid attention. The mirror showed me arguing with the local fire wizard. The king tightened his grip on his sword.

Edmund rode away from Fiona's croft. Maggie hunched over and cried.

I swallowed bile. One thousand franks for that mangy cur.

The mirror moved on to the riot, then to Sam and me with Richard Collins. The Enchanter stopped the scene and pointed out that Richard was an aristo, like the way he was waving his sword hadn't already spilled his secret in front of half the country. Yet another thing to feel guilty about.

When the mirror showed me yelling at the Fire Warlock, several thousand people sucked in their breath as one. Frostbite. Why show that? Both of us looked like asses.

The Fire Warlock turned his head and winked. I rolled my eyes and fought down a ruder gesture. Master Jean breathed in my ear, "Now all Franks will know what the nobles wanted kept secret."

Maybe that was worth looking like an ass for. And if the king made a fuss, you'd look like butter wouldn't melt in your mouth, wouldn't you, Master Jean?

When I handed the payment for the gate over to the Earth Guild, some aristos laughed. Cheering and clapping from the balconies drowned them out. The queen clapped. The mirror clouded over.

Maggie hugged me, and whispered, "Dad and Uncle Will would have been proud of you."

"I'm sorry," I said. She shook her head, and dribbled tears on my shoulder.

The White Duke hunched over with his head in his hands. The prince's eyes were huge and round. The king looked like he'd had three beers too many to figure out what he owed the barmaid.

The Enchanter said, "Master Duncan, do you agree with this representation of your life?"

I swallowed and nodded. Maggie raised her voice, clear and strong. "That's my brother!"

"Thank you, Miss Archer. Earl Eddensford, do you agree with this representation of your brother's life?"

The earl looked green. He made two attempts before he choked out, "Yes, Your Wisdom. I wish it weren't true, but it is."

"Thank you, Earl Eddensford. Now we come to the events of July seventh."

Earl Eddensford met my eyes, and flinched. Somebody should tell him his brother being a pissant wasn't his fault. No more than the riots would be my fault—I'd done what I could to calm things down. That wasn't quite true; I hadn't done everything I could in Blacksburg, but nobody told me what to do until too late. Damn these witches and wizards and their secrets. I didn't want to find out too late, again. The weight was backbreaking, like shouldering a sledgehammer the size of an ox. Those witches and wizards kept talking about hammers. The king had one, they said, but he'd forgotten how to use it. They didn't know hammers. I knew them, their heft, their balance. Put one in my hands…

My hands closed around a wooden shaft.

Master Jean sucked in his breath, sharp. The Fire Warlock turned his head and gawped. I looked down. Nothing. What the hell was this? The shaft dug a valley into my shoulder.

The Earth Mother's voice echoed in my head. *The Water Office is shackled to the king. Break the shackles.*

I closed my eyes, and saw a glowing chain stretching from the king to the Frost Maiden, and a glowing hammer. I twisted under the weight, and pushed at the shaft. It didn't budge.

You must break them before she calls you to account.

I twisted and pushed. It wasn't fair, her telling me to use magic. What could I—a halfpenny wizard, not even a member of a magic guild—do that a warlock couldn't?

The mirror clouded over. The Frost Maiden gave me a hard stare, then rose to take over for the Enchanter at the edge of the stage. Maggie and Doug eyed me like I was a rabid dog, but I had to get out from under that weight or my back would break.

The Frost Maiden talked about Lord Edmund. "He is no longer subject to our laws, but I do not doubt he has been called to account at a higher court. Were he still with us, he would be called to account here. As had been widely believed and accepted as right, the Water Office will not give a nobleman's illicit desires precedence over a common woman's virtue. The penalties imposed on the nobleman will be the same as if he had assaulted a noblewoman."

Maggie squealed. The building shook as the commoners in the balconies yelled, whistled, hooted, hollered, and pounded their feet. The king seethed. The queen clapped.

We are out of time. Break them now.

A muscle in my back spasmed. I closed my eyes, gritted my teeth, and heaved. The weight lifted from my shoulder, and fell.

Breakfast with the Duke

The harsh clang of breaking metal drowned out the other noises. I fell, hitting my head on the Frost Maiden's empty chair. My chest burned, muscles cramped, arms turned to jelly. Hands grabbed me and pulled me back onto the bench. The Earth Mother laid hands on me and eased the pain in my chest and back. Sweat trickled into my eyes and mouth. I leaned back and looked at the Earth Mother.

"Thank God you lived through that," she said.

"What did he do?" Several voices demanded.

She shook her head and glanced over her shoulder at the king. He was frowning, watching the Frost Maiden. The three water wizards huddled around her. Voices rose and fell. Hands waved. The Frost Maiden's ring blazed with a steady, bright light, casting weird shadows across the ranks of cawing aristos.

"I cast an illusion spell," the Air Enchanter said. "No one outside this circle can see or hear us."

"He used the king's hammer," the Earth Mother said. "The one King Stephen forfeited rights to."

"I got that much," the Fire Warlock said. He picked up the Frost Maiden's chair and set it upright. "But—"

"And it would have killed a weaker man. I wouldn't advise doing it again."

I mumbled, "You told me to." My head swam.

"How could he swing the king's hammer?" Master Jean said. "It is as ringed with spells as the king himself."

"Hammers are Earth Guild, Jean," she said. "Your guild isn't the only one with secrets."

Master Jean gave her a look that would have scorched a commoner. "So what has he done?"

"He broke the Water Office's shackles to the king."

"Ah." He straightened up and stared at the Frost Maiden's back. "Marvels and wonders, you said."

The luscious woman who turned to face us had sparkling eyes and roses in her cheeks. She smiled at me. I gulped, and quivered like a raw apprentice mooning over the master's daughter.

The water wizards filed back into place. The lead man rubbed his hands and fought down a grin. Master Charles squeezed my shoulder on his way past.

The Frost Maiden faced the muttering crowd and held up her hand for silence. "You have witnessed an event that has not happened in centuries: the breaking of old patterns as the Water Office responds to the weight of public opinion. The Water Office is no longer bound to favour one class at the expense of all others. A commoner with truth on his side need no longer fear to approach the Crystal Palace, and Justice Hall shall regain its proper name." Her voice rang like a trumpet. The king stared.

"And now," she said, all business again, "I shall demonstrate the truth of the Water Office's reform." The roses in her cheeks faded. "Grandmaster Duncan Archer, I summon you to hear your fate."

I was on my knees in front of the Frost Maiden. I wasn't sure how I'd gotten there. If Doug hadn't been standing beside me with a hand on my shoulder, I would have fallen over.

The Frost Maiden looked up at the balconies, holding out her empty hand. "You see, I do not carry the hourglass. No one, today, will die at the behest of the Water Office."

The balconies got noisy again. She held up her hand. "Save the celebrations for later. We still have much to cover before the day is over."

She waved her hand at me. "You have seen the qualities of this man. The Water Office understands Frankland needs more men like him, not fewer. To make his life forfeit for an act of self-defence, even one causing a nobleman's death, does not serve the cause of justice, nor will it benefit Frankland."

She went on, covering the same ground she'd covered at the trial. The aristos were almost within arm's reach. I could have been back in

Blacksburg, in the days before the riot, only now it was the aristos about to boil over. The hairs on the back of my neck rose.

There was death in the air, and it might yet be mine, even if it didn't come from the Water Office.

The Frost Maiden said I couldn't strike the first blow in a fight. The aristos didn't seem to care. The angry mutterings a few feet away kept on. Then she began talking about blood money. The muttering changed to satisfied snickers. The king leaned back in his throne, smiling. The dukes gloated. Doug's fist beat on my shoulder.

She said, "Earl Eddensford does not need a smith's support to survive. Therefore, the bulk of the reparations Grandmaster Duncan must pay will go where it may do the most good. For the next ten years, he will give one-fifth of all he earns to Frankland's neediest widows and orphans."

I gaped. Doug gaped. I looked at the earl. The earl gaped.

She said, "Nonetheless, the Water Office will not allow a precedence to be established that does not include reparations to the dead man's family."

She gave me a long look. Doug's fingers dug holes in my shoulder. I held my breath.

"The Water Guild Council has determined that in this case, and in this case only, the fair amount due is one gold frank."

Doug leaned on me. I smacked both hands on the floor or he would have knocked me flat, and he was supposed to be holding me up.

The crowd roared. The king bellowed. A cold breeze blew through the ballroom. The noise died to an angry rumble from the aristos.

"Save the celebrations for later was not a suggestion," the Frost Maiden said. "Each time I am interrupted the hall will become colder." She turned to the men on the king's right hand. "Earl Eddensford, are you satisfied with this judgement?"

The earl licked his lips, eyes moving between the Frost Maiden and the king. "Yes, Your Wisdom, I am." The angry rumble grew.

She asked me a question. I couldn't make it out. I owed one frank. I could go home. Someday I'd scrape enough together to buy a horse. I could—

Doug whacked me, hard. "Aye, Your Wisdom. He's satisfied."

"Very well. That is all. Return to your seats."

"Stay there," the king growled. "You've asked the earl and the smith if they're satisfied. You haven't asked us."

The Frost Maiden raised an eyebrow. "If both parties in a dispute are satisfied, Your Majesty, there is no need for you to be involved."

"But what if we're not satisfied? We can override the Water Office, if we wish."

"Please, Your Majesty, I beg you not to." The earl was on his feet, swaying, like he was the condemned man facing the Frost Maiden. "Please do not heap further dishonour on my house."

The king said. "But the price of an earl's son…"

"Edmund was not worth it, Your Majesty. This family has already suffered for his sins. Any blood money you require them to pay me, I will return to them, doubled. I cannot take their misery on my conscience."

There was not a whisper in the ballroom. When the Air Enchanter cleared his throat, I nearly jumped out of my skin.

"Perhaps, Your Majesty," the Enchanter said, "you should wait until we have heard the third case. A few minutes delay won't hurt, and you can deal with all three cases at once."

The king gave the earl another hard stare, then shrugged. "Go on, then."

My body slid into place on the wooden bench, but my soul danced on a mountaintop. I was king of the world.

Maggie's face glowed. "One frank," she breathed. "Duncan, did you do that?"

I threw up my hands and looked at Master Jean. He nodded without taking his eyes off the king. I fell several thousand feet down the side of my mountain. Wherever Master Jean was, it wasn't the top of the world. He hadn't relaxed at all.

"And now, Your Majesties, lords and ladies," The Air Enchanter said, "we shall review the events on the morning of Lord Edmund's death."

I twisted my neck to see.

The mirror cleared, showing the White Duke and his guests, making a din over breakfast. A clerk stood by the duke's chair, reporting on some business. A door at the other end of the room opened, and Jake Higgins came in, leading Reverend Angus.

I snarled. The fire lad was right; I should have escorted that trouble-making preacher to Edinburgh myself. Whatever the Frost Maiden did to him, he'd deserve it.

Jake led him to the duke's side, and started out. The duchess's head snapped up. Her shrill voice carried over the other noises. "What was that about the Archers?"

The preacher said, "I was informing His Grace that the blacksmith, Duncan Archer, has returned to Abertee after being in the Blacksburg riot. I was about to suggest that the duke take action before the blacksmith causes trouble here."

The duke looked alarmed. His duchess said, "Excellent suggestion. Thank you for coming to inform us. Rupert, are you paying attention?"

The clerk coughed. "Excuse me, Your Grace, but I don't believe he means to cause trouble. I had heard he was back in Crossroads, and had ordered out of Abertee a man who had played a part in causing the riot. Mr Archer said he had the authority as the new head of the Blacksmith's Guild. He was showing off a certificate signed by a swordsmith."

The duke brightened. "Got it, did he? Good for him."

The duchess screeched, "Good? Rupert, you are a first-class idiot. Didn't you hear what the man said? That smith was in the riot."

"He was," the preacher said. "He admitted it, himself."

The clerk said, "But, Your Grace, the story from Crossroads was that he helped someone the rioters attacked."

She snapped, "Of course that's the story he'd tell to make himself look good, but he's a troublemaker. Those Archers are always complaining about something or other, as if they expect us to spend our money on their roads or dams or such. I'd be glad to get rid of the whole lot of them."

The duchess waved the clerk away, and he bolted. Jake Higgins had backed into a spot by the door where he blended in with the footmen.

The duke said, "But dear—"

"Don't 'dear' me, Rupert. We've put up with those Archers for too long. It's time we evicted them."

"We can't evict them, they're freeholders."

"Can they prove it? Of course not." She looked down the table. "Would any of you be willing to ride over to that backwater and tell those Archers to leave?"

"But dear—"

Jake crept close to the table, between Lord Edmund and the duke's son. He said softly, "The blacksmith's sister is the best-looking lass in Abertee."

Maggie whimpered. I punched the back of the Fire Warlock's chair. He grunted.

Doug grabbed my arm and pushed it down. "You won't hit him. I will."

In the mirror, Lord Edmund smirked. "Well, then, it might be worth the trouble." The duke's son snickered. Lord Edmund raised his voice. "I'll go, Your Grace. I don't mind."

The duke went white. "No, wait, don't. I'll tell them to go the next time they come with a complaint."

"Don't be ridiculous," the duchess said. "They'll talk you into letting them stay, just like they've talked you around on everything else you've argued with them about. No, if Edmund goes, it will get done. He's not a soft sap like you."

She swept out of the room, Lord Edmund and Jake Higgins right behind her. The room cleared out until the White Duke was alone at the table, horror on his staring face.

The weight, once again, built up on my shoulders. I should have known that sour hussy was behind it. She had caused no end of trouble for everybody in Abertee, the duke included. Somebody ought to take her down a notch. She glared at me, her nose pinched like she smelled something rotten. Her son looked like a cat that had swallowed a juicy mouse.

The Fire Warlock had promised to deal with the man responsible. Reverend Angus wasn't in sight. Oh, God, he hadn't gone after that pissant Jake Higgins, had he? Jake deserved whatever he got, but he was small fry. I wanted that preacher shut up for good.

The mirror clouded over. The Frost Maiden walked to the centre of the stage, and faced the White Duke. "Your Grace, you have been charged with and found guilty of dereliction of duty. I summon you to hear your fate."

The King's Sword

A duke, called to account? My jaw dropped. The king bellowed. The ballroom got cold.

"Your Majesty," the Frost Maiden said, "please do not interrupt until you have heard the sentence."

The king had lost his hammer, but he still had a sword. The aristos made a din but I couldn't take my eyes off the king. He slid the sword several inches out of its scabbard. I knew that sword. A year ago Brother Clive had let me swing it.

"Stop this farce," the king said. "He is a duke; his behaviour is our concern, not yours. He may do as he pleases, as long as he does not usurp our position."

"No, Your Majesty. A duke may not do as he pleases. He is as bound by the requirements of his position as Grandmaster Duncan is by his. However, it is true this case should not have come to the attention of the Water Office. The Water Office is the court of last resort, only to be used if a nobleman is not called to account by his superior."

"What you don't see," the Fire Warlock growled, "is that Sorceress Lorraine and the Water Office are trying to protect the nobility from the Fire Office."

"Explain yourself," the king said. He watched the Fire Warlock with narrowed eyes, his hand busy with his sword. Brother Clive's swords were the best, Brother Randall had said—he beat the spell in with every stroke.

"Abertee went straight from being the one corner of Frankland I was least worried about, to one about to boil over, and it was his doing." The Fire Warlock jabbed a finger at the cowering duke. "Or, rather, his not doing what he should've, and letting his wife kick a hornet's nest. Things have quieted down since the end of June—no more riots, mostly because the nobles were on their way here, and the Water Guild blocked all trials. But it can, and will, heat up again, and when the next riot happens—that's when, not if—things are going to be different."

The Fire Warlock was on his feet, walking along the line of dukes, glaring down at them. "The next time there's a riot, the nobleman who caused it, or let it happen, will burn, just like the rioters."

"You can't do that!"

"I can, and will. The Fire Office has come to see you shielded good-for-nothings as being as much of a threat to Frankland as the rioters are. It's been a long time getting there, but it's there now, and he's the one"—another stab of the finger at the White Duke—"that got it there, by letting his bonehead duchess push out the man most responsible for keeping the peace in Abertee."

The Fire Warlock rounded on the king. "And your only hope for saving your ignoble cousins is to let the Water Office have first dibs on them. If the Water Office convinces the Fire Office they'll be held responsible, it won't make me burn them. Which is it going to be, Your Majesty? It's up to you."

From several yards away, I felt the heat pouring off the angry wizard. Master Jean was half out of his chair, straining at the bit like a horse before the start of a race.

Don't lose your temper, he'd said. Don't give the Fire Office free rein, he'd meant. The burnt circle from the last Scorching Time where York had been was a mile wide. Big enough to wipe out everybody in Paris, packed into this ballroom and the streets and parks nearby.

My mouth went dry; my hands shook. No wonder Master Jean was scared silly.

The weight on my shoulders grew. I cursed under my breath.

The queen whispered in the king's ear. He nodded, white-lipped. "Go on."

Master Jean settled down, but didn't relax. The aristos were boiling. Too stupid to be scared.

Maggie nudged me and nodded towards the White Duke's son. She whispered, "He was friends with Lord Edmund. When he's duke…"

Hard to imagine even an aristo gullible or wicked enough to be friends with that rotten scum, but gossip said the lad took after his mum, not his dad. The lad smirked as the duke shuffled forward to kneel at the Frost Maiden's feet. If she took his title away and made his son duke, God help us.

"Your Grace," the Frost Maiden said, "you should not be here alone. Have you no one to stand with you? Your son? Your wife? A friend?"

The White Duke shook his head and mumbled.

"That's not right," Maggie said. Doug and I looked at each other.

The Frost Maiden raked the line of dukes with her eyes. "Will not one of you, his kinsmen and peers, come to his aid?" They all looked away.

Doug took a deep breath and shifted his weight forward. I stood up. "I'll stand with him, Your Wisdom."

Heads turned to stare. The Frost Maiden said, "I beg your pardon?"

"He's one of ours. From Abertee, I mean, and I'd do it for anybody in Abertee." Besides, it was only fair; I got him into this mess.

"Your Grace?" she said.

He looked like a dog begging for scraps. "Please."

The weight on my shoulders got heavier. I stood beside the duke, cursing myself. Letting Doug stand here would have been the sensible thing to do.

The Frost Maiden said, "Your Grace, as a duke you are required to protect the people in your domains from lawlessness, but you made no move to prevent Lord Edmund from abusing the women of Abertee. Your wife, who does not have the authority, attempted to evict a family of law-abiding freeholders on false grounds, and you let a man with a grudge against that family use Miss Archer as enticement to persuade Lord Edmund to carry out your wife's errand. You have been found guilty as charged, of gross dereliction of duty.

"There is, first, the matter of prevention. The Water Office will not, for this offence, take the district of Abertee from your domain, but I warn you it may do so for a future offence. As recompense, the women Lord Edmund attacked in Abertee will henceforth, as long as they live in your domain, be exempt from taxes and rent."

The commoners, almost as one, let out a massive "Hurrah!" She stared up at the balconies. They went quiet, but the mutterings from the aristos grew, and didn't quiet when she stared at them. A cold breeze blew across them, but it only seemed to make them angrier.

"And finally," she said, "as punishment, and as a reminder of the pain those women under your protection will live with for the rest of their lives, you will never again, during your waking hours, be warm."

The White Duke's teeth chattered. There was a moment of total, shocked silence, before the aristos shot to their feet, yelling and shaking their fists, surging toward the stage and the balcony stairs. The noise grew as the commoners joined in the yelling. I crouched by the duke and wished for a hammer.

A stinging spray of sleet sent the mob reeling backwards. Wind howled. The sleet turned to snow.

My fists closed on empty air. Even with a hammer, there'd be nothing to swing at. We were snow-blind. The mob had disappeared. A yard away the Frost Maiden was a blur, her throbbing blue ring casting eerie shadows. Screams sounded where tongues of fire danced through the white.

Even if I had that hammer, maybe I couldn't swing it again. The Earth Mother had warned me not to, and the magic she had used on me was wearing off. But if the opportunity came, I had a use for it, her advice be damned.

The snow thickened, muffling the screams and yells and dimming the flashing lights. The Frost Maiden was lost in the blizzard. I was sure I wasn't alone only because the quivering duke was leaning against me.

More than once I'd heard powerful magic backed the Royal Association of Swordsmiths. Nobody had explained what that magic was, but if there was any, now would be the time for it. I yelled into the wind, "I need your help. Can any smith, dead or alive, give me a hammer?"

The shaft of the king's hammer was in my hands again. I ran my hands up and down the smooth wood, and crowed. I would swing it, and be glad, even if it killed me. The snow cleared. I was adrift in a quiet pocket with the duke and the Air Enchanter, walled in by swirling white.

The Earth Mother walked out of the snow. "And what are you planning on doing with that? It wasn't my doing, this time."

I shrugged. "Maybe I won't get a chance."

The air warmed; my teeth stopped chattering. The pocket expanded, and took in first the Fire Warlock, and then Master Jean, his eyes afire. The royal family on their thrones came next.

"King Stephen," the Earth Mother said, "you have failed even those closest to you. I charge you with dereliction of duty."

The king had murder in his eyes. He yanked his sword out and came towards us, swinging. I heaved. With a flash as bright as the Frost Maiden's ring, the sword shattered.

BARBARA HOWE

272

The Warlock's Agent

Shards of the king's sword bounced off an unseen wall between us. A red-hot poker ripped through my chest. I fell on my face.

The Earth Mother, swearing like a tinker, rolled me over. I lay on my back in the snow, freezing and burning, and watched ghosts swirl around us. Uncle Will was there with a hayfork, and Master Randall with a sledgehammer.

Stark raving mad, I must be. Better not tell anybody.

The king, on his knees, whimpered, "You can't. You can't."

Master Jean's words burned with the cold of a clear winter night. "We have warned you, time and again, that a reckoning is due. That reckoning is upon you. You cannot win if you persist, against all sense, in fighting all four Offices."

The Frost Maiden was a shadow on the storm's edge. "Take up your mirror, Your Majesty, and see the likely outcome if the Water Office tries you on the charge Mother Celeste made against you."

The pain in my chest was easing. The ghosts, an army of smiths, were fading. I twisted my neck to watch the king and queen. She screamed and dropped her mirror.

Master Jean said, "None of us desires this outcome. If you act in the interest of all Frankland's citizens, it may not come to pass. The choice is yours."

"This is treason!"

"Is it, Your Majesty?" the Frost Maiden said. "The Water Office understands treason to be betrayal of the country, not the king."

"Enchanter Paul, do something!"

"Your Majesty, the Air Office does not approve of favouritism. It recognises an implicit contract between the king and all Franks, and wants that contract honoured. It will not protect you."

The queen knelt in the snow beside the king, "Dear, I think you must give in. Everyone could see what Rupert and Edmund did was dreadful. You don't want the people to think you're a fool, do you?"

Drawing breath to laugh hurt. The Earth Mother thumped me on the chest. "Stop that."

Her teeth were chattering, too. Master Jean circled around, and laid warm hands on us without taking his eyes off the king.

The Fire Warlock said, "Make up your mind, right now, or the whole country will know your sword shattered."

The king whispered, "What do you want me to do?"

"Take the Great Oath."

The king's eyes were wide and staring, and his hands shook. "My father and grandfather ordered me not to, and I'll not. I'll not let them down. Go ahead and kill me."

The queen screamed, and wrapped her arms around her husband's shoulders. Master Jean edged closer to the king.

Enchanter Paul said, "There is another way. If Your Majesty accepts that the Water Office's judgments are fair, and signs the contract I have proposed, neither the Water Office nor the Fire Office will harm you."

The king dropped his head in his hands and moaned. The queen pleaded with him. Out of nowhere, a desk appeared, with pen, ink, parchment, wax, and seal. The king groaned and reached for the pen. Master Jean, gloating, backed away and faded into the snow.

The Fire Warlock gave me a hand. "Think you can stand up?"

My back ached; my legs were jelly. "Maybe."

"It won't be for long."

"What's he signing?"

"Wait. You'll find out."

The king handed the parchment to the Enchanter. The Earth Mother said, "I withdraw my charge."

The wind changed, and blew the snow off the stage. The White Duke was still on his knees, shaking. I pulled off my coat and wrapped it around his shoulders. It wouldn't do him any good, but it made me feel better.

He pulled the coat close. "Thank you." He blinked up at me, only the top of his head showing over the collar. "Funny that, seeing your uncle again."

I stared down at him, and jumped when the Frost Maiden said, "Your Grace, are you satisfied with this judgment?"

I'd nearly forgotten what had started the blizzard. The snow was melting off the half-frozen aristos. They looked confused and groggy, like they'd had a bad dream and were having trouble waking up.

The duke raised his head, and stared, first at the king, then at the other dukes. The king looked over his head. The other dukes turned away.

He croaked, "What happens if I say no?"

"The Water Office may be merciful, but mercy is not guaranteed, and you must present a strong argument for why you deserve it."

His jowls quivered. "I can't. I guess I'm satisfied, Your Wisdom."

"Miss Archer, as representative of the women Lord Edmund attacked, are you satisfied with this judgment?"

Doug and Maggie huddled together, whispering. The king dug his fingernails into the arms of his throne. The queen watched, wide-eyed, her hands fluttering.

Maggie stood and said, "No, ma'am."

The duke whimpered. Master Jean edged forward. The mob raised its ugly head.

"How can he live like that?" Maggie said. "I think I'd kill myself if I could never be warm again. It may be just, but it's not good for him, and he's not been a bad duke when his wife wasn't bullying him. Couldn't you give him a chance to get warm? If he did something kind, like, say, taking care of the women that were hurt worse than I was?"

The king puffed the air in and out of his cheeks like a slack sail, flapping in the breeze. The gaggle of dukes looked like lost sheep. The queen beamed at Maggie.

The duke's head rose out of the collar. "Please, let me do that. I would. Please?"

The Frost Maiden closed her eyes. The blue light flickered, and then it was snowing again, a light powder, glistening and sparkling like diamonds where it caught the light shining in the windows. It dusted heads and shoulders without chilling us, and for a few seconds everything gleamed, like the ground on a sunny morning after a hard frost. Then it melted away and was gone.

"It shall be so," the Frost Maiden said. "The Water Office is pleased with the mercy Miss Archer has shown today. Fortune shall smile on her."

She nodded at us. "You may return to your seats."

The duke scuttled away, still wrapped in my coat. The other dukes drew away from him. I staggered to the bench.

"Are you all right?" Maggie whispered. "What happened?"

I shook my head. "Shh."

"Given the special circumstances," the king said, "with Lord Edmund being so badly behaved, we accept that the judgments in the case are fair." He glared at the Frost Maiden. "We accept that in this one case only."

The aristos seethed, but no one moved. Some brave soul in the balcony cheered. A few others joined in, and then many. The king glared at the Frost Maiden, but the prince goggled at the balconies. I snorted. It must never have occurred to them that we might want to approve of them.

It was over. We had won. I could go home.

The Fire Warlock was on his feet. "Earlier the king said he called us here today to hear both Sorceress Lorraine and me account for ourselves. We've heard from Sorceress Lorraine. Now it's my turn. Your Majesties, the Fire Office was set up to ensure Frankland's safety and security. It's done a good job of protecting us from external threats. No one argues with that. It hasn't done as good a job of dealing with internal threats. After the recent riots, no one argues with that, either. There's a lot of history there, but I'm not here today to give you a history lesson. The question is: what changes can we make to do a better job in the future?

"Protecting Frankland from both external and internal threats is too big a job for any one wizard. A nearly impossible job sometimes. Not even a Fire Warlock can be in half-a-dozen places at once. King Stephen has given his approval to an experiment the Air Enchanter suggested. For this experiment I will appoint a number of agents to help me keep an eye on affairs inside Frankland. These agents will have the power to mediate disputes, including between nobles and commoners. They will enforce the charters governing the districts. They will report to me regularly about problems and unrest, and will have the authority to call on me for help if anything seems about to get out of hand."

I forgot my aching back. That sounded like what the head of the Blacksmith's Guild did in Abertee, only better—if the agents were commoners. Being able to go to the Fire Warlock if the duke or any of his guests got out of line would give the agents more leverage.

The Fire Warlock said, "The agents could be men or women, nobles or commoners, talented or mundanes. Commoners will have the same shields as the nobles, as long as they are serving as the Fire Warlock's agents, but the shields won't pass to their children."

Doug thumped me on the shoulder. I grinned. Give them enough to do the job, but don't let their children grow up to be brats. Good so far.

"The people appointed to be these agents would need to be special people—hard-working, dedicated, generous, honest, out-going, friendly with all ages and types of people, willing and able to give everyone, from a duke to the lowest ditch-digger, a fair chance. Not easily intimidated..."

Leave everything to the witches and wizards, Granny Mildred had said. Frost me if I would. I was half off the bench, reaching for that golden hammer, when the Fire Warlock said, "That's why the best choice for the first agent is a man who's already shown he can and will give even the Fire Warlock a piece of his mind when necessary. What about it, Grandmaster Duncan?"

"Aye, Your Wisdom."

The hooting and hollering in the balconies turned into shouts loud enough to be heard in London. "DUNCAN! DUNCAN!" The king's shout was lost in the din. The Fire Warlock made no move to quiet them. Neither did the Frost Maiden.

The king glared at me. I stared back. After a moment, the king looked away.

The Enchanter held up a hand. A stiff breeze blew through the hall and the balconies quieted down.

The king said, "We've heard from both the Water Sorceress and the Fire Warlock, yes, but we've been reminded the Offices don't like favouritism. I charge you, Sorceress Lorraine, with playing favourites. You've been trying for years to get the Water Office to favour the commoners, and you gloated when it did. You must retire, and give way to someone who'll be fair."

He settled back on his throne with a self-satisfied smirk, and a nasty glare at Master Jean.

The Frost Maiden sat still, not saying anything, for a few moments, before standing and walking to the edge of the stage. She turned to face the king. "Guilty as charged, Your Majesty. I accept your ruling, and will retire."

Water spread out on the floor beside her, and a young woman stepped out.

"My apprentice," the Frost Maiden said, "is trained, and ready to accept the burden of the Water Office. Sorceress Eleanor, I charge you to be fair and just to all Franks."

The Earth Mother said, "Now wait a minute—"

"Take this ring, Token of the Water Office, with my blessing."

The Frost Maiden held up her hand. When the ring, glowing deep blue, fell off her finger and into the other witch's hand, she took a step backwards, her eyes rolled up in her head, and she dropped towards the floor.

Off Her Pedestal

I might have beaten the Enchanter to the falling witch if the Fire Warlock hadn't slammed into me when I shot off the bench. We teetered; the Earth Mother pushed past us and we both went down. By the time I picked myself up, the Enchanter had caught her and lowered her to the floor.

Her empty sleeve lay flat and tangled. The neck of her dress had gotten pulled awry. The new Frost Maiden tugged the dress back in place, hiding her arm's scarred stump.

"Idiot!" the Earth Mother said. "She had no business taking that ring off. The Office was the only thing holding her up. She lost an arm, for God's sake. She should have been in bed, not walking and talking and using magic non-stop for half the day." The king shrivelled under her glare. "She was willing to give her life for her country, and this is the thanks she gets? I hope you're satisfied. We're taking her to the Warren, and not in those nasty bumpy carriages either. We're going now, protocol be damned. Charles?"

The sorcerer picked the old Frost Maiden up. Water spread around him and the Earth Mother, and they disappeared.

Nobody moved. The queen, with one hand to her mouth, clutched at the king's arm, and whispered. Without waiting for the signal for us to rise, they trotted down the aisle just short of a run, with the prince and the dukes hard on their heels.

Master Jean slid out a side door. I caught up as he climbed into the first carriage. He nodded as I followed, then closed his eyes and slumped against the cushions.

The carriage lurched forward into the singing, dancing, shouting sea of commoners. Jewellery, perfumed handkerchiefs, and other trinkets flew in the windows. I tucked a flower into a buttonhole, chucked the women's knickers back out, and slammed the windows shut. I could hear myself again.

"Thank you," Master Jean said.

"Don't thank me for the magic. This flimsy carriage couldn't block that much noise."

"The Earth Guild spells on the windows are not my doing."

"Seems odd to be in a carriage with you. Everybody says you warlocks jump through the fire to go anywhere."

"I prefer to do so, but it is not without risk, and one is more likely to lose control when one is tired."

"So you weren't sure you could haul the king's arse away to one of the scorched circles if the Fire Office lost its temper. No wonder you were scared."

His eyes popped open and he sat bolt upright. "Dear God. How did you know?"

"I guessed, even before his sword shattered. I couldn't figure anything, short of the prospect of wiping out the royals and aristos, and Paris with them, that would make you so skittish."

He put his head down in his hands. "Was it so evident? I must be in worse shape than I imagined."

"Maybe not. I wouldn't have guessed if I hadn't been watching you for weeks now, trying to figure you out. And then, with you and the Fire Warlock saying goodbye…"

"You do not comprehend how dangerous it is to broach this subject. You were able to say what you did because the situation has resolved, and you were speaking in hypotheticals. We must never speak of it again, nor will you tell anyone what you did behind the curtain of snow."

"Hey, now, I'll say—" My guts cramped. My head pounded. Sweat ran down my forehead. "Fine. I won't." The pain went away. I leaned back against the cushions, breathing hard. "You put a spell on me."

"A geas, for your safety. These are Fire and Earth Guild secrets. We cannot divulge them."

"Why the hell not? If the aristos knew what happened there in the snow, it would scare the dickens out of them. Some of them might even grow up."

"I repeat, we cannot. It is not my choice." His eyes were hard, his mouth a thin line. "The Fire Office will not allow knowledge of such a lapse of authority to spread. Someone of lesser rank, yes, we could use as an example, but not this one."

The party going on in the streets didn't make up for the sour taste in my mouth. Women threw kisses at me. Men doffed their hats. My wee nephew could crawl faster than the carriage was rolling. "Maybe you will have to rebuild the Fire Office, too. I could've died, and all I did was…"

"All you did was save many thousands of lives, crush the nobles' hopes of overt royal support for retaliation, and wrench Frankland, if not back into balance, at least far less out of balance than it was."

"Aye, sir, I can see that."

"We are still on the brink of civil war. Make no mistake about it. The nobles will not acquiesce in the changes we have wrought, but when the conflict is over, the changes will stand, and Frankland will be the stronger for them. Do not belittle what you have done."

"Aye, Your Wisdom. Thanks."

He smiled, folded his hands behind his head, and slept.

Master Jean led the way through the tunnels to a bedroom in the Warren. The Frost Maiden—Sorceress Lorraine, that is—might have given me the gimlet eye for sticking my nose in, but she smiled.

"The man of the hour," she said. "You have become the commoners' greatest hero, and they do not understand the half of what you have done for them. We are deeply in your debt. More deeply than we can ever repay."

I shrugged. "Today you didn't say I couldn't go home."

"As soon as you pay the earl his gold coin, you are free to go."

Except for bright blue eyes, she was as pasty white as the sheets she lay on, and her bones were as sharp as Master Jean's. She couldn't have weighed over six stone, and with her arm gone, she looked like a cast-off doll—a doll with a warm smile. She was still gorgeous, but a woman, not a goddess. Not my woman, of course, but a woman who could love and be loved.

"I got what I wanted, ma'am. Most of it, that is." Let her and the sorcerer stroking her hair enjoy themselves. I'd take up the problem of Hazel with the new Frost Maiden. "Nothing you need to worry about, anyway. You've done fine by us."

"Indeed," Master Jean said. "You have accomplished a feat I did not believe possible. In the space of a single morning, you transformed yourself from an enemy of Frankland's common people into a martyr and their new heroine. Congratulations."

"I assure you," she said, "I had no intention of collapsing in front of the entire assembly."

The Earth Mother snorted. "I told you not to retire yet."

"Yes, Your Wisdom. I should have listened to you, but I had been thinking of retiring for some time, and when the king made his charge, the timing seemed right. I meant to throw him a bone to help him recover his dignity. I made things worse, instead. I regret that."

"Do not chastise yourself," Master Jean said. "None of us could have done better, in your place."

Mother Celeste said, "You were splendid, dear, and it turned out far better than I had dared hope. A celebration is in order."

The sorceress said, "I agree. When I have regained some strength, I will invite everyone involved in the reforging to a feast."

I couldn't help it. I shivered.

Sorcerer Charles laughed. "The Crystal Palace isn't the best place for an event like that. We'll find another venue more comfortable for everyone."

Master Jean said, "You were thinking, perhaps, of having the feast on board a ship? An evening cruise along the southern coast would be… thrilling."

I gawked. He winked.

The sorceress smiled. "That was not my first choice, but if you insist…"

"The Earth Guild will be delighted," the Earth Mother said, "to host the feast for you at the Warren. We prefer to keep our feet on dry land, thank you, even if the Fire Warlock Emeritus is losing his marbles."

The Earl of Eddensford and his wife were waiting for me in the Warren's Great Hall. I fished a frank out of my pocket and dropped it in his hand. "Thank you, sir, for standing up to the king for us. And I'm sorry about your brother. I'd be broken up over mine."

The earl squeezed the coin until his knuckles turned white. A muscle in his face twitched. "I envy you your brother. When the news mine was dead reached me, I felt little other than relief. I apologise to you for the ordeal he inflicted on you and your family."

The earl's wife took his hand, and gave me a smile that warmed me all the way down to my toes. "Let's go give this away, why don't we? There are lots of places where it will do more good."

After watching them go, I turned back to the Great Hall, and came face-to-face with the only other man my size in Frankland.

"I said you were the best man for our test case." The Fire Warlock held out a hand. "Thank you, my friend."

We shook. "Guess you were right."

"To be the first agent, too. We'll need to have a long talk about what being agent means, but—"

"You didn't say if I get paid for it. With giving away a fifth of all I make, plus taxes, I'm still going to have a hard time making ends meet."

"We'll pay you for your time, but if you can't make ends meet on what you're going to be pulling in as a smith, you don't deserve it. You're going to be rolling in it."

"Like rocks I am. Master Clive and Master Randall were comfortable, but not rich, and they'd been making swords for longer—"

"I doubt you'll ever get around to making a sword. Clive and Randall didn't have the richest men in the country and their wives watching them make a one-of-a-kind gate for an irritating little braggart of a baron. You're going to be flooded with orders from all the landed gentry wanting their mascots immortalised in a gate or door or what-have-you that makes their neighbours and friends turn green with envy. And they saw what you charged the baron. They'll pay whatever you ask. Wouldn't want their so-called friends to think they couldn't afford it."

"Good Lord."

He laughed, and clapped me on the shoulder. "You're not on probation anymore, either. Grandmaster Henry's not stupid. He knows the Swordsmiths' Guild's reputation would be mud if they kicked you out now."

"But... But... Oh, frost it. About being an agent..."

"We'll talk about that tomorrow, and about that fool preacher. Your duke will go along with whatever we suggest; he can't be feeling too kindly towards the man either. But that'll wait. Go enjoy yourself today. There's a party already in full swing in Crossroads."

"If you come, I'll buy you a beer."

He grinned. "I might. See you."

The Earth Mother's magic was wearing off; my chest burned and my arms were too weak to pick up a newborn lamb. I sat on a bench against a wall and massaged a cramping calf. I could go home. Sleep. See my nephews, brother, sister, sister-in-law…

Frost it. I'd gone off and left Doug and Maggie in Paris, and had no idea where they were or how they were getting home. How I was getting home, either, for that matter. I should have asked the Fire Warlock.

The hall was alive with a jostling, swirling, happy swarm of witches and wizards. A year ago, I would have laughed at anyone saying I'd see this eight-sided hall, one of the most famous places in Frankland. I'd never expected to see the Fortress, or Paris, either, and Injustice Hall was just a bad dream.

So much I'd gained in one year: new friends, a master's certificate, a spot in the Swordsmiths' Guild, fame, and maybe even fortune. A few things I'd lost, too: the freedom to come and go as I pleased, Charcoal, Master Randall, and Hazel.

The Water Guild owed me more than they could repay, she'd said. We'd see about that. But maybe Hazel wouldn't want to come back to Abertee, after Granny Mildred had pushed her out.

I stood, and nearly fell on my face. Still a bit unsteady on my pins, and my back ached. I needed a healer. I needed…that steadying touch on the arm, pumping life back into me. That cute, freckled face turned up to mine. That soft voice saying, "Duncan, I am so glad—"

I pulled her close. "They've let you come to say goodbye?"

Hazel buried her face in my shirt. Her shoulders shook. I stroked her hair and said, "I'm sorry. I'm so sorry." Her shaking got worse, as hard as Maggie would shake when she'd been a bawling little tyke. I bent down, then jerked upright. She was laughing.

I swung her onto the bench, where she was almost eye level. "Let me in on the joke."

She nodded with her hand over her mouth. I chewed on my lip while she struggled to talk.

"My trial was run by a level-three water wizard who wasn't part of the Reforging Coven. He didn't believe they had fixed the Water Office. He thought it would kill you, and he doesn't like earth witches, any of us."

"Go on."

"And he prides himself on coming up with creative penalties—making the punishment fit the crime—so after Sorceress Lorraine told him Granny Mildred couldn't stand me being in the same house with her, he decided the appropriate penalty was to condemn me to continue reporting to her in Abertee."

My ears must be playing tricks. "You have to stay in Abertee."

"Yes. I was shocked, too. Happy, but confused. Mildred wasn't angry with me. She sent me to the Warren because she worried I'd be in danger in Abertee after everyone heard what I'd done."

"But Maggie said—"

"Last night, after the trial, Mother told me—"

"Mother Astrid?"

"Yes. She said Mother Celeste and Sorceress Lorraine agreed that both guilds need to believe there will be non-trivial consequences for aiding a fugitive, especially now that a commoner can get a fair trial, the Water Guild will be more serious about capturing fugitives. But Warlock Arturos said he'd be damned if he'd let them make me suffer for teaching you mindwarping, since half the Water Guild would be dead now if I hadn't. So they created a conspiracy to make the rank and file in both guilds think I had no friends in Abertee."

"They…the Frost Maiden…" I put out a hand and leaned against the wall. "By the Warlock's beard. The Water Office didn't demand you be sent away?"

"No. The presiding Water Guild member has always had the authority to pick any district, and apparently the Water Office was satisfied that I understood the gravity of what I'd done, and wouldn't do it again. But the presiding wizard warned me that if you did survive, and we ever spoke again…"

I tightened my grip on her waist. "Go on."

She bent her head down. I had to strain to hear her. "He'd take away my ability to dig."

I talked into her hair. "Fire and frostbite. That's just awful."

"Don't overdo it. We don't know who's watching."

When I could keep a straight face, I pulled back a little. "You say Granny Mildred's not angry."

"No. She said I'll—" Hazel's freckles disappeared under a wave of red. "Never mind. She wants me to stay. She's going to apologise in public, making it sound like she changed her mind when the trial went well."

"Good. Who else knows?"

"Your brother. They let him in on it after Maggie had her row with Mildred. They didn't want to risk someone else sticking up for me, and Doug was working himself up into a lather."

I should've known. Doug and Maggie had always made me proud, and I wouldn't have to fight with either Mildred or the new Frost Maiden. For the heaviest man in north Frankland, I felt light as a feather. Hazel's freckles were coming back. "I know what Granny Mildred said to make you blush."

"Oh?"

"She said you'll make a fine Archer."

Her freckles disappeared again. Her eyes shone like stars. Her mouth begged for a kiss. I obliged.

She pulled away before I'd had nearly enough. "They're watching."

I looked around. Smiling faces ringed us.

Mother Astrid said, "You have my blessing, children. It's hard to imagine either of you could do any better."

Granny Mildred said, "I hope you've learned something from all this."

"Aye, Granny, I have," I said. "Us common folk have power, too, and we need to speak up for ourselves instead of ducking problems and waiting for the magic folk to fix them."

"Is that so?" She looked confounded. "You mean I've been giving bad advice all these years?"

"I'm afraid so, Mildred," Mother Astrid said. "We all have been."

"Maybe I'm too old to mend my ways. But you're not, you young scamp. What I meant was, I hope you've learned when to keep your mouth shut."

"Hell, no. I learned that those folk who are my betters can take somebody telling them the truth."

Mother Astrid laughed. Mildred said, "For Heaven's sake, sonny, that's not—"

"It'll do," Doug said. He and Maggie took her by the elbows and walked her towards the tunnels.

Maggie said, "Let's go, before the party gets too loud for Abertee to hear you tell Hazel you're sorry."

I followed, with my lass on my arm. I was whistling before we even reached the tunnel.

End of The Blacksmith

The story continues in

The Wordsmith, Reforging: Book 4